# DENIM & DIAMONDS

Copyright © 2025 by Penelope Ward and Vi Keeland

All rights reserved. No part of this publication may be reproduced, distributed, or transmitted in any form or by any means, including photocopying, recording, or other electronic or mechanical methods, without the prior written permission of the publisher, except in the case of brief quotations embodied in critical reviews and certain other noncommercial uses permitted by copyright law.

This book is a work of fiction. All names, characters, locations, and incidents are products of the authors' imaginations. Any resemblance to actual persons, things, living or dead, locales, or events is entirely coincidental.

**DENIM & DIAMONDS**
Cover Designer: Sommer Stein, Perfect Pear Creative
Editing: Jessica Royer Ocken
Formatting and Proofreading: Elaine York, Allusion Publishing,
 www.allusionpublishing.com
Proofreading: Julia Griffis
Cover Photographer: Wander Aguiar Photography
Cover Model: Lucas Loyola

# DENIM & DIAMONDS

**PENELOPE WARD
VI KEELAND**

I peeked one eye open and found a bearded man standing on the other side of the bed wearing a pair of boxer shorts and holding a gun. He looked vaguely familiar.

"Well, then stop pointing that thing at me!"

"Sorry." He lowered it. "What the hell did you scream like that for?"

I blinked a few times. "Who the hell are you?"

"Jesus Christ," the guy mumbled. "You don't remember last night?"

My eyes bulged. Last night? *Oh my God.* Did I sleep with this lumberjack? I looked down and was relieved to find I still had all my clothes on, boots and all.

The guy shook his head. "You'd remember it, sweetheart. Trust me."

"*What?*"

"You just checked to see what you were wearing, so I'm guessing you were questioning whether we had sex. We didn't. And if we had, you'd remember it."

"Why is that?"

The corner of his lip twitched. "How's your noggin?"

The pain I'd felt when I first opened my eyes came roaring back with a vengeance. I reached for my head. "Who are you, and what the heck did I drink last night?"

Lumberjack bent and lifted the mattress, casually tucking the rifle between it and the boxspring.

"Is that where that gets filed?" I asked.

His lip twitched again. "It is. And an extra dry martini, shaken not stirred, with a lemon twist, dash of orange bitters, and two bleu cheese olives."

I felt my nose wrinkle. "*What?*"

"You asked what you drank last night. That's what your prissy order was. Though that's not actually what you drank."

# CHAPTER 1

*February*

*Ugh. My aching head.*

I lifted it from the pillow and looked around the room. *Where the hell am I?* This was definitely not my room at Sierra Wellness Center, and why the heck are my eyes burning so much? I must've left my contacts in last night. I blinked a few times, attempting to get rid of the dryness. It helped, but when my vision came into focus, I found myself staring into the eyes of...a giant moose.

"Holy shit!" I jumped from the bed and landed on my ass on the hard floor.

*Clunk-clunk. Click.*

*Clunk-clunk. Click.*

My grandfather had loved old westerns, so I knew the unmistakable sound of a shotgun being pumped and cocked. I squeezed my eyes shut and raised my hands into the air. I might've also peed my pants a little. "Don't shoot! Please don't shoot!"

"What the hell, Red?" a deep, throaty voice growled. "I'm not going to fucking shoot you."

"A dry martini is not prissy."

"In this town it is, especially the way you order it."

"What did I drink if my order was too *prissy* for you?"

"Vodka."

"With?"

"Ice."

"No wonder my head is killing me. Why would you give me that?"

Lumberjack's eyebrows shot up. "Because you asked for it when I told you I didn't have orange bitters, bleu cheese olives, or lemons, and I was all out of vermouth."

"*You* told me you didn't have it? So you're who... the bartender?"

He frowned. "Yeah. I'm the bartender. Is that below your standards or something? I also own the place."

"I didn't mean it like that... I just..." I shook my head and looked around the room. For the first time, I realized the moose wasn't alone. He had friends—a deer with big antlers, a bear, and some other thing I thought might be an elk. "Did you kill all these animals?"

Lumberjack folded his arms across his broad chest. "Is that a problem?"

"I'm guessing for *them* it was."

He walked around the bed and held a hand out to me—I was still sitting on the floor. I hesitated, and he shook his head. "It's my hand, sweetheart. Not my dick."

My nose scrunched up. "Crass much?"

"Rather be crass than condescending."

I put my hand in his. "I am *not* condescending."

"No?"

"No."

He helped me to my feet. "If you say so."

I brushed my clothes off. "Do you have a bathroom I can use?"

Lumberjack pointed. "Maybe while you're in there, you can pry the stick out of your ass."

I narrowed my eyes. "You're rude."

He sighed. "Just go do what you gotta do, Red."

"*Red*. That's original." I attempted to lift my chin into the air and keep a bit of my dignity as I walked to the bathroom. But the screech I let out when I shut the door was anything but dignified. "Umm...Lumberjack?" I was afraid to move.

Footsteps came closer on the other side of the door. "Is that supposed to be me?"

"Did you know there's a giant *dog* in your bathtub?"

"I did indeed."

The Saint Bernard tilted his head at me, curiously. "You could've warned me."

There was silence for a few seconds, then, "Hey, Red?"

"Yeah?"

"Oak sleeps in the bathtub."

"Is Oak the dog?"

"Yep."

"Does he bite?"

"He sleeps in the bathtub because he's afraid of his own shadow. I think you're safe."

"Great," I mumbled.

I had one of those bladders that got overly excited once it saw a toilet, so I didn't have time for any more small talk. I walked to the porcelain throne and peed while the giant dog stared. *Fitting. I had a moose and deer watch me sleep.*

Oh, and it turned out I actually *had* peed my pants a little. This morning just kept getting better and better. I slipped my thong off, flushed, and went to the sink to wash my hands. Looking up, I caught my reflection in the mirror. *Oh God.* I didn't look much better than the poor mounted heads. My auburn hair was plastered to one side of my face with what might be drool, puffy green eyes were streaked with red lines from not taking out my daily wears, and dark raccoon circles rimmed underneath. I washed up and did my best to fix my hair and face, but there wasn't much that could make this hangover look any better than it felt.

At least when I opened the bathroom door, the smell of fresh coffee wafted through the air. I found Lumberjack in the kitchen—which technically was also the bedroom and living room in his studio apartment. His back was to me, so I took a moment to appreciate the view. Broad shoulders, narrow waist, and what looked like a pretty muscular ass under those boxer briefs. He was tall—super tall, actually, maybe a foot bigger than my five foot four. Definitely not my normal type. I tended to go for a runner's body—lean and trim, whereas this guy could best be described as *burly*.

Without turning around, he pointed to the counter next to him. "Coffee's there. And I figured you could use some Motrin."

"God, yes. Thank you." I walked over and lifted the steaming mug. "You wouldn't happen to have any creamer, would you?"

"Definitely not."

"Milk?"

"Nope."

"So I guess dairy-free cashew creamer blended with oat milk is out of the question?"

He looked over at me, frowned, and went back to what he was doing without saying a word.

I brought the mug to my lips. "Okay then…"

Lumberjack poured a second coffee in silence while I swallowed two Motrin with scalding black coffee. When he was done, he leaned a hip against the counter and looked at me.

"How many vodkas did I drink last night?" I asked.

He shrugged. "Three maybe?"

"The bar had dark paneling, right?"

"Yep."

I attempted to fit together the bits and pieces of things I could remember. "And a jukebox? I remember putting on Taylor Swift. But then it broke, I think?"

Lumberjack smirked. "I have a secret kill switch behind the bar that cuts the power. Usually have to use it at two AM when drunk fifty-year-olds put on Billy Joel and sing along. I cut you off the third time you played 'Shake It Off.'"

"Not a Swiftie?"

"Don't mind her. But I didn't like the way some of my patrons were looking at you while you were dancing."

"How exactly were they looking at me?"

He tipped back his mug and drank. "You probably shouldn't go out by yourself and get hammered."

"Why? Because I'm a woman?"

"Because you're a fucking lightweight. And the wrong person could've taken you home."

I sighed. He had a point. I didn't know this guy from Adam, but I didn't feel unsafe here with him. "You're right. Thank you for taking care of me."

He nodded once.

"It's just been a really bad week." I shook my head. "A really bad few months, actually."

"Is that why you're at that bougie mental hospital?"

I frowned. "Sierra Wellness Center is *not* a mental hospital. It's a voluntary wellness facility."

"Whatever." He shrugged. "Are you famous or something?"

"Why would you ask me that?"

"Because a lot of celebrities have come through town to spend time there since it was built three years ago."

"Oh." I shook my head. "I'm not famous. My handbags are maybe, but not me."

"Handbags?"

"I own Amourette, the purse company."

"Never heard of it."

"I don't think they would style well with your moose head and shotgun."

"Guess that stick was too far up there to pry it out in the bathroom, huh?"

"I was trying to be funny."

"You're about as good at that as you are drinking."

I smiled. "What's your name? Or should I just continue to call you Lumberjack, like I have been in my head since I woke up at gunpoint?"

"Name's Brock."

"Huh…"

"Huh what?"

I shrugged. "It fits you."

"And what's yours?"

"February."

His brows jumped. "Like the month?"

"Exactly like the month."

"Who names their kid February?"

I sighed. "We don't have time for the story of my mother." *But speaking of time…* I looked around for a clock. "What time is it anyway?"

"Eleven."

My eyes widened. "In the morning?"

"Well, you didn't knock out until four, so it's not like you slept that long."

"God, I'm *screwed*. My ladder is definitely going to be gone by now."

"Your ladder?"

"That's how I snuck out. My room is on the second floor. I paid one of the maintenance guys to leave a ladder at my window, but he said he'd have to get rid of it before the sun came up."

"Why do you have to sneak out? I thought you said the place was voluntary?"

"It is. But if you leave, they discharge you from the program. And if I get kicked out, I'm screwed."

"How are you screwed?"

"It's a long story. But I have a board of directors at my company, and there's this dumb morality clause in my contract and... Let's just say this is my punishment for doing something stupid."

"I have no idea what you're talking about. But it sounds like you're in deep shit."

I laughed. Maybe I needed the mental health timeout more than I wanted to admit. "How far away from Sierra are we?"

"About a mile."

"Oh good." I gulped back the rest of my coffee. "I should get going."

"I'll give you a ride."

"It's okay. I can walk if you just point me in the right direction."

He looked down at the boots I'd slept in—the cute, knee-high leather ones with chunky four-inch heels. "I'll drive you."

*Okay then.*

Brock's apartment was on the second floor. When we got down to street level and stepped outside, I realized where we were. "You live above the bar?"

"Yep."

"Well, that's convenient to get to work."

There were two pickup trucks parked in the driveway on the side of the brick building. Both had decals that read *Hawkins Log Cabins*. Brock opened the passenger door on the bigger of the two trucks and offered a hand to help me get in.

"Thank you."

The temperature had really dropped overnight, and I only had on a flimsy silk dress. Brock got in, started the truck, and noticed me shivering. He peeled off his flannel and held it out to me. "Truck's diesel. Takes a minute for the heat to warm when it first starts."

I waved him off. "It's okay."

"Lean forward."

Not sure why, but I followed his instruction. Brock wrapped his flannel around my shoulders. It was warm from his body heat and felt good, so I slipped my arms into it. "Thank you."

"Yep."

"Do you work for a company that builds log cabins during the day?"

He shifted the truck into reverse and backed out of the driveway. "Own it."

"I thought you said you owned the bar?"

"I do. Also own the grocery store in town and the laundromat."

"That's a weird combination of businesses."

He shrugged. "Economy went to shit a few years back, so the logging mill in town closed down. No work meant no cash to spend in the grocery store or laundromat, so those closed down, too. I had a little bit of money I didn't need from an inheritance, so I bought what I could to help people get back to work."

"That was very noble."

"It's a small town. Everyone helps each other."

"That does *not* happen in Manhattan."

"And that's one of the many reasons I've never been there."

"You've *never* been to the City? But you live in Maine, and it's only a ten-hour drive or a two-hour flight."

He shrugged. A few minutes later, we pulled up to the entrance of Sierra Wellness Center. There were some people milling around out front, so I ducked.

"Do you think you can drive around to the back of the building? That's where my room is. Maybe people will see this truck and just assume you're doing some work here."

Brock waved as he drove up the long driveway.

"Who are you saying hello to?" I asked.

"Fuck if I know. Not even quite sure how the hell I got roped into keeping you at my apartment."

"Roped in?" I felt offended. "I'm sorry if I was such a hassle."

He looked over at me. "You were."

"How was I a hassle?"

"You play shitty music, wouldn't tell me where you lived to take you home, and I had to carry you up the stairs where you proceeded to snore the entire night."

I did snore. "Oh."

"Yeah. *Oh*." The truck made a turn, and Brock slowed to a stop. "The coast is clear from the coppers. You can get up from down there now."

"Thank you."

Of course the ladder I'd used to climb out last night was no longer there. I looked around for something—anything—nearby to use to climb in. But it was just us and a shitload of trees fifty feet away. I nibbled on my fingernail. "Do you think you can pull up to that third window? Maybe I can reach it if I stand in the bed of the truck."

"That's not going to work."

"Well, do you have a *better* solution?"

He mumbled something under his breath that I didn't catch, but pulled the truck next to the third window. We both got out and looked up.

"Shoot," I said. "It's too high. This isn't going to work."

"I seem to have heard that somewhere before."

I put my hands on my hips. "You don't have to be so cocky about it."

Brock shook his head and walked around to the back of his truck. He lowered the rear gate and climbed up, then extended one hand and pointed to the bumper with the other. "Put your foot on there, and I'll pull you up."

"But I'm still not going to be able to reach the window."

"Just do it."

My foot had barely touched the bumper when Brock hoisted me into the bed. He walked over near my window and kneeled down on one knee. "Get on my shoulders. I'll lift you."

"Are you sure? I'm not as light as I look."

"I lift logs bigger than you all day long."

"Okay..."

Brock held out a hand, and I climbed up to sit on his shoulders, trying to be as ladylike as I could while wearing a dress. But once I was on, he didn't move. "Am I too heavy?"

"Nope."

"Are you afraid you're going to fall?"

"Nope."

"So why aren't you moving?"

He cleared his throat. "Are you...not wearing underwear?"

*Oh.*

*My.*

*God.*

I wanted to die. I'd completely forgotten that I had taken off my pee-peed underwear earlier in the bathroom. Here I was, legs over this man's shoulders with my vagina pressed against the back of his neck. I started to swing my leg off to get down, but he gripped my ankle.

"We made it this far. Might as well finish."

I covered my face. "I seriously want to die right now."

Before I could say anything else, Brock climbed to his feet. I wobbled but stayed on. "Go ahead," he said. "Stand on my shoulders, and you should be able to reach."

"Do you promise not to look up?"

"I managed to not turn around and bury my face between your legs, so I think we're in the clear."

*Oh my.* That gave me a visual. Me facing the other way, my legs dangling down big, burly lumberjack Brock's back, while he buried his face in me...

"Anytime now," Brock grumbled.

"Oh—right."

Luckily, my window was still open, and when I stood on his shoulders, it was easy enough to climb in. After, I stuck my head back outside. "Thank you for... everything."

He chuckled. "Take care, Red."

I stayed at the window and watched Brock the burly lumberjack get back into his truck. As it pulled away, I felt oddly sad. Though people here had to be looking for me by now, so I grabbed a change of clothes from the drawer and ran into the bathroom to get dressed, only to realize I was still wearing Brock's flannel. It wasn't even off when someone knocked at my room door. *Shit.* "I'll be out in a minute!"

I finished changing as fast as I could, then scooped all the clothes from the bathroom floor and opened the cabinet under the sink. As I tossed everything inside, something dropped to the floor. A little book. My dress didn't have pockets, so it must've come from Brock's flannel. I reached for it and thumbed to the first page.

"Oh...this is interesting."

# CHAPTER 2

*February*

"What do you think is the purpose of that book?" Morgan asked, twirling a lock of her blond hair.

"I'm not sure."

I'd just finished telling my new friend at the center about the little book I'd found in burly Brock's flannel shirt. He seemed to enter the date and a note for each day of the week. Things like: *Helped an old lady cross the street* and *Changed a tire for someone on the highway.* He appeared to be keeping track of good deeds or something.

"The last one was the best!" Morgan teased.

I rolled my eyes. "So embarrassing."

*Took in a silly, drunk woman before she got herself killed.*

"I need to start sneaking out of this place, too," she said. "Find my own hot lumberjack. Does he have any brothers? It's way more fun out there than in here."

Morgan Flowers was a twenty-two-year-old influencer staying at Sierra after a near nervous breakdown that had warranted a social media hiatus. Despite her massive number of followers, Morgan had a lot of anxiety when encountering *actual* people in real life. Her stay at Sierra was an attempt to become more grounded, placing more value on herself and less value on the opinions of those on the Internet. So far, she'd done almost nothing but vlog the experience for the future entertainment of none other than—you guessed it—internet strangers.

"Do you mind turning the camera off when we're talking about my personal life?" I scolded.

She adjusted her lens. "I'm not going to use the sound. It's just B-roll for my vlogs. You'll be a silent talking head beneath my commentary."

"Doesn't it go against the privacy policy here to be taking so much footage?"

"Since when are we following the rules, Miss Ladder Climber?" She giggled. "Or should I say Commando Hot Lumberjack Climber? Anyway, not sure about the camera rules. I never specifically asked, and I sort of smuggled the equipment in. As long as *you're* okay with me showing your face. And I thought you said you didn't mind, that we don't have anything to be ashamed of by being here?"

"We don't, but that doesn't mean I want a camera shoved in my face every five seconds. I didn't realize how attached to that thing you'd be."

She nodded and sighed. "Okay. I'll shut it off for a bit." Morgan put the camera away and reached for Brock's shirt, which was lying on my bed. She brought it to her nose. "Mmm... Smells exactly how I'd imagine a big, hot lumberjack would." She groaned. "Shouldn't have sniffed that. Now I'm horny. A lot of good that does me being stuck in here."

I watched her a moment, feeling...something. Why did her reaction to his shirt make me jealous? I mean, I barely knew the man and certainly wasn't able to stake a claim. But in my head, Brock was *my* pseudo-kidnapper, no one else's. He'd had my *bare ass* on his shoulders just this morning. *Ugh.* I cringed. That whole situation was less than ideal.

"Are you gonna see him again?"

"Well, I think I should return the shirt and the notebook, don't you? I mean, how else is he going to chart his daily good deeds?"

"I think that makes a good excuse to see him, because you know seeing him again is really what you're looking for." She smirked.

Feeling my cheeks heat, I denied it. "It's not like that."

"I thought you said he was hot."

"He *is*, but my attraction to the guy can't mean anything. I mean, what am I gonna do? I don't live here, and technically am not even supposed to be leaving the premises."

"What else is there to look forward to for the next three weeks? If you're not gonna sneak out and see the burly bartender again, maybe I will." She crossed her arms.

My heart fell to my stomach.

Morgan snapped her fingers. "A-ha."

"What?"

"Your face just turned so red. Now I know you're bullshitting me. You *do* like him a little." She laughed. "Maybe *more* than a little. And I was only kidding, by the way. Just trying to test you."

"I don't know him from a hole in the wall, Morgan. You can't like someone you know nothing about."

"You know he's protective and he likes to kill animals."

"Which, by the way, is an oxymoron." I laughed.

"Are you calling me a moron?"

"No. I said *oxy*moron."

"Sorry. I'm a little traumatized from the mean comments on my post yesterday. Someone actually did call me a moron."

"How are you posting when they took away our phones?"

"I snuck in a second one. I haven't been checking it, only posting once a day. I can't go dark. My followers will think I'm dead."

Morgan wrapped Brock's shirt around her shoulders, which caused a sudden rush of adrenaline as jealousy shot through me again. I definitely needed mental help. Good thing I was in the right place.

♦ ♦ ♦

Thankfully, I got George the maintenance guy to put my escape route back that evening, because I had to sneak out to the bar to return Brock's shirt.

I made my way down to the ground successfully, but after the mile-long trek to the bar, I discovered that Brock was nowhere to be found.

"What's got you down, pretty lady?" a man who looked to be in his seventies asked me.

"Oh..." I shook my head. "Nothing. I was looking to return something to the bartender from last night, but he doesn't seem to be here."

"Brock Hawkins, you mean?"

"Yeah. He owns the bar, too, right?"

"Yep. He owns half the town."

"So I've heard."

The man stuck out his hand. "Name's Hank. I'm not working today, but I bartend a few nights a week."

I took it. "February."

He narrowed his eyes. "What about February?"

"That's my name. *February*."

"No kidding. That's different!"

If I had a nickel for every strange reaction to my name...

The man sipped his beer. "So what's your interest in Brock? You said you're returning something to him?"

"His shirt." My face felt flush as soon as I said it. *His shirt*. I realized how that sounded and quickly added, "He gave it to me because I was cold. And, anyway, I'm just returning it."

I needed a drink.

"Well, if you have romantic interest in Brock Hawkins, you certainly wouldn't be alone. Not only is he quite respected in this town, but many of the single gals have their sights set on him. Not just because he's a good-looking dude, but as you can imagine, they see dollar signs. Can't blame him for shying away from all of 'em."

I hated the idea of women trying to use Brock for his money. I mean...*using him for that hot body, maybe*. But gold diggers? *No*. They had to go. "What do you mean when you say Brock shies away from women?"

"Not my place to tell Brock's business..." He looked over his shoulder and lowered his voice. "He turns all *offers* down, if you know what I mean. But let's just say he has good reason to be wary of women lately. His last woman left him high and dry."

"Left him? What happened?"

"Rumor has it his ex wanted a life outside of this small town. Didn't want to be stuck here. She knew Brock couldn't leave, with all his businesses and brothers and such. So she left him. Brock hasn't been seen with anyone since. Brokenhearted, I guess."

That made me a little sad for the guy. And I also felt kind of wrong talking about him behind his back, so I ended my conversation with Hank. "Well, thanks for the talk."

"No problem, January." He winked.

*Yeah.* I walked over to the bar and called to the bartender on duty. "Excuse me."

He turned. "What can I get ya?"

"Oh, nothing to drink. But when you see Brock, can you give him this shirt? It belongs to him." I held it out.

He took it. "Sure thing."

"Thanks so much."

Since I'd skipped the alcohol during my quick visit to the bar, I began my walk back to Sierra Wellness completely sober. I deserved a gold star or something, given this disappointment of a night.

While it bummed me out that I didn't have a chance to see Brock, I was probably better off, since this whole thing had become one big distraction from the real reason I was here. I needed to focus on my mental health and go back to the City with a clear head.

*Clear your head, not give head, Feb. Don't misunderstand the assignment.* I laughed to myself as I walked.

About five minutes later, I heard footsteps behind me.

My pulse raced.

The road was dark, and if anything bad happened to me out here, good luck calling for help—especially with no damn phone.

I picked up my pace, but the next thing I knew, something came charging past me.

It was a dog.

"Oak! Slow down, you big-ass goon!" a familiar voice shouted.

Brock raced past me and caught the dog by the leash. I ran to catch up with them.

"I guess live animals are a bit more challenging than the dead ones back at your place, huh?"

His eyes widened. "What the hell are you doing walking on the road this late, Fancy Pants?"

"Actually, I think a better name for me would be No Pants, wouldn't it?"

"You said it, not me. I wasn't gonna go there."

"Why did Oak run away like that?"

"He goes nuts when the streetlights cast a shadow. He tries to run away from himself. But then in the midst of that, some little animal crossed our path, and he tried to chase it."

"Aw, he just wants a friend for the bathtub."

Brock's expression remained serious. "You didn't answer my question. What are you doing out here?"

"I went to the bar to return your shirt."

"You didn't need to risk your life to return my shirt."

"This is hardly risking my life."

"Really? And how the hell are you gonna fend off someone all by your damn self out here? You wouldn't be able to call nine-one-one fast enough before someone came up behind you."

"Actually, I don't have a phone, so I wouldn't be calling anyone. They confiscate all devices at the center."

"Wow." He tugged on the leash. "No phone on top of everything else. They don't teach common sense in handbag school, do they?"

"No, I must've missed that module, along with the taxidermy lesson. I guess you're just a *whole lot* smarter than me, Lumberjack."

He grinned. "I take it your ladder is safely in place tonight, if you snuck out?"

"Yes. Rest assured, no other man's shoulders will be corrupted."

The low rumble of his unexpected laughter vibrated through me. "Well, that's good. Lucky me."

We stood facing each other. "I left your shirt and notebook with the bartender on duty." I crossed my arms. "By the way, why did you write that I was *silly*?"

"Thanks for invading my privacy."

"I couldn't help it. It fell out of your pocket, and I didn't know what it was."

"Uh-huh."

"You didn't answer my question. Why am I silly?"

"Because only a silly woman would put herself in the situation you did last night. I could be an ax murderer for all you know."

"No, you couldn't, with your little acts of kindness. You just *look* like one." I scratched my chin. "Actually, if you murdered those animals on your wall, maybe you are."

"I didn't kill those animals. I just wanted you to think I did."

"*Someone* killed them."

"It wasn't me. I inherited those heads." He frowned. "Why did you read my notebook?"

"Because I'm nosy." I tilted my head. "What's the deal with those entries anyway?"

He placed his hand on my arm, leading me away from the road. "There's a car coming. Come sit over here, off the road."

We moved to a rock in a grassy area a few feet away. The dog rested on the ground between us.

"Those notes are personal," he said. "But since you chose to butt your nose into my business, I record one good deed a day, yes."

"Why?"

"It's something my grandfather taught me. My mother's father. My dad wasn't around much growing up. Gramps helped raise me. He used to keep a record just like mine in a similar notebook. He'd always say, if a person could perform one good deed a day, that would cancel out any bad things he might've done." Brock shrugged.

"So it's like a superstition?"

"Maybe a little. But that would be *silly*, wouldn't it?" He winked. "Anyway, I figure there's no harm in making an effort to contribute to society one bit at a time. Recording one good deed a day helps keep me accountable. That's all."

"Well, that's impressive. Although, from what I hear, you have enough fans around here as it is. You're big shit around these parts. You have panties dropping left and right."

He arched a brow. "You have the nerve to bring up panties dropping after what you put me through this morning?"

When he smiled, it made my heart flutter. But soon enough Mr. Grumpy returned.

His forehead crinkled. "Where are you getting this intel about me, anyway?"

"I have my ways..." I teased.

"Spill, Red."

I laughed. "Hank the Gossip Bank?"

Brock growled. "Great."

He suddenly stood and pulled on the dog's leash. "Come on."

I thought he was talking to Oak, but then he turned and gestured for me to get up. "Let's go."

"Go where?"

"To my truck so I can drive you back to your place."

"No way." I shook my head. "I'm done playing damsel in distress. And I don't need a big lug to climb tonight since I made sure George was gonna leave me the ladder."

"It's not safe for you to be walking home this late."

"If *you* can walk out here this late, so can I."

"I'm a giant man with a giant dog. You're a tiny woman with no goddamn phone and for all I know, no fucking underwear."

I couldn't help but laugh. "I'll have you know, I *am* wearing them tonight. Although, I considered sticking them in your flannel pocket as a token of my appreciation. But something told me your grumpy butt wouldn't have appreciated it. You might have thought that was a bit *silly*, so..."

"What *is* silly is you trying to disregard real danger, just to prove a point."

I pointed my index finger at him. "Oh, I know what this is. You must not have a good deed for the day yet. That's why you want to drive me home."

"My good deed today is refraining from throwing your ass over my shoulder right now and walking you to my truck." He exhaled. "And why don't you have a damn coat on if you're walking a mile?"

"How *silly* of me..." I grinned mischievously, enjoying this exchange a little too much. "Actually, that was an easy mistake. I wore your flannel on the way here and hadn't accounted for the fact that I wouldn't have it on the return trip."

His voice softened a bit. "You're really not gonna let me drive you home? I think that's dumb."

My teeth chattered. "I'm already halfway there. It makes no sense to walk back with you only to have you drive me. I'll be fast. You don't need to worry about me."

"Let me walk you then," he insisted.

"No, please don't."

"Why are you really here in Meadowbrook?" he asked. "What are you running from?"

"I'll tell you if you tell me why your girlfriend left town."

Brock grumbled something under his breath.

After a long moment of silence, he took off the plaid flannel he was wearing.

I held up my palm. "I don't want it."

"Take it, Red. Don't be stupid. It's cold."

"You are the grumpiest man I've ever met." I chuckled as I gave in, gladly wrapping his warm shirt around me. It smelled a bit different than the last one, still woodsy and delicious, though.

"Be careful," he warned. "I'd tell you to call me when you get there, but you have no damn phone."

"I'll howl into the night." I giggled. "Even better, I'll send your dead heads a telepathic message that I got there safely."

"Dead heads? Like Grateful Dead?"

"I'm talking about your stuffed deer and moose."

"Oh," he muttered.

"You're a little slow tonight, Brock. Must be the cold air freezing your brain."

"The only thing freezing my brain tonight is the city girl who thinks it's safe to walk on the side of a dark country road with no phone, no jacket, and—I don't care what you say—probably no goddamn underwear. I'm just trying to make sure you don't turn into roadkill."

I walked backward away from him. "Tell you what… if that happens, you can have first dibs on hanging me on your wall, Lumberjack."

He shook his head. "Watch your ass, crazy woman. And hurry home."

Heeding his advice, I did add some pep to my step as I took off. He wasn't wrong at all about the dangers of walking late at night. But somehow the prospect of seeing *him* had seemed worth the risk. To be honest, I was pretty sure Brock Hawkins was the most dangerous thing on this road.

I made it back to Sierra safely, wishing there was a way I could let him know I was okay.

As I reluctantly removed his cozy shirt so I could take a shower before bed, something fell out of the pocket. How had I not felt this earlier?

I bent to pick it up.

No way.

*His phone.*

# CHAPTER 3

*February*

Seriously? No freaking password? Who the hell does that? Between the good-deed journal and now an unlocked cell phone, Lumberjack might as well have written all his secrets in a diary and handed it over.

Though I *shouldn't* read it.

That would be another invasion of his privacy. Perhaps I could just check out the apps he had? Those weren't too personal. Right?

I still felt a little guilty as I swiped from the home screen to the second page and perused the icons.

*CNN News*

*Sports Line*

*Fitness Pro*

*Marathon Man*

*Home Depot*

*Tinder*—Hmm... Interesting. Lumberjack has a hook-up dating app.

I stared down at the flame icon, feeling incredibly tempted to click in and see what type of women he swiped right on. But that would *definitely* be crossing a line. Yet my finger was still hovering over the app when Morgan popped her head into my room. Her eyes lit up when she saw the cell phone in my hands.

"You have a second phone, too?"

I shook my head. "Actually, this one is Brock's."

"Hot mountain man gave you his phone?"

"Not intentionally. I snuck out to return his flannel and little book. He wasn't at the bar, but then on my walk back, I ran into him while he was walking his dog."

"You just *happened* to run into him again?"

"I know. But he lives and works nearby, and his dog has to go out." I shrugged. "Anyway, we talked for a few minutes, and after, he made me take the flannel he had on for my walk back. I'd left the other one with the bartender. The phone was in the pocket."

"Jeez." She sat down on the bed next to me and plucked the cell from my hand. It was still illuminated. "How did you get in? Didn't he have a password?"

"Nope. No password."

"That's absurd. Who doesn't have a password?"

I shrugged again. "Someone with nothing to hide?"

She started to scroll. "I'll be the judge of that."

"Uh…" I reached over and swiped the phone from her hands. "You certainly will not. If *I'm* not going to invade the man's privacy, *you* aren't either."

"You're seriously not going to check out what's on his phone? A cell is a gold mine of information. If I'd had free access like this to any of the men I dated before we started dating, it would've saved me a lot of heartache."

"I'm not planning on dating Brock."

She grinned. "So just fucking him, then?"

"There will be none of that either. I'll probably never see the man again."

"Of course you will. You have to give him back that phone."

◆ ◆ ◆

Later in the afternoon, Lara, another patient I'd made friends with, came into my room. "Hey. You want to catch the five o'clock meditation class with me?"

"Yeah, sure." I pretended to fix my bedding while slipping Brock's cell phone under my pillow. I'd spent *way* too many hours staring at the thing today anyway. A little clearing of my mind was in order.

Meditation classes were taught by Trinity, one of the mental health therapists. She happened to be my therapist, so we already knew each other. She walked over while I was setting up my mat.

"Hey, February. How are you today?"

I smiled. "I'm doing well."

"How have you been sleeping?"

"Eh. About the same." Sleep had become an issue for me about a year ago. I could *fall* asleep, but I never seemed able to *stay* asleep. Even when I went to bed with a clear head, I woke up at two in the morning thinking about things going on at work or in my personal life. Insomnia was actually one of the reasons I'd snuck out to the bar the other night. I'd spent all day talking about the reasons I'd checked into Sierra Wellness Center, and I knew I'd be tossing and turning without a bit of liquid encouragement help me to drift off.

She smiled. "We're going to do some exercises you can try at night before you go to bed. I'm glad you came today."

"Me too."

The class began with Trinity playing a Tibetan singing bowl. She asked us all to focus on the peaceful sound it made, taking three deep breaths in through our noses and breathing out through our mouths. Then she instructed us to take a moment to think about a happy place. My mind immediately went to having coffee with Brock in his apartment, which was bizarre since I barely knew the man, and waking up hungover with a shotgun pointed at me wasn't exactly *happy*. But nothing else came to mind, so I went with it. Listening to the rhythmic hum of the bowl, I imagined myself in Brock's bed again—how good he'd smell, how his big, protective body would keep me warm. I'd snuggle close while he lay on his back, and I'd rest my head on his thick chest. He'd stroke my hair while I listened to his heartbeat. I felt so peaceful, so relaxed.

And that's the last thing I remembered thinking about when I woke up some time later.

Pushing up to my elbows, I was now the only student in the class. Trinity sat at the front of the room writing in a journal. "Oh my God," I said. "I can't believe I fell asleep. I'm so sorry. How long was I out?"

She shut her book. "Not too long. And there's nothing to apologize for. I take students falling asleep in meditation class as a compliment."

I stretched my arms over my head and bent to the left, then the right. "I can't remember the last time I napped. Maybe in college?"

"You must've needed it." She smiled. "I have another class in a few minutes. You're welcome to join. But if you go out to the gazebo on the west side of the building, you'll probably catch a beautiful sunset right about now. I sometimes sit there at this time when I don't have a class to teach."

"Oh. That sounds great." I stood and rolled up my mat. "I think I'll do that."

I walked outside and was greeted by a lavender-and-pink sky. The setting sun cast a golden glow over the trees surrounding the gazebo. It was so still and peaceful, and I realized I felt more relaxed than I had in ages. Maybe there was something to this mediation stuff after all? Or maybe there was something to fantasizing about a certain lumberjack. I wasn't sure which it was, but I sat quietly, enjoying the serenity. When it grew dark, I made my way back inside and decided to stop at the business center. Patients weren't allowed to use cell phones or electronic devices, but we were allowed fifteen minutes a day of computer time to take care of whatever we needed to. I generally used my time to email my administrative assistant, Oliver, who also happens to be my closest friend.

But today, I was so relaxed that I decided not to ruin it with work. Instead, I typed a quick note to my sister, letting her know I was doing okay. After, I still had a few minutes of time left, so I went on Instagram and typed in *Brock Hawkins*. Not surprisingly, he didn't seem to have an account. But while I was on, I noticed a tag from Morgan, so I clicked to see what kind of nonsense she'd posted today that had probably gotten a few hundred-thousand likes.

The video was of her smiling at the camera. I recognized the background as her room here. She nibbled her bottom lip before whispering, "I just read the *dirtiest text* I've ever read in my life." She fanned herself. "I had no idea that mountain men could be so descriptive. I need to get out of the big city more often."

I froze. *Mountain men?*

"If y'all want me to read another Tinder message, just like this video. If we hit half a million, I'll read another. A million? I'll read two!"

*Tinder!* Oh no.

Whatever calm I'd been feeling was replaced by a racing heart. I clicked to sign off from my Instagram account and rushed back to my room—only to find Brock's cell no longer under my pillow. *Damn it!* I sprinted to Morgan's room and found her sitting on her bed, holding her cell out and talking like she was recording.

"Where is it?"

She lowered her phone. "Where's what?"

"Brock's phone. I know you have it, Morgan."

She pouted. "God, your face is so tense. You should try one of the meditation classes they offer here."

"I don't need *meditation*, Morgan. I need *Brock's phone*!"

She rolled her eyes but opened the bedside table and slipped out the cell. "One of us had to go through it. You don't know anything about this guy you keep sneaking out to see."

"I'm not sneaking out to see Brock, and neither of us needs to know anything about his personal life."

Morgan grinned. "Not even about the app he has that controls a vibrator remotely? Or the pictures of his giant dick and washboard abs? What about the texts from his ex that say she can't stop thinking about how hard he fucks her? At least let me tell you about those." She looked down at her cell phone and turned it to show me the screen. "Four-hundred-and-twenty-thousand people want me to tell them about the Tinder messages, and it's only been fifteen minutes since I asked if they wanted to hear another one."

I frowned. "I can't believe you think it's okay to invade a person's privacy like this. It's *wrong*, Morgan."

She shrugged. "Maybe. But if what that man wrote is *wrong*, I don't want to be *right*."

"You're unbelievable," I huffed and marched out of the room with the cell phone.

Morgan yelled after me. "Wait! What will I read to my followers? I promised them two more messages!"

"Here's an idea..." I turned back to look at her. "Read them a goodbye note. Then turn your phone in to your therapist and actually try getting some help. Because I think you need it."

♦ ♦ ♦

Hours later, I lay in bed, staring at the ceiling in the dark. I wasn't happy with Morgan, but I'd managed to stop seething over what she'd done. Though not because I was any less mad. It was more that my focus had shifted. To Brock. To the photos that were only a few swipes away. To his dirty texts. To the *remote vibrator app*. That last one had been the center of my attention for the last hour, and I couldn't help myself... I finally gave in and slipped the phone out from under my pillow.

On the third screen in, I was pretty certain I'd found it.

BuzzBuddy.

The name might've been funny if I were in the right mood. But I'd had a bug up my ass ever since Morgan had spilled about all the crap on Brock's phone.

I stared down at the dumb app icon—a pink vibrator with a lipstick kiss on the side—anxious to click in. Though even *that* felt like an invasion of Brock's privacy, and I couldn't bring myself to do it. Instead, I went to Google and typed in BuzzBuddy.

*BuzzBuddy—control your woman's pleasure, even when you can't be with her.*

Beneath was an article that explained how the app worked. Essentially, it connected to an insertable vibrator that could be controlled remotely. The end user could do things like increase the vibrations and add G-spot stimulation. There was also add-on hardware available, things like a clitoris massager and a prostate gland stroker. *Jeez.* The thing supposedly even had the ability to determine when a woman had an orgasm. I continued to scan the article, half reading and half not, until a certain sentence caught my attention.

*The BuzzBuddy also records session history, including dates, times, and length of playtime.*

That got me thinking...

*Maybe I can just take a quick peek.*

It wouldn't be like I was reading his personal thoughts and messages.

It would only be some *facts*—dates and times.

Who knew? Maybe Brock hadn't even used the thing.

I gnawed on my lip as I closed out of Google and swiped back to the app.

Let's face it, I was never going to sleep without checking it out now.

And I was at a mental-health facility, for God's sake. I *had* to do what was best for my mental health, right? Sleep was too important.

I rolled my eyes at myself and groaned, yet I clicked into the stupid app anyway.

My heart raced as I poked around. It wasn't easy to navigate, but eventually I found an option called *Session History*. Clicking in, my eyes grew wide.

"Holy crap."

There were *pages and pages* of sessions. Seeing them all in black and white made me a little nauseous. But one entry in particular stopped me in my tracks. Because it had been recorded two nights ago—while I was sleeping in bed right next to Brock.

"*Unreal. Un-freaking-real.*" I whipped the covers off and got out of bed. Not only did I not want to see anything else in this phone, I wanted the thing out of my possession immediately. So I dressed as fast as I could, tucked the phone into my back pocket, and locked the door to my room. I was just about to climb out the window—without even knowing if the damn ladder was outside—when something dawned on me.

A man who has virtual sex with one woman while another is lying in his bed doesn't have respect for anyone. So why was I being so respectful and not looking through the rest of his phone? The answer: I wasn't anymore.

Without further debate, I went right to his photos. The first picture I called up was of a weird tattoo—I wasn't certain, but I thought it might be a squirrel running down a thigh. A *very thick thigh*... Was that Brock? I swiped again. And the next photo made my jaw drop...

♦ ♦ ♦

"Hi. Is Brock working tonight?"

The bartender shook his head. "Sorry, it's his night off."

"Oh."

"Can I get you something to drink anyway?"

If I wasn't going to be able to give Brock a piece of my mind, I definitely could use a drink. "I'll have a dry martini, shaken not—" Remembering what Brock had said about my *prissy* drink, I stopped and shook my head. "You know what? I'll just have a vodka and cranberry, please."

He knocked on the bar twice. "Coming right up."

A young man slid onto the stool next to me. He flashed a dimpled, crooked smile.

"Hey there. I think you owe me a drink?"

I smiled, even through my anger. "And why would I owe you a drink?"

His smile widened. "Because I dropped mine when you walked in. You're so damn beautiful."

I chuckled. "Cheesy. But cute. Though I think I'd need to see some ID to buy you any alcohol. Are you even old enough to be in here?"

The kid shrugged. "Nah. But the owner doesn't care." He extended a hand. "I'm Axe."

"Is that your real name?"

His lip quirked. "No, but it'll sound a heck of a lot better than *Arthur* when you're moaning it."

This kid was really adorable. Ridiculously over the top, yet somehow it worked for him. Charisma, shaggy hair, and a dimpled smile were a dangerous combination. I bet he was popular with girls his own age. There was also something familiar about him. "How old are you, *Axe*?"

"Eighteen. Well, close enough. I'll be eighteen next year."

The bartender returned with my drink. He wagged his finger at the kid next to me. "Leave the ladies alone, Arthur."

He pointed. "*She* hit on *me*."

"Yeah, right." The bartender moved two fingers back and forth, simulating walking. "Go back to the booth and finish your homework, or I'm kicking your ass out."

Axe, or *Arthur*, groaned. "You suck." But he also slinked off to a booth.

I drank my drink quietly after that, debating whether I should leave Brock's phone with the bartender or come back another night so I could give it to him myself, along with some choice words. As I finished off the last of my cocktail, Axe returned. He'd just started to say something when a booming voice interrupted.

"What did I tell you about sitting at the bar?" Brock's face was stern.

"I was just getting the nice lady's phone number," Axe said.

Brock looked to me. "You giving this kid your number?"

His tone pissed me off. *He* pissed me off. So I folded my arms across my chest. "What business is it of yours if I am?"

Brock scowled and pointed at the kid next to me. "I've told you ten times, you don't sit at this bar for four more years. Now you've lost the right to even come in here. From now on, you go somewhere else to do your homework."

"How can I go somewhere else when you took my car keys?"

"You have two damn legs. *Walk*."

"Can I at least have my phone back?"

"Will you leave if I give you your phone?"

"Absolutely."

Brock took a deep breath and blew it out. The kid was trying his patience. He turned to me. "Any chance you found a phone? I took this little shit's cell because he got suspended *again*. But I can't find it anywhere. I think I might've left it in the flannel I gave you last night."

I felt all the color from my face drain. "It...it wasn't your phone?"

"No. It's my dipshit little brother's."

I swallowed. "Your brother?"

He nodded.

"I, uh..." I took the phone from my back pocket and held it out hesitantly. "Is this it?"

The kid swiped it from my hand. "Thanks! Gotta go."

My head was still reeling as I watched him jog from the bar. I hadn't been looking at pictures of *Brock's* dick? I'd been looking at his *seventeen-year-old* brother? His little brother used *the BuzzBuddy app*?

Oh God.

"You okay, Red?"

I covered my face with my hands. "Not really."

"What's going on?"

I shook my head. "I'm mortified to even tell you."

"Shit." He chuckled. "This sounds good."

I still had my face covered, so I spread two of my fingers and peeked out. "If I tell you, you have to promise you will *not* torture me about it."

"Not sure I can do that until I hear what it is."

I sighed. "I peeked in your phone—at least I thought it was your phone until two minutes ago."

"Okay..."

"I hate to tell you this, but your little brother has some *interesting* apps on there."

"Oh, I know." He shook his head. "Freaking BuzzBuddy. The little peckerhead got suspended because of the damn thing. He was using it on some girl while they were in school, and one of the teachers heard the humming. That's why I took his phone and his car away. Our mother, God rest her soul, would've chopped off his balls for having shit like that."

My heart squeezed. I hadn't known he'd lost his mother. "I'm sorry. Your brother is so young to not have a mom."

Brock nodded. "Art is the youngest. My mom had six boys."

"Who does he live with?"

"My aunt. That's what my mom wanted. But my brothers and I all keep an eye on him and help out." Brock gestured to the booths on the other side of the bar. "You up for another drink? Maybe we can go sit over there for a while?"

I smiled. "I'd like that."

"Good." He winked. "Because you owe me one after I didn't bust your balls about going through the phone when you thought it was mine."

Brock and I spent the next two hours talking. He told me more about growing up with five brothers, and I finally came clean about the real reason my board had sent me for a mental-health break.

"Let me get this straight... You had no clue the mic was on, and everyone in the audience at some hurdy-turdy fashion show heard you having sex?"

I sipped my drink. "Pretty much. With my competitor. And we sort of cursed at each other through the whole thing. I *loathe* the man. Though sadly, it wasn't our first time."

Brock went quiet.

"What are you thinking right now?" I asked. "I'm not generally promiscuous like that, if that's what's running through your mind."

"That wasn't what I was thinking."

"Then what is it?"

He met my eyes. "That I'd like to punch the fucker who got to have sex with you."

A little flutter moved through my belly. I smiled. "The feeling is mutual. I was jealous of whoever you were sexting with. By the way, you should tell your little brother to delete some of the racy pics he has on his phone. He's underage, and if he sends them to people, it could be considered dissemination of child pornography." As soon as I said the words, my eyes flared. "*Oh my God, Brock*. You have to get your brother's phone back!"

Brock's brows pulled tight. "Why?"

"Because I was pissed at you and left you a parting gift on it. I took a pic of me giving you the finger."

He shrugged. "That's not a big deal. My brother's seen and done a lot worse."

"No, Brock! You have to get it back. I didn't just give you the finger. I wanted you to see what you were missing, so I held it up *between my bare breasts!*"

# CHAPTER 4
*Brock*

I'd booked it out of the bar so damn fast there was probably smoke left in my wake. My pulse was going a mile a minute. This woman was going to be the death of me. It was hard to believe I'd only known her a couple of days, because she'd consumed me from the moment she blew into town.

No way in hell I was going to let my brother see that photo. *That's why I'm speeding down the road*, I told myself. But I had a vested interest in getting to that photo—for myself. As crazy as February drove me, there was no denying how gorgeous she was. Knowing she'd sent a nude photo for my eyes only made me a little crazy. It also made me realize how damn hard up I was, and how much I needed to be careful not to let my carnal desires get in the way of common sense.

Going over the speed limit, I raced to make it to my aunt's before my brother happened to go through his photos and notice it.

I reluctantly slowed down when I spotted an old man on the side of the road. He was holding his side, limping, and looked like he was struggling to walk. Shit. *Why do I always attract this stuff?* Normally, this would be my good deed of the day, to stop and help. But if I did, I'd run the risk of not getting to Axe in time.

After I passed the man, guilt consumed me. So I stopped my truck and put it in reverse.

I rolled down the window. "Are you okay, sir?"

His voice was frail. "Just played cards at my friend's house. Thought I could make it home carrying this bag, but I'm feeling awfully tired. Got a cramp in my arm."

"Where do you live?"

"On Groveland..."

I tilted my head. "I can take you home."

His mouth curved into a smile. "That's very kind of you, Brock."

"You know my name?" I asked, surprised.

"Everyone knows you around these parts."

I got out and helped lift the little old man into my truck. "What's your name?" I asked.

"Jim."

I forced a smile. "Hi, Jim."

Once he put his seatbelt on, I took off. Hope he didn't mind my lead foot, because I had no freaking time to waste here.

Jim turned to me. "I'm very grateful for your help."

Tenser by the second, I groaned under my breath. "No problem."

"You seem to be in a rush. I hope I'm not making you late for something."

I laughed at the thought of explaining the truth to him: that I was in a race against time to view a pair of tits before my brother had a chance to. But instead, I said, "Nothing important enough to not get you home safely."

After I got to the old man's house, I helped him out of the truck. I was about to take off when he held up his shaky finger and asked me to wait outside. He said he needed to give me something.

*Shit. What now?*

He walked toward his house at a snail's pace, and then I waited, not so patiently.

I bounced my legs as the minutes passed. *What the hell am I waiting for?* I should just go. But that would be a total dick move.

I shook my head at myself. What a dumbass I was to give February my shirt without checking the pockets first. Served me damn right to be in this position.

About five minutes later, the man finally came out of the house carrying something. Once again, it took him forever to get from point A to point B. It would be a miracle if Axe wasn't whacking off to February's photo as we spoke. Pretty sure I'd totally screwed myself.

The man handed me a small plastic bag. At first I thought it was weed, but then I realized there were two cookies inside. "Here are some treats my daughter made. I hope you enjoy them. Thank you again for driving me home."

I couldn't help but smile at the sweet gesture. "Thanks, buddy. I appreciate it."

"Bless you," he said.

The cookies looked good, but I doubted they were worth the consequences of this delay. This time I couldn't afford to wait for Jim to safely reenter the house. I drove off and was lucky I didn't get a ticket as I rushed to my aunt's.

Thankfully, I could see my brother through the window, so I knew he was home.

Out of breath, I knocked on the door.

He opened a few seconds later. "What the hell? Why are you knocking like that?"

"I need your phone."

He narrowed his eyes. "Why?"

"Never mind why. Just give it to me."

My brother shook his head. "Fuck that. I just got it back. Why would I give it to you again?"

"Axe..." I scolded.

"What?"

"Give me the fucking phone..."

"Not until you tell me why you need it."

I searched his eyes for a moment because I needed to know if he'd seen the photo. He looked genuinely confused, which told me I might still be safe. My brother wasn't the type to hide his amusement very well. So, while I still didn't know how I was gonna get the phone from him, I breathed a sigh of relief that I wasn't too late.

"I just need to see the phone for a minute. I'll give it right back."

He crossed his arms. "Not until you tell me why."

My brother had a point. There was no logical reason for him to hand over his phone when I had just given it back to him. If I was going to get it, I had to do something rash, something a little insane, which was exactly how I felt when it came to that woman.

I leapt forward before Axe had a chance to react, reaching into his back pocket where I knew he typically carried his phone.

His hair was all messed up when I let him go. "What the fuck is wrong with you, man?"

"Give me five minutes. I'll be back with it then."

"I thought you said a minute," he called after me as I ran out of his house.

Escaping into my truck, I took off down the road so he couldn't see what I was doing.

I parked on a side street, and my finger shook as I pulled up the photo library.

Sure enough, the most recent photo was the most beautiful set of tits I'd ever seen staring back at me. As promised, February's middle finger was right between them. Sweat beaded on my forehead as I imagined what would've happened had my brother found this first. I'd dodged a bullet.

I took a few minutes to just stare at the photo, my mouth watering as I imagined pulling one of those perfectly pink nipples into my mouth, sucking hard. I'd been in a dry spell lately, and this was probably the last thing I needed—especially since I'd already vowed not to let anything happen with this woman, even if she was tempting as all hell. That didn't change the fact that she was only traveling through town and was probably the last woman I should be messing around with. But isn't it always the one you can't have that you want?

Blood rushed to my dick as my finger rubbed gently over the screen, tracing her creamy mounds. *Fuck. One more minute*, I told myself. Then you have to let go. Only one more minute, and then I'd delete the damn thing and never look at it again. I'd have to remember to delete it from the trash folder on his phone as well.

After my minute was up—maybe it was ten minutes—my fingers hovered over the delete button. But I couldn't. I couldn't do it. As far as I was concerned, this photo was gold. I texted it to myself instead before deleting the photo from Axe's library and from the deleted photos file. Maybe now I could go on with my damn night and start functioning like a normal human instead of a feral cat.

I drove back to my aunt's house. As expected, Axe was pissed.

He held up his hands. "What the hell is wrong with you?"

I handed him the phone and calmly said, "Thank you."

"You're not gonna tell me what this is all about?"

"Not unless you want to explain all the shit you've been up to, Vibrator Boy."

He smirked. "I have nothing to hide."

"Stay out of trouble, please."

He called after me. "Seriously? You're gonna leave me hanging like this?"

Ignoring him, I left.

When I returned to the bar, February was still waiting there.

"Jesus, that took forever," she huffed.

With a scowl on my face, I didn't say anything. I tried not to look at her for fear my eyes would travel below her neck and it would be obvious that her breasts were still at the forefront of my mind.

"Well?" she finally said. "Was it successful?"

"Oh, I got it, all right."

She swallowed. "Did you...manage to delete the photo from his phone?"

I finally looked her in the eyes. "Yeah. Thankfully. He hadn't seen it."

"How do you know?"

"He would've told me if he had."

February's eyes fixed on mine. She seemed to be expecting me to say something more, but that wouldn't be happening. I wasn't about to admit that I'd looked at that photo for a second, let alone stared at it for several minutes until it became permanently fixed in my brain. Not wanting her to sense any guilt on my face, I moved behind the bar and got to work—or at least pretended to, wiping everything down and arranging bottles, even though the actual bartender on duty tonight was attending to someone right beside me.

Much to my chagrin, February leaned her arms over the counter. "I'd like to order a drink, please."

"No," I snapped.

"Excuse me?"

My eyes darted toward her as I stopped wiping. "No."

She tilted her head. "Why?"

"Because we're not gonna have a repeat of the other night, where you're drunk off your ass and I have to pick up the sloppy pieces."

"I'm only going to have one more drink."

I raised my brow skeptically at her.

"I'm serious, Brock. I don't make the same mistake twice."

I groaned. "What do you want, then?"

She rested her chin on her hand. "Surprise me."

As much as I wanted to just pour her a damn water with lemon, instead I prepared a Tom Collins and slid it toward her with a cherry on top.

Of course I couldn't help watching as she took the cherry into her mouth. My dick twitched as I forced myself to resume wiping down the counter.

She took a sip and moaned. "Mmm... This is so good."

Some of it dribbled down her shirt, and I felt my dick stiffen at the vivid recollection of what was behind that material.

I really needed to get laid—with anyone but this gorgeous traveler.

She licked her lips. "You shouldn't have made me something so tasty if you didn't want me to have another."

"Well, I won't be making you another. So I hope you enjoyed it."

She slurped the last of her drink and moved the ice around with her straw. "Why are you grumpier than usual tonight?"

"Because I would've preferred not to have to chase your tits down to save them from being plastered all over the Internet."

"Was that your good deed for the day? Keeping my boobs from going viral?"

"Actually, no."

"Aw, really? What was it, then?"

"Gave an old man a ride home," I muttered.

"You're so sweet deep down, Brock."

"You don't know me enough to come to that conclusion. Be careful about assuming I'm so sweet and respectful. I'm one notch away from losing it with you."

She squinted at me.

I raised a brow. "What?"

"I don't believe you would actually lose control. I don't know why...but I trust you."

"You shouldn't." I gritted my teeth.

"You know..." She sighed. "It kind of makes sense now."

"What makes sense?"

She looked at me with a mischievous grin that made me want to lift her over the bar and smack her ass. She'd lit some kind of fire inside of me, one that needed to remain at a subtle simmer until she left town.

She once again attempted to slurp the last of the liquid from her glass before slamming it on the counter. "It kind of makes sense that phone wasn't yours."

The mention of the phone reminded me of the photo, which of course made my blood pressure rise. "Why is that?"

"The vibrator app—it doesn't line up with your personality."

"In what way?"

"I couldn't picture you going to such great lengths to get a woman off. You're more of a straight shooter."

"You're right about one thing."

"What's that?" She smiled.

"I wouldn't need a damn app to get a woman off. Never needed *any* help pleasing a woman."

Her face reddened, and that seemed to shut her up—until it didn't.

"Speaking of that, why did your ex leave town?"

*This again?* "Excuse me? What does that have to do with any of this?"

She shrugged. "It doesn't. I'm just curious about it."

It angered me that Hank had been spilling my business to February, especially when she'd probably drawn the wrong conclusion. Yes, my ex left town, but it *wasn't* cut and dried. People had been whispering ever since she left, assuming I'd been dumped. But that wasn't the whole story at all.

February shook her head. "I'm sorry for prying."

"You should be. You've been getting your information from the town gossip, but no one actually knows what happened between my ex and me *except* her and me." I slapped a dishtowel against the bar before throwing it over my shoulder. "But let me be clear. Her leaving was a *good* thing for both of us and had nothing to do with my ability to please a woman, if that's what you were implying."

"I wasn't implying anything. I was just being nosy."

"You're an awfully nosy person for someone with her own secrets, who mysteriously shows up in a random town to stay at that hokey wellness center. I'm sure *you* have a much bigger story than I could ever tell about myself. I bet it's more complicated than that microphone tryst, too."

"I might have some daddy issues and be generally fucked up, yeah. But no one is perfect. More people should try to get help for their issues and know when to slow down. I don't think the wellness center is hokey at all, and I'm happy I came. It's a good thing for me."

"Is that why you spend so much time trying to sneak out of it, because it's so great?"

"Speaking of which..." She looked over at the clock on the wall. "I'd better go."

"Don't..." The word came out of my mouth a little too quickly for my liking. As if my dick had decided to speak in place of my mind.

"Why?"

"Bartender working for me tonight has to leave early, so I've gotta close. Wait for me. I'll drive you back."

"I can't. I promised my friend Morgan I'd help her with something. I totally forgot about it."

Her cheeks turned red, and I got the impression she was lying. I certainly didn't want to force her to accept a ride with me if it made her uncomfortable.

"I'm gonna walk," she insisted.

That didn't exactly sit well with me. But it had been a long, *frustrating* day, and I wasn't sure I trusted myself to spend any more time with her. Besides, it wasn't like I could force her to wait for me or carry her over my shoulder to my truck, as much as that sounded enticing.

I let out a long breath. "Can you find some way to let me know you got home safely?"

"Morgan has a phone she snuck in. I can probably text you from her number."

I grabbed a pen and paper and jotted down my number. "Figure out a way to let me know you got home."

"Or else what?" she challenged.

"Or else I'm climbing up your ladder and seeing for myself."

"I kind of like that idea."

I glared. "No, you don't."

"You're sure of that, huh?"

"You need to *not* like that idea. You get my drift, February?"

"You're sending me mixed signals, Brock. Earlier you were admitting to being jealous at the thought of me and another man, and now you're warning me not to like the idea of you climbing into my room. You're a cock tease."

"I didn't realize you had a cock."

She rolled her eyes. "Well, you know what I mean..."

"I'm a tease? You fucking sent me a photo of your tits."

"What did you think, by the way? You never said."

I felt my face heat.

"That good, huh?" she asked.

I remained silent for a while, refusing to chime in.

She finally gave up on an answer and started to strut away.

"Hey, Feb," I called.

She turned. "What?"

"You have my number. Be sure to send photos to the right place from now on."

"You wish," she said before disappearing out the door.

*Yes.*

*Yes, I do.*

# CHAPTER 5
*Brock*

I looked down the block before flipping the OPEN sign in the window to CLOSED and grumbled to myself. "Good. Maybe she'll never come back."

Though that thought made my chest grow tight. It had been five days since I'd seen or heard from February. The last message I'd received was from an unknown number the night she'd returned my little brother's phone. It read *I'm back*, and apparently that was that. Though it hadn't stopped me from watching the damn bar door every night I'd worked.

"Hey!" my brother Elvin yelled. "Grab me a shot of Casamigos, will ya?"

"Your legs broken or something?"

He pointed to his casted ankle.

"Shit." I hung my head. "Sorry. I forgot." A few weeks ago, my oldest brother had snapped his tibia when he fell off a roof at a jobsite. He hadn't been wearing a safety harness, so the dumbass was lucky it wasn't his neck.

Tonight was our monthly card game. All the Hawkins boys played except for Axe. I grabbed five shot glasses and lined them up on the bar before filling them with one continuous pour. Two of my brothers weren't here yet, but they should arrive any minute.

"Tequila for everyone." I walked over to the table and started passing out shots. "Don't say I didn't get you anything at Christmas."

I had two left on the tray when the front door burst open. Trevor strutted in with a gloating smile and held up a big Tupperware container. "Sorry I'm late. My new lady, Emma, wanted me to bring the homemade seven-layer dip hot."

Everyone groaned. Maddox cursed as he dug into his pocket and threw a fifty-dollar bill on the table. "Fucking unbelievable."

I chuckled. "Told you. You underestimated the man and bet way too low."

Trevor was the second youngest brother and the ladies' man of the bunch. A little over a month ago, he'd shown up to card night with some elaborate Mexican dish a woman he'd gone out with had cooked for him to bring. By the end of the evening, we'd started a betting pool on how many weeks in a row Trevor could get a different woman to cook something Mexican for poker night. I'd picked thirteen. Maddox hadn't been as confident and had only picked five, so he'd been hoping Trevor would show empty-handed tonight. No such luck.

Elvin grabbed the deck of cards from the middle of the table, slipped them from the case, and started shuffling. "I vote we change the rules of the bet to allow for duplicates. That carne asada what's-her-name made last week was freaking delicious."

Trevor set the platter in the middle of the table and flipped a chair around to sit backward. "What the hell *was* her name?"

I shook my head. "It was only a week ago, you idiot. Your dick's gonna fall off at this pace if you keep it up."

"I'm pretty sure your dick falls off from nonuse, too," Maddox said. "So both Trevor and Elvin are gonna look like Ken dolls from the waist down soon."

"What are you talking about?" Elvin stopped shuffling. "Linda promised me sex a week from Tuesday if I cleaned out the garage this Saturday."

Maddox shook his head. "I'm never getting freaking married."

I filled two pitchers of beer behind the bar and brought them over to the table. "Where the hell is Fritz? He's never late."

"Oh. I almost forgot..." Trevor peeled the top off the plastic container, and a smoky smell wafted through the room. "He texted me. He got a last-minute call for a pickup, so he's either gonna be late, or he might not make it at all, depending on how things go."

"He still didn't find a replacement driver for Pete?"

Our brother Fritz owned the local tow shop. He was currently down a few drivers.

"Nope. He hired some guy last week. Dude showed up Monday, worked one day, then quit because he got a better job. Fritz is working eighty hours a week."

"Let's get started without him then. If he shows, we can deal him in later."

The guys all anted, and twenty minutes later I was down almost a hundred bucks. I'd lost every damn hand. So when the front door swung open, I was grateful for some new blood to mix things up. I yelled without looking up. "Get your ass to the table. I need you to break this shitty streak I'm stuck in."

But the voice that answered wasn't my brother's. "That sounds like you're saying I'm your lucky charm?"

*February.*

All heads whipped to the front door, including mine.

"*Damn.*" Trevor cooed. "I don't know who you are, but you can be *my* lucky charm."

I elbowed him in the ribs before jumping to my feet.

"What the fuck?" he complained.

"*Watch your mouth.*"

"My mouth? What the fuck for?"

I ignored my brother and headed to the door to greet February. Her cheeks were all rosy. "Why the hell don't you have a jacket on?"

"I didn't have anything that went with my outfit."

February had on a burgundy, form-fitting, V-neck dress with a bright teal belt cinched tight around her narrow waist. It accentuated her killer figure, showcasing the beautiful tits I knew were under there since I'd spent *waayy* too many hours looking at that middle-finger picture this week. I grumbled and removed my flannel. "Here. This goes just fine."

She looked around me as I draped it over her shoulders. "Am I interrupting something? I noticed the sign on the window said closed, but the door was open."

"Nothing important. It's just card night. I close early one Sunday a month to play poker with my brothers."

"Oh." She thumbed over her shoulder. "I should go then."

She should *definitely* go—what with my nosy brothers and how damn sexy she looked tonight—yet

I found myself shaking my head. "Stay. I'll make these guys be on their best behavior."

"Are you sure?"

"I haven't heard from you in a while. Thought maybe you were done with sneaking out."

"The maintenance guy that I bribe for my ladder has been out sick, and my friend Morgan's phone was confiscated, so I couldn't text you." She smiled and tilted her head. "Shame. I had big plans to make that photo I'd sent you into a series."

Yep, it was a bad idea to have her stay. A *bad, bad* idea. But before I could come to my senses, my brother Elvin yelled, "Are you playing this hand or what?"

I raked a hand through my hair and lowered my voice. "I have three aces. I need to play this one out."

"Mind if I watch?"

"Just ignore the jackass brothers, *especially* Trevor."

February and I walked to the table together. Each of my brothers had a look of surprise on his face, except for Trevor, who was too busy checking out my guest. I kicked his chair as I passed. *"Don't be a dick."*

"What did I do?"

I grabbed a chair from a nearby table and positioned it next to where I was sitting with a nod. "Everyone, this is February. Feb, these are three of my idiot brothers—Elvin, Maddox, and Trevor."

"You must not be from around here. I *definitely* would have noticed you." Trevor smiled. His tone made me want to punch him.

February politely smiled back as she sat. "I live in New York. I'm just...visiting for a while."

I tossed two chips into the pile and lifted my cards. "Raise."

The betting went around the table, yet all eyes stayed on February.

"You ever play poker, February?" Elvin asked.

"Once or twice. But I'm not very good."

"Call," I said and flipped over my cards. *Three aces and a king high.* All of my brothers tossed their hands onto the table without bothering to show what they had.

Trevor tipped his chair back until the front feet came off the floor. "Looks like maybe she really is your lucky charm. That's the first hand he's won all night."

"Oh really?" February turned to me as I swept the chips to my side of the table. "Do I get a cut of the winnings for my part?"

"Sure do. You want a beer or a beer?"

She chuckled. "Tough choice. I guess I'll go with a beer."

Elvin gathered all the cards and shuffled once again. "What kind of a name is February? I've never heard of it before."

"My mother went through a phase where she believed she was remembering things from her past lives. She went to see this medium who claimed to channel the spirit of my mother's past life from two-hundred years ago—a prostitute named February."

My brows jumped. "Seriously?"

"Yep." February reached for my beer and knocked back a healthy gulp. I have no idea why, but it was sexy as fuck.

"So you're named after a hooker?"

"I am indeed. The medium also told my mother she was once a man named Chuck who robbed banks. So I think I made out on the deal."

I lifted my chin to February. "You gonna drink the rest of my beer or you want me to make you your prissy cocktail? I picked up bleu cheese olives at the market the other day."

February's eyes lit up. "If you say you also have orange bitters, I might propose."

My lip twitched. I'd picked that shit up, too. "I'll make it. But I'm stirring it, not shaking." As I stood, I glared at my brothers. "Be *nice*."

Trevor grinned. "Oh, I'll be *very* nice."

I wagged a finger at him. "The martini won't be the only thing getting stirred if you don't cut the shit."

As I worked behind the bar, I listened to the conversation at the table.

"So how long are you in town?" Elvin asked.

"Almost another three weeks."

"What do you do back in New York?"

"I design purses."

"No shit. You know, Brock did some designing back in the day."

I had no idea where this conversation was going, but I knew it couldn't be good. I yelled over. "Whatever he's about to tell you is a lie."

"Really?" Elvin smiled. "So you didn't sculpt stuff out of cat shit?"

I closed my eyes. "*Fuck*."

February laughed. "He made sculptures out of cat shit?"

"Yep. Brock was probably five or six when we used to go to this park on the outskirts of town. It had a few swings and a slide with a sandbox. The local stray cats treated it like a litter box. Brock thought the shit was clay and started sculpting crap for our mom."

"Did you know it was cat poop?" February asked.

"Of course. I'm not an idiot like my brother."

"Why didn't you tell him?"

"What fun would that have been?" Elvin shrugged. "Our mom had a snowman made of three round cat turds and twigs on her windowsill until the day she died. I tried to get it when we cleaned out her house, but Brock beat me to it."

February turned in her chair. "Do you still have the shit sculpture?"

I shook my head at my brother. "I'm going to kill you, Elvin."

My brothers all laughed while I finished stirring—*not shaking*—a prissy martini. I set it down in front of February and waited for her to sip.

"Good?"

"Oh my God. This might be the best martini I've ever had. What brand of olive juice did you use?"

"They're homemade. This little Italian market has an olive bar with all different kinds of stuffed olives."

Trevor raised a brow. "You went to Rizullo's?"

"Yeah."

"They moved last year, didn't they?"

"Yep."

"They're like forty miles down south now, in Noahsville. What were you doing down that way?"

I wasn't about to tell my brother I'd driven there just to get the olives. I cleared my throat. "Gave an estimate."

"To who?"

"A potential customer."

"What was their name?"

"You writing a damn book or something?"

My brother tapped a finger to his lip and grinned. *He knew.*

I attempted to thwart whatever was about to come out of his mouth next. "Who's dealing?"

"I am," Elvin said. "You want in, February?"

"Umm... Like I said, I'm not very good."

Maddox smiled. "Those are our favorite people to play with."

From that point on, either February or I won *every single* hand of cards. We cleaned out all of my brothers. I leaned back in my chair when we took a break. "I thought you didn't know how to play?"

"I didn't say that. I said I wasn't very good. And I'm not, compared to my uncle who taught me. He's a professional poker player in Vegas."

I smiled. "So you suckered us."

"Not *us*. *Them*. You I let win twice, but only because you got all the stuff to make those amazing martinis."

Normally we took a stretch break and then played for another hour or two. But Elvin grabbed his jacket and crutches. "I have an early job tomorrow morning, so I'm going to call it a night."

Maddox nodded. "Me too."

Trevor sipped his beer. "I can stay."

Elvin shook his head. "*Let's go, jackass.*"

"Why?"

"Because it's time for you to go find some other woman to prey on. Pretty sure this one's taken."

I rolled my eyes. But I couldn't say I was upset my brothers were clearing out. The last thing I needed was alone time with February, yet that's exactly what I wanted. The two of us walked the guys to the door. Of course, when Trevor took February's hand to shake it, he lifted it to his mouth and kissed the top with a smirk. I'd make him pay for that.

"Walk me out, bro?" Trevor said.

My eyes narrowed, but I told February I'd be right back and followed the dumbass to his truck.

"What's up?"

"February seems really great."

"Okay..."

"And she's smoking hot."

My jaw clenched.

Trevor chuckled and pointed to my face. "You're turning purple."

"Is that what you made me come out here for? To bust my balls?"

"Well, yeah. But that's not the only reason."

"What do you want?"

Trevor put a hand on my shoulder. "I just wanted to remind you that ladies who wear sexy boots like that and carry designer handbags don't stick around this small town for long."

I frowned. It wasn't what I wanted to hear, but he was just trying to look out for me after what had gone down with the last city woman I'd dated. So I nodded. "It's fine. We're just friends."

"Oh really? So you wouldn't mind if I went back inside and asked her out?"

I scowled.

Trevor laughed and opened the door to his truck. "That's what I thought. But you enjoy the rest of your evening anyway."

Back inside the bar, I found February cleaning up the poker table. "You don't have to do that."

"I don't mind." She stacked the poker chips inside their case. "Your brothers are great."

"They're pains in the asses."

"It's nice that you get together every month."

"Elvin's wife also hosts dinner every other Thursday."

February smiled. "My only sister lives in California. It must be nice to have family around."

"Sometimes. But don't let them know I said that." We finished cleaning up the table. "You want another prissy drink?"

She nibbled on her lip. "I should probably get going, too."

She was right, yet somehow I couldn't bring myself to tell her that. "Stay for one more."

Our eyes met, and she was quiet for a long beat before nodding. "Okay. One more."

I whipped up her fancy drink, poured a beer for myself, and we went and sat in a booth. I kept my eyes on her while she tasted the martini.

"What?" she asked.

"Nothing."

"You weren't just thinking about nothing. I saw the wheels in your head spinning. Tell me what's on your mind."

"I was just wondering who you hang out with like this at home in New York."

"No one." She shook her head. "I work late, often until midnight, and then go home to an overpriced empty apartment." She smiled. "You want to know a secret?"

"What?"

"I don't even have dishes in my kitchen cabinets."

My brows pulled tight. "Where are they?"

"Nowhere. I don't have any."

"Why not?"

She shrugged. "My ex took them when he moved out, and I never bothered to replace them."

"Your ex? How long ago was that?"

"The divorce was finalized three years ago."

I had no idea she'd ever been married, but I didn't find that information half as disturbing as not having dishes for three years. "How do you eat?"

"I have most of my meals at the office, but sometimes I get takeout at home." She laughed and pointed to my face. "You look horrified. Does it help if I tell you I do have utensils? And a few coffee mugs."

"Not really."

Her smile widened. "I mentioned my lack of dishes to my therapist this week, and she was very bothered by it, too. I'm not sure why it doesn't seem to faze me."

"Why did your ex take the dishes? Were they his before you got married or something?"

She sipped her martini. "They were his grandmother's. She gave them to us as a wedding gift. He offered to replace them for me, but I told him not to."

"Did you work until midnight when you were married?"

She shook her head. "No, I didn't have to back then. Maybe eight or nine, some nights. I had a business partner. Tyler did half the work, maybe even more. He and I started Amourette together right out of college."

"What happened to him?"

"He died. About a month after my divorce was finalized."

"Shit. I'm sorry."

"Thank you. He was in a car accident on his way out to the Hamptons for the weekend." She picked up the toothpick with skewered olives and used it to stir her drink. "That's when I started working a hundred hours a week. Last year, I sold part of my company to a big conglomerate. I wanted the resources they were going to bring more than the cash infusion, but that's turned out to be a nightmare. They try to micromanage things and want to mass produce my product line overseas rather than make them locally." She laughed. "And I have no idea why I'm telling you all of this. I have a therapist at Sierra who would be thrilled if I told her any of it, and yet I can't seem to open up to her. The dishes thing just sort of slipped out one day."

I shrugged. "I don't mind."

She lifted the toothpick to her mouth and used her teeth to pull off one of the olives. "Anyway...a failed marriage, a dead business partner, and I also made some bad financial decisions like investing in a factory that went belly up, and yeah, I guess I probably could use this forced vacation. Though it would've been nice to decide to take it on my own."

"Would you have ever done that? Checked into Sierra, I mean."

She smiled sadly. "Probably not."

"Sometimes things happen that we might not have picked for ourselves, but they turn out to take us in a new direction that turns out even better."

February's eyes dropped to my lips. I wanted more than anything to lean in and kiss her. When her gaze rose and met mine, I got the feeling she knew it. After a few seconds, she looked away and knocked back the rest of her drink. "I guess I should be going."

I nodded. "I'll drive you."

"Thanks. I won't fight you about taking the ride tonight. These boots aren't the most comfortable to walk a mile in."

We were both quiet for the drive back to Sierra. Once we passed through the gate, I turned my lights off and pulled around to the back of the building. Too bad her ladder was waiting for her. I wouldn't have minded her having to crash at my place again.

"Thank you for letting me hang out. And for the ride back."

"Anytime." I dug into my jeans pocket and pulled out an old iPhone. "Here. You said your friend's cell was confiscated. Take this one. It's ancient, but it works. It's the bar's telephone, but no one ever calls it."

"That's sweet, but it's okay."

"Take it." I extended my hand farther. "I don't like you not having one for an emergency."

February smiled. "An emergency? Or not having one to send the next pictures in the series?"

I winked. "Whatever you need it for."

She laughed and took the phone. Then she grabbed the door handle and started to get out. But she stopped and turned back to me. "Can I ask you something?"

"What?"

"Why haven't you kissed me?"

I blinked.

She continued before I could figure out how to answer the question. "It's looked like you wanted to a few times, but then you never do."

My eyes jumped back and forth between hers. "You're right, I have wanted to kiss you."

"But..."

"But you're leaving in a few weeks, and it's probably not a good idea."

February smiled and leaned in to kiss my cheek. After, her mouth moved to my ear. "Such a shame.

Some of the best times I've had in my life started out as *bad ideas."*

# CHAPTER 6

*February*

Group therapy sessions were the worst. While I definitely found some value in my one-on-one appointments and also some of the relaxation classes here, the group sessions were different. They consisted of a bunch of people talking over each other, one big brain dump of thoughts and feelings, without us ever really getting anywhere. I had enough issues of my own without having to spend time working out other people's problems. And there was rarely a common denominator among us.

Morgan complained about her social media exhaustion and depression from having "low views." Stephanie from Boston lamented that she'd woken up this morning and couldn't get a certain song out of her head. So now she thought she was going crazy and it would be stuck there forever. Angie from Baltimore was feeling disconnected from reality, like she was outside of her own body.

I hadn't said a word this morning and wished I could somehow get out of this session.

As if the universe heard my plea, my secret phone buzzed in my purse. I looked around, hoping no one had heard the vibration. Going to check it would be my excuse to leave this miserable session.

"Excuse me." I stood. "I have to use the bathroom."

I escaped from the group therapy room and checked my phone out in the hall. Much to my delight, it was a text from Brock—the first since he'd given me the cell two days ago.

> Brock: Any chance you could sneak away during daylight hours? Or are you perpetually a vampire?
>
> February: There's a first time for everything. What did you have in mind?
>
> Brock: I'd like to offer a getaway car if you can swing a daytime escape.
>
> February: Where would we be going?
>
> Brock: It's a surprise.
>
> February: Give me a hint.

The dots moved around as he typed.

> Brock: You might end up getting sticky.

*Sticky.*

Hmm... *Sex* was sticky...

Imagining his body on mine, I got a chill down my spine. Sticky, hot, sweaty. Something told me that wasn't the kind of stickiness I'd be getting, though. I knew better.

> February: Sounds naughty.
>
> Brock: LOL. Get your mind out of the gutter, Red. This is actually the most innocent place you could imagine.

**February:** Should've known with you.

**Brock:** What's that supposed to mean?

**February:** Just that you've been nothing but a Boy Scout since we met.

**Brock:** Lord knows you're not making it easy.

**February:** How do I dress for this sticky outing?

**Brock:** Casual.

**February:** I can be ready in twenty minutes. But I'll need some help sneaking out.

**Brock:** I can park outside your window next to the ladder and be on the lookout. I'll text you when it's safe to come down.

A half-hour later, after announcing to the center staff that I was feeling ill and retreating to my room for the rest of the day, Brock texted that the coast was clear outside.

I climbed down the ladder carefully and ran to his truck. Brock took off fast. Escaping in broad daylight felt even more dangerous than doing so at night.

When I turned to look at him, all I could think was *holy hell*. Brock was wearing a baseball cap backward. Pieces of his longish, brown hair stuck out of the opening at the front. I could've sworn the muscles between my legs tightened. He looked so freaking hot.

"The hat suits you."

"Happy you approve," he said, glancing at me before returning his eyes to the road. "And once again, you didn't bring a jacket."

I looked down at myself. "Whoops."

He winked at me. "It's all right. I've got you."

*God, why does he look sexier than ever today?*
"Okay, so now you need to tell me where we're going..."

"Well, seeing as though you're only in town for a limited time, I was thinking it would be a shame if you didn't get to see more of it."

It touched me that he wanted to show me around. But it wasn't the town I wanted to see more of. It was *him*. "So...come on. Tell me where we're going."

He flashed me a smile. "The fair."

My mouth dropped open. "Like a carnival?"

"Yep. Except ours is legendary and probably better than your average carnival."

"Oh my God." I clapped. "Are you serious? I'm so happy right now."

"Just a warning..." He smirked.

"What's that?"

"I'm pretty much a master at the ring toss—and all the other games, for that matter. So prepare yourself for defeat."

"As long as I get to keep the giant stuffed animal you win, we're good."

"Not sure you'll be able to take that back to the City, but I plan to win you one anyway."

"You can keep it at your place. It will give me a reason to come back and visit. Oak needs a friend in the bathtub." I winked.

He laughed. "Oak would violate it, and you'd never see it in the same condition."

*Wish Brock would take some lessons from his dog.* I sighed.

Brock was probably the manliest man I knew, but something about his vibe today gave off boyish charm. It had to be that damn backward hat.

My excitement grew as we pulled up to the fair. Spotting a Ferris wheel always gave me chills. There was something so magical about it.

Brock found a spot for his truck, and we walked together to the entrance.

The moment we stepped through, the smell of fried dough and popcorn became all-consuming. My stomach growled as nostalgia came over me. While the carnivals I'd been to as a kid weren't quite as large as this, I was immediately taken back to my childhood.

But unlike my childhood, the most popular attraction here? Brock Hawkins. Everywhere I looked, women stared at us. Brock and I continued to be watched as we waited in line at the ticket booth.

I cleared my throat. "What's the deal with all the people staring at us?"

He looked around. "Who?"

"Well, women, mostly." I surveyed the area. "You really don't notice it?"

He shrugged. "Can't say I do."

"You're pretty oblivious, then. The women here seem very interested in you. Any idea why?" I *knew* why. But I still wanted to see what he said, whether he'd admit what a catch he was.

Brock shrugged. "I guess they have nothing better to do."

I slapped his arm playfully. "Do you not realize what a hot commodity you are?"

"If you mean because I have money, I guess that's sad."

"It's not just that, Brock. You're the whole damn package. A good-looking man with a good head on his shoulders—and yes, one who makes a good living—is not easy to find. These women are salivating." *Heck, so am I.*

"Well, I guess they're also probably drawing some conclusions right now, aren't they? Seeing as though I'm with you. I bet that's also why they're staring. They're wondering what the deal is with us."

*Join the club.* I chuckled. "Well, I'm happy to play the role of most-hated woman in town until I leave."

When we finally got to the front of the line, Brock asked for two-hundred tickets.

My eyes widened. "Two hundred? What the heck are we going to do with that many?"

Brock grinned. "We're gonna have some fun, Red."

There was that boyish charm again—the magic of the hat. I was here for it.

Brock reached for my hand, and I got goose bumps as I practically skipped alongside him. His touch warmed my entire body. Finishing this stint at Sierra would be much easier if I weren't so damn attracted to this man in every way.

Over the next couple of hours, Brock and I played countless games, ate our way through the fair, and rode the Ferris wheel. And yes, we used every single last one of those tickets. Brock won me a giant stuffed cow, which we walked back to his truck so we didn't have to carry it around. Pretty sure I was going to have Brock take it home to Oak and tell him to have fun with it. How the hell could I climb the ladder with that thing anyway?

Eventually the afternoon sun gave way to a golden evening, and a chill took over the air. Without me having to ask, Brock took off his flannel, wrapping it around my arms and enveloping me in his intoxicating smell.

Wearing his shirt was becoming one of my favorite rituals.

"I feel like it wouldn't be a day with you if I didn't end up wearing one of your flannels."

"That's because you never wear a damn jacket."

"There's not even a little part of you that *likes* me wearing your shirt?"

His jaw ticced. "I can't say I mind the way it smells when you give it back." He sighed. "Don't mind it at all."

Satisfied with that answer, I closed the shirt over my chest. "I've had a lot of good days in my life, Brock. But this one might have made my top ten."

"Well, damn. I'm honored." He smiled.

"I feel like I'm in a movie. This town is like a place you go to forget about your troubles."

"That's an illusion," Brock countered. "Want to know the reality?"

"Okay..."

"The fair is a nice escape, but I know many of the people here. And some of them don't have a pot to piss in. They probably save up for weeks just to afford to enjoy themselves for one day here."

"Well, that's very sad, actually."

He nodded. "And I can probably point to any person here who *seems* happy and tell you a story about them that would surprise you."

"What about him?" I challenged, pointing to an old man sitting on a bench. He was eating cotton candy and seemed content.

"That's Randy Lindley. Lost his wife earlier this year. Used to always see them around town together. It's like his other half is missing now. This is his first season here without her."

*That's so sad.* "Oh." I frowned. "I'm sorry to hear that."

He pointed to a cute little girl who looked to be about five or six. "See her? She doesn't know it, but her father is cheating on her mother. Saw him down at the bar the other night with a woman who wasn't his wife, Josephine."

My stomach sank. "Jesus, that's horrible." Just the thought gave me PTSD and reminded me of my own dad.

I pointed to a random woman. "What about her?"

"Cheryl Brown. Her husband was injured while on active duty. He uses a wheelchair now. Doing okay, but they have a ton of medical bills. Three kids." Brock shook his head. "Bryce deserved better than that."

"Well, you've brought me back to reality, Mr. Hawkins, and managed to depress me at the same time."

He smiled sadly. "Not trying to depress you, Red. Just making the point that no one's life is easy, and there's plenty of heartache, even in an idyllic town like this. Here's the thing, though. Despite everything that anyone here is going through, they're still here, enjoying themselves. We have to find these little moments that help make up for the tough times. That's why I wanted to break you away from that place to experience this. It's good for the soul." He stared into my eyes. "I hope your time here in town is worth it, that you're able to go back to the City with a fresh outlook."

I could see the reflection of the carnival lights in his beautiful eyes. "Well, that sounded suspiciously like goodbye, Mr. Hawkins. And I don't know if I like it..." As we looked out toward the chaos, an evening breeze caressed my face.

After a couple of minutes of comfortable silence, I turned to him. "What's *our* sad story?"

"What do you mean?"

"You know, what would someone say about us if they were privy to our situation? Two seemingly happy people, assumed by all to be a romantic couple, but the truth is..." I paused. "You fill in the blank."

Brock crossed his arms and seemed to think about it for a second. "They'd say, 'See that knockout with Brock Hawkins? She's not really his girl, just a mysterious woman passing through town with an expiration date.'"

"Ouch. That's abrupt and tragic." I laughed. "Well, I feel fortunate to have this experience anyway. It's very grounding being here. Back in the City, everyone is constantly moving and paying no mind to each other. It's disheartening to live in that world day in and day out. Just the fact that you can point to someone and know their story... How many people do I pass on the daily that I'll never see again, let alone have a true understanding of their personal struggles?"

"Who broke the girl out of prison?" someone interrupted.

I turned to find Brock's brother Trevor standing beside us. Brock must've filled him in on the reason for my stay in Meadowbrook.

Brock rolled his eyes. "When did you get here?"

"Been trolling around for a few minutes. Ran into three different women who've made me Mexican food in the past six months, so that's awkward." He turned to me. "You're looking even more beautiful tonight, Red."

Brock gave him a look of warning. "You don't get to call her that."

A look of amusement crossed Trevor's face. "Oh, it's like that, huh?"

Brock gritted his teeth.

It gave me pleasure to see him so protective. Hard not to read into it. Maybe there was hope after all, even if I wasn't sure what I was hoping for.

Trevor turned to his brother. "How about we play some games? See who can win her the bigger prize?"

"I think we both know who was born with the bigger prize, brother," Brock cracked.

Trevor winced. "Ouch."

He hung with us for a few minutes before his attention was diverted by a woman who would probably be making him huevos rancheros next month.

Brock and I eventually decided to leave the fair, but he drove us around Meadowbrook for a while, showing me more of the town. He took me by his high school and the house he grew up in. Then he showed me the log cabin he was currently building. It got to a point where he was no longer showing me anything but just driving around aimlessly. I had a theory: Brock wasn't ready to say goodnight to me just yet.

I reached over and placed my hand on his leg, which felt a bit brazen. "How long can we drive around before you admit you're just stalling?" I asked.

"I don't want to bring you back to my place, so this is the only choice I have."

Exactly what I'd suspected. "Are you forgetting we've already slept together?" I joked.

"Hardly." His eyes darted toward me. "You wouldn't use the term *slept together* lightly if you knew the real deal." He winked.

"Why did you text me today? Was it really just because you felt bad that I'd be leaving town without experiencing more of Meadowbrook?"

"Are you trying to get me to admit I wanted to see you?"

I arched a brow. "Did you?"

Brock didn't answer until he'd pulled into a spot across from my ladder. Then he turned to me. "I suppose I did want an excuse to see you. Even if that's not very smart."

After a long moment of silence, Brock spoke again. "See that guy over there? Brock Hawkins? He's had a tough year between a failed relationship and a couple of business ventures gone south. He was living day to day, going through the motions, until this beautiful woman showed up out of nowhere at his bar. He's thought about her every day and has had nothing but adventures ever since she rolled into town. At first, he thought she was a little...*extra*, but he's since realized she's vulnerable, real, and unlike anyone he's ever met before. Even though she's leaving soon...he wishes he had more time with her." Brock smiled sadly. "That was a better commentary than the one I gave you before." He reached out and took my hand in his.

It felt so good to be touched by him, my small fingers lost in his big, masculine ones. "See that girl over there? February Shaw?" I said, looking down at our intertwined hands. "The last thing she wanted was to be sent away to a wellness center to work on herself. She thought it was gonna be the worst experience of her life. Until one morning she woke up staring at a moose head. She realized this small town had a lot to offer, especially one Brock Hawkins, a man who, while grumpy on the outside, continues to warm her heart with the sweet things he does, not only for her, but for almost everyone he comes across. She's never met anyone like him. She thinks he's remarkable. And she *really* wishes she had more time with him, too."

Our eyes locked, and I swore this was it: Brock was going to finally lean in and kiss me. I licked my lips in anticipation. But he never moved. He just let go of my hand. As much as I understood why he was holding back, I wished he'd give in a little...just for one night. Or even one moment.

I finally gave up, placing my hand on the car door to leave. "I'd better go inside."

"Yeah." He nodded. "You'd better go while the coast is clear."

"Thanks again for today."

"My pleasure, Red."

He stayed in his truck, watching me as I walked away.

I turned back toward the truck. "Hey..."

He rolled down his window. "What's up?"

"Do you have a good deed on record today?"

He thought about it for a second. "Yeah."

"What was it?"

After a long pause, he said, "This. Dropping you here instead of taking you back to my place and doing all the things I wanted to. You'll thank me later."

# CHAPTER 7
*Brock*

"What's going on, big brother?" Trevor swiveled one of the stools at the bar and hopped on the seat backward.

"How old are you that you still have to sit like that?"

"I'm more comfortable this way."

"Do you do that when you take a date out to dinner at a nice restaurant?"

He winked. "My dates prefer to cook for me."

"Probably because you have no manners and sit like that in public."

Trevor lifted his chin. "I'll take a Coors Light. Thanks for asking."

I poured my pain-in-the-ass little brother a beer and filled a glass with seltzer for myself.

"So..." He sipped. "What's going on with you and Miss Fancy Pants? I was surprised to see you two yesterday."

I didn't have to guess who he was talking about. "Nothing."

He arched a brow. "Really? I can't remember the last time I saw you walking around a carnival."

"Just being hospitable. Showing a visitor around the area."

Trevor chuckled. "Yeah, right. I seem to remember a tourist who stopped in a month or two ago and asked you for directions to those caves people like to visit nearby. You told him to *buy a fucking map*."

"That guy had it coming. He also asked for a pumpkin beer with sugar on the rim."

My brother smirked. "Also noticed you had the ingredients to make a certain fancy cocktail for Miss Fancy Pants the other night when we were playing cards. Even drove forty-five minutes to get stuffed olives."

I said nothing because...what could I say? Trevor was right. I wouldn't even make margaritas for people who tried to order them. And when douchey city folk came in and tried to order beer made of apples or pumpkins or some shit, I charged them double for Budweiser so they wouldn't stay long. Yet I'd gotten up extra early this morning to take that long drive for olives again, just in case February came in anytime soon.

"I'm not judging." Trevor smiled. "I'd drive for olives for a woman as hot as February. I'm just surprised *you're* doing it."

"You're not the only one," I grumbled.

"So what's the deal with her? You hittin' that?"

I pointed at him. "Watch it."

"How would you like me to ask? Are you and Miss Fancy Pants making mad, passionate love?"

I rolled my eyes. "Christ, you're annoying."

Trevor laughed and drank his beer. "Seriously, though. She seems cool. There aren't too many women around here who can play cards, hold their own with four Hawkins assholes drinking beer, and walk a state fair for hours in high-heel boots and a smile. I'm happy for you, bro."

"There's nothing to be happy for me about. February and I are just friends."

"Why is that? She's looked pretty into you the two times I've seen you together."

"Because she lives in New York."

"So?"

"Been there, done that. No thanks on going in for seconds."

"You mean because of what happened between you and Nina?"

"Unlike you, when I make a mistake, I learn my lesson."

"Did you talk to February about her long-term plans?"

"I don't have to. She has a whole life in New York City. Born and raised there, owns her own company—just look at her. Does she look like she belongs here in Meadowbrook?"

Trevor shrugged. "It looked like she was enjoying herself in Meadowbrook last night at the state fair. And it also seemed like she had fun the other night when she played cards with us."

"The woman would rather freeze her ass off than wear a coat that doesn't match her outfit."

My brother rubbed his chin. "I seem to remember she was wearing your ugly flannel last night at the fair. You want to know what I think?"

"Definitely not."

"I'm glad you asked. I think you're making excuses not to see where things can go with this woman because you're afraid to get hurt again."

"You don't know what you're talking about."

"I see the same woman as you, bro. She's a designer-wearing fashionista who probably spends more money on her hair and nails than we do on truck payments. There's no arguing that point. But if you keep looking, you'll also see a woman who didn't hesitate to play carnival games, got her coiffed hair all messed up going on rides, and enjoys a corn dog as much as she does her fancy drinks. Stop trying to put her in a box. She can be more than one thing, even if you can't."

I thought about it. Maybe my idiot brother was right for a change. February did seem to have a good time at the fair and playing cards. In fact, she'd spent most of the time we'd been together smiling. Maybe I wasn't giving her enough credit. I rubbed my beard, thinking out loud. "You think she would stay here part time if I went there part time?"

"I don't know, but I think you're getting ahead of yourself. Why don't you try slowing down and just taking it step by step?"

He had no idea how bad I was dying for step one—*a damn kiss*. I had barely slept last night after dropping February off. My body physically ached for the woman. Though, if I was going to take the first step, maybe I could sneak in two steps at once and cop a feel of those luscious tits that had been haunting me. I'd spent *hours* staring at the photo she'd sent me. Sometimes doing more than just staring, too.

Trevor knocked back the last of his beer and pushed it to my side of the bar.

"You want another?" I asked.

"Nah. I have a hot date. I met a woman at the fair last night."

"What's this one's name?"

Trevor grinned. "No fucking clue. She told me, but I forgot. I'm going to have to tell her I need to use the bathroom when I pick her up and hope there's some mail lying around on the counter."

I shook my head. "You're unbelievable."

"I am, aren't I?"

A few minutes later, I was refilling beers for a few of my regulars when a guy walked in. He had on a three-piece plaid suit with pants so short his bare ankles were showing. The dude looked as out of place as February had the first night she'd wandered in here. He sauntered up to the bar, and I would've bet my truck the fucker was going to order wine or ask to use the bathroom.

"What can I get you?"

"I'll take a cabernet. A two thousand nine or earlier from the Napa Valley, if you have it."

I frowned. "Got Sutter Home. The bottle's got a few inches of dust on it, if that's old enough for you."

He smiled. "How about a vodka and seltzer then?"

"I can do that."

He looked around. "Where's the restroom?"

*Two for two.* I inwardly smirked and pointed. "That way."

Plaid Suit came back a few minutes later, and I hit him with a three buck, I-wear-three-piece-suits surcharge and went back to the other end of the bar to talk to Hank, who was here as a regular this evening, rather than the bartender he was two nights a week.

He lifted his chin in the direction of the plaid suit. "New York or California?"

I shook my head. "Didn't ask."

"I got twenty he's from the Big Apple."

I looked over. The guy was probably early thirties and had hair he spent too much time on, but he wasn't bad looking. Sort of reminded me of a Ken doll. It irked me that I thought he'd look the part standing next to someone like Feb. "Not taking that bet," I grumbled. "He's definitely from New York."

Hank shrugged. We spent the next fifteen minutes debating whether or not it made sense for me to put solar panels on the house I was building for myself. Then Plaid Suit lifted his arm like I was a damn taxicab.

Hank caught it too and smirked. "Probably jerks off looking in the mirror."

I chuckled but went down to see what the guy wanted.

"You want a refill?"

"Please."

I poured two fingers of vodka into a glass and grabbed the seltzer gun.

"Can you make that a double?" he asked. "I'm visiting a woman who drives me fucking nuts."

"Is there a different kind where you come from?"

He smiled. "Guess not."

I finished mixing his drink and slid the glass over to him. When he took it, I couldn't help but notice the big, shiny Rolex on his wrist. "You from New York?"

"How'd you know? My accent?"

I shook my head. "We don't get a lot of suits coming in here."

He eyed the deer head hanging over the bar. "That's probably because we're afraid you'll shoot us."

I smiled. Maybe he wasn't as big of a douche as he looked. "Taxidermist gets freaked out when we bring him Wall Streeters. He's worried his stock portfolio will suffer."

Plaid Suit sucked back half his double vodka. "What's a taxidermist do on Tuesdays?"

"What?"

"Nothing special. Just the usual stuff."

I chuckled. "So why does a city boy travel all the way to northern Maine to visit a woman who drives him fucking nuts?"

"Sex, of course. It's addicting. She's freaking gorgeous, too. If only I could tape her mouth shut." He looked at his big watch. "Speaking of which, I should get going. Visiting hours end at four."

A sinking feeling settled into the pit of my belly. "Visiting hours? She in the hospital or something?"

"Nope. At a wellness-type place. It's called Sierra something. GPS said it was only about a mile down the road from here."

I gritted my teeth. "Woman you're visiting from the area?"

He shook his head. "New York. Don't ask me why her board couldn't pick a place closer to home."

I swallowed. "Her...board?"

The guy knocked back the rest of his drink, pulled out his billfold, and peeled a fifty off, tossing it on the bar. "Long story. But I'll leave you with one piece of advice. Make sure the mic is off when you bend your archnemesis over the table it's sitting on."

♦ ♦ ♦

Hours later, I was still stewing.

"Hey, Brock. Can I get another beer?"

"You've had enough."

Bill Foster's brows jumped. "What are you, the Budweiser police?"

I pointed to the door. "Go home to your wife."

"Seriously?"

I glared at him and leaned over the bar. "Do I look like I'm fucking joking?"

"Jesus Christ. Who pissed in your damn Cheerios?" Bill pushed back from the bar and spoke to the guy he'd been sitting with. "Let's get out of here. There's a bar on the other side of town where the owner actually wants to sell drinks."

Hank watched the two guys leave, then got up from the stool he'd been sitting on for hours and walked behind the bar.

"What do you think you're doing?" I growled.

He took out two shot glasses and a bottle of tequila and poured. Holding one out to me, he shrugged. "Being a friend. Don't know what crawled up your ass. Don't care if you don't want to talk about it. But drink this. It'll help take the edge off."

I hesitated, but eventually I slugged back the shot. February had never mentioned that today was visiting day, and we'd spent the entire afternoon together yesterday. She certainly hadn't mentioned that some guy she was sleeping with was coming for a visit either.

I set the shot glass back down in front of Hank. We made brief eye contact, and he nodded and poured another. I wasn't much of a drinker—a couple of beers here and there, but rarely hard alcohol. The second shot burned less than the first going down, so I figured that was a sign to keep going.

By the fifth shot, my rigid jaw had loosened enough for me to finally speak. "Thank you."

Hank nodded. "Anytime, my friend. Go do what you gotta do. I'll close up tonight."

Fortunately, I lived upstairs, so I didn't have far to stumble to make it home. But *un*fortunately, I took the bottle of tequila with me when I left. Three more shots, and I started talking to Oak, my trusty Saint Bernard.

"Women suck. Do you know that?"

He tilted his head and lifted an ear.

I nodded. "Yeah, you're smarter than me. Maybe I should sleep in the bathtub, too."

Oak laid his giant head on my lap. "Is that the type she likes?" I shook my head. "Who doesn't wear fucking socks with a suit?"

I rested my head on the back of the couch and shut my eyes, still grumbling. "Think his hair was frosted or some shit. Probably uses hairspray, too. I should've lit a match near him to check."

I must've nodded off for a while because sometime later I woke to a light knock at the door. Oak rushed to the bathroom—into the damn tub—and left me to fend for myself. I was groggy and started to think I might've imagined the knock, but then I heard it again.

I opened the door to find February standing on the other side. She smiled. "I thought you were working tonight?"

I frowned. "What the care do you hell?"

Her brows dipped. "What?"

"What the care do you hell?" *Wait. No, that's not right.* I shook my head and attempted to unscramble the words. "What the care do you hell?" *Fuck me.*

"Are you...drunk?"

"What are you doing here, February?"

She blinked a few times. "I came to see you, of course."

"What for? No-sock-wearing-motherfucker not get the job done?"

Her lips pursed. "I'm not sure what your problem is, but I think I should go."

I leaned forward and spoke in her face. "You know what my problem is, Red?" She didn't back down in the slightest. I have no clue why, but that turned me on. Though I tamped down the feeling. "Your buddy stopped in and told me what a great lay you were."

February's face twisted. "What?"

I nodded. "Mr. Three-Piece-Suit. Told me *fucking you* was addicting."

Her head pulled back. "You spoke to Tobias?"

"Tobias?" I scoffed. "Figures that's his name."

"I don't understand. How did you speak to Tobias?"

"Does it matter how I found out your secret?"

"My secret? Tobias coming was not a secret."

"Well, you sure as hell didn't mention it to me, and we spent the entire day together yesterday."

"That's because I had *no idea* he was coming."

"Sure you didn't."

"Are you serious right now? You don't believe me?"

"It doesn't matter what I believe."

"It does to me."

"Why?"

"Because I care about you, you big doofus! And if

you weren't so pigheaded, maybe you could see that you care about me, too!" She looked away for a few heartbeats, and then pushed up on her tippy toes and got right in my face. "Why did it upset you when you found out Tobias visited me?"

I gritted my teeth. "You know why."

"Yes!" She raised her hands into the air and waved them around. "I do know why! But you can't even admit it to yourself."

I stared at her, saying nothing.

"How would you feel if I told you I let Tobias *touch me*, Brock?"

My face was on fire, and it felt like steam was billowing from my nose and ears.

"No response?" She moved closer. "How would you feel if I told you I let Tobias *fuck me* then? Would that make you jealous?"

I closed my eyes, doing my best to hang on to my last shred of control. "Please stop."

"Not until you tell me you were jealous!"

"Of course I was fucking jealous!"

"Then why don't you do something about it already?"

My chest heaved up and down. She was so damn beautiful, so damn perfect, so not afraid to call me on my shit. I couldn't resist her anymore. Cupping her cheeks, I backed her against the wall. I wanted this woman more than anything I'd ever wanted in my life, and it scared me to feel that out of control. So I took a deep breath and attempted to pull together whatever restraint I had before bending to kiss her. Just as my lips were about to connect with hers, she put a hand on my chest.

"Brock...wait." February's eyes met mine. "I've learned a lot about myself these last two weeks, and I am not going to allow myself to be used by people anymore. I want this as much as you do, maybe more. But not like this. You're drunk."

*Fuck*. She was right. I hung my head. "I'm sorry."

She smiled sadly. "So am I. But if you ever want to kiss me while sober, just call. I'll be waiting."

♦ ♦ ♦

The next morning, I was kicking myself in the ass for the way I'd acted last night. I needed to see February. There was no way I could wait until the next time she snuck out. So I took a calculated risk and walked in through the front door of Sierra Wellness Center.

"Hi. I'm here to visit my sister. I think I might be a little early for visiting hours."

"Actually, I think you're a little late," said the woman at the desk. "Yesterday was visitors' day."

"Yesterday?" I did my best to look shocked. "You're kidding me?"

The woman shook her head. "Visitors' days are always on Sundays. I'm sorry."

"Shoot." I rubbed the back of my neck. "I drove all night to get here in time. Took me *twelve hours*."

"Oh my gosh. That's a long way."

"Yeah. My sister's always been there for me. I'm a single dad with *four kids*, and she's helped me out a lot, so I wanted to be here for her."

The woman covered her heart with her hand. "That's so sweet."

"Is there any way I could just maybe…say hello? So she knows I was here at least?"

"It's against policy, but let me check with her counselor."

"Thanks. I really appreciate it."

Fifteen minutes later, I walked into a small visitors' room. February was already inside. Her eyes widened when she saw me. "Oh my God. You're my surprise visitor who drove twelve hours?"

I stalked over to her. "Sorry about that. I couldn't wait to see you, and that's the best I could come up with."

"Is everything okay?"

I pulled back her chair, lifted her out of it, and wrapped February in my arms. "It will be in a minute, and for the record, I'm stone-cold sober."

# CHAPTER 8

*February*

It felt like time stood still as Brock placed his ginormous hands around my face and began to devour my lips. The entire room faded away, and I couldn't have cared less if anyone walked in. I'd waited too long for this moment.

Brock tasted so damn good as our breaths collided. I couldn't get enough. My body bent back as he leaned over me, pressing his hard chest against my breasts. How long had I been missing out on this experience? Brock was one hell of a kisser, intense yet tender. Just like *him*, honestly.

My hands found their way to his thick, brown hair, tugging and raking. If only we weren't in this room, but rather alone in my bedroom, maybe just maybe Brock would lose his inhibitions and give me what my body had been longing for since shortly after I met him.

He groaned over my mouth. "These lips are going to be the death of me."

"It's about damn time you kissed me, you big dummy."

Brock smiled over my mouth.

"Oh my goodness. February, why are you kissing your brother?" a voice interrupted, prompting me to jump back.

I turned to find the woman who worked the front desk standing there. *Busted.* I went to open my mouth, but Brock gave me a look. "Sorry. I should clarify that I'm actually her *stepbrother*, not her blood brother."

It hit me now why they'd given Brock access. He'd said he was family. They were better about allowing family visitors. They probably thought it was some kind of emergency, when the only apparent emergency was in Brock's pants.

"Sorry..." I said to her. "My *stepbrother* and I have really missed each other."

Brock shrugged.

The woman said nothing before walking away, looking mortified. After she left, Brock and I broke into laughter.

"I can't believe you told them I was your sister."

"Well, I don't have a sister, so..." He winked. "Always wanted one."

Looking out in the hall to make sure the coast was clear, I took his hand and led him down to my bedroom.

Once inside, he placed his lips on mine and rasped, "We're hiding in here now?"

Nodding, I threaded my fingers through his hair. "Until you get kicked out."

I was ready to climb him like a tree when we were once again interrupted.

Morgan barged into the room, walking backward, and holding her phone in camera mode. She must've either gotten her previously confiscated phone back, or had smuggled yet another one in. Morgan had been so into her vlogging that she backed right into Brock.

"Oh my goodness! You're literally a ton of steel. Just like I imagined." She held out her hand. "Nice to meet you, Lumberjack. Surprised they let you into this place."

Brock narrowed his eyes. "Still calling me Lumberjack?"

"It's sort of the nickname we've given you," she said.

He turned to me. "Well, I suppose with the way I've acted some days, there are worse things you could be calling me behind my back."

Feeling my cheeks heat, I shrugged before realizing that I should probably introduce them.

"Brock, this is my friend Morgan. She's the person whose phone I've used while here. She loves to document her life, so being friends with her means being included in multiple vlogs that have yet to be disseminated around social media."

"Well, it's nice to meet you. Any friend of February's is a friend of mine."

Morgan's eyes glimmered. "Rumor has it you have some brothers?"

"As a matter of fact, I do. One of them is a little too young for you, but he'd give you a run for your money on social media. He likes playing around with his camera as well."

I laughed thinking about how *social* Axe had been.

"Oh, I think I know that brother." She winked. "Saw a little too much of him."

"Too bad she can't cook here in this place," I cracked. "She's out of the running for Trevor."

Morgan blinked in confusion. "What?"

"Never mind." I chuckled. "Actually, would you mind giving us some privacy? I have a feeling he's going to get kicked out soon."

"Oh, yeah...sure." Morgan grabbed her camera. "Nice to meet you, Brock."

"You too." He nodded.

After Morgan left, I locked the door, and Brock's expression turned serious.

"Considering you're right—that we probably don't have a lot of time—I do need to talk to you."

I straightened. "Okay..."

He cradled my cheek. "As much as it might seem like I came here just to kiss you, I want to discuss what happened last night."

"What about last night specifically?"

He slid his hand down. "First off, I want to apologize for the way I acted."

"I have to say, it was the first time I've witnessed you so out of control. Can't say I hated it. But you were drunk, so it really doesn't count."

"Well, I hate being out of control. It's why I don't drink much very often. But last night, as I explained, I had my reasons."

"Your reason, as you admitted, is that you were jealous." I winked.

"Can you blame me?" He exhaled. "But I shouldn't have handled myself that way."

"Well, I'm happy you heeded my advice about kissing me when you were sober."

"How could I *not* take advantage of that?" His expression darkened. "I hope I'm the only man who's gotten to do that in the past twenty-four hours."

My smile faded. "Nothing happened with Tobias, Brock. I told you, we hate each other."

"So what did he want? You didn't elaborate last night."

"He wanted what you can probably imagine he wanted."

"Actually, he *told* me what he wanted when he stopped by my bar. Idiot couldn't even try to play it off like he had a more legitimate reason to come to see you."

"He didn't get very far. I met him down in the lobby and basically sent him on his merry way. I didn't invite him, and he shouldn't have come here."

Brock gritted his teeth. "What made him think that was a good idea when *he* was essentially the reason you ended up here? That's inconsiderate."

"He's indirectly the reason I'm here, I suppose, yeah. But I have to take accountability." I sighed. "But Tobias is egotistical and thinks the world revolves around him."

He drew in his brows. "Why did you even like a guy like that?"

"I never liked him as a person. It was just... Well, you know what it was about. It was more of a rebellion than anything else."

"Yeah, but that gets old, doesn't it?"

"Yes, but the beauty of messing around with someone like Tobias is that you don't have to worry about getting your heart broken."

Brock nodded. "Okay, I guess I can understand that."

"I'm not interested in him, Brock. I'm not interested in anyone but you at the moment, and that really sucks for me."

"You've gone from the Plaid Suit to Plaid Shirt? Is that what you're saying?"

I giggled. "Plaid Shirt is most definitely my thing, yes."

He flashed the most gorgeous smile as he pulled on my shirt. "Look, I know you're not gonna be in Meadowbrook much longer, but I would like to spend the rest of your spare time here getting to know you better. At the same time, I don't want to hinder your recovery or distract you from the reason you came to town in the first place. So I need you to direct me as to what you're up for."

"Well, most of my treatment is during the day. As you know, my obligations end when the sun goes down. Seeing as though there's nothing I love more than sneaking out to see you, there's no reason we can't continue that."

"All right. Got it. No more daytime kidnapping." He grinned. "But how about dinner at my place tonight?"

"You're actually inviting me to your *apartment*? This is huge," I teased.

"Is that good with you?"

"Absolutely. I've missed it since my accidental sleepover."

"Text me when you're able to get away so I can come get you. No more walking on the road at night. Those days are over. You hear me?"

"Yes, Grumpy."

He groaned and pulled me to him, enveloping my lips with his and kissing me passionately. Then, without another word, Brock reluctantly pulled away and left.

The one benefit to Tobias's visit was that it had lit a fire under Brock, and I was totally down for that.

Morgan reentered my room soon after Brock left. I was still massaging my swollen lips with my fingertips.

She plopped down on my bed. "Well, he's even hotter than I imagined."

I sighed. "He is." I joined her on the bed and stared up at the ceiling. I fell into a daydream, replaying those kisses.

"Uh-oh," she said.

I turned to her. "What?"

"You're falling for the guy, aren't you?"

"Am I delusional for allowing this to continue? I mean, this can't end well..."

"Says who? You make the rules in your life. Who's to say you can't have the best of both worlds?"

"Long-distance relationships don't work."

"They don't work if you believe they won't." She tilted her head. "Have you not learned anything since we've been here about the power of belief?"

"I'm still practical, Morgan. Distance is a bitch. It's hard enough to make a relationship work, but when distance is involved, it's nearly impossible. It's okay in the beginning maybe, but then the logistics wear you down after a while, especially when the couple has moved beyond the honeymoon phase."

"Have you ever been in a long-distance relationship?" she asked.

"No. But I've had friends who were."

"You're basing your impression on hearsay. Someone else's experience will not necessarily be your reality."

I sighed. "I thought I was supposed to be the older and wiser one here."

♦ ♦ ♦

The aroma of cooking hit me the moment I entered Brock's apartment that evening. "Something smells yummy."

"Making a stew."

"Stew. That's so...*manly* of you."

"It's the one thing I know how to make really well. Hope you're hungry."

Was I ever, albeit not for food. But I'd take it.

The ambience in Brock's place really hit the mark tonight. *Cozy*. He had a fire going in a small pellet stove. And Oak was nestled on the couch, taking up most of the space. I'd describe the vibe as warm and welcoming, were it not for the taxidermy heads that always put a damper on things. Even now, they were looking at me...

I chose to ignore them and took a deep breath of the spicy scent. "Well, thank you for cooking and for having me here. I could most definitely get used to this."

He shook his head. "You'd tire of it fast. I imagine your dinners in the City are a bit fancier than stew in a crockpot."

"Yes, but that doesn't make them any better. Going out gets old. *This* is novel. I can't remember the last time a man made me a home-cooked meal."

"Well, don't get too used to it, unless you like stew. I don't have a big repertoire. Beef stew is pretty much it. Maybe a little pasta and red sauce."

"I like that, too." I winked. "But sadly, I don't have enough time left to get used to anything."

He frowned. "That's true."

"Honestly, not once since I've been here in Meadowbrook have I missed my life in the City. That's saying something."

"But you're still going back."

I crossed my arms over my chest. "Let's not put a damper on this night by reminding ourselves."

"I can agree to that." He nodded. "Let's keep it upbeat tonight."

Brock set the table and served us each a steaming bowl of his hearty stew. I was impressed. Not only had he added potatoes and carrots, but some fresh thyme.

"This looks absolutely amazing, Brock."

"I brought all of the ingredients to make your favorite drink, too, but it doesn't really go with stew. You want me to make you one, or do you feel like something else?"

Getting even a little buzzed didn't fit with my mood tonight. "You know, I'd actually like to stay sober."

"Well, needless to say, after yesterday I'm perfectly okay with that."

"Anything to drink is fine."

Brock took two ice-cold seltzers out of the fridge for us. The cold, fizzy liquid complemented the hot stew perfectly.

After Brock served me a second helping, I was totally stuffed. "Mr. Hawkins, that was the tastiest dinner I've had in a long damn time."

"You liked the moose meat, eh?"

My eyes widened. "Moose?"

"That's what you just ate."

"It is?" My jaw dropped.

He chuckled. "No, it was regular beef. Relax."

"Not sure why that freaked me out. Maybe because of the giant moose head that's been judging me from your wall since the moment I walked in. Don't want to think about eating the other half of him."

"I just wanted to see how adventurous you were…"

"I'm adventurous, just not when it comes to what I put in my mouth." I froze, realizing how that sounded.

He arched a brow. "Interesting…okay. I was kind of hoping for the opposite." He winked. "Kidding."

"Oh, I know you are, Mr. Cautious."

"Don't tempt me, Red. I don't have as great a hold over my inhibitions as you seem to think."

"Well, certainly not with any alcohol in your system, as last night indicated."

"I had no alcohol in my system when I took your beautiful lips earlier, though. Sober as a judge for that." He groaned. "If we'd been truly alone, not sure I would've stopped there."

"You're alone with me now." I raised an eyebrow. "How are you managing to control yourself?"

"By not starting anything…as much as I want to."

We moved over to the couch, and I silently willed him to kiss me again. What would be so bad about two adults engaging in a little carnal fun, anyway? No hot mics around here… But my brain answered that question for me: This would be more than just sex for both of us. Our hearts were getting involved, so we had to tread lightly. I'd never gotten attached to anyone in such a short amount of time; this was new for me.

"I know it might seem like I'm not interested in anything serious based on my reckless behavior with Tobias, but I would like to find someone I can spend my life with. I feel like I've given you the impression that I'm only out for a good time. I may have divulged too much about the situation that brought me here. But that whole thing was entirely insignificant and separate from my true desires."

"I'm not judging you, Red. I promise. Despite having made a couple of dumb decisions, you've never struck me as someone who takes things lightly. Well, except for jackets. You definitely take wearing a jacket lightly."

"And you don't take *anything* lightly. But I like that about you."

With that, Brock leaned in and kissed me senseless. My brain short-circuited as my back pressed against the cushions under the weight of his body. Our tongues collided, and I felt my panties getting wet. For the first time, I began to doubt whether we could get through this evening without having sex. And I was starting to feel a little chicken.

"I don't take kissing you lightly," he said as he came up for breath.

"What happened to your plan to not start anything?" I panted.

"My plans always change when it comes to you, Red."

I straightened the wrinkles in my shirt. "Well, as much as I'd like to spend the night, I don't think we should sleep together. It *would* complicate things."

"Thank you for the formal clarification. Unfortunately, I agree."

"I have no desire to go back to the wellness center, though. It's too cozy and warm here."

He shrugged. "So don't. Sleep in my bed tonight. I'll crash here on the couch. Then I'll drive you back in the morning."

While it was tempting, I shook my head. "I can't do that."

"Why not? You've slept in my bed before *with me*. Can't get any more dangerous than that, and not a thing happened."

He had a point. I could totally do this.

"If you want me to spend the night...then yeah, okay." I smiled.

"I want to fuck you hard is what I want." His eyes seared into mine. "But that won't happen. Doesn't mean I won't dream about it."

And now I felt tingly all over.

We snuggled together on the couch, and despite our plan for me to move to the bed, Oak had plans of his own. He rested his chin on my lap and fell asleep. His head was like a giant paperweight.

"Well, I can't move now. I don't want to wake him."

"He's exhausted from violating the cow I won you at the fair for three days straight."

"He's horny."

"He's not the only one around here lately." Brock grinned mischievously. "And this would be the first time he's slept out here in the living room in...I don't know how long. He's usually in the tub by now." He chuckled. "You make him feel comfortable enough to risk being attacked by his own shadow."

"If that's my claim to fame, Hawkins, I'll take it."

Brock leaned his head against my shoulder. "He must sense what I sense."

"What's that?"

"That you're nothing to be afraid of. You're vulnerable and beautiful. And honest."

"Well, I'm happy you feel that way."

"I wish I didn't. I wish you'd give me a reason not to be devastated that you're leaving."

Our eyes locked.

"Seriously, let me move him if you'd like to get up," he finally said.

I shook my head. "I can think of far worse places to be stuck than on a comfy couch with a fire blazing. And believe it or not, I like how his face feels on my lap."

Brock smirked. "I've got a face, too."

"I guess I walked right into that one."

"Trust me, though, if it was *my* face on your lap, neither of us would be sleeping."

Rather than retreat to his bed, Brock grabbed a giant plaid blanket and draped it over us.

Oak never moved that night.

And neither did we.

# CHAPTER 9

*February*

"You've got to be kidding me..." The following afternoon, I stared down at the invitation I'd just opened. "What balls."

The date printed was almost exactly a month from now. Which also happened to be the date of a board meeting. *Great. Just great.* Nothing like being beat up *twice* in one day.

"February?" I looked up to find Morgan standing at my door. "I thought you said you had therapy at one today?"

"I do."

She pointed to the clock on my wall. "It's five after."

"Shoot." I shuffled the mail strewn all over my bed into a pile. "I guess I lost track of time."

"Is that all fan mail? God, you get almost as much as I do."

"Not quite. These are all *bills* and other work stuff. I had my assistant send me my mail so I could keep up with things."

Her nose wrinkled. "Yuck."

"Tell me about it." I opened the nightstand and tucked the stack of envelopes inside. The wedding invitation was still on top of the pile as I slid the drawer closed. At the last second, I plucked it out. *This should give me something to talk about today.*

Morgan was still parked at my door. I wagged a finger at her as I passed. "No snooping. It's just invoices and contracts."

She held her hands up. "No worries. I don't have any interest in bills."

Trinity, my counselor, was already seated in her chair when I arrived at her office. I knocked lightly, though the door was open. "Sorry I'm late."

She closed the notebook on her lap and smiled. "No worries. I was running a few minutes behind anyway, so it worked out well. Come on in, February."

I took the seat on the couch across from her with the envelope in my hand.

"How are you today?" she asked.

I sighed. "I've been better."

"What's going on?"

I held out the offending mail. "I got this today. You've mentioned more than once that I don't talk enough during our one-on-one sessions. Well, I have a lot to say about this."

She opened the oversized envelope and slipped out the gaudy invitation. "Johnathan Augustus and Ilona Jones request the honor of your presence on May 14 to celebrate their joyful wedding vows." Trinity looked up. "I take it this isn't something you're feeling joyful about?"

I shook my head. "Johnathan is my ex-husband."

"I didn't realize you'd been married. When we talked about relationships, you mentioned you'd had one serious one, but it didn't work out."

I nodded. "Johnathan was my one serious relationship."

Trinity opened her handy-dandy notebook and jotted something down before looking up again. "How long were you married?"

"Three years."

"And how long ago did you divorce?"

"Everything was finalized a little more than three years ago."

She nodded. "Can I ask what led to the divorce?"

"You can. But I'm not sure I'll ever know the truth. Johnathan and I dated for seven years before we got married. He was my high school sweetheart. After the wedding, everything seemed to be going well, at least to me. We never really fought or anything like that. Then one night, he told me he didn't love me the way a husband should love a wife. At first, I blamed myself. My business had just started to take off, and I worked a lot. I sometimes didn't get home until eight or nine, and I went into the office on the weekends. Johnathan put in a lot of hours, too, but not as many as me. I suggested we go to counseling, but he didn't want to try. He basically gave me the '*it's not you, it's me*' speech.

"After he moved out, I beat myself up over the things I should've done. I could've come home to cook dinner once in a while, and I shouldn't have stopped wearing pretty lingerie to bed like I'd done before we were married. I thought I'd made my husband feel neglected." I stopped and stared out the window. "Then two months after our divorce was finalized, I had lunch with Ilona—*my best friend*. As soon as we sat down, she started to cry and told me she and Johnathan were seeing each other."

Trinity blinked. "Your ex-husband is marrying your best friend?"

"My *ex*-best friend now. But yeah." I took a deep breath in and blew it out. "Ilona and I had been best friends since elementary school. She swore up and down that nothing happened with Johnathan until after we were divorced. But I'll never know the truth."

"I'm very sorry that happened to you. It must've been a difficult time in your life."

I shrugged. "It was. Thankfully, I had my work to keep me busy."

"How did Johnathan leaving make you feel?"

I thought back, something I didn't do often. "Alone, I guess. Abandoned. I remember one day I was looking at some old pictures of my mom. They were taken a few months after my dad left us for another woman. And I thought to myself—I *feel* like she *looked* at that time."

"How old were you when your parents split up?"

"Twelve."

Trinity opened her notebook and scribbled for a while.

I smiled sadly when she finally looked up. "You wrote an awful lot. Did you just figure out what Colonel Sanders put in his secret recipe for fried chicken?"

She smiled back. "Not quite. But I think we've gotten to the bottom of your commitment issues."

"I didn't realize I had commitment issues..."

"We've talked about a few men you've had flings with recently—Tobias, for example. But you haven't dated anyone seriously since your divorce."

"My work keeps me extremely busy. I don't have time for a relationship."

"Do you think it's possible that you use work to avoid getting too involved with men because you've been hurt by the important ones in your life?"

I sighed once again. "I don't know. Maybe? I honestly try not to think about my dad or Johnathan."

"That's understandable. But there's a difference between not having time to date and not *making* time to date. We've talked a lot about your job. If you wanted to, could you hire some sort of an operations manager to help shoulder some of the workload? Would that be financially possible?"

I had way more money than I had free time, so I nodded. "I could afford it. But it's really difficult to find someone to trust to run a company you've built from the ground up."

Trinity tilted her head. "Have you interviewed a lot of people for the position?"

*Busted.* She was a smart cookie, and I couldn't help but smile. "Not a single damn one."

Trinity chuckled. "Sometimes we tell ourselves we don't have time to do the things we don't want to do or that we're scared to do. But it's important to make time for the things that really matter in life. For example, our health, love, family, and personal development."

I was quiet for a few moments. One thing I'd learned since arriving at Sierra was that the counselors often had a better perspective when looking at problems from a distance than the patients did close up. So I decided I might as well come clean on the rest of what was going on in my life.

"I started seeing someone recently."

"Do you mean Tobias?"

I shook my head. "No. Brock. He's really great."

She smiled. "Well, that's exciting. Tell me about him. How did you two meet?"

I nibbled on my lip, not sure how to explain without getting myself in trouble. Trinity misread what was going on in my head.

"There's no judgment here, February."

"It's not that... It's—well, let me ask you something. Is everything I tell you in here confidential?"

"Of course."

"So you can't discuss what I tell you with the administration?"

Trinity shook her head. "You signed paperwork when you were admitted that says I can share private information with other members of the medical staff if it is critical to your care. Like, if we were changing one of your medications, I might need to discuss that with the nurses in charge of dispensing. But I don't discuss what we talk about in here, if that's what you're worried about."

I still wasn't positive I wasn't going to screw myself by telling her the truth, but I needed to talk to someone about my feelings for Brock. So I decided to take the risk. "I've sort of been sneaking out at night and going to a local bar. I climb out the window in my room and go down a ladder."

Trinity's jaw fell open. I chuckled. "I told you about my best friend and my ex getting married and me having sex on a hot mic, and that's the first time you've shown any real reaction."

She smiled. "I'm sorry. I'm supposed to be trained to not show surprise or judgment, but the thought of you climbing down a ladder in the dark just caught me off guard."

I smiled back. "It's fine. I know it's a little nutty."

"So this man Brock, you met him at a local bar?"

"He owns it, yeah."

"Tell me about him."

"Well, he's *nothing* like any man I've ever dated."

"Do you mean physically or his personality?"

"Both. Physically, I usually date guys who look like my ex-husband or Tobias—tall, trim, clean-shaven, and well-dressed. Brock is tall, but that's where the similarities end. He's burly, with broad shoulders and a beard, and he usually wears flannels and jeans. But it's more than that. Brock has a different set of priorities than any of the men I've been with. He has five brothers, and he spends a lot of time with them. He also prioritizes the people who live in his small town over the size of his apartment."

"Those all sound like pretty good qualities in a partner."

My face fell. "That's the problem. I don't think I can be a partner to him."

"Why not?"

"Well, for one, I live in New York City, and he lives here. I like to shop and travel, and I barely see my sister once a year. Brock doesn't like big cities and has deep roots here in Meadowbrook, and…I don't want to get hurt if we can't work it out."

"Do you like him a lot? Think he could otherwise have long-term potential?"

I didn't have to think about those answers. I nodded. "I'm crazy about him, and while it's only been a couple of weeks, something in my gut tells me he could be something special in my life."

"Have you spoken to him about your concerns? Shared your fears with him?"

I shook my head. "I'm not good at that. I don't like to look weak."

"Sharing your fears with someone isn't being weak, February. It's just the opposite. It's being brave."

♦ ♦ ♦

Later that night, I snuck out my usual window, and Brock picked me up just outside the entrance to Sierra.

"Hey you." I pulled the truck door shut.

Brock hooked his big hand around my neck and drew me to him. "Come here."

Our lips met for the second time, and less than ten seconds later, I was ready to climb over and straddle the man.

Brock broke the kiss with a groan, tugging at the crotch of his jeans. "Jesus, woman, you turn me into a sixteen-year-old boy."

I smiled. "I feel the same way."

He shook his head. "You up for me to take you somewhere other than my place or the bar?"

"Sure. But I only have an hour or so. I got a roommate this afternoon. They usually don't double up, but they're at capacity right now, so it'll be a few days before something opens for her and I get my privacy back. Anyway, she's having some blood-pressure issues, so they're coming in to take her BP every couple of hours. They took it right before I called you to pick me up."

He put the truck into drive. "I'll take whatever time with you I can get."

Brock linked his hand with mine and held it for the ten-minute drive. Eventually we slowed and pulled down a dirt road that ended at a big lake. The moon bathed the area in beautiful light.

"Wow," I said. "This is amazing."

Brock cut the engine. "This is where we used to come in high school to make out."

"Are those your plans for this evening?"

He reached behind my seat and pulled out a duffle bag. "I wanted to show you more of Meadowbrook, but sucking your face is definitely on the agenda."

I laughed, and Brock got out of the truck and came around to open my door. He spread a blanket on the grass, then took out a lantern, a bottle of wine, and two glasses. While he uncorked the merlot, I looked around and tried to stay in the moment, but I couldn't seem to get my mind off the conversation I'd had earlier with Trinity.

I'd been preoccupied ever since my appointment. I didn't have much time left here in Meadowbrook. Maybe my counselor was right, and I should have a conversation with Brock about how I felt about him and the things that made me nervous about pursuing a relationship after I left.

Brock passed me a glass of wine and told me some facts about the lake, but my mind was stuck elsewhere. Not surprisingly, he noticed.

"You okay?"

I forced a smile. "Sure. Why?"

He tilted his head. "I don't know. You're quiet... off."

"I'm just a little tired," I lied. "But I'm not too tired for some of what you mentioned was on the agenda for the evening." I crawled over to Brock and pressed my breasts against his chest before pulling his mouth down to meet mine. The kiss was nice, *really* nice, even—but I quickly realized I was slipping back to my old ways, and I didn't want to do that with Brock. So I stopped sort of abruptly.

My fingers felt my swollen lips as I spoke. "I'm sorry. I'm lying to you."

Brock's tone remained even. "Okay. About what?"

"About being tired. I'm not. My head is just somewhere else, and I didn't want to talk about it so I kissed you. I have a bad habit of using sex to distract men from talking about anything real."

Brock took my hand. "Talk to me. What's going on, Red?"

I took a deep breath. "I got an invitation to a wedding in the mail today."

"Okay..."

"The groom is my ex-husband."

"Oh." He was quiet for a moment. "Did it upset you because you're not over him?"

"God, no. I'm definitely over Johnathan."

Brock shrugged. "It is just him moving on then?"

I shook my head. "It's more than that, actually. If it's okay, I'd like to tell you about what happened."

"Of course."

I spent the next fifteen minutes telling Brock about my relationship with my ex—how we met in high school, how Johnathan had been the only man I'd ever been with on my wedding night, how I'd supported him financially while he went to law school. I concluded with the happily *never* after of my story—my ex and my ex-best friend getting together and the wedding invitation that had arrived today.

"Believe it or not," I said. "I'm really not upset that he's getting married. It will always sting that he's with my ex-best friend, but him moving on isn't what has me so preoccupied right now. It's the realization that I've let my marriage and other things that have happened to me control my dating life." I looked into Brock's eyes. "I'm afraid to get hurt again, Brock."

He pulled me into a hug. "I'm sorry that happened to you. I really am. And now I might want to kick that idiot Johnathan's ass even more than I want to kick Tobias's."

I smiled. "You'd crush both of them with one hand tied behind your back."

Brock stroked my hair. "Thank you for sharing all of that with me. Just so you know, you're not the only scared one sitting on this blanket."

"You're just trying to make me feel better. You're not afraid of anything."

"That's what I might've said a few weeks ago. But a certain fiery little redhead has me scared shitless." He cupped my cheeks. "I'm in deep, Red. I have no idea how the hell it happened so fast, but it did. And I hope you can find a way to put your fears behind you and not let them control your future. Because I see good things coming your way—coming *our* way—if you're willing to accept them."

Brock and I held each other for a long time after that. It was everything I needed and more. Too soon, though, I had to get going. I was so close to completing the wellness program and didn't want to get kicked out now, so we headed back to Sierra.

Brock shut off the lights on his truck as he drove up the long driveway and parked around back, next to my ladder. Our goodnight kiss was gentle and sweet. After, he leaned his forehead to mine.

"So tell me," he said. "Am I going to need a tux, or will a suit be okay?"

I felt my brows pull together. "A tux? For what?"

"For the wedding next month. I'll go with you, if you want to go."

# CHAPTER 10

*Brock*

A few days later, the bells on the door chimed as I entered the one tuxedo shop in all of Meadowbrook.

A man immediately greeted me. "How can I help you, Mr. Hawkins?"

I didn't recognize him, but he apparently knew me. "I need to be measured for a tux, please."

"I'll get someone right out."

"Thank you." I nodded.

Looking around at the mannequins dressed to the nines, I felt very out of place. I'd made fun of Plaid Suit, and here I was getting fitted for one myself. I'd make sure the pants were longer than his had been, though.

"Well, well, well, if it isn't Brock Hawkins," a voice said from behind me.

I whipped around. Squinting at the short blonde, I realized her face looked familiar. *Shit. Just what I need.* Sasha Brinkley. I dated her in high school.

I ran a hand through my hair. "Sasha. How have you been?"

"I'm well. What brings you in here? You're not finally getting married, are you?"

"No." I shook my head.

"Was gonna say. Pigs must be flying, if that's the case." She laughed.

"I'm attending a wedding out of state and want to make sure I have a tux in time."

"That figures. Would've been the talk of the town if *you* were off the market."

"Not really sure how my relationship status is anyone's business, but okay…"

"I heard about what you did to your ex. What was her name? Tina?"

"Nina." I gritted my teeth. "And excuse me? What the hell are you talking about? *What I did?*"

She smirked. "Drove her out of town…"

This was pissing me off. I shouldn't encourage any more discussion of this, but I felt the need to defend myself. "Where exactly are you getting your information?"

"People talk around here, Brock. You know that."

"I didn't drive anyone out of town. That isn't what happened at all. Nina's a grown-ass woman with a mind of her own."

She shrugged. "Well, maybe she left of her own accord. But I'm pretty sure women don't leave town entirely unless their hearts are broken."

"You don't know what the hell you're talking about, Sasha. And I suggest you spend less time entertaining the Meadowbrook gossip mill and more time doing your damn job." I glared at her. "Can you kindly just measure me?" I shook my head. "Actually, no." The last thing I needed was Sasha's hands down by my balls or some shit. "Can you get someone *else* to do it, please?"

She rolled her eyes and left in a huff.

A man came by a few minutes later, taking a tape measure to me. He didn't say a damn word, which was exactly the way I liked it.

I had both of my arms sticking straight out when I glanced at the window and noticed Trevor walking by. He did a double take before a look of amusement spread across his face.

*Great. Just great.*

He entered the shop wearing a shit-eating grin. "What's this all about?"

"What does it look like?"

"Don't tell me you're eloping with Fancy Pants? If that's the case, might I be the first to say, 'I told you so'?"

"I'm accompanying her to a wedding next month. It's black tie."

"Interesting. And where might this wedding be?"

"New York."

Trevor's eyes went wide.

After the guy finished taking my measurements, I went to the register to put down some money while my nosy brother waited for me. Sasha flashed me a dirty look from across the store.

As we walked out of the shop together, Trevor started grilling me.

"I'm surprised you're going out of town for some wedding," he said. "The last time we spoke, it seemed like you had written off anything happening between you and February. Now you're getting fitted for a tux and traveling to New York?"

"Yeah, well, I'm just taking it day by day."

"Cool. I just, you know, wanna make sure you're staying true to yourself."

I wasn't following. "In what way?"

"*You* in a tux shop? It's like the apocalypse, man."

"I'm not changing for anyone, Trev. It's just a damn wedding. One day. Calm your nutsack."

"Just keep in mind that you're sending her a clear message that you're interested by going to this wedding. Nothing wrong with that. And I'm all for it. But if you *don't* plan to try to make things work once she leaves, you may not want to lead her on."

"I thought just the other day you were supporting me pursuing her," I noted. "Why are you trying to mess with my head right now?"

"I *do* support it, so long as you don't lose yourself in the process, you know?"

"You don't need to worry about that. I've got too many damn responsibilities in this fucking town to ever forget who I am, even if I wish I could sometimes. Couldn't lose myself if I tried."

"All right. All right." He chuckled. "Hey, wasn't that the girl you dated in high school working in there? What was her name? Sasha?"

"Yeah. She had some nerve. Came over to me and started talking shit."

"What did she say?"

"She mentioned that she'd heard about *what I did* to Nina—whatever the hell that means."

"What *did* you do to Nina?"

"That's exactly the point. People are just making shit up."

He laughed. "Well, if there's anything people in this town are good at, it's talkin' crap and making shit up."

I tried to laugh, and I wished I could just shake it off. But the mention of Nina had gotten inside my head a bit. I'd never actually explained to February why my ex left town. And once she learned what happened, she might doubt whether we could make this work.

♦ ♦ ♦

Later that evening, I was back at my house when I got a text.

**February: I won't be able to meet you tonight.**

I hadn't been sure whether we had plans, but I was hoping she'd sneak out as usual. However, at first, I was relieved. Given how hard it had been to control myself around her lately, it was probably safer to have a night off. But it also bummed me out, since she didn't have much time left here in Meadowbrook.

**Brock: Why can't you come out?**

**February: I'm sick.**

**Brock: Crap, really? What are your symptoms?**

**February: Just feel run down. Maybe some kind of virus. I've been in bed all day. My new roommate went to another room to sleep so she doesn't catch it.**

**Brock: Damn. I'm sorry to hear that, Red.**

**February: It's okay. I'll live.**

**Brock: Get some rest.**

**February: xo**

I turned to Oak. "I told her to get some rest, but I should go over there. What do you think?"

He stared at me.

"Or is that too much? She's sick. Maybe she doesn't want me there. No one wants guests when they're sick, right?"

Oak tilted his head.

"But she's probably not eating if she's sick. She needs to eat. She needs chicken soup."

He let out a single bark.

"Now you're awake because you heard the word *chicken*, you big lug!"

He barked again.

"You think I should do it, don't you?"

He fell to my feet and rolled his big body around on the floor.

"You just want chicken. I can't trust you for shit." I sighed. "But you *do* think I should go get the stuff to make soup? I'd have to go to the store. Tell me what to do, Oak."

*Ruff!*

"Damn you, you old romantic." I grabbed my coat. "All right. I'll go."

♦ ♦ ♦

*This is going to be interesting.*

I had the soup carefully sealed in a container in a bag. I needed to hurry so it didn't get cold because I wasn't sure if Feb had a way of heating it up. I couldn't remember if she had a microwave in her room.

I'd thrown my own ladder into the back of my truck and set it up right before I sent her a text.

**Brock: Open your window, Red.**

*Please don't be asleep.*

When I noticed the window slide open, I began to climb the ladder.

As I made my way up, February called down to me. "What are you doing, Brock?"

"Brought you some soup," I said, careful not to jostle the contents of the bag too much as I climbed.

She took the bag from me as I crawled through the window.

"Be careful with that," I warned. "It's hot chicken soup. I don't want it to leak."

Her mouth dropped open. "You made me soup?"

I nodded. "You have to eat it fast before it gets cold."

"You didn't have to do this."

"Well, Oak told me to. He said he owed you for the nice sleep the other night." I winked. "Lie down and relax. I'll prepare you a bowl."

I took out the two bowls I'd brought, figuring I'd have some with her.

She covered her mouth. "You brought bowls?"

"Well, you don't even have plates at home. Figured you didn't have bowls here. I brought spoons, too."

As I handed her a bowl, I looked more closely at her face. Not a sniffle in sight, and she had makeup on. My stomach sank. February didn't seem too sick.

"On second thought..." I stood. "I'll leave you with the soup."

"Stay." She rose from the bed. "You brought two bowls, which was very sweet. Clearly you were planning to join me."

"Yeah. But now I'm thinking better of it. Probably shouldn't risk catching whatever you have." I tried to give her the benefit of the doubt.

She frowned. "I promise to keep my distance if you stay and have some soup."

So I caved, lying next to her in bed—fuck distance—while we ate together.

"This was incredibly sweet, Brock. Thank you," she said when she'd finished. "And it was really good, by the way. Who says the only thing you know how to make is stew?"

"Well, I'm glad you liked it." I winked. "And no biggie. I needed a good deed of the day anyway."

February elbowed me. "I should get sick more often." Her smile faded.

I started to worry again about what was really going on. Something still seemed off.

"I should probably get going." I moved off the bed.

"Please stay. I want to talk to you."

Lying back down next to her, I said, "Okay. What's up?"

"Did you come for any other reason than to bring me soup?"

"I've had a lot on my mind today, actually…"

"Like what?"

"I wondered whether I went a little too far in telling you how scared I was about my feelings for you. I don't want to scare *you*." I hesitated. "And…there's some stuff you don't know about my past relationship. I never explained why Nina left town. And I kind of feel like getting that off my chest for some reason."

A look of concern crossed her face. "Why don't you tell me now?"

"It's not very complicated. But it's not what people think. Everyone knows Nina left. They assume she wasn't happy here in Meadowbrook and that she either dumped me or I *drove her out of town*—whatever that means."

She chuckled. "I picture you driving her out as she sits in the cab of your big red truck."

"Right?" I shook my head. "Ridiculous." I sighed. "Anyway, that wasn't it."

"So what happened?" She rested her chin in her hand.

"Nina wanted me to make a full commitment to her. And I wasn't ready to do that. She'd been wanting to move out of town, but that wasn't the whole story. She'd told me she would stay if I'd commit. But I wasn't ready—with her."

"Well, you can't be forced into something as important as marriage."

"The thing is...she didn't even want kids or a family. She just wanted to get married. It felt like more about having a ring on her finger than anything else. Something felt wrong."

"And you don't want to get married at all or..."

"I didn't say that. But I knew it didn't feel right to marry *her*. And when she gave me the ultimatum, it all became clear."

She cocked her head. "So you might be open to marriage someday?"

I needed to be honest. "I'm not sure if marriage and kids are for me. I've always said that. But I am open to finding the right person and seeing how it plays out. I feel like what's meant to be will happen."

"Thank you for being open with me, Brock." She caressed my arm.

I arched a brow. "Will you be open with *me* now?"

She let out a shaky breath. "What do you want to know?"

"I want to know why you made up a sickness to get out of seeing me tonight." I stared into her eyes. "You don't look sick, Feb. You're *not* sick. Am I right?"

February closed her eyes for a moment. "I *am* sort of sick, but not with a fever or cold."

"What's wrong?"

"I'm sick to my stomach. But it's nerves, not a virus."

"Nerves over what?"

"I might be in trouble." Her voice shook.

My heartbeat accelerated. "Talk to me. What's going on?"

"I looked at the calendar today and realized…" She hesitated.

"What?"

"I'm a week late for my period. That never happens."

A sinking feeling developed in my stomach. My eyes widened. "You think you're pregnant?"

"I don't know. I shouldn't be. But I *could* be. It's a remote possibility."

This situation had gotten a hell of a lot more complicated in a matter of seconds. *Are you kidding me?* The timing on this…especially since I'd just admitted I might never want kids.

I rubbed my temples. "I assume you have good reason to suspect it's possible?"

"I used protection with Tobias, if that's what you're asking. So it doesn't make sense."

"It *would* be his, though, right?"

She nodded. "He's the only person I've been with recently, Brock."

I let out a sigh of relief. At least there were no additional surprises.

She exhaled. "I feel terrible having to admit this to you. But I can't lie to your face any longer. This is the reason I've been off today."

"Why haven't you taken a test?"

"I've been too scared to sneak out and get one. This has only been going on since this afternoon. That's when I realized the date. Being here at Sierra has made me lose track of time." She shook her head. "I don't really want to know. But I *need* to know."

"Well, fuck, you shouldn't be sitting here wondering. The stress alone will kill you. Let me go out and get you a test." The room was spinning. *Who am I kidding?* This was partly for me, too. *I* needed to know so I could move on with my life.

She clasped her hands together. "That would be amazing."

I grabbed my jacket. "I'll be back."

Wasting no time, I climbed down the ladder to my truck and headed to the pharmacy. The ride over there was a blur. The entire way, I said a silent prayer that the test would be negative.

I got there just in the nick of time, before they were about to close.

Unfortunately, the old man at the counter was a family friend. I cleared my throat. "Evening, Mr. Hayes."

He looked at me funny when he saw what I was purchasing. "Something you want to tell me, Brock?"

"Nope. And there's nothing *you're* gonna tell anyone about this, either." I slipped him a fifty-dollar bill. "Catch my drift?"

"I saw nothing." He winked, placing the money in his pocket.

I got in my truck and raced back to Sierra with the test. Thankfully no one had screwed with my ladder, and it was still there.

After I texted February, she opened the window as I climbed up.

"Got the last kit on the shelf. Can you believe it?"

"Wow," she breathed.

I placed my hands on her shoulders. "It's gonna be okay. I'll stay with you until we know."

"I'd better get this over with." She read the back of the box. "After I pee on the stick, I have to wait three minutes."

"I'll be here waiting."

"Thank you, Brock. Truly." She placed her hand on her chest. "Gosh, my heart is beating so fast right now."

"Go get it over with, Red. No sense in putting it off." *My heart can't take it.*

February disappeared to the bathroom, leaving me alone in her room.

The wait was excruciating. My mind kept catastrophizing. If she turned out to be pregnant, the chance of us working out would be nil. This situation would've been tough long-distance without a baby in the picture. But with a baby? Next to impossible.

I thought back fondly to earlier tonight when my biggest problem had been whether she was faking an illness. I would've given anything to go back to that time.

I checked my phone. It had been five minutes. She had to know by now. The fact that she hadn't come out wasn't a good sign.

*Fuck.*

*She's pregnant.*

*I know it.*

I had to think fast. *What will I do?*

I still wanted to explore this.

That was my truth.

I must've been fucking crazy.

But if that woman came out here and told me she was having a baby... I wasn't going anywhere—I knew it in my gut.

*Well, damn.*

You learn something new about yourself every day.

*I need to know if I'm losing my mind.*

*Where the fuck is my dog when I need him?*

I paced.

The door burst open.

"It's negative!" She beamed.

I let out all of the air I'd been holding. "Oh, thank fuck!"

# CHAPTER 11

*February*

"Hey, Trinity." I popped my head into my therapist's office a few days later. "Do you have a minute?"

She smiled. "Of course. Come on in."

"Is it too late to add names to the guest list for tomorrow? For family day?"

Trinity shook her head. "Not at all. How many people would you like to add?"

I nibbled on my lip. "One. But I'm not even sure he'll come."

"That's not an issue. The guest list is just for security purposes, so reception knows who they should let in. Who do you want to add?"

I took a deep breath. If saying his name freaked me out this much, maybe it wasn't a great idea to invite him after all. "You know what, I think I changed my mind."

Trinity smiled warmly. "The purpose of the one-on-one counseling sessions we do during family day is to help you mend relationships before you go back home. If you're struggling to decide whether you should even invite someone, a session might do some good."

I blew out two cheeks full of air. "It's my dad. We've been estranged for a long time."

"Well, the decision is obviously yours. But letting out pent-up emotions and clearing the air can be cathartic. You and I have talked a lot about the different work stresses that contributed to you coming to Sierra Wellness Center, and that makes sense because those are the issues you've dealt with recently. But sometimes the things we don't deal with on a day-to-day basis can weigh just as heavily on our mental health."

I sighed and nodded. "Okay. Can we add Joseph Shaw to the guest list?"

"Of course."

I filled out a form before leaving Trinity's office and then headed to one of the small telephone-lounge rooms. Since we weren't allowed to have cell phones, there were several places we could go to make phone calls in private. They all had comfy chairs and couches. I'd only used the rooms for work calls so far, so I hadn't noticed the box of tissues on the end table. *Might need those for what I'm about to do.*

I hadn't seen my dad in more than a decade. And it wasn't because he was a great distance away. As far as I knew, he still rented a house in Queens, a twenty-minute train ride from me in Manhattan. I stared down at the phone, thinking how much I'd changed recently. Three weeks ago, I would've never imagined that this place might actually help me. I'd only come to Sierra because my board of directors had forced my hand. When they'd suggested I might be having a nervous breakdown, I'd laughed at them. These days, though, I wasn't so sure they were wrong. Maybe it was the pregnancy scare, or maybe it was the hormones—I'd finally gotten my period this morning—but I felt like I should keep pushing myself to find peace. And that meant it was time to fix things with my father.

I picked up the phone and dialed. If I didn't call right this moment, I might chicken out. I wasn't even sure if his home number was still the same one I knew. Heck, he might not even *have* a house phone anymore—most people didn't these days.

My heart raced as the phone connected.

One ring. *Thump-thump.*

Two rings. *Thump-thump-thump!*

By the time the third ring started, my chest was pounding so hard I thought I might go into cardiac arrest. I considered hanging up, but at the last second someone answered.

"Hello?"

*My dad.*

I didn't say anything.

"Hello?" he repeated in a sterner voice. "Is someone there?"

I sat up stick straight and cleared my throat. "Uh, yeah. Hi, Dad."

A pause. "February? Is that you?"

"Yeah, it's me."

His tone softened. "How are you, honey?"

My eyes filled with tears. "Not so good, actually."

"Where are you? Are you hurt?"

I smiled sadly. "No, no. It's nothing like that. I'm fine, at least physically anyway. But..." I gnawed on my lip. "I'm at a wellness facility."

"A what?"

"It's a place people go when they need a mental-health timeout. I was working a lot and under a lot of stress and... Well, let's just say I'm here, and it's helping."

My dad was quiet for a beat. "I'm sorry to hear that. Is there anything I can do?"

"Actually, there is. That's why I'm calling. Tomorrow is family day. They have these counseling sessions and stuff and..."

I'd made it over the biggest hurdle—*making the call*—yet I couldn't bring myself to ask him to come, to ask him to do *anything* for me.

Long seconds ticked by in silence, and eventually it was my dad who spoke.

"What time should I be there?"

♦ ♦ ♦

"Hey." I held the old phone up for a better angle and smiled at Brock's naked chest. "Boy, I called at the right time. Are you naked?"

He chuckled. "Just came upstairs for a minute to change my shirt. Tossed out a drunk who was starting trouble, and the jackass spilled his beer all over me."

"How about you set the phone down on the counter so I can get the full view from a distance?"

"You can have the full view, live and in person, anytime you want it, sweetheart. Just say the word, and my clothes will come off."

"Is that a promise?"

"One you can take to the bank, Red." He finished putting on a T-shirt and brought the phone closer to his face.

The abs had been nice, but this view wasn't so bad either. "Sorry I couldn't sneak out tonight to visit you. The maintenance guy was sick today." I yawned. "Excuse me. That came out of nowhere."

"Tired?"

"I think it's more mental exhaustion than anything physical."

"Oh yeah? Everything okay?"

I lay back on my bed and held the phone up to my face. "Ask me that at this time tomorrow, and I'll let you know."

"What's going on?"

"I invited my dad for family day tomorrow. It was a last-minute decision. I called him this afternoon."

"You haven't really talked about your father. Do you not get along?"

I shook my head. "He screwed over my mom when I was pretty young, and I've never really forgiven him or gotten over it."

"And now you feel like you're ready to do that?"

I shrugged. "I'm not sure. But I think my relationship with him and my relationship with my ex have had far more of an effect on me than I allowed myself to accept before coming here. I think it contributed to my not wanting to get close to men or open up to anyone."

Brock smiled. "I'm proud of you, you know that?"

Warmth spread through my chest. "Thank you."

"I'll have the truck gassed up and ready to go if you need to talk after you see him tomorrow."

"I appreciate that."

"So do you have anything you need to do for the rest of the night? Any counseling or stuff?"

"Nope. I think I'm going to take a nice, warm bath. I haven't fully taken advantage of this ritzy place's spa products and the big, beautiful tub in my bathroom."

Brock was quiet for a minute. "What I wouldn't give to be there while you're naked in that bath."

I smirked. "That might be able to be arranged."

His eyes grew wide. "Oh yeah?"

I laughed. "Don't get too excited. I didn't mean in person—at least not tonight. But how about a little FaceTime fun? Do you think you can get someone to cover the bar in maybe a half hour?"

"I'll shut the fucking thing down if I have to."

♦ ♦ ♦

I'd just set the phone up on a shelf in the bathroom and stepped back to see how I looked when a feeling of panic washed over me. Maybe I'd taken this too far. I should probably change... But as I reached for the phone, it rang. I lifted it close to my face as I answered to avoid showing what I had on.

"Hi."

Brock's face fell. "Did you change your mind?"

"No, I just..." I looked over at the tub full of bubbles then down at the teddy I wore. It was black and lacy with a thong. It made me feel insanely sexy. *Fuck it. I'm doing this.* "Let me set the phone up." I positioned the cell back on the shelf and took a deep breath before stepping into the camera's view.

"Holy fuck," Brock grumbled. "You look incredible. Do you sleep in that type of thing every night?"

I chuckled and shook my head. "No. I borrowed it from my friend Morgan. She does some risqué selfies for her social media."

"Turn around for me." His voice turned husky. And here I'd been worried my lumberjack might not be comfortable with a little FaceTime fooling around.

I did a slow pivot, stopping when my back faced the camera.

"Bend over, beautiful. Show me that ass."

A shiver ran through me. I *loved* the way he took control right from the get-go. Somehow I knew that's how things would be with him in bed, too.

I put two hands on the tub, bent at the waist, and gyrated my hips around playfully.

"Always hated FaceTime," Brock said. "But now I get it."

I chuckled and gazed over my shoulder. "Are you done looking?"

"Not by a damn mile. But turn back around." Brock stayed quiet for a long time, just looking. When he spoke again, his voice was low. "Take it off. Slowly."

I slipped the thin straps from my shoulders and took my time peeling the lacy material down my body. My eyes stayed glued to the phone screen, watching Brock's face. He ran his tongue along his bottom lip as I shimmied the teddy to the floor.

"Fuck me..." He groaned. "You're bare."

"Do you like women like that?"

"I don't like *women*, Red. I like *you*. And I'll take you any way you come. But, yeah, I think bare is sexy as shit. I can't wait to lick that beautiful pussy."

*Oh my. Yes, please!*

"Just give me another minute to look at you, and then we'll get started. I promise."

*And here I thought we'd already started.* My engine was definitely revving.

After a while, Brock lifted his chin. "Thank you. Climb into the tub, babe."

I slipped into the bath. The top had a few inches of bubbles so I was no longer exposed.

"You good?" he asked.

I nodded. "It feels incredible. Maybe you should take a bath, too."

"Another time. Right now, I want to focus on you. I'm not even going to touch myself. I just want to tell you all the things I want to do to you and watch you come. Is that okay?"

I smiled. "That sounds pretty perfect to me."

"Good. Now close your eyes. Slide your hand into that warm water and find that swollen bud of yours."

I closed my eyes and did as he instructed. Orgasm wasn't generally easy for me—not with a man and not alone. It happened maybe fifty percent of the time. But the electric bolt that shot through my body as I spread my legs and touched my clit told me tonight was going to fall on the winning side of that ratio.

"Rub a small circle." Brock groaned. "God, you're so damn sexy. I can't wait to put your legs over my shoulders and bury my face between them. I'm going to make your body tremble until you come on my tongue and then drink every last drop of your sweetness."

I rubbed faster and harder, imagining exactly what he'd said.

"Slip your finger inside, sweetheart. Only one."

I parted my flesh and began to finger myself. It felt good, but I needed more. I was tempted to add a finger or two. The bubbles were blocking the view, so Brock wouldn't know. Yet I controlled myself and pumped in and out with only one finger.

"I wish I was there with you right now. I'd straddle your face while you touched yourself. Grab a fistful of your hair in my hand, and fuck your mouth and throat until I heard you gag."

*"Oh God."*

"You like that?"

I nodded. "I need more, Brock..."

"Slip another finger in, then another. Fill it up, just like I'm going to do with that tight pussy."

My fingers pumped faster, and my breaths barely kept up.

"Gorgeous. My cock's inside you, and you're so tight, so fucking wet. I'm about to explode. I can feel you swelling all around me, gripping me like a fist."

I felt the orgasm building with every word Brock spoke. My mind focused on nothing but the ferocious need to break free. The building could've burned down around me, and I wouldn't have been able to stop.

"Come, sweetheart. Let it all go."

I climaxed nearly violently, my body shaking and twitching through every pulse-pounding wave. It was the most intense orgasm of my life, and the man who gave it to me hadn't even touched me yet. My chest heaved up and down as I struggled to catch my breath. "Brock..."

He cleared his throat. "Yeah, Red?"

My eyes fluttered open, and I felt a lazy smile creep over my face. I looked at the phone for the first time since we'd started. "That was crazy good."

He smiled. "I'm glad. Stay in the bath and relax for a while now, yeah?"

"I think I'll do that."

He winked. "'Night, beautiful."

"'Night, Lumberjack."

"Call me tomorrow after family day ends. Okay?"

"I will."

After we disconnected, I expected the reminder of what tomorrow would bring to tense me back up. But not even that could wake my sated body. I was too consumed with what I'd just done. *If video sex was that good, I can't wait to experience the real thing with this man.*

# CHAPTER 12

*February*

I couldn't stop rubbing my hands together as we sat down.

My father pointed his eyes to my lap. "The first time I remember you wringing your hands like that was the sixth-grade spelling bee."

My brows pulled together. "You weren't at the spelling bee."

He smiled sadly. "Yes, I was. I was in the back row. I came to a lot of things without letting you know I was there."

"Why would you do that?"

He shrugged. "It was a big day for you, and I didn't want to make your anxiety worse."

*I wouldn't have had anxiety if it weren't for you.*

I stayed quiet for a long time.

Trinity looked back and forth between us. She tilted her head. "What are you thinking right now, February?"

"I don't think I should say."

She spoke to my dad. "Would you like to hear what's on your daughter's mind? Even if it's hurtful?"

He nodded. "We can't get past it until it all comes out."

Trinity looked to me. "Take your time."

I sighed. "I was thinking I didn't have anxiety before Mom's thirty-fifth birthday."

Dad's face fell. "I'm sorry." He looked over at Trinity. "I made my daughter keep quiet about something I shouldn't have. What I did shouldn't have happened at all, but at the very least, I should have owned my actions and come clean to my wife." He paused and looked at me again. "I'm so sorry, February."

"I thought you were out shopping for Mom's birthday gift when I saw your car in the back of the store parking lot. I thought maybe for once, you hadn't gambled away all of your paycheck and were going to remember Mom's birthday the next day."

My father looked to Trinity. "February was out riding her bike, minding her own business, happy as can be, and she found me in the car with another woman."

I scoffed. "She was riding something else."

"Not that it excuses any of my actions, but I was an alcoholic with a gambling addiction."

"Was?" Trinity asked.

He nodded. "I've been sober for seven years now. Haven't gambled in eight."

That information took me by surprise; my chest tightened. "I didn't know that."

"I wasn't a good father, and I was an even worse husband. I've made more mistakes than I could count in my life. But it haunts me to this day that I forced you to keep quiet about what you saw." He hung his head.

When he lifted it and looked at Trinity again, there were tears in his eyes. "I manipulated my own child, told her that if she shared what she'd seen, it would break up our family and be very painful for her mother."

"To this day, I have trouble looking Mom in the eyes because of the secret I carry with me." I looked at my therapist. "They split up a year later. Mom told us it was because she couldn't take the drinking anymore. But then when I was seventeen, we ran into a woman on the street. She stopped us and apologized to Mom. That's when I learned my mother knew he'd had affairs and didn't tell us. That woman wasn't even the same woman I'd caught him in the car with. Apparently there were many. Still, my mom tried to protect my sister and me, even after he'd cheated on her. Yet he was selfish enough to make his own daughter lie and live with guilt."

Dad wiped a tear from his cheek. "I did all that and more. If I could go back and change things, I would. I swear to you, I would. But I can't. All I can do is apologize." He reached out and touched my hand. "I'm sorry, February. I'm *so, so* sorry for the things I've done that hurt you."

I looked down at his hand covering mine. "Mom has been encouraging me to make amends with you for years."

Dad shook his head. "She's still the kindest human I've ever met."

I tasted salt in my throat and swallowed. "She is. Some things never change."

He squeezed my hand. "But I like to think that I have."

Over the next two hours, there were a lot more tears—from my dad and from me. But toward the end, there was some laughter, too. Trinity stayed in the background most of the time, only guiding us when necessary.

Eventually, a low chime on her phone sounded. She pushed the button to turn it off and smiled. "Sorry about that. I always set alarms because I have a tendency to lose track of time. There are only about five minutes left of family day visiting hours. I'll leave you two alone, and you can walk your dad out."

"Okay. Thank you for everything, Trinity."

My father stood and extended a hand. "I appreciate everything you've done for us today. Please take care of my little girl."

Trinity smiled. "She doesn't need much taking care of. She's doing great on her own."

I walked my father outside. There were people milling around near the door, so we walked toward the parking lot.

"How much longer are you here?" he asked.

"Another week."

"Can we see each other again when you get out?"

I nodded. "I think so. How about I call you?"

"I'd like that." Dad looked me in the eyes. "Thank you, February. I know we have a long way to go, but I appreciate you allowing me back into your life. I promise I won't let you down this time."

We hugged, and I watched him get into his car and disappear down the long driveway. Today had been heavy, yet I felt lighter. I had a sense of hope I hadn't felt in a very long time. Maybe I could get to a healthy place with my dad, and with relationships again. That last thought made me excited to tell Brock about today.

I stayed outside for a few minutes, enjoying the warmth of the sun on my face. When my stomach growled, I realized I hadn't eaten anything since last night, so I headed back inside. The hidden cell phone Brock gave me buzzed from my pocket. I dug it out and opened it, finding a local number flashing. No one ever called except Brock, so I answered with a smile.

"Hello. How did you know I was thinking about you?"

"Oh," a woman said. "I think I have the wrong number."

"I'm sorry. I shouldn't have answered like that. Are you trying to reach a bar called The Brook?"

"I am. Well, I'm trying to reach Brock Hawkins, actually."

"He's not here at the moment. Can I take a message?"

The woman sighed. "I've left him four messages already on his personal cell phone. I figured I'd try the bar since he isn't returning my calls."

An unsettled feeling came over me. "Umm... I can make sure he gets the message, if you want to leave one with me."

"Thank you. Will you please ask him to call Nina? It's important."

*Nina...as in his ex?*

Maybe there were two Ninas. At least I hoped there were.

"Will he know where you're calling from? A company or a supplier or something?"

"He should know, considering we dated for almost a year."

# CHAPTER 13

*Brock*

There was nothing more peaceful than being out in the woods. The towering trees. The earthy air. The rustle of the leaves.

Trevor and I were working on one of a few log cabins I'd been building. This wasn't the one I planned to live in; that one was a lot bigger and a bit farther off the beaten path. But this smaller cabin was one I'd sell or rent someday as an investment property.

It was a wonder I hadn't chopped a damn finger off because since last night, I'd been replaying that FaceTime session with February in my head nonstop.

At one point Trevor stopped what he was doing to bring me my phone.

I took it. "Why are you giving me this?"

"You left it on that rock over there. I saw it light up. You missed a call from Nina." He snickered. "What the heck does she want?"

I stuck my shovel into the ground and looked down at the screen. Letting out a deep sigh, I groaned. "I don't understand why she keeps calling."

"*Keeps* calling? She's called you more than once?"

"Yeah." I placed the phone in my back pocket. "It's not the first time she's called this week."

"You're not answering?"

"I haven't, and I don't plan to."

My brother narrowed his eyes. "Isn't that kind of rude?"

"Yeah, well, so is using women to make you Mexican food and then ghosting them." I rolled my eyes and sighed. "I don't actually think it's rude, no. Isn't she the one who left town? Why should I answer her calls if I don't want to talk to her? There's nothing to talk *about*."

He shrugged. "I don't know. Just seems rude not to return someone's call."

I raised my voice. "I know what she wants, and I'm not interested."

"All right. All right." He resumed working. "But you think she wants you back?"

"Well, she tried to get me to commit to her. That didn't work. So she left town. Pretty sure she believed her disappearance would change my mind. But that strategy doesn't always work. Sometimes distance doesn't make the heart grow fonder. Sometimes you grow even *further* apart. Since she's been gone, I've realized even more how incompatible we were."

"Is it that, or is it that *someone else* came on the scene not so long after she left and mended your broken heart?"

February most definitely had taken my life by storm. But even if she and I were opposites, we were *compatible*. And if there *had* been a broken heart to mend, she would've helped with that. But contrary to the rumors in this town, I wasn't devastated by my ex leaving. It turned out to be more of a relief than a heartbreak.

"My feelings for February don't change the fact that Nina was never right for me," I told Trevor. "But as far as February goes..." I shook my head and smiled, thinking again about our virtual sex last night.

After a moment, he burst out laughing. "Damn, *that* good, huh?"

I couldn't help grinning. "Yes, my brother. It is that good."

"You devil." He lowered his voice, though our only company out here was wild animals. "You had sex with her?"

I didn't feel comfortable giving my brother details. So I tried to be vague. "We didn't have sex...in person. That's all I'll say."

"Well, shit. That sounds kinky. No wonder you don't give a shit about Nina's calls."

"It's not that I don't give a shit about Nina. You don't just stop caring about someone you were with for a while. But I see now that we weren't right for each other. And it's not gonna help her if I entertain whatever it is she wants from me. That would be like opening an old wound. End of story."

Trevor dropped the subject as we got back to work, and I began chopping wood.

Several minutes later, I'd just swung my ax backward, getting ready to slice into a huge log, when a voice stopped me.

"Hey!"

I turned to find February behind me. *What the hell?*

"What are you doing here? I nearly took your head off."

"Sorry. I didn't realize this was a danger zone."

I put down the ax. "How did you know where I was?"

"I went to the bar, and the bartender on duty gave me the address. I used the GPS on your phone to walk here."

"Hey, February," my brother called out.

"Hi, Trevor..." She smiled, but it seemed strained.

*Something is off.*

"You shouldn't be walking alone. But you already know that. This is a very desolate area."

"What choice did I have if I wanted to come find you?"

"You could've called, and I would've come to you. You know that."

"I didn't want to stop you if you were working." She looked down at the ax on the ground. "Obviously, you're busy."

"Let's talk over here." We walked toward the back of the property where we could have some privacy. "What's wrong, February? You look like something is bothering you."

"You're right." She exhaled. "Something *is* bothering me."

"Talk to me. What's going on?"

She frowned. "I got a phone call earlier on your phone."

"Okay..."

"It was your ex-girlfriend."

*Crap. What the fuck?*

"I asked her if I could take a message, but she just told me to tell you to call her back. Apparently, you haven't been returning her calls."

"There's nothing going on there, February. I don't understand why she's trying to reach me all of a sudden. But that's correct—I haven't been taking her calls."

"She said it was important."

"It's *not* important." I shook my head. "She's trying to get back with me. And I want no part of it."

She looked up at the sky. "I shouldn't be upset, but it rattled me a little, that's all. With me leaving soon, I'm just extra sensitive, I guess."

"I'm sorry."

"Why *haven't* you taken her calls?" She crossed her arms. "Is that how you treat someone you used to be involved with?"

"Trust me, it's for her own good."

February cocked her head. "Why?"

"Because it's over between us. Nothing good can come from opening up the lines of communication again. She left. She made her decision. It was the right one. And I have no interest in entertaining what she has to say. Anything I tell her about what I've been up to since she left isn't going to please her, because I've been happier than ever. I'm sorry if my attitude about the whole thing seems shitty, but I feel like my refusing to talk is in *her* best interest, too."

A look of worry crossed February's face. "You really think she's trying to get back with you?"

"I suspect that."

"Why?"

I paused, unsure whether to elaborate. "Before she left, Nina had seemed sure I would change my mind. She'd bet that I'd come to my senses by her birthday, said she'd come back and we'd meet up at the place where we first met. Her birthday is approaching. That's why she's calling."

"So you're standing her up?"

"I'm doing what's best for her instead of wasting her energy. Why would I want to let her down a second time?" I sighed. "I've also been in a good headspace lately. I don't want to disrupt that. I'm setting boundaries. You know what I mean?"

Her shoulders seemed to relax. "I can understand that rationale," she said. "When Tobias came here, it felt like the last thing I needed. I'd been so happy otherwise and was relieved when he left. So I can relate to having boundaries."

"Sometimes we have to. As I get older, I'm learning that. It's bad enough that everyone in this town seems to think they're entitled to know everything about my life."

February wrapped her arms around herself. "It just seems weird because I'm leaving soon, and all of a sudden she's calling you. Feels like bad timing."

"I get it." I took off my flannel and wrapped it around her, because once again, she had no damn jacket on. "I'm sorry you've been overanalyzing her phone call when it truly means nothing."

She closed the flannel over herself. "It's okay."

I rubbed her cheek with the back of my fingers. "If anything, my experience in getting to know you has helped me confirm that I made the right decision in ending things with Nina."

She sighed. "I might have overreacted because I had that therapy session with my dad earlier today. It was good, but it made me very emotional, and then that phone call came in. It was just a lot at once."

"Ah." I nodded in understanding. "That's right. This was family day. Let's go sit over here for a minute."

I led her to the back of my truck, where we sat on the tailgate.

She spent the next several minutes telling me about the experience today with her father.

"Thinking about your dad's cheating has put you on edge," I said. "And then you get a phone call from my ex and somehow tie the two together. I'm sorry. I realize how bad that timing is."

"It's not your fault."

"I've never cheated on anyone, Feb."

"Never?"

I shook my head. "Never. Broken more than a few hearts, but never cheated."

"That's commendable."

"Not really. It's just the right thing to do. There's no reason to cheat on someone when you can just end things if you're not happy."

She arched a brow. "How many broken hearts are we talking here? Maybe I should walk away now so you don't have a chance to break mine. I don't want to be the one hundred and seventeenth."

"Really, woman? Because I'm fairly certain that if anyone is going to end up with a broken heart in this situation, it's me." I looked her in the eyes. "Do you have any idea how badly I've fallen for you?"

"Badly enough to give up your life here and move to the City?"

*Well, shit.* That question had crossed my mind multiple times, but I certainly wasn't expecting her to hit me with it right this second. Not like there was a gray area to the answer, either. It was pretty much yes or no.

Shit or get off the pot. The difference between being together or not.

I hesitated, which likely didn't help my case. But I couldn't answer the question without thinking it through.

"Your silence on the matter pretty much gives me my answer, Brock."

"Don't make assumptions because I think before I speak."

"Look..." She placed her hand on my arm. "It wasn't a fair question anyway. It was rhetorical. Because I know your entire life is here. I'd be a shitty person if I expected you to give all of that up and move to an unfamiliar place. That's why this situation is so complicated. We may want to be together, but it very well may be impossible."

My brows drew in. "Sounds like you've already made your mind up that this is a dead end." I blew out a frustrated breath. "What are you saying, February?"

She stood. "I think I'm saying we should stop seeing each other before we both get hurt." Her eyes watered. "I have to go."

I shot up. "What? Wait. Let me at least drive you. We can talk this through. I—"

"I'm sorry, Brock."

I couldn't get another word in because she ran off faster than a bat out of hell—once again still wearing my shirt.

# CHAPTER 14

*February*

*Now I'm the one avoiding phone calls.*

I stared down at the cell in my hand and realized it was the first time it had rung all day. It had been five days now since I'd seen Brock. On the first day, he'd called four times. On the second, three. On the third, two. Now today—it was just the one call. That's likely how fast I would fade from his thoughts once I was back in New York.

5

4

3

2

1

*February who?*

Tears welled in my eyes.

It had been absolute torture to cut off all contact with him. But why dig myself deeper when nothing would ever come of it? It would only make it more painful in the end. Yet I somehow couldn't imagine walking out that door tomorrow and going back to the City without seeing him.

"Yoo-hoo..." A voice interrupted my thoughts. I looked up to find Morgan standing at my bedroom door. She tilted her head. "Boy, you were really somewhere else. I said your name three times."

"Did you?"

She nodded with her hands behind her back, then walked in and held out a small gift bag. "A little something to remember our time here."

I smiled sadly. "I don't have a parting gift for you."

She plopped down on the bed next to me and set the bag on my lap. "This isn't really a gift. It's more closure."

Inside was the black teddy I'd worn the night of my video sexcapades with Brock. I'd hand washed it and returned it to her the next day. "Umm... How is this closure? Seeing this is more the *opposite* of closure."

Morgan covered my hand with hers. "Not if you put it on and go say goodbye one last time..."

I started to speak, but Morgan put a hand up. "Hear me out before you respond. You're better at giving advice than I am. I don't know what I would've done without you these last few weeks. But every once in a blue moon, something smart comes out of my mouth. I think what I have to say is important."

I squeezed her hand. "Everything you say is important, Morgan. You don't give yourself enough credit."

She rested her head on my shoulder. "You need to see him one more time, February. Talk to him. Look at what happened with your dad when you tried to shut him out. Relationships that are important to us are like open wounds. If you walk away without closure, they fester and never heal. But if you allow it to close, you can move on. You'll have a scar, but we can live with those."

I sighed. "Maybe you're right."

Morgan smiled. "Hang on." She dug into her pocket and took out her cell phone. Holding it up to me, she pressed record. "Say that again. But leave off the *maybe* part."

I chuckled and bumped my shoulder with hers. "I'm going to miss you, my zany friend."

She winked. "No, you're not. You're going to see me every day. On Instagram."

♦ ♦ ♦

I raised my hand to knock, then lowered it.

*What if he has company?*
*What if Nina is in there?*
*What if...*

No. No. No. I'm being ridiculous. Brock would never do that to us.

*Though there is no us anymore, is there?*
*You haven't even spoken to the man in five days.*
*And he moved on pretty quickly after things ended with his ex, didn't he?*

My palms started to sweat. This was ridiculous. *I* was being ridiculous. Yet when I raised my hand to knock again, I still couldn't do it. Fear crippled me.

Though when I heard a deep voice behind me, I certainly jumped high enough.

"Just gonna stand there all day?"

*Brock.*

I covered my racing heart and turned around. "You scared the crap out of me."

"Sorry."

"I went to the bar to look for you, but they said you took tonight off."

He shoved his hands into his pockets. "I was working on a cabin."

"At midnight?"

"I have a personal project I work on whenever I have time. A log home I'm building for myself."

"Oh. I didn't know that."

Brock nodded. We fell quiet as we stared at each other, but the ever-present sexual tension was still there. It crackled in the air all around us.

"You want to see it?" he asked.

I nodded. "I'd love that."

Back downstairs, Brock opened the passenger door of his truck. Once I climbed in, he took off his flannel and wrapped it around me before going to the driver's side. "You should really wear a jacket."

Unfortunately, that was pretty much the extent of our conversation for the fifteen-minute drive. I had no idea what to say, and it seemed Brock didn't either. The silence was awkward. The roads were dark, and Brock stared straight ahead.

When we turned off the highway and headed down a dirt road toward a wooded area, I attempted to break the ice. "You're not taking me out into the woods to kill me, are you? I don't want to die wearing a blue flannel over a red dress."

Brock shook his head and parked. "Wait here. I have to turn on the generator."

A minute later, the entire area was illuminated by floodlights. The view took my breath away. *Wow. Just wow.* Nestled deep in the woods, a wide, welcoming porch stretched across the front of a big log cabin. I could easily envision rocking chairs and some hanging ferns, and maybe a rustic lantern over the tall front door.

Brock opened the passenger door and held out a hand. Somewhere nearby, a brook babbled.

"This is incredible. You built this yourself?"

He nodded. "Every last bit of it. Cut down every log and handmade every cabinet in the half-done kitchen. I'll probably be ninety by the time it's finished, but I wanted to do it all myself."

"I can totally picture Oak pulling a fish out of that brook I hear running."

"He better. Or I'm not putting in a bathtub for his lazy ass."

I smiled, though being here was a painful reminder of how different Brock and I were. The man built log cabins in the woods out of trees he cut down with his bare hands, and I'd never even been camping. "It's really beautiful, Brock."

"Thank you."

"Can I see inside?"

He nodded.

I'd thought the outside was impressive until I walked into the house. I walked over to the biggest stone fireplace I'd ever seen. "You built this all by yourself, too?"

"Collected all the stones from around the property. It's been put to good use already since the place doesn't have heat yet."

"Can we...make a fire?"

Brock caught my eyes. He stared for a few seconds before nodding and looking away. "I have cedar logs piled on the side of the house. I'll be right back."

While Brock worked to collect the wood and start the fire, I wandered around in awe. On the front side of the house, large windows framed views of the forest. In the back, they showcased a giant lake. It made the inside feel like it was part of the outside, giving the cabin a sanctuary-type feel. It was so peaceful, I almost forgot I'd come to say goodbye. *Almost.*

Brock set a few sweatshirts in front of the roaring fire. "Best I can do."

"I can't think of anything that would be better."

We sat side by side on the floor for a long time, staring into the fire in silence. My insides were in turmoil. I'd come to say goodbye, yet my heart never wanted to leave.

"Why did you come to see me tonight, Red?"

I turned to face him, but he kept staring into the fire. "I'm leaving tomorrow. I couldn't go back home without saying goodbye."

"No? Why is that?"

I took a deep breath. "Because I've fallen for you, Brock."

"Funny way of showing it." He scoffed and shook his head. "I'm pissed at you, Red. You didn't even try to fight for us. I thought I meant more to you than that."

I tasted salt in my throat. "I'm sorry."

"What for?"

"Everything."

"I'd rather you fight than apologize."

"How am I supposed to fight for us when we don't live in the same world? You love it here, Brock. Look at where we are this very minute. You're building your own home log by log, and I have a company to run in New York City and a board of directors to convince I'm not a crackpot." Tears streamed down my cheeks, and my voice broke. "I can't ask you to give this up for me any more than you can ask me to give up my life for you."

Brock had been keeping his distance, but he turned to face me and wiped my tears. After, he took me into his arms and held me tight. I felt him all around me—his scent, his touch, his love. And it made me want him *in* me. I looked up and kissed him. "I want you so much."

Brock wrenched his mouth away. "I can't. I can't make love to you and have you run out on me and never come back. I'm too angry."

"Then don't make love to me. *Fuck me.* Fuck me with all the pent-up anger you have because I'm leaving you in the morning."

His eyes darkened. I thought he was going to break, but instead he stood. "I can't do that to you. I won't hurt you."

I shot up and grabbed his hand. "It'll hurt me *not* to ever have you. I want you so much, it physically hurts."

Brock's jaw clenched.

My heart pounded. I felt desperate, desperate enough to shrug the flannel from my shoulders and pull my dress over my head.

Brock's eyes dropped to my red lace bra and panty set and darkened to almost gray, though I couldn't be sure if it was from anger or desire. But it didn't matter. I wanted him. I *needed* him.

*"Please..."*

For a few heartbeats, I thought he was going to tell me to get the hell out of his house. His jaw was rigid, and I could practically see steam billowing from his nose. But then he spoke.

"Turn around."

*Oh God*. Two words. That's all it took, and I was on fire. I ached for this man.

"Walk to the kitchen counter," he gritted. "Don't turn back around."

My body pulsed with electricity. I would've done anything he said. I stepped to the kitchen counter and held on to the edges.

Brock walked up behind me. The sound of his belt buckle coming undone and zipper going down was the most erotic thing I'd ever heard. "I don't have any fucking condoms."

"I don't care. I have an IUD, and I trust you."

He wrapped one arm around my waist and hoisted me up to my toes. His other hand pushed me down against the countertop. "The only thing you should trust right now is that you're not going to be able to walk right tomorrow."

Brock laid his body over me and whispered in my ear. "I'm going to leave marks."

I whimpered. "I want you to."

He reached between my legs, pushed my underwear aside, and groaned when he touched me. "Fucking wet. You knew I'd give you whatever you wanted. I'm just a fucking toy to you."

"You're not a—"

Whatever I was about to say was lost when I felt him nudging my entrance. His smooth, hot cock was hard as steel. All of the air left my body as he pushed inside. Brock buried himself in one rough thrust, not stopping until his hips were flush against my ass. One of us was shaking, but I couldn't be sure which.

"Is this what you want?" he growled. "You want to feel how angry I am with you?"

"Yes," I hissed. "Yes, please."

Brock grumbled a string of curses as he pulled out to the tip and slammed back in deep. He did it again and again, over and over. It was harsh and angry, but nothing had ever felt so good. I was going to be sore as hell tomorrow, probably have a bruise or two on my ass, but right now I felt nothing but pure ecstasy. My orgasm hit brutally hard, which seemed fitting considering the mood.

"Brock!"

He kept going, thrusting harder and harder. My legs shook, and I couldn't seem to catch my breath.

"Fuck," he groaned. "Fuck. Fuck. *Fuuuuck!*" His roar echoed around the empty room as he sank deep and stilled. I could feel his heat seeping into me, and my body pulsed all around him.

After, we were both panting. Brock stayed bent over me, his front to my back. He turned his head and rested his cheek against my body. When I felt wetness, I knew he was crying.

"Brock..."

"Don't—"

I swallowed and nodded.

We stayed that way for a very long time, both crying silent tears and holding on tight. Eventually, Brock disappeared into what I suspected was a bathroom and came back with a towel. Without saying a word, he cleaned me up.

I turned to face him. "Can we stay here for a little while?"

His jaw clenched, yet he nodded.

We sat back in front of the fire, and I rested my head on Brock's lap. Eventually I must've drifted off to sleep. When I woke, the sun was coming up, yet I found Brock in the same position he'd been in when I'd nodded off.

"Have you been sitting there like that this whole time?"

"I got up to add wood to the fire a few times."

"You didn't sleep?"

He looked over at me. "I can't let you leave with what we did earlier. You deserve better." Brock took my hands, weaved our fingers together, and brought them both to his mouth for a kiss. "When I get over the anger, I'm going to remember you for what you are: a woman worth the risk of getting hurt, a woman who isn't an angry fuck, but someone you make love to."

Tears filled my eyes once again. Brock pressed his lips to mine, and every pent-up emotion I'd been holding back found its way into the kiss. It was passionate, beautiful, even. In that moment, I made the decision to give myself to him fully, even if I might never be the same after.

Brock guided me to lie back and climbed on top of me. When he lined himself up at my opening this time, he kept his gaze locked on mine while he pushed inside. He glided back and forth lovingly, taking his time and going slow. Once he was fully seated, his eyes closed briefly. "I've always thought a little place by the lake was heaven. I was wrong. Being inside you is better. You feel incredible, February."

We moved together, our bodies rocking in unison, kissing like the lovers we were right now. It was the most connected and emotional experience of my life.

Brock became my world, and in the moment, I never wanted to live anywhere else.

Too soon though, the tension grew to be too much. As much as I didn't want the moment to end, it was coming, fast and furious. Brock's thrusts grew harder, his jaw tightened, but neither of us could stop it.

"Brock..."

"Right there with you, sweetheart." His voice was strained. "I feel you squeezing me."

My orgasm took root, and my eyes fluttered closed.

"Open, February. I want to watch you give everything to me, at least this once."

That was all it took. I moaned as my body contracted and pulsed, feeling waves of warmth spread through my chest. When I started to come down from the high, Brock sped up his thrusts. He looked into my eyes as he released, and I will never, ever forget the moment.

He kissed my lips gently for a long time after, still gliding in and out. Brock pushed my sweaty hair back from my face. "Crazy about you, Red."

I turned and kissed the palm of his hand with a smile. "Crazy about you, too, Lumberjack."

♦ ♦ ♦

We pulled up to Sierra after the sun was already up.

"You want me to drop you at the door?" he asked. "They can't kick you out when you're being discharged today anyway."

I smiled. "Nah. I'll use the ladder for old times' sake."

We drove around the back of the building, and Brock pulled up at our usual spot under my window. He killed the engine.

After I gave him his phone back, I made sure he had my actual cell phone number.

"I don't know how to say goodbye to you," I whispered.

"So don't." He pushed up his shirt sleeve, revealing his wrist, and unhooked a bracelet he always wore. It was a simple silver bar. I'd noticed it a few times before but had never gotten around to asking if it had any significance—one of the many things I'd never get to ask.

"Give me your wrist," he said.

I held out my hand, and he clasped the bracelet around it.

"My grandparents got together a month before my grandfather went into the military. She was a jewelry maker and made him this. The numbers engraved on the bar are the coordinates to the land you were on today—where I'm building my house. It was their land for fifty years. I want you to have this in case you ever decide to come back. That way you'll always know where to find me."

# CHAPTER 15

*Brock*

Everything sucked this morning.

The skies were gray.

The morning news was depressing.

My eggs were runny.

My coffee couldn't get hot enough, even though I'd nuked it five times. Now it tasted like mud.

Oak hadn't done his business when I'd taken him out earlier, so now the rest of the morning would revolve around his damn bowels.

I closed my eyes for a moment. Was it that everything sucked today, or did things just *seem* worse because I'd had to say goodbye to her earlier this morning?

As I stood in my kitchen and pondered this over my mug of awful coffee, Oak wagged his tail by the door.

"Oh, *now* you want to go?" I groaned.

I grabbed the leash and took him out for a walk.

"You'd better go this time," I said as it started to drizzle.

*Of course* it was raining now, too.

After he freaked out over his own shadow for about five minutes, Oak finally took care of things on the side of the road. I bent to pick it up with my trusty plastic bag. "This is a *shitty* morning all around, isn't it?" I told him as I tied a knot in the bag.

After we returned to the house, Oak circled around me in the kitchen, his paws scratching against the tile. Something was still bothering him.

"What? You were just out. What the hell is wrong with you?"

He looked up at me as he tried to catch his breath after the walk.

"You trying to tell me something? You'd better not be judging me for being here and not with her this morning, because I feel bad enough about the way she and I left things."

He barked at me.

"But seriously, Oak, this is really it? All of these weeks of pent-up frustration, the best sex I've ever had, and now it's just *over*?"

Oak growled.

"You're lucky she and I weren't here last night. You would've gotten an eyeful. Or maybe you would've liked watching, you old perv. I saw what you did to that stuffed cow."

*Ruff!*

"How good *was* it, you ask?" I shook my head. "I don't normally brag to humans, but I know my secret is safe with you." I sighed. "Anyway, Oak, to answer your question, the sex was so effing good that I lost my damn mind and gave her my bracelet. *That's* how good. Because the chance to have another night with her means more than a family heirloom, apparently."

I went to heat up my coffee for the thousandth time.

"It doesn't seem right that she's still technically here in town and I'm not spending these last minutes with her." I stopped the microwave. "I need you to talk me out of going over to Sierra right now. Because I *really* want to."

Walking over to the counter, I grabbed a pen and notepad. "Let's go over the pros and cons. I know you like this kind of analysis."

Oak plopped down onto the floor, looking a bit bored by my dilemma.

"A big con is that seeing her would only make it harder to say goodbye and prolong the agony." I wrote *goodbyes suck* in the con column.

I pointed my pen at him. "A pro would be seeing her one more time. But another con would be that I could do or say something dumb—like suggest we try the long-distance thing, which you and I both *know* is a bad idea, right?"

Oak continued to rest his chin on the floor.

"But a big pro would be that *she* could suggest it, which would mean a long-distance relationship wouldn't be something she viewed as a negative. Knowing she'd be open to it and wouldn't think I was crazy might make me more likely to consider it." I threw my pen onto the counter. "That's two cons and two pros, if you've been counting. We're at a dead heat."

He let out a loud bark.

"What's that you say? A huge pro would be that if I go, I'd at least not have to spend the rest of the day wondering what would've happened if I had?" I scratched my chin. "You make a good point. And it would be one more moment I'd get to spend with her.

One more moment would be worth it, wouldn't it?" I grabbed my keys and headed toward the door before I could change my mind.

"Damn you, Oak, and your damn...romanticness. You need to get a life of your own and stop interfering in mine. You're turning me into a goddamn sap." I slammed the door behind me.

I drove my truck to a convenience store on the way and grabbed a bunch of snacks for Feb to take on the road, since I knew she was renting a car to get back to the City. I didn't have time to waste, but the snacks would give me a reason to stop by other than just being unable to let her go.

When I pulled up to Sierra, I noticed the ladder was gone. That wasn't a big deal; it just meant I couldn't surprise her by showing up at her window.

I called her cell phone, but there was no answer.

*Crap.*

Having no choice but the main entrance, I went straight to the front desk.

"How can I help you?" a woman asked. Thankfully, she wasn't the same employee who'd witnessed our stepsiblings' kiss the last time I was here.

"Hi, I'm February Shaw's brother. I was hoping to catch her before she leaves today..."

The woman's smile faded. "Oh. She was discharged about a half hour ago. She already left."

My stomach dropped. "What?"

"I'm sorry."

I hung my head. "Thanks."

Carrying my big bag of snacks, I'd turned toward the door when a voice called from behind me.

"Hey, Lumberjack!"

I turned to find February's friend Morgan.

I waved. "Hey..."

"What are you doing here?" she asked.

I sighed. "Well, I thought I'd catch February before she left. But it seems I'm too late."

"Oh my gosh. That's so romantic. You wanted to get her not to leave?"

"Not exactly. But I wanted to see her one more time before she hit the road."

She frowned. "That's too bad. I think she would've loved to see you. She was down about leaving this morning. She decided to leave early because she felt it was better to rip the Band-Aid off and get a head start if she was leaving anyway."

My chest felt tight. "She was down, huh?"

Morgan nodded and took out a phone. She looked around and lowered her voice. "Come look at this."

She led me down a hallway and showed me some footage of an interview with February that she'd apparently done this morning.

I could hear Morgan ask, "Closing thoughts on your time here?"

February fiddled with my bracelet around her wrist. She seemed melancholy as she answered. "Closing thoughts are that I'm happy to be leaving Sierra but not happy to be leaving Meadowbrook."

"Any specific reason you're not wanting to go home? Most of us are dying to get back to our normal lives by now. I know I am."

"I feel like I'm leaving a piece of myself here. That's all I'd like to say on camera."

"From what I suspect, it's a big piece." Morgan laughed.

I rolled my eyes.

"What's the biggest lesson you learned while at Sierra?" Morgan asked her.

February paused. "Having the right person around can change how you see life. Material things become less important when you're surrounded by the right relationship. Experiences are what matter. And each experience is more valuable than the last. Not exactly a lesson from Sierra but more from...the ladder extension school." She winked.

After that, February walked away from the camera, and the video ended. But boy, she was still wearing my damn flannel. And her parting words told me she was still thinking of me this morning, too.

I said goodbye to Morgan, leaving her with the bag of snacks, minus one thing I kept for myself.

With a heavy heart, I drove back to my house.

When I arrived, there was a note taped to my door.

*I guess I just missed you. On my way, but thought I'd try for one last kiss before I hit the road. Guess it wasn't meant to be. Take care, Brock.*

*xo Your Red*

We'd just missed each other? When I'd gotten up this morning, I'd been certain this wasn't my day, but now I *knew* I was cursed.

The first thing I did when I got inside was call her.

She picked up right away. "Hey..."

"I can't believe you came by."

"Where were you?"

I let out a long breath. "I was at Sierra—tried to see you one last time."

"Are you kidding?"

"I wish I was." Pulling my hair, I paced.

"I assumed you not being home was a sign, since it would've only made me sadder to say goodbye again, but now I feel even worse knowing you came to see *me*."

"I picked you up some snacks for the road, but honestly, Red, that was just an excuse to see you one last time."

"Aw, man. Snacks? I got a few things myself, but I could've used more. What did you get me?"

"I didn't know what you liked, so it was a little of everything: chips, candy…Big Red gum because of your nickname. I gave the whole bag of stuff to Morgan, but I kept the gum."

"You're so thoughtful. If I wasn't thirty miles down the highway now, I'd turn around just for the Big Red. And maybe a kiss, too."

"It was all just a ruse to taste your lips anyway."

"Well, *I* wasn't even gonna use an excuse. I tried to come to you for the very same thing. I heard Oak behind the door. He kept barking at me. I felt bad because I would've loved to give him a hug goodbye, but I couldn't get to him."

"He knew about my plan, so he was probably trying to warn you that I was looking for you."

"What?"

"Never mind." I chuckled. "Anyway, I'm sorry we missed each other."

"What did Morgan say?" she asked.

"She showed me the video interview she did with you this morning. It sucked to see you looking so sad. But I have to say, you in my shirt really did it for me."

"I'm still wearing it now. I love smelling you on my ride. Sweet torture."

I groaned. "Damn."

"Why didn't you call me earlier and tell me you planned to come by?"

"I thought I'd surprise you. But I did try to call when I got to Sierra. Went straight to voicemail."

She sighed. "Yeah. Service has been patchy out here. That's why."

"I figured it was something like that."

"Thank you again for the bracelet. It means a lot. I want you to know I'll always cherish it."

I plopped down on my couch and rubbed my eyes. "Don't be afraid to use it, you know?"

After a few seconds of silence, she said, "What if I come to my senses, years down the line, use the bracelet to come find you...and you're married? What then?"

I scratched my chin. "Well, then I might have to go on a *very long* trip to the store for some milk."

She giggled. "You're bad." She sighed. "You're never gonna believe what song came on the radio as I was leaving Meadowbrook."

"What?"

"'Wild Horses' by the Rolling Stones. If you listen to the words, it kind of reminds me of us."

"Well, I don't think I've ever paid attention before, but I'll definitely listen to it."

The line went silent, and I realized the call had dropped.

*Shit.*

I tried to call her back, but it went straight to voicemail.

My phone rang about a minute later, and I immediately answered. "Everything okay?"

"I'm sorry. That was on my end. Damn patchy service again."

"No worries, Red." When she started breaking up, I added, "Be careful driving, okay? Text me when you get home."

"I will."

After we hung up, I sat there in a daze.

Oak came over and placed his chin on my leg.

I rubbed between his ears. "You tried to warn her that I was looking for her, didn't you?"

He whimpered.

"I know," I muttered. "We tried."

♦ ♦ ♦

That evening, Tim Weaver, who owned one of the local convenience stores, sat at my bar.

"Rang up that ginger beauty, February, this morning," he told me. "She grabbed a few things for the road. Told me she was headed out of town, back to New York City."

"Yeah. She left this morning."

"Not sure if I should be telling you this, but…"

My eyes darted toward him. "What?"

"Her eyes were red. Looked like she'd been crying."

*Fuck.* I stopped wiping the counter. "Yeah?"

"You do something to upset her?"

"None of your damn business, but no." I gritted my teeth.

I never wanted to see February hurt, certainly not at my expense. While I hadn't *intentionally* hurt her, I'd let things go too far with us the other night, and the aftermath had made things even more painful today.

Making love to her was worth all of it, though. But it was no wonder both of us felt broken.

Later that night, "Wild Horses" came on the music streaming service I used at the bar. I just shook my head, powerless against the universe. Anxious to know why it reminded her of me, I tried to listen to the words through the noise in the bar. But I couldn't figure out their exact meaning—something about a failing relationship and some kind of heartache. Still, this song would always remind me of *her*.

Speaking of Red, she must have been home by now. I'd told her to text me, but I felt like hearing her voice, so I picked up the phone and dialed.

After a few rings, she answered. "Hey, Brock."

She sounded down.

"Hey. Just checking to make sure you got home okay."

"Unfortunately, no. I'm stuck in traffic. It's been stop and go most of the way here. There are tons of accidents because of the weather. It's dark and rainy now, and I have another fifteen miles to go. At this rate, it could still take hours."

"Aw, baby, I'm sorry. What a long day for you."

"That's what I get for driving. I should've just flown. It would've been a short flight. The drive up was great. Used it to clear my head. But the ride back is just torture."

"I wish I was with you. I'd drive so you could rest."

"You know what I wish?" she asked.

"What?"

"I wish I could go back to the night I spent on your couch in front of the fire with Oak on my lap. I'd give anything to be in that cozy spot right now."

I closed my eyes for a moment. "That was a damn good night. Not quite as good as last night, but a close second."

"Absolutely *nothing* tops last night," she agreed. "I haven't been able to stop thinking about it."

"Me neither, beautiful." I groaned, remembering the ecstasy of being inside of her.

"Will you stay on the phone with me for a bit?"

I was supposed to be working the bar, but heck, I owned the place and made the rules. I temporarily stopped service and retreated to the back room, where I stayed on the phone with February for the next hour.

After we hung up, I vowed to follow through with my promise to attend the wedding with her. She hadn't mentioned it again, and I wondered if maybe she didn't actually want me to go. But heck, I had a tux on order, and I couldn't bear the thought of not seeing her again. So I needed to make it happen. *Wild horses* couldn't keep me away.

*Damn, that's corny.*

*It's been a long day.*

I was just about to close down the bar when my brother Maddox walked in.

"Hey, dude. What are you up to?" I asked.

He beamed. "I got the best freaking news today."

"Well, it just so happens I could use some good news. What you got?"

"Wait, what's wrong?" His brow furrowed.

"February left today."

"Shit. That's right. Trevor told me." He patted me on the shoulder. "I'm sorry."

"What's going on with you?" I asked.

"The insurance finally approved my surgery. They set a date for the operation."

I felt myself smile. "That's amazing, man!"

Maddox had been dealing with an old sports injury for some time now, and it had been impeding his ability to work his construction job. While he owned part of the business, he did a lot of hands-on work, too.

"You still good to fill in for me at the site while I'm out of commission?" he asked.

"Yeah. Of course. Anything you need."

"That really means a lot, man."

"Anytime."

"And I can count on you to pick me up from the hospital and shit? Take me back to your place until I can recover? I hate asking you to do that, but it'll be easier than you having to come to my house with Oak."

"Yeah. Whatever. Don't worry about it. When did they schedule your operation?"

"Well, they had one opening and said if I didn't take it, I'd have to wait two months. So it was a no-brainer. The surgeon is super booked. It's on a Friday, two weeks from yesterday."

"Cool."

But almost as soon as I'd said that, I realized what that Friday was.

The weekend of the wedding in New York.

# CHAPTER 16

*February*

*"I'm getting divorced."*

I shook my head with a chuckle as my assistant walked into my office. Oliver had on a purple-checkered three-piece suit with a hot pink tie and matching hanky. His thick, horn-rimmed glasses sat on top of his head.

"Good morning to you, too. And you shouldn't throw stuff like that out into the universe. No one else would put up with you."

He slumped into the guest chair on the other side of my desk. "I sat on the gosh darn *porcelain* this morning, and it was cold and *wet*!"

My nose wrinkled. "What are we talking about here? And I wish you would start cursing again already. *Gosh darn* sounds bizarre coming out of your mouth."

"Antonio used *my* bathroom. And no, I'm no longer a truck driver. This is the new me. I speak like an aristocrat now."

"With a Brooklyn accent…"

The week before I left for Sierra Wellness Center, Oliver and I had showed next year's spring handbag line at a fashion show. We were backstage rushing to get things ready when the one and only Donatella Versace had walked in. Oliver hadn't noticed her enter the room and was busy barking curses at a vendor who'd shown up late with one of the outfits a model was supposed to wear. Donatella was gracious and complimented our line, but before she left, she told Oliver he was handsome but would be even more so if he didn't use such *foul language*.

"I'm not sure I can handle you talking like an altar boy." I shrugged. "But back to your divorce. You and Antonio don't share the bathroom?"

"Definitely *not*. We have three bathrooms—the one in our bedroom is for communal peeing." He clasped his hands together and then lifted the top one to demonstrate a lid opening. "That seat stays up at all times." He gator-chomped his hands closed. "The other two are for pooping—his and his poop stations. Antonio uses the one in the guest room, and I use the one in our mother-in-law bedroom. This morning, I went to use *my bathroom*, and the seat was up! My boar of a husband not only violated our potty pact, but he *sprinkled when he tinkled*!"

I shook my head. "I think you'll get over it. Besides, you would shrivel up and die without Antonio, and you know it. Who would cook your breakfast and dinner every day? Who would prepare your morning cappuccino exactly as you like it, with one-point-five teaspoons of sugar—God forbid it be *two* teaspoons—and a dash of cocoa powder? Who would make your welcome home lemon-drop martini at six fifteen promptly every day? Who—"

Oliver held a hand up. "Whose side are you on?"

"Yours, always. But you're making a mountain out of a molehill. You should be happy that you *have* a partner—one who moved from Italy just to be with you and has stuck around for twenty years even though you threaten divorce three times a week." I frowned. "I can't even get a man to move here from Maine."

"Oh, honey." He leaned forward and patted my hand. "I told you I'd show you my secret blow-job techniques. My flute recitals can make a man give up living in a ten-bedroom palace in Milan for a three-bedroom dump in Queens."

Antonio really had lived in a ten-bedroom house in Italy, but the three-bedroom place in Astoria his family had bought them as a wedding gift was far from a dump. The inside could've been featured in *Architectural Digest*.

I sighed. "I wish it were that simple."

"Have you spoken to him?"

I shook my head.

"Texted?"

"Not since the night I got back."

Brock had asked me to send him a text when I got home, which I did. He'd sent back a sentence or two. But that was it. I hadn't heard from him again.

I'm not sure what I expected to happen between us once I left Meadowbrook. It wasn't like we'd made plans to keep in touch. But I hadn't thought things would come to such an abrupt end. The day after I got back to New York had been super busy. I'd spent fourteen hours at the office putting out fires and whipping things back into shape. Yet I'd still checked my phone a few times, expecting to see a text from Brock at some point.

But none came. So I figured I'd wait until he was ready. Unfortunately, I was still waiting two weeks later.

"Why don't you just pick up the phone and call him?"

"I don't want to make it harder for him." I looked down at the silver coordinate bracelet on my wrist. I hadn't taken it off since the morning Brock put it on, not even to shower. "Besides, at this point, there's nothing left to say."

"Say, *come visit me.* I miss you."

The thought of Brock standing in the middle of Manhattan made me smile. "He's never been to the City. He'd hate it here."

"He wouldn't be coming for a tour of the subway, rats, and graffiti. He'd be coming for a tour of *you.*" Oliver shrugged. "You'll stay indoors and boink the whole time."

"That would work if he were just a hook-up, but he's not. He's an all-in type man. When he decided to build a cabin, he cut down the trees for the logs and collected stones to build a fireplace. When the small town he grew up in struggled because the biggest employer shut down, he opened businesses to put people back to work. He's loyal and dedicated, and he deserves a woman who will be just as dedicated to him."

"You can do dedicated. You're dedicated to this company."

"That's part of the problem. This company takes up all my time."

"Sell it! Antonio worked in the family business—selling high-end collectible cars worth more than our house. Here he climbs telephone poles for ConEd."

"But Antonio hated his job in Milan. I love what I do."

"You could always cut back and work less."

I motioned to his iPad, which he'd walked in carrying. "Call up my schedule. Show me the next month."

Oliver pressed some buttons and turned the screen to face me. There were colorful appointments and tasks crowding every day—even Saturdays and Sundays. "You're a little full right now," he said. "But that's only because you were out for a month. It will get better."

I shook my head. "I've been saying '*next month will be lighter*' for more than nine years now. It doesn't happen. Running a business is like chasing a butterfly. Just when you think you catch it, it flutters and makes you run to keep up."

"Well, you need to figure out something. Because I can't take the mopey, sad face anymore. You look like the Mona Lisa."

"People think the Mona Lisa is beautiful."

"*Idiots* think she's beautiful."

I laughed. "Did you come in here with any actual business to discuss? If not, I have a lot of work to do to prepare for the four-PM board of directors meeting I'm dreading."

"No, but why is there another board meeting so soon? You just had one two weeks ago when you got back. Aren't they usually a monthly thing?"

"They *were*. But I'm pretty sure certain members are trying to keep a close eye on me, to make sure I don't crack."

Oliver stood. "This is like your Friday from hell. The board followed by Lame and Blame's wedding tonight."

"Is Johnathan Lame or Blame?"

"He's both, sweetheart. And, by the way, my offer to be your plus one is still open, if you change your mind. My tux is pressed and ready to go."

"Thank you. I appreciate that. I really do. But I'm just going to show my face and then slip out."

"Are you at least wearing the green dress that slits almost all the way up to your hoochy-coochy and dips down to your tater tots?"

"I was just going to wear the black one I wore to the Dolce & Gabbana fall launch party."

Oliver's nose crinkled. "That's high fashion, not hello f-me. It's your ex marrying your friend, not me and Antonio renewing our vows. You want to steal all the attention from the bride."

When I'd mailed back the invitation and said I would attend, I'd hoped *my* attention would be stolen tonight—by the sexy lumberjack who'd volunteered to go with me. But I dreaded the thought of going at all now, much less alone.

"I'll think about it."

Oliver walked to the door. "I'm going to return a few calls and then pick up the new leather samples we ordered. Let me know if there's anything I can do to help get ready for the meeting later."

"Thank you."

♦ ♦ ♦

"This was just delivered for one of the board members." Later in the afternoon, Oliver walked into my office holding a package. "Do you want to take it with you, or should I bring it up?"

"Which board member is it for?"

He scanned the plastic FedEx wrapper. "Arthur Connolly."

*Ugh.* The leader of the witch hunt. I despised that man. Sadly, he reminded me of my grandfather. Not because he was old, though; he was probably in his late sixties. But because of the way he talked down to women—like I should be getting his coffee rather than running a company. I lifted my chin, motioning to the corner of my desk. "Just put it on top of that pile I'm bringing, please."

Oliver was almost out of my office when something on the package he'd set down caught my eye. I reached for it. "This package is from Lucchi?"

"How do you know that?"

I pointed to the top right corner of the address label. "This is their logo."

Oliver walked back and looked over my shoulder. "You're right. It is. I didn't notice. Why is a board member getting something delivered from our biggest competitor?"

Unease grew in the pit of my stomach. "I have no idea."

"Have you discussed Lucchi at any of your board meetings?"

I shook my head. "Definitely not."

"Well, let's open this baby and find out."

"We can't. That's an invasion of privacy."

"To you maybe..." Oliver plucked the package from my hands and ripped it open before I could even finish objecting. He grinned. "*Oops!* Silly me. I wasn't paying attention and assumed it was part of our mail since that's usually the only thing that gets delivered here. I'll apologize to Mr. Connolly." Oliver pulled a thick stack of documents out of the envelope and eyed the letter on top. "You're selling part of Amourette to Lucchi?"

"No, of course not." I took the documents from my assistant's hands. Flipping through the pages, my eyes widened when I saw the amount listed as the purchase price. "Oh my God. *This* is what the board meeting today is really about."

"What?"

"A few months ago, I told the board I wanted to expand our manufacturing facility so we could produce faster to keep up with trends. Arthur Connolly is a banker, so he volunteered to look into where we could get the best loan terms. These documents are for the *exact* amount of the loan I wanted to take. That bastard is going to try to get the board to sell part of my company to Lucchi, rather than take on debt."

"He never mentioned anything to you about it?"

"No, and I would've told him not to waste his energy. Because I will *never* sell anything to Lucchi. I regret selling a piece of the company to the investors I brought in during our last expansion. They're the ones who made me answer to this horrible board of directors. There is no way in the world I'd ever answer to *Tobias Lucchi*. It's bad enough I hate-screwed him more than once." I whipped open the top drawer of my desk, yanked out my purse, and started marching to the door.

Oliver called after me, "Where are you going?"

"To get some answers."

"But the board meeting is in forty-five minutes."

"It won't take me that long. That is, unless I get arrested for murder..."

Luckily, Tobias's office was only a few blocks away. I'd been there once before, and that was a mistake I didn't want to remember. The receptionist was on the phone when I walked into the lobby. I didn't have time to waste, so I spoke anyway.

"Excuse me. I need to speak to Tobias. It's urgent."

She gave me an annoyed look and held up a finger, then returned to what sounded like a personal call. But I was too impatient to wait until she figured out who was picking up little Ashley from school today, so I shook my head. "Don't bother. I'll let him know I'm here."

She stood and called after me as I marched through the double glass doors that led to the back offices, but I didn't stop until I got to the big corner space. Tobias was on the phone when I flung the door open and let myself in. His brows drew together at first, but he quickly got over the initial shock, and a smarmy smile crawled up his face.

*Ugh. Don't even...* I held up the package of documents. "What the hell is this?"

"Marty, I'm going to need to call you back." Tobias hung up his desk phone and stood. "You're looking as beautiful as ever, February."

"Don't bullshit me." I waved the documents in the air. "Tell me how this came about."

He stepped around his desk. "You look upset."

"*I am fucking upset!*"

Tobias walked past me and closed his office door. After, he put a hand on my hip from behind. "Don't worry. I'm here to help you work out those frustrations."

I smacked his fingers away. "*Don't fucking touch me!*"

He held two hands up, looking a bit nervous. "Keep your voice down. My staff doesn't understand the dynamics of our relationship. They might jump to the wrong conclusion."

"We don't *have* a relationship. We used to *fuck*. Past tense. But I've recently been reminded of my value, and you are far beneath the acceptable limit."

"Is this foreplay? I know arguing with me gets you off, but something seems different right now."

"*Something is different, you dipshit*! I just received these documents, and I have no idea what the hell is going on. I'm not selling you my company."

For the first time since I walked in, Tobias grew serious. His forehead wrinkled. "You didn't know Connolly solicited me to buy a piece of Amourette?"

"No, of course not."

"He made it seem like everyone was on board. I had no idea you didn't know."

"If that's true, why didn't you mention it when you showed up at Sierra uninvited?"

Tobias frowned. "You didn't exactly give me a chance to speak. I believe your exact words were, '*Leave and don't ever come back or I'll get a restraining order.*'"

I held his eyes, looking for a sign that he was lying, but couldn't find one. "Arthur really contacted you?"

"Why would I lie? It would've pissed you off more to say I initiated the offer, and you know I like pissing you off."

I took a deep breath and nodded. "Thank you."

A smile tugged at the corner of his lips. "How about thanking me with a quickie?"

"Not if your life depended on it, Lucchi."

Fifteen minutes later, I was back at my office. I rode the elevator straight up to the conference room without stopping to get my laptop or the package of stuff I'd prepared for the board meeting. I was five minutes early, but all of the members were already milling around chit-chatting.

I took my position at the head of the table and cleared my throat. "Can I have everyone's attention, please?"

The room hushed, and all eyes turned and focused on me.

"Thank you." I looked directly at Arthur Connolly. "This meeting is no longer necessary. I'll be invoking the buy-back provision in our contract."

The half-dozen wrinkles in his forehead deepened. "What are you talking about? You don't have that kind of money."

"Not today. But I'll get it."

"From where?"

"None of your damn business. Though I'll tell you one thing, not a single cent will come from Tobias Lucchi."

Arthur's eyes widened.

I smirked, enjoying catching him off guard. "Meeting adjourned."

♦ ♦ ♦

Two-and-a-half hours later, I polished off my second glass of wine as I got ready for the wedding from hell. I looked in the mirror at my outfit. Oliver was right. This dress was fashion forward—almost art—but it wasn't very sexy. And after a day like today, coupled with the night I was about to have, I needed more. So I quickly changed into the near-scandalous green dress and finished getting ready. A town car was picking me up in less than ten minutes, yet I poured another half glass of liquid courage and chugged it.

Just as I slipped on my stilettos, the doorbell buzzed. The driver was early, and I still had to put my jewelry on. I walked to the door to let him know he'd have to wait, but when I opened it, my jaw nearly hit the floor.

"Brock? What are you doing here?"

# CHAPTER 17

*February*

"Hey, beautiful." He smiled.

*Oh my God.*

Standing before me was the most incredible sight my eyes had ever had the pleasure of seeing: Brock in a tux.

Brock with his hair slicked back in a way I'd never seen before.

The black tuxedo fit him like an absolute glove, and he smelled like pure heaven.

Before saying another word, he lifted me into the air and kissed me so hard I thought my lips might fall off. I felt light as a feather in his arms. With every second that passed, it felt like I was coming alive again. The depression I'd experienced since returning from Meadowbrook disappeared as I melted into him.

When he finally put me down, leaving me painfully aroused, I took a moment to catch my breath. "Well, hello to you, too, sir," I panted.

"Surprised?" He beamed.

"Beyond."

"I told you I'd come." His eyes lowered to my body. "You look freaking amazing, Red. God." Brock shook his head. "I thought red was the color of the devil, but apparently, it's green. That dress makes me want to cover you with my body all night."

"You have my permission to do that," I said, disregarding all of the progress I'd made in trying to distance myself. Brock was so much harder to resist in the flesh.

"Be careful what else you tell me I can do tonight. I might just take you up on it."

"Brock, what's happening here? I can't believe you came. I just assumed when we said goodbye—"

"A promise is a promise, Red. Did I not tell you I would accompany you to this wedding?"

"Yes, but you never mentioned it again. I assumed with the way we left things that you'd decided better of it."

"Gonna be honest. I *really* wanted to be here, but I didn't think I was gonna make it. Got fitted for a tux a while ago while you were still in town, but then my brother went and scheduled a surgery for today. I'd promised to help him recover at my place. But I was able to get my other brothers and a couple of locals to look after him in shifts for the weekend."

I shook my head. "I can't believe you went through all those hoops just to come to a wedding with me."

"Then you're underestimating how much you mean to me, Red." He rubbed the back of his hand against my cheek. "It's not about the wedding for me, though."

"You have no idea how much it means that you're here." I reached for him, wrapping my arms around his neck. "Work has been so stressful. And I've missed you every second of every day on top of that. To go from not knowing if I'd ever see you again, to this..." I pulled back and looked into his beautiful eyes.

Before I could blink, his mouth was on mine again. I didn't want to mess up his slicked-back hair, yet I couldn't help digging my fingers into it. The heat of his body felt like it would singe my dress right off of me. *Maybe we should just skip the damn wedding altogether.* A night *in* sounded like a much better idea.

Brock suddenly stepped back. "We're gonna be late. We should go."

"You sure we shouldn't just skip it?" I wasn't exactly being facetious.

"We can't, Red. We need to make a scene." He winked.

"Okay." I grinned.

"Plus, my driver is waiting."

The idea of Brock having a driver amused me. I couldn't picture him sitting passively in the backseat of a car. Anything other than him bulldozing his way through Manhattan in his big red truck didn't make sense.

"Your driver, huh? Since when do you have a driver and wear tuxes, Brock Hawkins?"

"I already paid him to stay and take us to the wedding."

"Cool. Thanks. I'll cancel my ride." I took out my phone.

With that task managed, Brock and I headed outside and into the back of the waiting black Town Car.

As the driver took off, Brock moved close. He reached over and found the slit in my dress, slipping his hand underneath it. The heat of his touch sent shivers through my body. He slid his palm all the way up my leg, stopping where my thigh met my hip.

"I'm suddenly having second thoughts about going." He groaned. "Kidding, but not really kidding."

"There's still time to turn around." I pulled on his bow tie. "I didn't think you could get any hotter, and then you showed up in this tux. You're nothing if not versatile."

His hand, still on my thigh, rose a bit higher.

"Fuck," he muttered. "Red, you look so damn beautiful."

Then I looked down and noticed the bulge in his pants. My nipples immediately reacted.

He forced his hand away. "I need to stop touching you before everyone in that church gets an eyeful."

I squirmed in my seat, willing myself to calm down.

By the time we arrived at the church, fashionably late, the wedding party was lining up inside the entryway, preparing for the procession.

As Brock and I zipped past them hand in hand, I couldn't help but notice Ilona's reaction. My former friend, dressed in her designer bridal gown, had a look of true surprise on her face. Many of the bridesmaids were also my former friends. The whispers behind us faded into the distance as we walked down the aisle together in search of a seat. I somehow knew they were all eating their hearts out right now, which brought me great satisfaction. Imagine if they also knew how wonderful this man was on the *inside*.

We made our way to one of the pews on the groom's side of the church. Technically, I could've chosen either side. That was the twisted advantage, I supposed, when your ex-husband married your ex-best friend.

Even better than the bridal party noticing us? When I saw my ex-husband's eyes land on Brock and me—particularly on Brock. I gave Johnathan a curt nod. Brock had no idea what pride I felt having him by my side. My ex nodded back, likely trying hard to figure this out.

*Good.*

Brock whispered in my ear, "That's your ex, I assume?"

"Yeah. That's Johnathan."

"He looks easy to snap in half if he ever makes you sad again."

I patted his knee. "Hopefully that won't be necessary."

When Ilona came down the aisle, a chill ran along my spine. Brock leaned over and whispered in my ear again, "She's got nothing on you, Red. He's crazy."

Later, as the priest spoke, Brock kept nudging me with his elbow, sarcastically challenging some of the points in the sermon.

*Surrendering control to God and trusting in His plan.*

"Thank goodness God's plan was not to have you end up with that douche," he whispered.

*Exploring mutual love and respect in marriage...*

"These two know a lot about respect, don't they?"

*Two being better than one.*

"That's your ex's motto anyway. She'd better watch her friends around him."

*Forgiving each other just as God forgives.*

"God might forgive. But karma? Karma's a bitch, and she remembers."

I shook with laughter throughout the ceremony. What I'd assumed would be one of the toughest hours of my life turned into anything but. I couldn't stop smiling.

When the ceremony ended, everyone lined up to greet the bride and groom near the entrance of the church.

When we finally got our turn with the happy couple, my ex put on his best fake smile. "February, *so* happy you could make it." He turned to Brock. "Who's this?"

I held my hand out toward my handsome date. "This is Brock Hawkins."

"Her *boyfriend*," Brock added.

Butterflies swarmed in my stomach. Even if that declaration was just for show, it made me weak in the knees.

Johnathan tilted his head. "How...nice. You never mentioned him, February. How did you guys meet?"

I froze for a moment, realizing I hadn't planned for this. I didn't want to admit where I'd been when Brock and I met—neither at the bar nor Sierra. Not that there was anything to be ashamed of, but my reasons for being in Meadowbrook were none of their business. Johnathan and Ilona might misinterpret it to mean I'd had a nervous breakdown because of *them*. That's how self-centered they were.

Brock seemed to sense my hesitation and quickly stepped in. "February was sightseeing up in the woods of Maine where I live. She got a little lost trying to find one of our local establishments, so I stopped to help. We got to talking, and honestly, the rest was history."

That was simple enough, and if you thought about it, it could even be considered true. I had been *lost* when I'd met Brock. Just not literally.

"Well, doesn't that sound like a Hallmark movie?" Ilona chimed in. "I suppose you were wearing a plaid, flannel shirt and drove a big red truck, perhaps with a Christmas tree strapped on the top?"

I narrowed my eyes, unable to tell if that was meant to be funny or insulting for some reason. *Everything but the Christmas tree, bitch.*

"Don't forget the ax for chopping wood." Brock winked, not missing a beat.

"Ah, yes." She laughed.

After we walked away, I teased, "Thanks for not telling them the *actual* way we met."

"That I carried your drunk ass to my bed? They'd draw the wrong conclusion there. But it's none of their freaking business, anyway."

"I like how you think, Hawkins."

"I like *you*." He wrapped his arm around me as we returned to the spot where he'd paid the driver to wait for us.

When we arrived at the swanky reception, Brock and I kept to ourselves. It was like our own private party as we drank champagne and sampled hors d'oeuvres.

After dinner was served, I couldn't believe my ears. The DJ had put on the Rolling Stones' "Wild Horses."

"You're kidding." Brock dropped his fork. "It's our song, Red. You have to dance with me."

I'd previously told him I preferred not to dance tonight, but he was right; we couldn't pass this one up.

He took my hand and led me to the dance floor.

As Brock held me close, he spoke in my ear, "You know, I've heard this song more than once since you left town."

"Really?"

"It's like the universe was trying to tell me what a jackass I was for letting you go so easily. Figures it played tonight, too. That's not a coincidence, either."

I couldn't help but notice how fast his heart was beating against mine. He'd proven in many ways tonight how much he cared about me.

He looked around as we continued to sway to the music. "I've been so transfixed by your beautiful eyes, Red, I didn't even realize we're the only ones dancing to this."

"It's *our* song." I winked. "They must know that."

After our dance, Brock and I were on the way back to the table when he pulled me toward the photo booth instead.

He wriggled his brows. "We can't leave without photos."

We took a bunch of photos with various props. We stuck out our tongues, made faces, and kissed. This playful side of Brock had me on cloud nine. I wondered if these images would merely be keepsakes of a relationship long gone someday, or if there was still a chance for us? Would we show these to our grandkids? I shook my head at that thought. Brock turning up here certainly gave me hope. But it was most likely *false* hope. One good night didn't change the fact that we lived separate lives.

We'd returned to the table for some cake when Johnathan and Ilona came walking in our direction, hand in hand.

*What a buzzkill.*

I straightened in my seat. "There's the happy couple..."

Ilona looked between Brock and me. "Happy couple? I should say! You two look pretty happy yourself."

"You know what?" I turned to Brock. "I really am."

Brock smiled as his eyes lingered on mine.

Johnathan interrupted, "Everything in life works out the way it's supposed to, doesn't it? I'm happy you and I both are where we were meant to be, February." He patted my shoulder. "Have fun."

They moved on to greet the next table.

Brock placed his hand on my thigh and squeezed. "If he touches you again, I might have to clock him. And where he's meant to be is hell."

I laughed a little, but sadness washed over me.

"What happened there?" Brock asked.

"Hmm?"

"In like a split second, your smile dimmed, and you lost the light in your eyes. Was it what he said?"

"It didn't upset me, per se. But he reminded me how much I wish our situation were simpler. It's been great spending this day with you, but this weekend will be over in a flash. Him being happy for me just made me wish things were the way they seemed."

Brock took my hand. "We don't have it all figured out, Feb, but that doesn't make what we're feeling any less real."

I shook my head. "God, I'm sorry. I lost it there for a moment. I'm back. I promise."

"We have plenty of time to lament the distance between us when we go back to living apart at the end of the weekend. But try not to let it ruin the two days we have."

"You're right. This time is precious. I'm shutting off the thoughts in my head. Believe it or not, that had been mostly working."

"Good girl."

The way he said *good girl* momentarily took my mind to a naughty place. I wouldn't have minded kneeling at his feet while he dominated me in that tux tonight.

"Are you getting lost in your head again?"

I felt my cheeks heat. "Not the way you think."

Brock excused himself to the bathroom. Shortly after, the DJ announced that the bouquet toss was about to begin.

*What the hell...*

I rose and stood toward the back of the crowd of ravenous single women, not expecting anything to come of it.

When Ilona threw the bouquet, everyone but me seemed to leap forward. One of the bridesmaids almost caught it, but it slipped out of her hands—landing on the ground by Brock's feet, just as he returned from the bathroom.

He casually bent, picked up the bouquet as if it were a piece of dust on the ground, and handed it to me. Then he leaned in and kissed me to the sound of thunderous applause.

"Now seems like a good time to get the hell out of here," he said after a moment. "You?"

"Sounds perfect."

With all eyes still on us, I tossed the bouquet to the cute little flower girl before Brock and I left hand in hand.

♦ ♦ ♦

Brock didn't say much on the ride home, nor did he put his hands on me, much to my chagrin.

So imagine my surprise when the moment I opened the door to my apartment, I found my back against the wall, Brock towering over me.

"I can't fucking hold it in anymore," he breathed, his eyes flickering with desire.

"You were so quiet in the car. I thought maybe—"

"I didn't want to look at you because I knew I wouldn't be able to wait until we got home. We need to be in private for all the things I want to do to you tonight."

My heart beat faster. Arousal raced through me, and he hadn't even touched me yet.

Just as I had the thought, Brock slid his hand through the slit of my dress and moved it up my leg.

"Are you ever planning on wearing this dress again?" he asked.

I swallowed. "Why?"

"Because I might want to ruin it right now."

"Do it," I dared. "Just keep your tux on while you do."

I felt a tug at the material of my dress and then a loud rip before our mouths collided. Brock kissed me hard as he ripped the dress a second time.

Raking my hands through his hair, I vaguely heard the sound of his belt buckle clanking as he undid the top of his pants. He then lifted me on top of him, my back against the wall.

Within seconds, I felt his cock at my opening, right before he pushed into me in one hard, swift movement. If I hadn't been so damn wet, it might've hurt. But instead, his filling me felt like absolute ecstasy.

We were both still mostly fully clothed as Brock thrust into me.

"I've wanted to fuck you in this dress all night, Red."

An unintelligible sound escaped me as I tried to curb the orgasm that begged to rise to the surface, faster and more powerful than any in my life.

"You're getting my pants all wet, Red. I *definitely* own this tux now." He laughed over my mouth.

"Good." Moving my hips faster, I rasped, "You're so hot in it."

"This beautiful pussy is mine tonight." He groaned. "*You're* all mine tonight. You got it?"

I answered by taking his mouth, our tongues colliding, circling, tasting, amidst frantic breaths.

Brock moved his hand behind my head as he moved in and out of me even faster. "Let me know when you're ready for me."

"Now..." I breathed.

I soon learned why he'd protected my head as he lurched forward when he came, his warm cum filling me. The feel of his wet heat between my legs timed perfectly with my own earth-shattering climax, which rolled through me in glorious waves.

He continued to hold me until our breathing slowed. Then he finally put me down, backed me against the wall again, and kissed me voraciously.

He placed an arm on each side of my shoulders, locking me in. "I was gonna ask you to show me around the City tomorrow, but I'm pretty sure all I want to do is *that* over and over again."

# CHAPTER 18

*February*

"You see? Manhattan isn't all that different from Maine..."

Brock raised his brows and looked around. "I'll give you that I didn't expect Central Park to be this big. But in the last twenty minutes, we saw a guy in only underwear and cowboy boots playing a guitar on the street, a guy on the subway who took off his shirt and started painting himself blue, and a woman on a bench eating what looked like a full Thanksgiving meal with chopsticks while sharing every other bite with a waiting *rat* and *pigeon*."

I chuckled. "The woman was very Snow White, wasn't she?"

"If you say so..."

I linked my arm with Brock's and steered us down the stairs to Bethesda Fountain. "Want to sit for a while?"

Brock shrugged. "Whatever you want."

We took a seat on the concrete wall that circled

the outer perimeter of the fountain and quietly people-watched together. To the left, a man chased twin boys who were probably around two years old. Each toddler ran in the opposite direction and tried to climb into the water.

"Have you talked to your dad since you've been back?" Brock asked.

I nodded. "Once. About a week ago."

"You call him or he call you?"

"He called me. He said he was going to be in Manhattan the next day and asked if I wanted to get together for lunch. But I had a packed schedule and was busy preparing for a board meeting, so I told him maybe another time."

"Was that a blow-off, or are you going to see him at some point?"

I sighed. "I guess I'll see him. We left it that he was going to call me in a few weeks, when things settled down at work. But after yesterday, I'm not sure that's going to be happening anytime soon."

"What happened yesterday?"

I filled Brock in on the board member I'd caught trying to sell part of my company, and how I'd made the bold—and possibly stupid—announcement that I was going to buy out the investors.

"You have the cash to do that?"

"I'm a little short…"

Brock was quiet for a moment. "I still have a little money left from the inheritance I got from my uncle, if you need it. It's just sitting in the bank."

"I need six-million dollars."

Brock's eyes flared wide. "Shit. That's a little out of my league."

I smiled. "I wouldn't take your money anyway. But it's sweet of you to offer. Thank you."

"Where are you going to get that kind of dough?"

"The bank, I hope. Two years ago, when I took on the investors, we had a business valuation done. They estimated Amourette at twenty million."

Brock whistled. "I didn't realize you were my sugar momma, Red. Hell, you're paying for dinner tonight."

I laughed. "Most of that estimate is goodwill for the brand, not actual physical assets."

"Still." He shrugged. "That's impressive. You started the company less than a decade ago, and now you've got a name worth that kind of money."

"I am proud of what I've built. Though it's cost me a lot personally to do it." I looked over and caught Brock's eyes. "And apparently, it's still costing me."

Brock wrapped his arm around my shoulder and squeezed. Silence hung heavy in the air. I hadn't meant to put a damper on the day when we had so little time together. So after a few minutes, I stood and tugged at his hand. "You up for me to show you two more places?"

"Is one of them inside of you?"

I smiled. "Okay, how about *three* more places today?"

Brock stood. "I'm up for whatever you want, as long as the day ends the same way it started, with you beneath me."

I liked the sound of that. *A lot.* Nevertheless, my heart grew heavy. *I wish every day could be like that.*

Brock and I rode the subway down to Penn Station. It was amusing as hell to watch him watch people. The young guy sitting across from us on this trip had a long, bleached-blond Mohawk and dozens of safety pins piercing his face. The older man standing to our left was clearly drunk. He wore a trench coat and wobbled while he held up a sign offering to show his dick for a dollar. A woman who must have been eighty took him up on it. Most of the time, I didn't even pay attention to the people around me on the trains. I was usually too busy answering emails on my phone or prepping for whatever meeting I was late to. The absurdity of New York had grown commonplace to me, but I couldn't imagine Brock ever getting used to it.

Once we were off the subway, we took the escalator up to street level, and I navigated the walk to the garment district—what's left of it these days, anyway. A lot of the shops were closed on the weekends, but Mood Fabrics was always open on Saturdays. I took Brock in and walked the long aisles. "My grandmother was a seamstress. She was a piece-garment worker at a knitting mill, which means she got paid per piece that she produced, not by the hour. The money wasn't great, and my grandfather had passed away when my mom was little, so Gram had to support the house herself. She made custom dresses on the side to help pay the rent, and this place is where she always came to buy her fabrics. I loved coming with her on Saturday mornings. I would spend hours perusing the fabric samples and dreaming up what I might make out of each. Gram was the one who taught me how to sew and started me on my journey in the fashion world."

"She ever teach you how to make a jacket?"

I laughed. "I swear, I have plenty of outerwear. I just didn't pack something that went with all my outfits when I was getting ready to go to Sierra."

Brock winked. "I think the one you had on this morning goes with anything."

My smile widened. I'd slipped on Brock's flannel with nothing underneath to go out to the kitchen and flip on the coffee machine.

"Come on." I tilted my head toward the stairs. "I want to show you something on the second floor."

I guided Brock to the cutting table, where a dressed mannequin stood nearby. Stopping, I did a little Vanna White hand waving. "This is Filomena."

"You named the dummy?"

"Actually, I named the dress she's wearing. It was my final exam project during my last semester at FIT. I got an A, and my teacher liked it so much that she put it on display in the lobby. One day, a pretty famous designer visited the school to give a lecture, and she spotted the dress and asked if she could wear it to her fashion show. *The* Carina Von Dusen wore my gown, and photos of her wearing it were splashed on the pages of *Elle* and *Vogue*. It opened so many doors for me."

I looked at all the beadwork on the dress, remembering the countless hours I'd spent hunched over in my tiny studio apartment, hand sewing them all on. The memory made me smile. "I couldn't afford all of the materials I needed to finish the project, so the owner of the store made me a deal. She covered what I was short, and I gave her the gown to display for a few months. They usually rotate different dresses on display, but Filomena's been here for nine years now. I could take her home if I wanted, but sometimes when I'm feeling frustrated or nervous, I walk here and visit in the middle of the day. My office is only a few blocks away, and it always makes me feel better."

Brock's eyes roamed my face. "You really light up when you talk about your work, you know that?"

I nodded. "I feel it on the inside, too. I may often hate the business side of things, but I love creating. Even after all these years, when I design something new, I still get the same high I felt when I would show my grandmother a shirt I'd made at age eight."

Brock nodded. "I get it. I feel the same way about building log cabins. When I was a kid, I would build them out of Lincoln Logs and show them to my grandfather. He was the one who taught me how to lathe logs. There's an art to it."

I suddenly felt overwhelmed with emotion. It could've been because I'd been talking about my grandmother, and she'd passed away last year. But I suspected it had more to do with the realization that neither Brock nor I was ever going to give up what we loved doing.

I swallowed and tasted salt, nodding toward the stairs. "Ready for our last stop?"

"Sure thing."

The final place I took Brock was the Brooklyn Bridge. We walked over the East River from Manhattan to Brooklyn Heights. "My dad's an identical twin," I said. "His brother lives in Dumbo. When my parents were married, we used to go to Uncle Mark's house for dinner every other Sunday night. After we'd finish eating, my dad and I would sneak out and walk to Manhattan and back so we didn't have to help with the dishes—at least we did before I caught him with another woman." I paused, realizing something. "I've driven over the bridge many times since then, but this is the first time I've walked it since the days when I crossed holding my father's hand."

Brock spoke quietly. "Today's bringing up a lot of old memories."

I smiled sadly. "Yeah, I guess a lot of my fondest ones are from a different time in my life. To be honest, I think I stopped making special memories in my personal life the last few years. I'm not sure I can come up with any I have with my ex-husband. Maybe that's the reason things didn't work out—I didn't put the time in to give us that chance, to go places and create memories."

Brock stopped. "The best memories are usually more to do with the person you're with, not the places you go." He cupped my cheek. "We could be walking down any street in any state right now, and I'd still always remember the way I feel at this moment. And it has nothing to do with a bridge."

I turned and kissed the inside of his palm. "You're a very smart man, Brock Hawkins."

He winked. "And a very hungry one. Think we can head back to your place now?"

"Yeah, definitely. We can stop and pick up some takeout on the way. What are you in the mood to eat? I keep a folder on my phone with my favorite restaurant menus."

Brock smirked. "Trust me, what I'm hungry for isn't on any menu."

♦ ♦ ♦

A streak of sunlight slipped between the blinds, rousing me from sleep. I found Brock standing next to the window in his boxer briefs. He stared out between the slats, looking lost in thought.

I pushed up to my elbows. "Hey. What are you doing out of bed so early?"

He rubbed the back of his neck. "Couldn't sleep."

"And here I thought I did such a great job wearing you out last night."

Brock smiled. He walked around the bed and sat down next to me. Lifting my hand to his mouth, he kissed the top. "I feel like a fish out of water here, Feb."

My heart squeezed. I pulled the sheet to cover my bare breasts and sat up. "Here in New York or here with me?"

"Definitely not here with you. This City just overwhelms me. It's got too many damn people and too much noise."

"It's undeniably different than Maine."

"How do you ever feel settled? Or relax with all the crap going on out there?"

I smiled. "I'm not sure I do. I basically run on adrenaline eighteen hours a day and then crash because I'm exhausted."

"That doesn't sound healthy."

I weaved my fingers with his and squeezed. "I loved the time I spent with you in Maine. It's beautiful up there and so peaceful. But if I'm being honest, I like the honking and sirens. I feel alive here in New York."

"I feel alive, too. Like someone put two paddles on my chest and turned the voltage up to full blast." Brock looked down at our joined hands and stayed quiet for a long time. "Is there anything important to you located above 82$^{nd}$ Street?"

"What do you mean?"

He shook his head. "I hate that damn subway. I figured the park is about a forty-five-minute walk from here."

"I'm not following..."

He looked me in the eyes. "I'm not sure I'm wired for the constant rush of this place, but if this is what you love and what you need, I'm willing to find a way to make it work for me on a part-time basis."

My heart started to race. "Oh my God, Brock. Really?"

He nodded. "Neither of us wants to give up everything. So why not both give up a little and see if we can work out fitting into each other's lives? Think you can meet me halfway, or at least a third of the way? Come up to see me some weekends?"

I whipped the sheet off and crawled over to straddle his lap. "I can definitely do that."

"Then I guess I got myself a girlfriend, if that's what you want?"

I nodded fast. "*I want. I want.*"

Brock held up a finger. "But no more subway. That shit is horrible."

"You've got a deal. We'll just do a lot of walking, *boyfriend.*" I smiled and pressed my lips to his, and we fell into a long, passionate kiss—one I hoped told him how happy he'd just made me. Lord knows, Brock certainly *felt* happy, at least part of him did anyway. He was rapidly hardening beneath me. When our kiss broke, I wriggled from his lap and stood.

Brock grabbed my hand. "Where do you think you're going?"

My answer was to drop to my knees and reach for the waistband of his boxer briefs. "I'm going to show you how happy you've just made me."

"If that's how you display happiness, you can expect me to keep you smiling *a lot.*"

I licked the wide crown and swirled my tongue around, looking up beneath my lashes as I took the taste of him into my mouth. "Show me, Brock. Show me how you like to be sucked."

"Fuck," he growled. "You couldn't be any more perfect."

Brock dug one of his big hands into the back of my hair and wound a clump tightly around his fist. "Open wide, sweetheart."

My body tingled with anticipation as I lowered my jaw and hovered over the length of him. He guided my head down slowly, then used my hair to gently pull me back up again. I hollowed my cheeks and sucked as he slipped out almost to the tip. "Just like that, beautiful. Suck my cock just like that."

He guided my head down again, the second time making me take him a little deeper. Brock's dick swelled in my mouth as we fell into a rhythm. When I moaned, his grip on my head tightened, and he started to move me faster. A switch seemed to flip, and he went from cautious thrusts to more carnal ones. Before he'd been holding back, stopping when he reached a certain point in my throat, not forcing me to take the full length of him. But now he pushed my head all the way down, letting out a string of curses as he hit the back of my throat. My eyes watered as I swallowed his thick, full length, and I felt a bite of pain when he yanked my head back up by my hair—though it turned me on more than I could've imagined.

"Babe," Brock growled. "I'm going to come. *Fuck*, I'm gonna *explode*."

The throaty sound of his voice and the way the words shook as he tried to restrain himself made me desperate to break his last bit of self-control.

Brock loosened his grip on my hair, giving me the chance to pull away before he came. But I didn't want to stop. Instead, I looked up at him again, letting him know I'd heard his warning before lunging forward and swallowing him to the root without any guidance.

"Fuck," he roared. "*Fuck. Fuck. Fuck!*"

Hot cum streamed down my throat, while Brock's body pulsed and jerked. He was still panting a minute later when I wiped my mouth and climbed to my feet.

"Jesus Christ, babe." He gulped air. "*That* might be able to get me on the subway."

I giggled. "I've actually seen that done *on* the subway."

Brock hooked an arm around my waist and pulled me to him. "Come here." He ran his knuckles down my cheek. "Thank you."

"You're very welcome."

"I really want to make this work, Red."

"I do, too."

"Just to be clear, I'm not saying that because of the incredible blow job."

I laughed. "Sure, you're not."

His lip twitched. "Alright, you might've given me a bit more incentive..."

I leaned in and rubbed my nose against his. "I really want it to work, too."

"I'm crazy about you, Red."

"I'm crazy about you, too, Lumberjack."

# CHAPTER 19

*Brock*

It felt so damn good to have February back in Meadowbrook, particularly waking up next to her on this Saturday morning. It had only been a week since I was in New York, so it was a treat to be with her again so soon. February had booked a flight at the spur of the moment yesterday afternoon. She'd left work early and arrived here in the evening. She'd only be here until tomorrow, so we planned to make the most of the short weekend together. *Could it really be this damn easy?* I guess time would tell.

While she gently snored, I looked up to meet the stare of the moose head on my wall, laughing to myself as it brought back memories of the first time February was in my bed. What she must've thought looking up at that thing. I remember how panicked she was. I never would've imagined the drunk woman from the bar would end up as *my* woman. I'd had no idea what I was in for. Yet here we were. I was happier than I'd ever been.

Of course, at the same time, I felt a pit in my stomach, because when you're feeling this high, typically there's nowhere to go but down. But one thing I knew for certain: I was willing to get my heart broken and take the chance that this might actually be it for me.

February wasn't the only one snoring. Oak also contributed to the sinus symphony in my bed right now. My dog, AKA Oak the-bathtub-sleeper Hawkins, was lying at the base of my bed by our feet. Last night, he'd climbed up onto the bed, rendering February and me speechless. Oak hadn't slept in the bed in years. Maybe somehow he'd remembered the night the three of us fell asleep on the couch in front of the fire, and he associated February with a feeling of safety. I'd be interested to see whether he returned to the tub after she left. Because the only two times he'd slept outside the bathroom in recent memory were nights that February had slept over.

*Damn.* I could get used to waking up next to them. The only bad thing about this new arrangement was that it would always involve having to separate from her again. There was no way around that.

February stirred and turned toward me. Her eyes slowly opened to find me watching her.

"Hey," she said groggily. "How long have you been up?"

"A while."

"You were watching me sleep?"

"I was."

"What were you thinking about?" She smiled.

"I was remembering the first time you were in my bed, among other things."

She laughed. "I try not to think about that. It was quite embarrassing." She rubbed her hand along my leg. "We've come a long way, though, haven't we?"

"We've come a lot since last night. That's for damn sure."

"Well, that too." She chuckled. "Probably my favorite part of being back here."

I wrapped my arm around her. "Any idea what you'd like to do today?"

"Put me to work."

My forehead wrinkled. "Excuse me?"

"Put me to work," she repeated. "Before I told you I was coming this weekend, you mentioned that you had work to do at the smaller cabin. Then after I told you I was coming, you said it could wait. But why don't we head over there? You can do the work you originally planned to, and I can help. That way you don't get too far behind."

She was going to help? I stifled laughter. I didn't want to insult her by admitting she'd probably be more hindrance than help. It was sweet that she wanted to come with me.

"I'm not sure you'll enjoy yourself, sweetheart. We should probably do something fun while you're here."

"Isn't that *your idea* of fun?" she challenged.

"Well, yeah. But you won't enjoy it."

"I *will* enjoy it. If me visiting is going to be a regular thing, you can't afford to drop everything each time I come, like it's some sort of vacation. It's not a vacation anymore. This is real life. Same as when you come to New York. It won't always be sightseeing. Some weekends we'll just be lying around decompressing from the week."

"As long as the lying around includes time inside of you, I'm good." I winked.

"Well, of course." She lowered her hand to my crotch, cupping my balls. "Sex with you has become my *favorite* way to decompress."

My dick hardened, signaling the fact that if she touched me even one more time, we might never leave this bed today, let alone get over to the construction site.

I arched a brow. "You *sure* you want to come to work with me?"

She nodded eagerly. "It will be like take-your-girlfriend-to-work day. I want to experience a typical day in your life."

One thing I knew? As long as February was around, nothing would ever be typical.

♦ ♦ ♦

When we showed up at the cabin, Trevor and Axe were already working. I braced myself for the ball-busting I knew was to come.

Trevor put his tool down the moment he spotted us. "Hey, Fancy Pants. Brock didn't tell me you were coming this weekend." He turned to me. "And I thought you told me you wouldn't be here today? To what do we owe the honor of your presence?"

"It was sort of a last-minute decision," I said. "February's idea, actually. She wanted to experience a day in the life..."

"Well, welcome back to Meadowbrook," he said to her.

"Thank you. It's good to *be* back."

"I have to say, I wasn't sure I'd see you around these parts again. I think Brock has been holding back a bit."

She looked at me. "Brock and I are trying out the long-distance thing, actually."

"Well, looks like we have a lot to catch up on, brother..." Axe looked at me and smirked. "I'm always the last to know anything around here. Comes with being the youngest." He nodded. "Anyway, good to see you, February."

"Thank you. Meadowbrook is much more interesting in the daytime. I want you guys to put me to work." She smiled proudly. "I want to help."

She was adorable, but this was going to be a disaster.

Trevor's eyes widened. "Uh...okay. You serious?"

I flashed him a warning look, hoping he wouldn't taunt her.

I ended up assigning February a few simple tasks, like transporting logs from point A to point B, figuring that was harmless enough.

"When did you get in?" Trevor asked February as she carried one of the logs over to him.

"Just last night. I called Brock in the afternoon when I booked my flight so he could pick me up from the airport."

"No wonder Brock left the worksite early yesterday," Axe teased. "He had a special delivery."

"He was all friendly toward the latter half of the day, too, remember?" Trevor added. "Now it makes sense."

My brothers were making me out to be a lovesick sap, even if all of that was true.

"It's none of your business anyway, you boneheads. I don't have to tell you my every move."

"Brock doesn't like to talk about you because he thinks we'll tease him, but in all honesty, we're happy for you guys," Axe said.

"You see, February, Brock actually has a very good reason to be cautious with information pertaining to his personal life," Trevor explained. "He was traumatized as a child when his feelings were outed in front of his entire class."

February frowned as she looked over at me. "What do you mean?"

I rolled my eyes and braced for the embarrassment.

"Brock tried to pass a letter to his childhood crush in grade school," Trevor continued. "The teacher caught him and read the letter to the entire class. Ever since then, he's kept his romantic interests to himself for the most part. That's why we always have to dig for information."

She covered her mouth to keep from laughing. "Oh no."

I had a feeling this wasn't the last of the embarrassing stories they planned to share today.

Unfortunately, February encouraged it. "I would *love* to hear more stories from Brock's childhood."

"Brock's childhood was before my time, sadly," Axe said. "But, Trevor, you must have more stories to share."

"I have plenty..." Trevor chuckled. "Like the time Brock decided to cut his own bangs. He looked like Jim Carrey in *Dumb and Dumber*."

February cackled.

"It was a dare," I explained. "But it didn't go as smoothly as I'd hoped."

Trevor looked over at me, amused. "Our mom ended up shaving his whole damn head."

"Damn." Axe laughed. "I wish I could remember that."

"I don't even think you were born yet, Axe. We have photos of it somewhere, though. I'll have to find them."

I held out my hand. "No need to dredge those up, please."

February walked over to where I was working and ran her fingers through my hair. "I can't picture you without this thick mane."

"Let's see...what else?" Trevor scratched his chin. "Oh! Speaking of his mane, Brock went through a phase in high school where he frosted the tips of his hair with bleach. Looked like a boy-band member. It was great."

February laughed. "Okay, now I *really* need photos."

"That can be arranged, too." Trevor winked.

"That I do remember," Axe chimed in. "I remember begging him to do it to mine so I could look like my big brother."

I needed to put a stop to this. "All right. Enough of this reminiscing, if you want to call it that. We should get back to work."

After about a half-hour of my brothers and me working together while February "helped," she let out a screech.

"Ow!"

I ran to her. "Are you okay?"

"I dropped this damn log on my foot. Not sure how it slipped out of my hands."

My brothers surrounded her.

She sat on the ground, holding her left foot as she looked up at us, her cheeks turning red. "This is mortifying. At least I wasn't wearing open-toe shoes."

I removed her shoe and sock and examined her foot, wiggling each of her toes gently. "How's this feel?"

She sighed. "Good. I think I'm gonna live."

I smiled. "Maybe you should rest for a bit."

"Okay," she said as she put her shoe back on.

This wasn't her thing. Which was fine. She didn't need to have beauty, business smarts, *and* be a freaking lumberjack.

Just when I thought she was safe, the pile of wood she'd been leaning against collapsed, nearly taking her down with it.

"Oh goodness," she cried. "I'm a walking disaster today, aren't I?"

I needed to end this. Now. "How about a change of scenery?" I suggested.

"Yeah, before she kills someone..." I heard Axe mutter.

"Why don't we go for coffee? I'm getting a caffeine headache anyway." I rubbed my temples, pretending to soothe the pain. "We got a fair amount of work done."

"Okay..." She shrugged, seeming a little defeated.

The two of us said goodbye to my brothers and headed to a local diner.

We each ordered a slice of apple pie to have with our coffee.

This was a much better environment for Feb. I admired her beautiful profile as she gazed out the window. The sunlight streaming through caught her eyes just right.

"What are you thinking, Red?"

She moved her gaze to me. "It's so good to be out and about in the daylight here with you."

"I forget how rare that is. Not anymore, though."

"I'm so lucky to experience this world away from the hustle and bustle. To have a reason to be here." February frowned. "I don't want to go back tomorrow."

"So don't." I rubbed my thumb along the mug. "Stay for a bit. You must have vacation days?"

"I do, but it's a bad time."

*Of course it is, you idiot.* She'd been away from work long enough when she was at Sierra. She must have tons to catch up on. "Right. Sorry to assume it would be easy to take time off."

A glimmer of hope crossed her face. "Although, people *do* get sick unexpectedly, right?"

"Sometimes they do. Yes." I smiled.

"Maybe I'll stay one or two days." She nodded. "I have to think about it."

"I'm happy you like it here," I said.

"I like *you*. That's first and foremost." She grinned. "But yeah, I feel at peace here. I didn't get a feel for what life in Meadowbrook was like before—aside from that time you took me to the fair. In some ways, being outdoors with you today did more for my mental health than the entire stint at Sierra." She shrugged. "Even if I wasn't very helpful."

"While you won't be constructing houses anytime soon, I still loved spending time with you."

"Your brothers are funny."

I rolled my eyes. "They're something, all right."

"You're lucky to have them."

I nodded. I definitely realized that.

February took a bite of her pie. "What's next on our agenda?"

"I don't know. Did you have something in mind?"

"As I mentioned, I want to get a feel for your normal routine. What would you normally do after a day of work?"

Probably shouldn't admit that first on the agenda would likely be taking a shower and whacking off. "I'd head home, get out of these clothes, then make something hearty to eat after working up an appetite all day. Maybe rub Oak between the ears for a while on the couch." I winked. "But you know, *today* I only have an appetite for one thing. Can you guess what it is?"

She licked her lips. "I might have an idea."

"What do you think about letting me spread you open tonight and making you come only with my mouth? For starters, of course."

Her face turned red, and I felt her foot move against my leg. Her eyes flickered with desire. I fucking loved getting her hot and bothered.

"Is that my answer?" I murmured.

"That's a resounding yes." She grinned.

On the way home from the diner, we stopped at Margie and Joe Reynolds' grocery store to pick up a few things. It was a mom-and-pop establishment that had been around as long as I could remember. Whenever I needed odds and ends, I went there instead of the bigger supermarket. We gathered ingredients for the stew I planned to make for dinner.

"I noticed you told them to keep the change," February said as we exited the store.

"Yep."

"Except you gave them two-hundred dollars when the bill was under fifty."

I nodded.

She rubbed my arm. "How often do you do that?"

I opened the door of my truck and placed the grocery bag on the seat. "It's the least I can do for them. I know they're struggling to keep it open."

"That's really sweet," she said as she hopped in.

After I started the engine, I explained further. "Well, I owe Mr. Reynolds, actually. When I was a kid, he used to let me get away with stealing candy."

"Aw, really?"

I nodded. "He caught me once and didn't say anything to my mother because he knew we were going through a rough time. You know what he told me?"

"What?"

"He said, 'Kid, all you had to do was ask. I'll give you the candy so you don't have to steal it.' And from then on, he did just that."

"Wow. What a nice man."

"Yeah. I never forgot that."

After a moment, February snapped her fingers. "And that was your good deed of the day. Am I right?"

I shook my head. "Actually, my good deed of the day was getting you away from that worksite before you damn near killed yourself."

We both got a good laugh out of that. But then my phone chimed. It had been sitting on the console between us.

February looked down at it. "You just got a text."

"Who is it?"

She picked it up, and her face turned crimson. "It's Nina. Your ex."

I clenched my jaw.

*For fuck's sake.*

The calls had stopped, and I'd thought we were over this. Today had been going so well...

"What does it say?" I asked.

February swallowed. "She's at your house and wants to know where you are."

# CHAPTER 20

*February*

"Oh my God." I pulled down the passenger-seat visor and checked the mirror. I looked like a hot mess. And we were just down the block from Brock's house. "Can you slow down a little? Drive slower."

Brock looked over with his brows drawn. "You change your mind? I can drop you back at the diner or take you over to the cabin? I told you I didn't think you should have to deal with this shit."

"No, I want to come. I just want to fix my hair and wipe off the mascara smudges under my eyes. I can't see your ex-girlfriend looking like a total disaster. Why didn't you tell me I was such a wreck?"

He shrugged as he pulled to the curb and shifted the truck into park. "I think you look great. But do whatever you need to. I'm in no rush to deal with Nina."

I patted down my hair and used my fingers to swipe away makeup. "You really didn't know she was coming?"

Brock stilled. "Look at me, Feb."

When I turned, he stared straight into my eyes. "I had no freaking idea. And the visit isn't a welcome one. As soon as we get to the house, I'll be letting her know that."

I blew out a deep breath and nodded. "Good. Because I just got my nails done this week, and I already chipped one lifting a dumb log. I don't want to ruin another one on this woman. I haven't RKO'd anyone since I accidentally knocked out my cousin Felicia's front tooth when we were eleven."

Brock's forehead wrinkled. "RKO? You mean KO, as in knocked out?"

"No, I mean *R*KO. You don't know this about me yet, because we haven't shared all of our deepest, darkest secrets, but I was a big WWE fan when I was little. I was obsessed with Randy Orton. He had this move—the RKO—where he would grab his opponent's head and take them down to the mat when they least expected it. I perfected it and used it on all my cousins and friends."

Brock's lip quirked. "You're full of surprises, Red. And to think, I was worried you might hightail it out of Meadowbrook because of an unexpected visit from my ex. And all the while, you're sitting there planning to kick her ass." He chuckled. "I didn't think it was possible to like you more, but this...I might propose later, woman."

"I don't usually condone violence. But you should know I feel very territorial when it comes to you, Brock."

He reached for my hand and brought it to his mouth for a kiss. "Feeling's mutual, beautiful." Brock looked over at the visor, which still had the mirror down. "And you don't hold a candle to Nina, or any other woman I've ever met, smudged eye makeup or not. So if you're done, I think we should go get this over with because there is only one woman I want taking up my time, and I'm currently looking at her."

My stomach fluttered. It was pretty amazing what this man could do to me with only his words. The unsettled feeling I'd had when I'd read that text message from Nina was suddenly replaced by confidence. I flipped up the visor without checking my face again and straightened my spine. "Let's go put the past behind us."

Thirty seconds later, we pulled around the back of the bar into Brock's driveway. Seeing a statuesque blonde at the top of the stairs, with her beautiful, long hair flowing down her back, put a dent in the cocky armor I'd slipped on only a minute ago. If Nina was that attractive from this view, I dreaded seeing what she looked like from the front.

Brock cut the engine, and the woman turned.

My jaw dropped immediately. And it wasn't because she was beautiful.

Actually, she might've been Miss America for all I knew, but I never made it up to her face. Because her *enormous belly* stopped me in my tracks.

My throat grew tight.

*Oh.*

*My.*

*God.*

My heart had been speeding since I'd read this woman's message in the truck, but now it pounded like it was trying to escape from my chest. I swallowed. "Brock, when did you two break up? How long ago?"

When no response came, I managed to unglue my eyes from the big belly long enough to look over at

Brock. His face mirrored mine—pale with a gaping jaw. "We split up at the end of September."

I used my fingers to do the math, and when my ninth finger went up, I felt my heart shatter into a million little pieces. "Brock..."

He shook his head. "It can't be. It fucking *can't* be."

Tears filled my eyes.

He unbuckled his seatbelt. "I need to know what the fuck she's doing here."

But I already *knew*. And deep down, he probably did, too.

Brock opened the driver's side door and jumped out. He looked back at me. "You still want to come with me?"

But all of my bravado had crumbled. I shook my head.

"You sure?"

A tear slid down my cheek.

Brock closed his eyes. "Don't go there yet, Red. We need to stay positive. I'll be back soon."

# CHAPTER 21

*Brock*

"Hi." Nina smiled nervously as I walked up the stairs to my apartment.

"What are you doing here?" I asked as I reached the landing.

She looked down at the truck parked in the driveway. "Is she your girlfriend?"

"Does it matter?" I took a steady breath, trying to keep my tone even when all I wanted to do was scream my head off. But I couldn't, not at a pregnant woman. "Why. Are. You. Here?" I asked again.

"Do you think we can go inside to talk? I really need to use the bathroom."

I just wanted her to say whatever it was she'd come to say—namely, that it wasn't my kid in her belly—and get the hell out of here so I could put this nightmare behind me and get back to my day with February. But Nina put her hand on her pregnant stomach, and there was no way in hell I could say no.

I unlocked the door and pushed it open for her. "You know where it is. I'll be back in a minute."

Once Nina went inside, I walked back down the stairs to the truck. I was relieved February was still inside. She rolled down the window, though she didn't say anything.

"She needed to use the bathroom. I'm gonna talk to her inside for a minute, if that's okay with you."

February shrugged. I figured that was the best I could hope for under these circumstances.

"I'll make it quick." I turned back as I walked away. "Don't go anywhere, okay?"

At least she nodded that time.

Inside the house, Nina was still in the bathroom. Oak paced back and forth outside the door. He looked as confused and upset as I felt, so I let him out the back door so he could go down to the fenced-in yard.

Nina came out of the bathroom and glanced around the living room. She smiled. "Nothing's changed."

I looked down at her stomach. "I'd say something has."

She looked anywhere but at me. "Do you want to go for a walk or something? Maybe take Oak? He looked like he could use some air."

"I'm not feeling much up for a stroll." I couldn't take it anymore. I snapped. "What the fuck, Nina?!" I yelled. "Whose kid is that?"

She jumped and started to cry. "Yours! It's yours."

It felt like someone had whacked me in the stomach with a baseball bat. I staggered three steps back. "How is that possible?"

"I'm due in less than a month, and we broke up a little over nine months ago. I haven't been with anyone else since before I met you, so there aren't any other possibilities."

"If that's true, why didn't you tell me?"

"I've been trying to call you for almost a month. You wouldn't return my calls."

"*A month*? Don't you think I should've known about this a little fucking *sooner*?"

She looked down for a long time. "I'm sorry. I really am. I didn't find out until I was three months along because I have an IUD, and I don't really get a period. When I took a test and it came out positive, I needed some time to figure things out. I never really wanted children, but I thought being pregnant would warm me up to the idea, that a little time would help me to settle into impending motherhood." She took a deep breath and finally looked up. "But I haven't, Brock."

"You haven't *what*?"

"Accepted that I'm going to have a child very soon." She held up a thick manila envelope that I hadn't even noticed and extended it to me. "There are two sets of papers in here. Adoption papers and sole custody papers. I had my attorney draw up both, but you should have your lawyer read the documents once you decide."

My head was spinning so fast I couldn't decipher what the hell she was saying. "Decide *what*?"

"Whether you want to relinquish your parental rights and put this baby up for adoption or take full custody yourself. I'm giving up my rights either way. You're the father, so you have a big decision to make, too."

I raked a hand through my hair, feeling sick to my stomach. *It can't be true. It just can't.* "I need a paternity test."

"Of course. I figured you'd say that. I already made you an appointment at a lab in Grovetown. It's tomorrow morning at nine. The office is about a half-hour drive, but I know Meadowbrook is a small town, and I thought you might not want to go to the lab here for privacy reasons. The test is just a simple mouth swab for you. I went in earlier today and had my blood drawn so they can run the test once they have your sample. Pregnant women have free-floating fetal DNA in their plasma, so they build a profile for the baby and compare it to the father's DNA. The woman said you can request rush results and get them back as fast as twenty-four hours." Nina leaned forward and again offered the envelope in her hand. "I'm really sorry to do this to you, Brock. It's just not what I want, and I couldn't bring myself to terminate the pregnancy."

I had no idea what the fuck to say, so I said nothing. Eventually, she set the envelope on the table and quietly walked to the door. "If you could let me know what you decide as soon as you can, I'd appreciate it. We don't have long to go."

"How long?"

"I'm due in less than a month."

She took a step out of my apartment and stopped. "Oh and Brock? The baby...it's a boy."

# CHAPTER 22

*February*

I watched as Nina walked to her car, got in, and drove away. When the taillights were no longer visible at the end of the block, my attention turned back to the second-floor door of Brock's apartment, waiting for him to come out. Every second that ticked by made my heart thump louder. Because if he needed a moment, that had to mean...

*Thump.*

*Thump. Thump. Thump.*

I shook my head.

*Maybe he just has to pee.*

*Maybe he's dealing with Oak.*

*Maybe... Maybe he realized we forgot to turn off the coffee pot this morning and now he's busy scraping some burned gunk from the carafe.*

I kept staring at the door, hanging on to shreds of hope, but with every moment that passed, it grew harder and harder to breathe. After a full ten minutes, there still wasn't any sign of Brock, and I felt like I'd used up all the oxygen in the cab of the truck. So I took one last gulp and opened the door. By the time I got to the top of the stairs, I was huffing and puffing like I'd climbed a mountain.

I found Brock in the kitchen, holding on to the back of a kitchen chair, looking down. His head lifted when he saw me at the door, and I didn't even have to ask what had happened. The answer was written all over his heartbroken face.

"It's yours, isn't it?" I whispered.

Brock nodded. His voice wasn't much louder than mine. "That's what she said."

"Do you believe her? Could she be lying to get you to pay child support? Is she financially secure? Maybe she just wants money from you?"

Brock locked onto my gaze. "She doesn't want any money. She doesn't even want the baby."

My eyes bulged. "What do you mean, she doesn't want the baby?"

He gestured to an envelope on the table. "She brought two sets of legal documents—one signs full custody over to me, and the others are adoption papers, in case I don't want the baby either."

*Oh God.* I slapped a hand over my mouth, feeling like I might throw up. I could hang on to hope when it might've been a ploy to get money. But this—her not wanting *anything* from Brock—what reason would she have to lie?

"Maybe she's wrong? She could *think* it's yours, but maybe there was someone else? Maybe she just *wants* it to be you."

Brock looked away. "I'm going to get tested in the morning. She already went to the lab and gave a blood sample. But I don't think she's lying."

"*No!* No, Brock! She *has to be* lying!" I yelled. "Maybe she had an affair with some deadbeat or drug addict, and she wants the baby to have a good father. Anyone who meets you knows you'll always do the right thing. You'd be a *great* dad." Tears flooded my eyes. "*She's lying! She has to be lying!*"

Brock rushed over and wrapped me in his arms. "I'm sorry. I'm *so, so* sorry, Red."

I swallowed a giant lump in my throat. "What are you going to do if she's telling the truth?"

He shook his head. "I have no damn idea."

♦ ♦ ♦

The next day, I found Brock showered and dressed, sitting in the dark at the kitchen table at six o'clock in the morning.

"What are you doing up so early? I thought your appointment wasn't until nine."

"It isn't, but the lab opens at seven. I looked it up online, and the website said they take walk-ins too. I want to get there early so I'm first. Results usually take three days, but I'm going to pay for a rush, which speeds it up to twenty-four hours. Twenty-four hours from seven AM is quicker than twenty-four hours from nine AM. I need this done as soon as possible." He paused. "Do you think you could change your flight and stay another day?"

I shook my head. I'd rearranged my schedule and packed a million things into tomorrow just to have the time here I'd already had. There was no way I could stay longer. Plus, I wasn't sure I wanted to be around when the results came in, when all hope was extinguished.

"I can't. I have a meeting with the bank about the loan I need to figure out and a ton of appointments at the office."

Brock nodded. "When you had your pregnancy scare, you said you didn't think you wanted children. Do you think you could date a man with a child?"

My heart clenched. "I don't know, Brock."

He looked so sad, so crestfallen. But I had to be honest with him. He nodded. "I understand. Will you at least stay until this afternoon? I'll go get this lab trip over with now, and then we can spend the day together and talk more?"

"I think you need some time to think. This is a big decision that you need to make on your own, so it's probably better if I leave on the flight I'm booked on this morning."

Brock looked up. "On my own? But it will affect you, too." Then his face fell. "No, it won't affect you. Because you're not planning on sticking around if it's my baby."

# CHAPTER 23

*Brock*

I'd just finished with the swab. My nerves were going a mile a minute because now that it was over, everything felt so final. There was no turning back from potentially getting the news that I was going to be a father. My life as I knew it might never be the same.

I returned to sit in my truck with my head resting against the back of the seat. As much as I didn't want to share this with anyone, I picked up the phone and called Trevor.

He answered, his voice groggy. "Hey, dude. Why so damn early?"

*Shit.* He was usually still sleeping at this time.

"I'm in trouble, man," I confessed.

"What's wrong?" he asked, sounding alarmed.

I scratched my head. "Sorry to scare you. I'm physically okay. But something's come up—something big and unexpected."

"Did something happen with February?"

I shut my eyes. "Not exactly. But it could mean the end of things with her."

"What is it?"

I took a deep breath and told him what had happened with Nina showing up.

Trevor was just as shocked as I'd been. "Ho-lee shit."

"Yeah."

"Well, it makes sense now why she's been so damn persistent in trying to reach you." He sighed. "I don't even know what to say."

"You and me both, brother," I muttered. "You and me both. I feel like I'm in the middle of a fever dream."

"I wish I could make this go away for you. Axe and I were just talking about how cool it was to see you so damn happy with February. And now this." He paused. "How's she handling it?"

"Pretty sure it's over with her."

"Why do you say that?"

"We said goodbye to each other before I left for the lab. She didn't want to wait for me to drive her to the airport, and instead called a car. I didn't argue because I needed to get this damn test over with, and she was probably better off not having to deal with another second of this nightmare. I wouldn't want this situation either, if I were her."

"Hold up. She *said* she couldn't handle it, or you're assuming that?"

"She didn't say it exactly. But she's in a state of shock, and when the fog lessens, she'll realize even more clearly that she wants nothing to do with this."

"How are you so certain of that?"

I paused, unsure whether to tell him about February's pregnancy scare.

"There was a time she thought she might be pregnant by an ex, and she said she wasn't sure if she wanted kids. She was relieved when the test turned out to be negative. And this wouldn't even be *her* kid. Why would someone who wasn't sure they wanted kids of their own want to raise someone else's?"

He sighed.

If Trevor couldn't come up with a rebuttal to make me feel better, that likely meant he knew I was screwed when it came to February now.

"When do you get the results?" he asked.

"Twenty-four hours. But you know how you just *know* sometimes? I already know I'm this baby's father. It's just a matter of figuring out what to do with that information."

"Maybe there's a reason this happened."

"Not sure I'm following you…"

"Maybe it was meant to be."

I ran a hand through my hair. "Okay. *Still* not following you."

"I'm not sure you would've ever decided to have kids were it not for an accident like this, Brock. Maybe this is your chance to experience something you never knew you wanted?"

"I haven't made a decision about raising this baby."

"Brock, seriously? I know you. You would never let anyone else raise your kid. You treat us *all* like your kids, and you're the best damn pseudo-father around. So, while you might not have officially made your decision, I already know how this is going to go."

I knew he was right, but I still couldn't accept that this was happening, let alone admit that I'd be keeping the baby.

I rubbed my eyes. "Maybe by some miracle he'll turn out not to be mine."

"Wait...*he*?"

"Yeah." I swallowed. "It's a boy."

Trevor went silent on the other end. "A boy?" he finally said.

"Yeah..."

"I'm gonna have a nephew?" I could hear the excitement in his tone.

I attempted to quell it. "Trev..."

"Sorry. I—"

"Don't get all emotional on me. We don't know shit yet."

"Right." He cleared his throat. "Yeah. Of course. But just know, if he *is* one of us, we'll all help you. This little guy will be raised by a band of brothers."

I couldn't help but laugh. "I think that sounds good in theory, but if you're not gonna be there to wipe his ass in the middle of the night, I'm not sure it counts."

"Okay, maybe you're right. But we'll help out however we can. I'll take some babysitting classes if I have to. Learn CPR."

"Now *that's* funny."

"I'm trying to be serious here."

"You'll have a better chance at seducing some woman to help me," I taunted.

"Hey, whatever works." He laughed.

"Anyway, I appreciate you wanting to help. But this is my mess to handle."

"Will you promise to let me know as soon as you find out the results?"

"Yeah, of course." I sighed. "I'll let you go. Oak's probably freaked out by my weird behavior. I need to get home to make sure he's okay."

When I got back, I stopped short at the sight of February still sitting on my couch. She'd had her head in her hands and jumped when the door opened.

My eyes widened. "I thought you were leaving..."

She stood and came over to me. "I was wrong. I realized the reason I wanted to leave was because I was scared. But once I thought it through, I figured out that leaving you wasn't what I wanted at all."

Hope filled me. "Are you sure? Because I don't need your sympathy, Red."

"This isn't about sympathy." She wrapped her hands around my cheeks. "My *heart* wants to stay. I couldn't leave you to wait for these results all alone."

There was that damn hope trying to seep through again, a glimmer of faith that maybe she wouldn't bail if the worst-case scenario came true.

"I paid for the expedited test. So we should know by tomorrow."

"I'll stay whether it's twenty-four hours or a week. I don't want you to go through this alone."

Pulling her into a hug, I breathed her in and reveled in her warm presence. "Thank you, baby."

The next twenty-four hours would be excruciating. But having her here would help me get through the wait. That said, what would happen *after* the twenty-four hours concerned me most. Suddenly, my guard went up.

"The thing is, Red, while I appreciate your support right now, any additional time I spend with you is only going to make it harder to let you go if you decide not to stick around when we get confirmation that this baby is mine."

"Neither of us can possibly know how we're gonna handle something that hasn't happened yet, Brock. I feel like we both need to take this situation moment by moment." She began to pace. "Am I freaked out a little? Okay...*a lot*? Yeah. But right now? We don't have the answer. What we *do* have is each other and the entire day ahead of us."

I placed my hand on her shoulder to stop her pacing and kissed her forehead. "Thank you for staying," I said.

"Of course."

Oak seemed to be patiently listening to us from across the room. *Jesus*. Had I even taken him out this morning? I couldn't remember. That's how I knew my head wasn't screwed on straight.

"I'd better take Oak out," I said.

"I just did. Before you got here."

"You did?"

"Yeah." She nodded. "He really needed to go."

"He didn't get spooked by his shadow and try to run?"

February shook her head. "Nope. We had a nice walk, actually."

"I don't know what you've done to my dog, but please keep doing it."

Another wave of sadness came over me as I realized Oak would miss February, too. My pessimism couldn't be stopped.

After a bit, she and I decided to get out of the house for a while. We went to the center of town, walked around, and got lunch, though I didn't have much of an appetite. It seemed everywhere we went today, we were surrounded by babies. And each time we passed one, February looked over at me for a reaction. My cheeks would burn, and I had no idea what to do with myself. Was she trying to gauge my decision?

At the moment, we were trapped in a line at the home improvement store. And sure enough, in front of us was a toddler giving me googly eyes.

Finally, February nudged my shoulder. "The universe is definitely messing with us today, huh? All these babies and toddlers everywhere."

"I thought it was just me." I stuck my tongue out at the little boy, which caused him to cackle. "Maybe they were always around, but now we're noticing them."

She shrugged. "Or maybe in a weird way, the universe is trying to prepare you..."

My stomach sank. This time out of the house was supposed to be a distraction. It had turned into anything but.

February and I stopped at a café for coffee on the way home. We sat across from each other, both mostly lost in thought, when I caught her staring at me.

"What's on your mind?" I asked.

"You could have a *son* right now, Brock." She shook her head. "A son."

Had the reality of it all only now hit her?

I nodded, and then decided the sooner she knew the better. "I need you to know that if this baby is mine, I'm going to raise it."

She narrowed her eyes, looking perplexed. "Of course. I wouldn't expect anything less."

"You knew that was going to be my decision?"

"Brock..." She smiled. "You're the gentlest giant I've ever had the pleasure of knowing. And you have the means to care for a child, so why would you give him up?"

I nodded. "I couldn't imagine giving up my child."

"You have the biggest heart. It's why I..."

She stopped herself, and now I might never know how she'd planned to end that sentence. Damn this fucked-up situation.

February reached over and placed her hand on mine. "At least you know. This might be harder if you had to decide."

"Well, there's still the fact that I know nothing about raising babies and have no clue how I'm supposed to work and take care of him."

"You're gonna be the best father. I have no doubt."

My brow lifted. "What are you basing that on?"

"Your treatment of others—people you aren't even related to. This little guy would be your flesh and blood. I can't imagine how much you'd grow to love him."

"All the love in the world can't help you raise a baby," I countered.

"You can get a nanny."

I chewed on my bottom lip. "I don't want just anyone taking care of my kid, Red."

She smirked.

I arched a brow. "What?"

"See? Already so protective."

Rubbing my temples, I admitted, "I'm scared. Not only because of how much my day-to-day life will change, but also because you and I had finally come to an understanding that we would try to make this work. I don't see how I could possibly be there for you the way you'd need me to now." I groaned. "Anyway, so much for taking this moment by moment, huh?"

She squeezed my hand. "It's okay. You're allowed to feel all over the place. We both are. There's no playbook for this situation."

♦ ♦ ♦

Oak was asleep in the corner of the living room when we returned to my place.

After a few minutes, February came up behind me in the kitchen, wrapping her arms around me and placing her cheek on my back.

I turned to face her and looked down into her beautiful eyes.

"What do you need, Brock?"

"I need to go back forty-eight hours to when my life felt complete."

"I wish I could give that to you. But what can I do right now?"

I rubbed my thumb across her lips. "You being here is everything."

"I want to do more." She reached up and threaded her fingers through my hair. "Use me to forget about your troubles tonight…"

*Whoa.* Wasn't expecting that. "You want me to fuck you so I forget about all this?"

"Tonight is the last night before we know something. There's still a chance that this might not be real, even if that's a long shot. But let's just escape from reality for the rest of the night. Then tomorrow we'll face everything."

I don't know what came over me, but I'd gone from stressed and scared to hornier than I could remember in a matter of seconds. Maybe stress did that to you. But suddenly I needed her more than my next breath.

Lifting February off the ground, I carried her over to my bed. But the moment I put her down, it became clear that I wasn't the one in charge tonight.

"Lie back," she commanded, gesturing to the bed.

I did as she said while she climbed on to straddle me. She slowly removed my clothes as I lay there, my cock stiff as a board. All I wanted was to bury myself inside of her and forget. Tonight was the last night before my life would likely change forever. I needed to mark it somehow, and there was no better way than this, making love to February. No matter what happened, I'd never forget this night.

When she began to disrobe, my dick hardened further, dripping with arousal, and I became desperate to feel her skin to skin.

She was stark naked as she pulled down my boxers, my dick bobbing forward, practically slapping her in the face.

February laughed as she wrapped her mouth around my cock and proceeded to give me the best head of my life. Up and down, deep into her throat, occasionally circling the tip with her tongue. My eyes rolled back from the sheer pleasure of her warm mouth fucking me.

I nearly came before she pulled back, my dick making a popping sound against her mouth at her sudden retreat.

Then she moved to hover over me, sinking down onto my shaft. I let out an unintelligible sound as I went balls deep into ecstasy.

"Fuck, Red," I muttered. "Fuck. You feel so freaking good."

February swayed her hips as she rode me, her clit rubbing against my groin with each gyration.

"You knew exactly what I needed, didn't you?" I rasped, digging my nails into her lower back.

Panting, she nodded as she picked up the pace.

I wasn't going to last another minute. Her riding me like this was too damn good to handle. I gripped her waist and pushed her down onto my cock with greater force.

When her body began to tremble, I let go, spurts of hot cum exploding out of me as I emptied inside of her. She screamed in pleasure as her own orgasm fully took hold.

After we came down, Oak barked in the doorway. He must've needed to make sure February wasn't hurt after the way she'd shrieked.

"It's all good, buddy." I chuckled.

She lay next to me. "I should probably feel weird that Oak just saw me naked."

"Are you kidding? You gave him his biggest thrill of his life."

"You're assuming seeing *you* naked isn't an even bigger thrill for him."

"Well, he and I have never had that conversation, so anything is possible." I turned my body toward hers. "Thank you for that. I managed to feel like a normal man again for twenty minutes."

"The pleasure was all mine."

That night, February and I fell asleep in each other's arms, Oak once again joining us at the foot of my bed. Just the three of us.

Was it the last time we'd ever do this?

The following morning, a phone call woke me.

My heart raced as I got a look at the caller ID.

*The lab.*

# CHAPTER 24

*February*

I held my breath as I watched Brock swipe to answer his phone.

"Hello?"

The room was eerily quiet, except for my heartbeat, which I was pretty certain the whole world could hear thumping away.

"This is he." Brock looked down while he listened, then rattled off his date of birth and what I thought might be the last four digits of his Social Security number. Meanwhile, I still hadn't taken a breath.

"Okay, yes. I'm ready." Brock's eyes rose and locked with mine. I heard the faint sound of a female voice saying a few words, and then all of the color drained from his face. I thought I might throw up. I knew the results without having to be told.

A warm tear trickled down my cheek, and I quickly turned my head and wiped it before Brock could see. A few seconds later, he thanked the person and hung up.

"It's your baby, isn't it?"

He nodded.

I'd heard the word *heartbreak* countless times, but I'd never thought of it as an actual physical description. Yet I could've sworn that's what was going on inside my ribcage. My chest grew tight, and I had to use all of my focus to push air in and out of my lungs. It was one thing to decide to have a relationship with a man who was your complete opposite—a man who lived a simple life, hours away in rural America. But *this*? How could *this* ever work? He'd never be able to come visit me like we'd planned. What would he do, travel with an infant on a plane to New York City?

Brock took a seat on the bed next to me. "What are you thinking right now?"

I shook my head. "I'm too embarrassed to say because it's all selfish."

He reached for my hand and laced our fingers together. His voice was hoarse when he spoke again. "I'm sorry, Red. I'm so damn sorry."

I swallowed a lump in my throat. "You're having a baby in a matter of weeks, and I'm sitting here thinking about how it will affect *me* and *us*, rather than considering the well-being of your child and what he'll have to go through without his mother around." I summoned the courage to look over at Brock again. He looked the way I felt—terrified, dejected, and maybe a little ill. "What are *you* thinking right now?"

He shook his head. "I'm scared shitless. I've never even changed a diaper, and I live above a bar. My house is years away from being done at the rate I'm building, and…where will the kid sleep? In the tub with Oak? I don't have a crib or a damn extra bedroom to put it in.

And how do you pick out formula and decide what to feed it? *He.* It's a *he*, not an *it.*"

Brock raked a hand through his hair and went quiet for a long time. "I have a job—*two* full-time jobs with the bar. I'm usually home to eat and sleep and that's about it. I don't want my kid raised by a nanny. I want him to have the type of life I had, with a full-time mom and a house with a bunch of siblings who are always fighting, yet the place is filled with love."

My lip trembled. A full-time mom? I'd never be that, even if we found a way to stay together. And a bunch of siblings? "Brock, I can't—"

"I didn't mean..."

I put my finger on his lips, stopping him from continuing. Whether he'd meant to say it or not, he was being honest, and I had to respect that. "It's okay. I get it. I really do. My mom worked full time after my dad left. She had to support our family alone, and one thing I learned in therapy was that my parents not being around may be the root of some of my issues. I worry about abandonment and have fears of getting too attached to people. Your child should have everything he deserves and more. And he will. One way or another, you'll make sure he never wants for anything, that he never feels alone or unwanted. Because that's the type of man you are, Brock. You work hard, but you love harder, and your commitment to the people you care about is inspiring. You make the world a better place. It's one of the things I admire most about you."

"Jesus, February." Brock pulled me into his arms and clutched me tight. "I just blew all our plans out of the water, and you're giving me a pep talk. I think *you're* the one who makes the world a better place."

We held each other for the longest time. Something deep inside me felt scared to let go. Like I might never get to hold him again. Brock didn't say it, but his tight grip made me think he felt the same way.

Eventually, he stroked my hair from my face. "I know you've already extended your stay once, but is there any way I can convince you to stick around one more day? It's selfish of me to ask, but I'm not ready to let you leave yet. I need you here, February."

I nodded. "I have to make a few calls to rearrange my schedule, but I can take the early flight tomorrow."

Brock nodded, visibly relieved. "Thanks, Red."

We didn't leave the house for the rest of the day. Brock called his brothers to cover him at work, and I had Oliver help postpone meetings. Oddly, after that, we mostly went back to the way things normally were. Brock cooked us dinner. We snuggled on the couch. Neither one of us spoke of the baby, or the future, or what would become of us. Probably we were in denial, but it might've been the only way we could make it through the day without breaking down.

At three AM, I slipped from the bed and gathered my things. Brock had planned to drive me to the airport for my six AM flight, but we'd only fallen asleep at midnight, so I didn't want to wake him. Today was going to be stressful enough, and he needed his sleep. So I gently kissed his forehead and went to the kitchen to write a note before calling an Uber.

When headlights pulled down the block, I took one last look at my sleeping giant. Even after everything that had happened, just looking at him made me smile.

I'd fallen in love with Brock Hawkins—madly, deeply, head-over-heels in love. I wasn't sure if this realization would change anything or make things worse, but when I walked out that door, I felt like I was leaving a piece of my heart behind. The big question was—would I ever come back again to visit it?

# CHAPTER 25

*Brock*

I picked up February's note for the fifth time and re-read it, looking for a hidden meaning.

*Brock,*

*Didn't want to wake you so I took an Uber to the airport.*

*Talk soon.*

*X*

*Feb*

*P.S. Relax and breathe. You're going to be a great dad.*

While the words were kind, I couldn't move past the ones that were missing—words like *we* and *us*. And *talk soon* wasn't the same as *see you soon*.

My cell phone rang, and hope flickered in my heart. But finding *Nina* flashing quickly extinguished the optimism. I debated not answering for the first two rings, but she wasn't something I could avoid, so I swiped.

"Hello?"

"Hey, Brock. How are you?"

"I've been better."

Nina sighed through the phone. "I got a copy of the results yesterday, so I assume you did, too."

"I did."

"I was trying to give you a little time, but I need to get back home. My doctor was against me traveling this late in my pregnancy, and I had to hide my belly when I boarded the plane because I read that some airlines won't let you fly after thirty-six weeks."

Jesus Christ, I hadn't thought of any of that. What the hell would she do if she went into labor here? Deliver with a stranger who didn't know her history? Did she even have a pregnancy history? Any medical issues with her or the baby? There was *a lot* I hadn't thought about. "Right, yeah. You need to take care of yourself."

"I'm booked on a seven PM flight tonight. Do you think we could get together for lunch today?"

The last thing I wanted to do was have lunch with my very pregnant ex, but I didn't have a choice. Time wasn't going to stop so I could get used to this shit. "Yeah, sure. The Clubhouse Grill okay?"

"Perfect. How about noon?"

I nodded, even though she couldn't see me. "I'll be there."

♦ ♦ ♦

Nina was already seated when I walked into the restaurant. Her hands rested on the top of her belly. I couldn't take my eyes off it as I took the chair across from her.

"How are you feeling?" I asked.

"Like a snowman who ate too many cookies." She patted her stomach. "This guy is already over eight pounds. The only good thing about that is the doctor won't let me go past my due date. They're going to induce me on the first if I don't go into labor by then."

I smiled half-heartedly. "I weighed nine pounds, thirteen ounces."

Nina smiled back. "I *knew* it was your fault. Seeing the size of your shoulders right now is also a reminder I didn't need."

We both grew quiet. There was so much to say, so much to figure out, but I had no clue where to begin. Luckily, Nina jumped in.

"I don't mean to rush you, but have you decided what you're going to do?"

"I'm not letting a stranger take my child."

Nina's shoulders relaxed, and she laid her hand over her heart. "Oh my God. I'm so relieved. You will be such a good father to this baby."

"I'll take full custody, but would you consider being in your son's life in some way? Maybe do the every-other-weekend thing? I can bring him to you, or I'll get you an apartment here. A kid needs a mother, Nina."

Her face fell, and she shook her head. "I can't, Brock. I need to make a clean break or I'll never move on."

"How the hell can you do that?"

"It's not a decision I've made lightly. I've had months to think about what I should do, and I've thought long and hard about what's best for this baby. It may seem like a selfish decision to you, but I promise it's not. I'm giving up this little boy because it's best for him. A child should not be raised by someone who is just *doing the right thing*. He should be raised by someone who *wants* him and is ready to dedicate their life to parenthood. I never wanted a child, Brock. I never planned to be a mother."

I could see pain etched in her face, and it made me feel like shit for using such an accusatory tone. Whether I liked her decision or not, it couldn't have been an easy one to make. "I'm sorry. Having a child is your choice as much as it is mine. I shouldn't have questioned your decision." I meant the words I said, but a small part of me still clung to hope. Maybe she'd have a change of heart after she saw the baby. Maybe she'd warm up to the idea and we'd be able to co-parent. "I'll take full custody, but if you ever reconsider and want to be involved..."

Nina smiled sadly. "I'm not going to, Brock. I'm moving to England as soon as the baby's born."

"England?" My neck pulled back. "What's in England?"

"I took a position there. It's with the same company I've worked for the last five years, but it's a promotion into a different division. I already have the movers and my flight booked. I'm leaving a week after I deliver, if I go full term. I need a fresh start."

I suddenly felt like my sweatshirt was too tight. I pulled at the neck. Nina either didn't notice how panicked I felt, or she was doing a damn good job of ignoring it, because she plucked some papers from her purse and got right down to business.

"I typed up my medical history and all the history I know about my parents and grandparents. Both my grandfather and dad had diabetes, and I had borderline gestational diabetes, so you should probably keep an eye on the baby's blood sugar. But other than that, most of the diseases in my family are from lifestyle choices, like drinking and smoking." She slid the papers over to me and held up a finger. "Oh, and while we're talking about medical stuff, do you want the baby to be circumcised?"

I blinked a few times. "Shouldn't he be?"

"The doctor said getting it done reduces the risk of urinary tract infections and also lowers the incidence rate of penile cancer when he gets older."

"Penile cancer?"

"Also, do you want to be at the birth? I'm delivering at Brigham and Women's Hospital in Boston." She pointed to the papers in my hand as if my head wasn't spinning. "That address and all of my doctor's contact information is on the third page there. But I can call you when I go into labor, if you plan on trying to come."

"Okay..."

"And names. You'll need a name for the birth certificate when I'm in the hospital. I assume you'll use Hawkins for the last name, but you'll need a first and middle. That is, if you want a middle one. I don't think that's required. Do you have any names in mind yet?"

"Uh, not really."

She smiled. "I always loved your grandfather's name, Patrick Hawkins. It has such a warm ring to it."

I stared at her like she had two heads. Still, she went on...

"The last page has a list of items you'll need, things like a car seat, a swing, a baby monitor. I realize this is a lot to take in, but we don't have too much time, so I thought I'd try to help in whatever way I can. I also put a few websites on one of those pages—a nanny service in the area that has very good reviews and an agency that can find you a wet nurse if you choose to go that route."

I felt my entire face wrinkle. "What the hell is a wet nurse?"

"It's a woman who'll breastfeed a baby when the mother isn't available."

"That's...a thing? Why not just feed it formula?"

Nina smiled sadly. "Breastmilk is rich in antibodies that can help protect a baby from infection." She reached into her purse and pulled out *What to Expect When You're Expecting*. There were dozens of colorful tabs sticking out from the side. "I also marked some pages I thought you might want to read. The section about wet nurses is one of them."

I started to feel dizzy, but powered through as best I could. Mostly I seemed to repeat things Nina said, and I was mentally kicking myself in the ass for not bringing a notebook and pen to write shit down. At least I didn't have to do much talking. Nina yapped all through lunch and then through the tiramisu she ordered, too. By the time the waiter came over with the check, I felt desperate to go outside and get some fresh air. I started to get up, but Nina put both hands on her stomach.

"He's awake."

"Awake?"

She nodded. "Apparently the baby's size isn't the only thing he got from his father. He's a very active little boy. I'm surprised he stopped rolling around and kicking while I ate lunch." Nina looked down and rubbed her belly before looking up. "Would you like to feel him?"

The thought scared the shit out of me, yet I found myself nodding. Nina took my hand and positioned it on the lower left side of her swollen belly. A few seconds later, I felt a flutter, followed by a very distinct tap. Then another and another. It almost felt like the little guy was knocking from the inside, asking if he could come out. It was the most surreal moment of my life.

"That's him?"

Nina smiled and nodded.

My eyes filled with tears. I was terrified and confused and a million other emotions, but in that moment, something ignited within me. *That's my baby boy.*

# CHAPTER 26

*February*

My phone chimed in the middle of a meeting at work. I looked down to find a text.

> **Brock: There are way too many nipples to choose from.**

My mouth went agape. *What?*

> **February: I thought men liked nipples.**

Brock: The kind that go on bottles, Red. How am I supposed to choose? There are too many different kinds.

> **February: Ah. You're baby shopping. All alone?**

> **Brock: Yep.**

> **February: Someone send help! LOL**

> **Brock: You're not kidding. I wrote out a list of stuff I needed. But I'm not clear on which brands are best. This shit is confusing as hell.**

I grinned as I imagined big Brock standing clueless in the baby aisle. Some hungry woman would spot him and offer to rescue him any minute now. I figured I'd beat her to the punch.

> February: Do you want me to FaceTime you? We can shop together.
>
> Brock: I'd never refuse a chance to see your face. That would be awesome. But aren't you in the middle of your workday?
>
> February: One of the perks of being the boss is that I can take a break whenever the hell I want to. I'll call you in a few.

After telling my coworkers I had an important phone call—technically the truth—I excused myself from the meeting and headed to my office, closing the door behind me.

While Brock and I hadn't made any formal declarations about the status of our relationship, we'd talked each day since I'd come home from Meadowbrook three days ago, and I lived for these little surprise moments of contact. Even if our future was unclear, I still wanted to be there to support him in any way I could from afar. Since neither of us knew how we were going to feel once his son arrived, it seemed best to just take it day by day for now.

I placed the call, and when his handsome face popped up on the screen, the butterflies in my stomach came alive.

"Hey, Brock."

"Hey, beautiful. How are you?"

"I'm good. How are you?"

"Better now that you're here." He smiled.

I leaned back in my seat and exhaled. "So...nipples, huh? That's where we're starting." He paused, looking defeated. "I decided to formula feed him. The whole wet-nurse thing freaks me out. I don't want him to be drinking some strange woman's breastmilk."

My eyes went wide. "You were considering hiring someone for milk?"

He shrugged. "It was Nina's suggestion—before she basically handed me a baby how-to guide and ran. She thought breastmilk would be better for him."

My cheeks felt hot, the need to punch that woman growing by the second. "Well, really nice of her to be so conscientious when she's not going to be the one feeding him."

"I know." He shook his head. "The fucking irony, right?" He sighed. "I feel guilty about not giving the baby what's best for him, but I need to go with my gut on this."

"There's absolutely nothing wrong with formula," I assured him. "I was formula fed. I turned out okay, right?"

He scratched his chin. "Hmm... Now, you have me second-guessing it."

"Hey!" I giggled.

"Kidding, Red. You're damn near perfect."

A chill ran down my spine. Our eyes lingered for a moment before I cleared my throat and willed myself to focus on the task at hand.

"Okay..." I typed into my computer. "Nipples. Let's do some research."

"Not exactly the kind of nipple play I like with you." He winked.

I quickly scanned some articles to find baby bottle recommendations and suggested a brand he was able to find at the store and place in his cart.

"Thank you, Red," he said after making his selection. "That's one less thing to worry about."

"Well, that was only one item on your list. We have a long way to go. What's next?"

"Diapers. I've narrowed it down to two brands, but how do you know which size?"

"I think the newborn size is pretty safe to start."

"But this is *my* baby. What if he comes out huge and skips right over that?"

He had a point.

"Then buy a few packages of the next biggest size, too. It's not like you won't need them eventually, you know?"

"Good point."

There should've been someone in Brock's life who could've gone baby shopping with him today. But his mom wasn't around anymore, and his brothers were probably as helpless as he was. Despite my need to protect myself, I wished so badly that I could be there in person.

"This list is long. It'll take us all day." He wiped sweat from his forehead, and I felt compelled to step in. Well, as much as I could from afar.

"Tell you what," I said. "Let me take this off your hands."

He drew in his brows. "What do you mean?"

"Send me the list. Take a photo of it and text it. I'll research the best products, and then I'll order everything and have it shipped to you."

He shook his head. "I can't let you do that."

"Why not? It would be my pleasure. I feel helpless over here. It's the least I can do."

He looked away for a moment. "Feb, I can't—"

"Non-negotiable."

He sighed, his shoulders slumping in surrender. "Well, thank you. It means a lot that you'd want to do this for me."

"You don't have a lot of free days before he's born. Go work on the cabin. Or start getting the apartment ready."

He nodded silently, just staring at me.

"Are you okay?" I asked.

"This whole thing is surreal. I don't know how to feel about anything. Sometimes I'm excited about getting to meet my son. And other times, I'm totally afraid. The one thing I'm absolutely sure of is that I miss you like crazy."

My heart fluttered, though I tried to squelch the feeling. "I miss you, too."

After we finished our call, I spent the rest of the afternoon shopping online for Brock. He'd insisted on giving me his credit card number and wouldn't send the list until I promised to use it. I was pretty sure I'd ordered him all the main things he'd need, choosing what the Internet agreed were some of the best brands. I'd even added some things that weren't on the list like baby spoons and silicone bibs. He wouldn't need those right away, but it would be nice to not have to worry about buying them when he did.

And there was one other item I couldn't resist throwing into the mix: little plaid footie pajamas that reminded me of one of Brock's shirts.

♦ ♦ ♦

At the end of the day, I was leaving the office when our public relations manager, Fallon, stopped me.

"Hey, Feb. Are you okay?"

"Sure," I said as we walked down the hall together. "Why wouldn't I be?"

"You left the meeting earlier very abruptly, and you've had your door shut all afternoon. Well, except when I stopped in to hand you a coffee."

"I'm fine," I assured her as we exited the revolving doors. "I just had some...personal stuff to take care of."

She looked skeptical as we faced each other outside the building. "Okay, if you say so."

I cocked my head. "You don't believe me?"

Fallon looked around as if to make sure no one was near us and whispered, "I saw you looking at baby stuff when I barged into your office. You closed your computer window when you realized I was standing behind you with your coffee." She lowered her voice further. "Are you pregnant?"

*Oh Lord.* She'd drawn the wrong conclusion. "No. Why would you jump right to that?"

"Isn't it obvious?"

"I'm not pregnant. I was shopping for a friend. It's not my baby."

As soon as those words exited my mouth—*not my baby*—I felt it in the pit of my stomach. Reality hit me all at once.

*Brock's having a baby.*

*Not my baby.*

The finality of it all threatened to choke me.

She snapped me out of my thoughts. "What's going on, February?"

Fallon was a friend. I could trust her. I needed to let some of this out, so we moved to sit on a stone ledge outside our building, where I explained everything that had happened with Brock.

Fallon offered a sympathetic smile. "I once dated a guy who was a single dad. His son wasn't a newborn, but pretty young, like three or four."

"And?"

Her expression dampened. "Mitchell was a solid boyfriend. Trustworthy and loyal. But he always had to put his kid before me. And that put a strain on things. If they have kids, you never come first. That's just the way it is. Some people are okay with that. Me? Well, I'm a selfish person. I need to be number one. So needless to say, it didn't work out."

I swallowed. "At least you figured it out before you got too attached to the kid."

She nodded. "Mitchell was amazing, though."

"Yeah," I muttered. "My guy is amazing, too."

*My guy.* But he *wasn't* really anymore, was he?

♦ ♦ ♦

Later that evening, I was attempting to relax at home when my phone lit up with a number that looked international.

Picking up, I squinted. "Hello?"

"February, bella. How are you?" came a strong Italian accent.

It was Giovanni Vitadinni, a potential investor I'd been wooing since I started to get the vibe that the bank might not be too keen on the loan I needed.

I feigned my best friendly voice. "Giovanni, it's great to hear from you, although it must be pretty late there."

"I'm an insomniac."

"Ah." I laughed. "Have you come to any decisions on what we last spoke about?"

"I'd like to discuss it further...but in person."

My eyes widened. "Oh?"

"Come out to Milan next week. You can stay in my villa. My wife, Francesca, would love to meet you."

*Next week?*

I couldn't just drop everything and fly to Italy. Then again, Giovanni was someone I didn't want to piss off right now. If he was inviting me out there, that meant he was considering becoming an investor at a time when I could really use his financial support...

"Let me take a closer look at my schedule, and I'll get back to you soon, if that's okay?"

"That's perfect, bella. Take your time. Just not too much time, eh? I'm eager to speak with you."

"Got it. Thank you. You'll hear back from me in the next day or two."

After I hung up, it occurred to me that if I took this trip to Milan, it would likely be during the time Brock's son would be born. Wouldn't I want to travel to meet the baby? Help Brock? That depended on whether Brock wanted me there. Then again, even if he did, it might not be in Brock's best interest for me to lead him on if I wasn't going to be there day in and day out—for the long haul.

My heart had been aching all day, ever since shopping for baby items. The rational part of me knew it was best not to involve myself much further. A huge part of my heart, on the other hand, begged to differ.

I needed a distraction. I opened my laptop and began googling photos of Milan to try to psych myself up for a potential trip to Italy next week.

*High-fashion mecca...great food...a freaking villa?*

*This is exactly what you need, February—get away and forget about Brock and babies.*

*Let Brock handle what he needs to because the sooner he gets used to life as a single parent without you around, the better.*

*Go as far away as you can.*

*This trip to Milan would be a godsend.*

I had to laugh for a moment when I noticed the two separate windows open on my computer. They represented the two parts of my life right now. One was Milan, with endless possibilities in terms of my career. And the other? My completed order of baby items for Brock, which represented my continued desire to be tied to him, even if that was a dead-end road.

I opened a third window and started googling information about *women who left their careers behind for men they loved.* I ended up in an online chat forum. A woman had posted about leaving her tech job to move across the country to be with her boyfriend, who happened to be a single dad. The end of the post simply said, *wish me luck.* The entry was dated last year.

Did she regret it? I typed into the comment section: *Any update? How did it go? Are you still together?* I knew I probably wouldn't get a response, so I closed the screen and went about my evening.

A FaceTime call from Brock came in just as I was getting ready for bed.

"Hey, you," I said in greeting.

"I wanted to thank you again for placing that order for me."

I'd forwarded Brock the confirmation numbers, so he knew what he'd be receiving and could track the shipments.

"It was truly my pleasure," I said, plopping down on my bed, stomach first.

"I don't know if you could tell earlier when we were on the phone, but I was basically having a panic attack at the store. And you freaking saved me, Red."

"I could see it in your eyes, Brock. No one should have to go through what you are, preparing for such a big life change with almost no notice."

"You really sent me a lifeline today. I was able to go to the worksite and get a ton done because I wasn't lost in that store, crippled by my fear, incapable of making simple decisions for the whole day." He paused. "Thank you."

"You don't need to thank me again. I wanted to do it. It was kind of fun in a weird way. No matter what happens with us, if you ever need me, I'm here."

Sadness crossed his face, but he shook his head, seeming to force himself out of the funk. "I moved some things around in my apartment. Wanna see?"

I moved to sit up against my headboard. "Show me."

He turned the camera so I could see the room.

"Wow. The crib's up?"

"I figured I'd put him in this corner."

Then the camera panned up to the wall above where the baby would be sleeping.

My mouth dropped open. "Get that deer head off the wall near his crib!"

"What? I figured he'd like a furry friend watching over him." Brock laughed. "No?"

"Are you kidding? He'll wake up in the middle of the night, look at that thing, and think he's having a nightmare!"

Brock chuckled as he continued the tour of his makeshift nursery.

"Where did you get that bureau?" I asked.

"I built it myself a few years ago. I'd had it in storage. I'm pretty bad at all the small things, but furniture? I've got that covered."

"And the crib? You didn't make that, did you?"

He shook his head. "Bought it. Pretty much the only thing I was sure I needed and didn't require help with. I put it together yesterday." He moved the phone toward the floor. "Check out this rug."

It was a big fuzzy bear rug.

"A bear. Perfect. Fits in great with the rest of the décor."

"I thought so." He grinned.

"Might as well introduce him to taxidermy and bears young." I chuckled. "You've gotten more accomplished than I imagined. Good job."

"Talk to me when I'm trying to figure out how to use all that stuff you ordered. This furniture is the extent of my expertise."

"One day at a time. You'll figure it out," I assured him.

I closed my eyes for a moment. Sadness washed over me as I once again reminded myself that during all those days he'd be experiencing "one day at a time," I wouldn't be there. And when I opened my eyes, I saw the same sadness reflected back at me.

"Talk to me, Brock."

He let out a long breath. "I should be more excited. It's like I don't know how to feel. One moment I'm okay, and the next, I feel completely panicked."

"That's called shock."

"Yeah, maybe." He frowned.

"Just because you feel a certain way now doesn't mean you'll still feel that way when he's here. I bet things will fall into place in a way you can't imagine."

Brock sighed. "I just feel like he deserves a better reception than a big, scared goon who doesn't know what he's doing—on top of having no mom."

My chest felt raw. "Think of the alternative, Brock. If you'd told her you didn't want to raise him, then what? I'm sure he would've found a loving home eventually, but he wouldn't have had either of his parents. He's gonna be so lucky to have you for a dad. And while I know nothing will make up for the fact that his mother isn't around, being with you is the next best thing to having both parents. When he's old enough, he's going to appreciate that his dad dropped everything to be the best father he could be."

His eyes seared into mine. "I *did* have to drop everything, didn't I?" He swallowed. "I lost you."

"You didn't lose me. You just..." I hesitated as silence filled the air and I felt myself shutting down. I had no idea how to finish that thought. "I'd better go. It's late."

"Okay." He smiled sadly. "Thanks again for today."

"Anytime, Brock."

After we hung up, I walked over to shut down my laptop, but before I logged out of my email, I noticed a notification. I'd received a response to my question in that forum from the woman who'd left her career to move across the country with her single-dad boyfriend.

But I was too damn afraid to click on it. So I shut my laptop and crawled into bed.

As I drifted off to sleep, an image of those little plaid footie pajamas floated into my brain. I smiled, equally lovestruck and pained by the reality of what never could be.

*Baby Lumberjack.*

# CHAPTER 27

*Brock*

"That can't be right." I lifted a piece of fabric dangling almost to the ground. "The kid will fall right through."

Nick, one of my laborers, scratched his head. "Let me tie it around myself. A baby sling is like a tie; it's hard to do when it's on someone else."

I yanked the hippie-looking fabric from my body, but the knot around my neck didn't budge. Fiddling with it didn't help, so I sighed and turned, pointing to my back. "Can you please give me a hand getting this thing off?"

Unfortunately, my brother Elvin pulled up at that moment. He looked at the baby-carrying contraption tied around my body and an amused smile spread across his face. *Great. Just what I need—ball busting.*

He hopped out of his truck, grabbed his crutches, and slammed the cab door closed. "What do we have going on here? Playing dress up, big brother? I didn't realize they made those things in three-XL."

"Go away," I grumbled.

Elvin chuckled. "You know, they make *formed* baby carriers that just snap around your back. Much easier than those sling things."

I turned to my worker, who had finally untied the knot. "Is he screwing with me?"

Nick shrugged. "No. They make ones that look like hiking backpacks, except you wear them on the front. You clip it in the back and the baby just slips in on your chest."

My eyes narrowed. "So *why the hell* would you use this thing then? It's like tying a blanket with holes around your body and expecting it to hold a kid."

"This is made of hemp and is good for the environment."

I shook my head. "I should damn well fire you."

Elvin smiled and thumbed toward his truck. "You ready to go, Brock? I promised Linda I'd be home in time for dinner tonight. I've been working late the last few days."

"Go where?"

"You said you'd take a ride with me to pick out roofing materials. Linda isn't too happy with the blue tarp I have covering the leak in the living room. When it's windy at night, it flaps around and wakes her up."

"Shit." I rubbed the back of my neck. "I forgot. I've been so busy with work and the bar, not to mention trying to figure out all this baby shit, that it must've slipped my mind."

"The forgetfulness only gets worse after the kid's born."

"Thanks," I mumbled. "Just what I needed to hear." I turned to Nick. "Think you and Tim can finish up milling the rest of the log pile without me?"

He nodded. "We'll get it done, boss."

"Thanks." I nodded toward my truck and spoke to my brother. "We'll probably be over the weight limit for your truck. Roofing shingles are heavy. So let's take mine. You always have half your bed packed with personal shit anyway."

"Just wait. That's where you'll be keeping your most valuable possessions, too, someday—when the kids take over every inch of space in the house and garage."

*Kids.* As in plural. I wasn't sure I was going to survive one, let alone multiple. But I kept my mouth shut, and Elvin and I climbed into my truck. Sullivan Roofing Supply was a twenty-minute drive.

"How you feeling about the baby coming?" he asked. "You seem a little calmer than the other day when I saw you."

I glanced over at Elvin. "I must be hiding it better. I'll kick your ass if you share this with any of our knucklehead brothers, but I'm scared shitless. I feel like I'm going to fuck up. Though at the same time, part of me is starting to get excited to meet my kid. I guess I've warmed up to the idea a bit in the last few days."

"It's only been, what, ten days since Nina dropped the bomb? It's good that you're already settling into the idea of being a dad. And you *are* going to fuck up. We all do as parents. We're still human, after all. Screwing up is basically part of the job description. Becoming a father is like assembling furniture from IKEA. Half the time you have leftover pieces, and sometimes you put it together backward. But hey, the kid will still turn out fine. Probably."

I shook my head. "Thanks for the encouraging words."

"No problem." Elvin's phone buzzed. He pulled it out of his pocket, checked the screen, and tucked it back into his jacket. "You'll do fine."

I sighed. "It's just not the way I pictured things when I thought about having a family someday."

"And I pictured myself living in the Lost City of Kitezh with Angelina Jolie."

I smirked. "I forgot all about your Angelina Jolie obsession when we were kids. Remember the time you wrote her a love letter and mailed it with that terrible drawing you did of her as Lara Croft from *Tomb Raider*? The sword looked like she had a big dick in her hands?"

"What are you talking about? You never mentioned that."

I smiled. "Mom and I laughed our asses off when you weren't around. Why the hell did you think I asked you if she wrote back a million times?"

Elvin shook his head. "You're such a dick."

"You all had pipe dreams. Fritz wanted to be a YouTuber who reviewed snacks."

"And Trevor wanted to be an actor. Remember when we convinced him he should make some videos to put together an audition reel, and you and Maddox wrote a script for him? He was supposed to pretend he'd just witnessed a murder and call the cops in a panic. Except Mad actually dialed nine-one-one, and the police showed up with lights and sirens blaring."

"Mom was pissed." I smiled. "Especially because we busted the coffee table filming the pre-murder fight scene."

Elvin chuckled. "I guess none of us is exactly living the dream we had when we were kids. What did you want to be when you grew up? I don't remember."

I stared at the road, not really seeing it. Good thing they were usually empty around here, and I could drive them blindfolded. "I wanted to build log cabins."

"Really?"

I nodded. "Grandpa gave me a set of Lincoln Logs when I was three. By four I was building shit out of twigs in the yard."

"*Huh.* I guess some dreams do come true."

I didn't have a single complaint about my job. In fact, I didn't have much to complain about when it came to my life. I spent my days doing what I loved and my nights keeping company with beautiful women or shooting the shit with the local guys at my bar. It was a simple life, but a content one. At least it had been until a certain coatless redhead wandered into it. February might not have been part of my dreams growing up, but these days I couldn't imagine a life without her.

"Dreams can change," I said.

Elvin looked over, and our eyes met for a brief second. That was all it took for him to know what I was thinking.

"You think you and February can figure out how to make things work?"

I frowned. "We *had* figured it out. We were going to take baby steps, alternate visiting each other on the weekends. But how the hell am I going to go to New York with a kid? How do you drive ten hours in a baby sling?"

My brother snickered. "You don't, asshole. You put him in an infant carrier and strap it down in the backseat."

"An infant carrier? You mean a car seat?"

"No, I mean an infant carrier."

"What's the difference?"

"They're sort of the same, except a baby goes in an infant carrier and a toddler goes in a car seat. A kid needs to be a certain size to move into the type where they sit up. I think it's like thirty pounds and thirty inches or some shit like that."

"Jesus Christ, I didn't buy an infant carrier. I bought a damn car seat."

"There's a Target down the block from the roofing supply place. We can stop and pick one up, if you want."

"What the hell else don't I have that I need? I don't have a clue how to take care of a baby."

"Relax." My brother patted my shoulder. "Everyone feels that way when they bring their first kid home from the hospital. Doesn't matter if you had nine months to prepare or nine days. You always feel unprepared. But you'll do fine."

I felt like I was unraveling. "I don't have anyone to cover me at the bar or at work, and I need to take a CPR class and learn to swaddle—*whatever the hell that means*—and I've watched a dozen YouTube videos on changing diapers and still couldn't figure out what type to get when I went to the store. I feel like I'm running out of time and don't even know what to prioritize anymore."

"The kid," Elvin said pointedly. "That's what you're going to prioritize for the rest of your life. Once that baby is in your arms, your decisions actually become easier, because nothing else seems important, other than keeping him safe and happy. Being a parent means your child trumps everything. If the ship goes down, that's who you're saving. If you only have enough money for food for one, you're going hungry." My brother snort-laughed. "When you're about to dip inside your woman after weeks of being turned down because she's exhausted and then that baby cries—you're taking care of the kid and coming back to a snoring wife and jerking off in the shower the next day. *Again.* That kid sets the priorities from the moment it arrives."

"Sounds like that last part is personal experience..."

"You have no damn idea, brother."

A few minutes later, we pulled up at the roofing store. Elvin unclicked his seatbelt but didn't reach for the door handle. "Listen, I know you're crazy about this February. Nevertheless, the bottom line is that you can love her all you want, but she's going to have to bend more than you now if you have any shot of making things work. She's going to need to love that baby so much that she makes him a priority too."

I felt more deflated than ever. February didn't even *want* kids, so how far could I expect her to bend before she broke?

♦ ♦ ♦

An hour later, we were almost back at my jobsite with more than a ton of roofing shingles when my phone rang. I didn't recognize the number, but I knew the area code—*Boston*. My pulse picked up as I reached for the panel on my dashboard and pushed the button to answer on speakerphone.

"Hello?"

"Hi, Brock. It's Nina."

"Is everything okay? Are you in labor?"

"No. I'm not in labor. And the baby and I are okay, but I am in the hospital."

*Shit.* "What happened?"

"I had a little spotting, so I went to the doctor for a checkup. He did an ultrasound, and it turns out I have placenta previa."

"What's that?"

"It's a condition where the placenta is low in the uterus and partially or fully covers the cervix opening. The baby is fine, but it means I'm at a risk of severe bleeding if I deliver vaginally."

I raked a hand through my hair. "Jesus Christ. Can they give you medicine for it, or fix it somehow?"

"No, but sometimes it corrects itself. As the uterus expands, it can naturally push the placenta back up. If it doesn't, I'll probably need a C-section. But they're going to keep me in the hospital for a day or two, to monitor things and keep an eye on the bleeding."

"Damn, I'm sorry. Is someone there with you?"

"My sister Kelly dropped me off. She had to go to work. But I'm fine. They have me on bedrest, which makes me miserable, so I'm not the greatest company anyway."

I was quiet for a few heartbeats. "Okay. Is there anything I can do?"

"No. I just wanted to keep you updated."

"Alright. Well, I guess give me a call tomorrow to let me know how things are going?"

"I will."

"Thanks. Take care, Nina."

I pushed the button on the dash to disconnect and felt more overwhelmed than ever. "What if something happens to the baby?"

Elvin looked over. "You can't think like that. She's in the right place. She'll get good care."

"Did Linda have placenta previa?"

Elvin shook his head.

"Should I go to Boston?"

"If you feel like you should be there, you should go."

"I still have so much shit to do here to get ready to bring a baby home."

"You need to do what your gut tells you. But I can promise you that half the shit we buy for babies, they don't really need. You need diapers, formula, and a couple of outfits. Hell, our grandmother didn't even buy a bassinet. She would just clean out a dresser drawer and put the baby in there for safe keeping."

I yanked at my hair. "*Fuck*. We never stopped to get a bassinet either. But I think I need one. I'm not using a drawer."

"Take a deep breath, Brock. That vein in your neck is starting to bulge. I'll grab one for you."

"What if the bleeding starts again so they do a C-section and I can't get there? What if there are no flights available?"

Elvin pointed ahead. "Slow down. You're about to miss our exit."

My jobsite was only a few blocks off the highway, so my head was still spinning when I pulled in.

"You want to swap trucks for the night?" my brother asked. "So you don't have to bring the haul to my place? You've got enough going on."

"It's okay. I'm just going to check what the guys got done here and then I'll stop at your house on my way home and help you unload."

He nodded. "Thanks. And I'll have a cold beer waiting if you want to talk some more. I feel like you might need a few minutes to yourself first anyway."

My brother wasn't wrong, though I needed a lot more than a few minutes to get my head on straight. The problem was, I didn't have time. What I really wanted to do was call February and talk to her about how I should handle Nina being in the hospital. But I wasn't sure it was fair to dump this stuff on her. I was lucky she was still speaking to me at all.

A few hours later, though, even after a beer with my brother, I still had no damn clue what I should do, so I wound up calling her.

February answered on the first ring, though I could see she was still at the office. "Hey, you. Can you hang on just a minute?"

"Yeah, sure."

She moved the phone away from her face, but I could still hear her talking. "Thank you for staying so late, Oliver." She laughed. "And for making sure I didn't strangle that thread supplier."

Oliver's voice was distant. "No problem, boss lady. Antonio made *meatloaf*, so you did me a favor. Every time he makes it, I feel like he's one bad decision away from making a nice loaf of bread. Don't stay too late tonight."

"I won't." February laughed. "Thanks again."

I listened to the sound of her office door closing and then her beautiful, smiling face returned. "Sorry about that."

"No problem."

Her face fell. "What's the matter?"

And here I thought I was doing a halfway decent job of trying to act normal. "How do you know something's wrong?"

"It's written all over your face. Your jaw is tense, and you have little creases on your forehead. What's going on?"

I sighed. "I'm sorry to call you with my shit. But I wanted to get your opinion on how I should handle some things."

"Is everything okay with the baby?"

I explained the call I'd received from Nina earlier today and told her some of the stuff I'd read online about placenta previa.

She shook her head. "I'm so sorry to hear that."

"So many things can go wrong, for the baby and the mother. Fetal distress—the baby can be deprived of oxygen due to disrupted blood flow through the placenta. Placenta accreta spectrum—that's when the placenta attaches too deeply to the uterine wall and causes hemorrhaging during delivery. Maternal shock, placenta abruption. It's not good."

"Okay, well, if you called for my advice, then the first bit I'm going to give is that you need to retire your Google MD. If you have questions and concerns, you should get your information firsthand. Maybe ask Nina if you can speak to the doctor so you can discuss your concerns. Google is only going to scare the crap out of you. Trust me, I once convinced myself that a pimple on the back of my neck was a tumor because I spent too much time researching online. By the time I got in to see the doctor, I'd already weighed the pros and cons of which chemotherapy I needed."

I sighed. "You're right. Nina didn't sound too concerned. I'm getting myself worked up unnecessarily."

"We worry when we care."

I was quiet for a beat. "Do you think I should go there? To Boston? Be there in case anything happens, or she goes into labor?"

I thought the screen had frozen, the way February went silent for so long. Eventually she smiled sadly. "I'll be honest, as the woman you're involved with, I hate the thought of you sitting beside your ex. But as someone who knows right from wrong, I think the right thing for your baby is to go be with them. It's also the only way you're going to have peace of mind."

I sighed. "I was supposed to come see you this week. I don't know how often I'm going to get there in the weeks after the baby is born."

"Actually, I was going to call you when I got home to tell you I need to go to Milan, so it sort of works out anyway. The potential investor I told you about—the one who owns half the leather supply in Italy—wants to talk in person."

"That's good, right?"

She nodded. "I should never have gotten into bed with the venture capitalists that took over my board. They know nothing about my business. But if Giovanni is interested, I think he'd make a much better partner. I've known him for years. He's smart. I could learn a thing or two from him."

"Giovanni from Milan, huh? Sounds like a male model. I hope all he's interested in is investing."

February smiled. "He's happily married and invited me to stay at his villa with him and his wife."

I had a lot of balls making that comment, considering I was probably going to get on a plane and go visit the woman carrying my child. But hearing the guy was married made me feel better anyway. "I'm relieved that I won't be letting you down if I decide to go to Boston. But I miss you, Red."

Her face went soft. "I miss you, too."

After a few more minutes, the cleaning crew knocked on February's office door. "I should get going so they can do their thing."

"It's late. Take an Uber, not that awful damn subway."

She rolled her eyes. "Yes, Lumberjack."

"Thank you."

"I haven't made my arrangements for Italy yet, but I'll probably take a night flight tomorrow or the next evening. I like to sleep on the plane to help adjust to the time. But give me a call after you talk to the doctors in Boston."

I still wasn't a hundred-percent sure I was going, but February already knew. It made me smile. "I will."

She blew me a kiss. "Talk to you soon."

Panic washed over me. "February, wait!"

"What's the matter?"

"I just…I want to say thank you for being here for me, even when what I need to talk about is hard to swallow."

"Of course. I care about you. I've told you before, but I want you to hear it again. No matter what happens between us, I'd like you to be able to rely on me."

The *no matter what happens between us* hurt like hell, but I couldn't blame her. "Thanks, Red. Get home safe."

She winked into the camera. "'Night, DILF."

# CHAPTER 28

*February*

Giovanni's butler appeared at my side. "Another limoncello?"

I held out my hand. "Oh, no, thank you. I should probably stop at one."

Lush greenery surrounded us as I sat with Giovanni's wife, Francesca, in the backyard of their palatial villa in Milan. Our table was in the middle of a garden. I took a deep breath of the aromatic herbs, a mix of basil, rosemary, and thyme.

Milan was so romantic. Given the circumstances of my life, that was both ironic and sad. I found myself too distracted to truly enjoy being here, my mind constantly wandering to Brock, my chest filled with a gnawing ache. As much as I tried to distract myself, the knowledge that Brock's life was about to change any minute now consumed me. I still had no real idea what that meant for us. It was hard to imagine how things could ever work between us once his son arrived, but I couldn't fathom a world without Brock.

I hadn't heard from him in two days, and my imagination was going wild. Had his son been born? Was the baby okay? Did something happen with the birth? Would Nina pull a fast one and change her mind about raising their son? Would Brock somehow develop feelings for Nina again after he witnessed her giving birth?

It was odd for him not to check in, so I assumed *something* had happened.

Francesca interrupted my thoughts. "Everything okay?"

She was about ten years younger than her husband—tall, with long black hair and thick, manicured brows. Giovanni hadn't joined us, since he had a business meeting. He'd said he wanted me to spend my first full day getting to know his wife. Her question made me realize how transparent my mood was.

My mouth curved into a strained smile as I prepared to answer her question. Was I okay? My first instinct was to lie. But at this point, I felt just about ready to burst, so I decided to tell the truth.

"No. Everything's not okay, actually, Francesca. And I'm so sorry to bring my emotional baggage to your beautiful home." My eyes stung, but I did everything in my power not to cry.

"Oh no." She frowned, seeming genuinely concerned. "Tell me what's wrong."

"I'm not sure you're ready for this one." I laughed sadly.

"Does this have to do with a man?"

"Basically...but it's complicated. It's—"

"Trust me. I've heard it all. I have a group of close girlfriends who are all single, and you should see the drama that unfolds in their lives. There's nothing that could surprise me."

"My boyfriend is having a baby with another woman," I blurted.

Francesca snapped her fingers. "Giorgio! More limoncello, please. I don't care what February says. She *needs* another."

I sighed. She was probably right. Drowning my sorrows was the only hope I had of getting through this day. Thank goodness I wasn't meeting with Giovanni for official business until tomorrow.

As Giorgio poured me another drink, I began to explain the Brock situation.

"Why haven't you called him, if you're concerned?" Francesca asked. "It will make you feel so much better to speak to him."

I ran my finger along the rim of my glass. "I guess... I don't want to interrupt."

She tilted her head. "But if he cares about you as much as you seem to think, won't he welcome hearing your voice, no matter what?"

That was probably true. In reality, my own fear had kept me from contacting him.

"I think I'm just afraid to know the truth. As long as the birth hasn't happened, I can pretend everything is normal."

"Well, if melancholy is your normal, I feel sad for you. What you're experiencing *now* hardly seems normal. Am I right?"

I hung my head and nodded.

"You can put an ocean between you and your troubles, but they're all still right here, aren't they?" She paused. "I hope you don't mind me asking, but what are you doing in Milan if you love this man and can't stop thinking about him?"

"Well, Giovanni wanted to meet with me here."

"Is that *really* why you came?" She cocked her head. "You could've told my husband it wasn't a good time. He would've understood."

"Pretty sure I'm running away," I muttered.

She nodded sympathetically. "Yeah."

I liked Francesca. She had a way of pulling the truth out of me, and without someone calling me out, I would've suffered even more in silence.

I took a sip of my drink. "If I'm here, it puts distance between us and removes the option to see him. I don't have to face this head on."

"You know, when I married Giovanni, he had two kids of his own."

"I don't think I realized that."

I'd known Giovanni had two sons but assumed Francesca was their mother.

"And you see?" She smiled. "Everything turned out fine. I look at them like my own. And I don't have the stretch marks like their mother." She winked.

But the two situations were hardly the same.

"Well, in this case, there would be no birth mother in the picture. Being with Brock would mean I'd be the only mother-figure in the child's life. And that's a tremendous responsibility. Being with him would also mean less time to dedicate to my business, my career." I exhaled as a flash of panic hit. "I should probably have my head examined for having this conversation with the wife of a potential partner."

She reached across the table. "Do not worry. This conversation stays between us. Anything we talk about has absolutely nothing to do with business."

My pulse calmed. "Thank you. I appreciate your discretion." Though I couldn't imagine her not telling her husband everything after I left.

"So you think it would be difficult to have both a relationship with Brock's child *and* a career?" she challenged.

"My life is in New York City. His is out in the country, in Maine." I stared out at a stone garden statue. "And I'm not sure I can give the child what he needs. Brock and his baby deserve it all."

Rather than offer further advice, Francesca snapped her fingers again, prompting Giorgio to return and pour me more limoncello. *This has to be the last one*, I told myself.

After lunch ended, Francesca left me alone as I headed to my room. But I quickly grew antsy. Though I was a little buzzed, I decided to take a walk around the stunning city to clear my head.

While out, I passed the Duomo di Milano cathedral and a beautiful shopping center with luxury stores. Once again, I thought about how I was supposed to be having the time of my life, while it felt like anything but.

A few blocks farther down, my eyes landed on a sign that said *Psychic Readings* in English. It was in front of a small building that seemed more run down than the others around it. Because of the English sign, I wondered if this psychic catered mostly to gullible tourists.

But I had nothing to lose—or maybe the limoncello decided that for me—so I entered the place to find a woman with a long, black braid scrolling on her phone. Her back was turned to me, and I could see she was watching videos of dogs. They looked like pugs.

"Hello?" I said.

She turned, put her phone down, and gave me a once-over. "Hello."

I cleared my throat. "I'd like a reading?"

The woman nodded, then got up and charged my card the fifty-dollar fee before returning to her seat.

"I'm Luna," she said. "And you are?"

"February."

She arched a brow. "That's your name?"

"Yes," I answered, annoyed. If I had a nickel for every person who questioned my name…

She nodded and gestured for me to sit across from her. Luna took my hands in hers as she closed her eyes. My heart beat faster. I wasn't sure I even believed in this stuff, yet the anticipation of what she might say still made my heart race.

Then she let go of my hands. "I sense a major shift coming in your life."

Licking my lips, I asked, "What kind of shift?"

"I'm being shown the symbols for both life and death. But I'm not sure how to interpret this."

Dread filled me. "That doesn't sound good."

Luna scratched her chin. "It's not very often that I experience this kind of confusion when reading people." She closed her eyes for a moment. "The death symbol could be a literal reference to death or just the death of a certain part of your life. Same goes for life. There could be new life, figurative rebirth, or the literal start of life."

I had *literally* just paid to be freaked out with no answers. My buzz was wearing off fast.

After another ten minutes of confusing, mixed messages that told me absolutely nothing, I decided to get the hell out of there. I stood and practically fled. Bells chimed on the door as I made my exit.

Back out on the street, I looked both ways multiple times, paranoid as I crossed, fearing my apparent impending death. A bike whizzed by, nearly hitting me. Tomorrow I was supposed to sit down with Giovanni to discuss our partnership. What a shame it would be if I never made it to our meeting. A flash of Brock's face entered my mind. *What a shame if I never get to meet his baby. Never get to see Brock again.* I had to fly back. What if the plane crashed?

As I walked down the cobblestone streets, I knew my anxiety had everything to do with the fact that I'd gone too long without speaking to Brock. Now it had manifested into stress-induced paranoia.

I finally broke down, deciding to call Brock's brother Trevor to see if he had any information. That was my compromise to avoid interrupting Brock, in case he was in the middle of the birth.

After he answered, I cleared my throat. "Hey, Trevor. It's February."

"February...everything okay?"

"Yeah. I, uh..." I shook my head. "I'm sorry. I had your number in my phone. From that time Brock sent the meme about the goat."

"Ah, yeah. That was funny." He chuckled. "Well, how can I help you, Fancy Pants?"

That made me smile. It was a semblance of normal—or what normal used to be. It brought me back to days I'd give anything to have again: nights by the fire in Brock's living room, Oak nestled next to us.

"I was just wondering if you'd heard from Brock. I didn't want to interrupt him for obvious reasons."

"He went to Boston. But I haven't heard from him since."

*He's in Boston.* I let out a long breath. "I see."

"Want me to text him? Find out what's—"

"No," I insisted. "Please don't. I just wanted to see if you knew anything. I'll wait to hear from him. Don't want to bother him."

"You sure? I was due to text him anyway."

"No!" I repeated.

The denialist in me who didn't want to know the truth had hijacked this conversation.

Trevor sighed. "I know my brother would want to hear from you, no matter what's going on. Why don't you just call him?"

There were so many answers to that question.

*Because I don't want to face reality.*

*Because I'm afraid of hearing in his voice that having a baby somehow changed him.*

*Because I'll have to face that another woman gave birth to his son.*

*Because once it happens, it might really be over between us.*

"I might call...at some point," I said.

After a long moment of silence, he added, "It's okay to be freaked out."

I swallowed. "I guess I'm not very good at hiding it, huh?"

"I don't think my brother expects you to be handling this well. Certainly not any better than he's handling it." Trevor laughed. "He doesn't know what the fuck he's doing. This is gonna be interesting to watch."

"You'd better do more than watch. He's gonna need your help."

"It'll be like the blind leading the blind, then." He cackled. "But yeah, I already told him I'd take babysitting classes and shit."

"That'll score you some points with the ladies."

"You think? Maybe I can score a hot single mom?" His tone turned serious. "Look, February, Brock wouldn't want you to be sad right now. I happen to know he cares very deeply for you. And I'm just...really sorry this whole thing happened." He paused. "Brock's been such a good brother. He deserves happiness. And you make him happy. I wish he could have it all. But I can also understand why you might not be able to stick around anymore. No one would fault you for that."

Heat rose from my neck to my face as my feelings consumed me, mostly guilt and sadness.

"All that said... If you have it in you to stick it out, to let my brother show you what he's capable of, maybe things won't work out so badly in the end. It just might take a while before he can give you the kind of attention you need."

This conversation had gone a bit deeper than I'd expected. But I was grateful for his candor. "I'd better go," I told him. "Thank you so much for taking my call and for the talk. I appreciate it more than you know, Trevor."

"I'll call you back if I hear anything, okay?"

"That would be wonderful. I appreciate it."

"No problem. Take care, February."

"You, too."

After we hung up, I somehow found myself in front of the psychic place again. How the heck did *that* happen? I looked around and realized that while I'd thought I'd been walking home, I'd walked in a circle, ending up where I started.

*Just great. Now you've totally lost your mind.*

That was my life lately, I supposed. Just when I thought I was making headway in getting over Brock, or at least accepting reality, I'd end up at square one, second-guessing everything.

I took the fact that I was here again as a sign to go inside and give Luna a piece of my mind for freaking me out.

But the moment I entered, she rushed to me, her eyes wide. "I'm so glad you came back!"

"Why?"

"I received further clarification. The symbols were very much about birth, not death. There is *definitely* a rebirth happening in your life, if not an actual birth." She leaned in. "Is there any possibility that you could be pregnant?"

Pausing to think, I realized I'd just gotten my period. "No. That's definitely not the case." Imagine that plot twist, huh? I cringed at the thought. "There's no pregnancy on the horizon. That's all I can tell you." *Not mine at least.* Now I worried the psychic was able to sense something pertaining to Brock's baby. I decided I didn't want to know anything else and exited before she could give me any other info.

Taking out my phone, I made sure to open a navigation app this time, so I knew where the hell I was going. I had the directions under control this time, but as I began to walk, tears rolled down my cheeks as I finally lost the last shred of my ability to manage my emotions.

And for the first time today, I knew I *needed* to call Brock. This couldn't wait any longer.

When I got back to the villa, I FaceTimed him from the privacy of the gorgeous guest bedroom I'd been staying in.

My heart pounded as I waited for him to answer.

When my beautiful man popped up on the screen, the sight nearly knocked the wind out of me.

Because he wasn't alone. He was holding a baby swaddled in a blanket.

# CHAPTER 29

*February*

I swallowed a lump in my throat while tears welled in my eyes. "Oh my God. He's here..."

Brock looked down at his baby with awe on his face. It made my heart squeeze.

"He is. And the poor little guy looks like his old man."

I swiped wetness from my cheeks. "What a lucky little boy. Can you hold him up a bit, or position the phone so I can get a better look at him?"

"Sure." Brock adjusted the baby in his arms and turned the camera so I could see his sweet face. Daddy hadn't been kidding when he said the two of them looked alike. The not-so-little boy had beautiful tan skin and green eyes. He had his dad's thick, dark brows and straight nose, too.

"He really is your mini-me. He's absolutely gorgeous, Brock. Congratulations."

"Thank you." He shifted the phone back to his face, but I could still see the baby staring up at him. "I'm sorry I hadn't called yet. It's been a whirlwind two days, and this is the first time I'm sitting down."

"When was he born?"

"About two hours ago. Nine pounds, eight ounces."

"Wow. Only two hours ago? And my, that's a big baby. Do you want me to let you go? I just wanted to see how things were going since I hadn't heard from you."

Brock yawned. "No. This is exactly what I needed—to hear your voice."

"Was it a long labor?"

He nodded. "Twenty hours."

"Is Nina okay? With her placenta previa and all?"

"She is. Tired, I'm sure. But the issue resolved itself at the very last minute. I flew out yesterday morning, and when I got off the plane, I had a message waiting from Nina telling me her water had broken and labor had started. They thought they were going to have to do a C-section, but when they did a sonogram, the positioning had changed."

"Oh, that's great."

He shook his head. "I understand now why women were made to give birth."

"Oh?"

"Because men couldn't handle that shit. Labor is damn awful."

"Were you…in the delivery room with Nina?"

"Yeah. She did better than me."

Was I jealous? Maybe a little. Though it was less about him being with another woman and more that he'd experienced such a monumental, beautiful thing with someone else. It made me sad that it wasn't *me* who'd gone through that with him. But that was my problem, so I put on my best happy face.

"I'm so relieved everything worked out. Did you pick out a name yet?"

Brock looked down at the baby. "Patrick. After my grandfather. Nina had suggested it when we met back in Maine to talk. My first instinct was not to take a name she'd come up with. But then I saw this little guy's face. He looks like me, and I look exactly like my dad. There was no way I could name him anything else."

"Patrick Hawkins," I said. "I like it. And I think naming someone after a person who was important in your life is like giving them a piece of history to carry with them always. It's definitely better than naming him October."

Brock chuckled. "I have to admit, I thought your name was a little odd when we first met. But now, it suits you."

"Because *I'm* odd?"

"No, because you're special and should have a name that matches."

Warmth filled my chest. I allowed myself to enjoy it for a moment before asking the next question. "Has Nina reconsidered about the baby? I wondered if seeing him would make her want to be involved in some way. It must be easier to *say* you're going to never see your child again than to actually do it."

Brock frowned. "Unfortunately, no. She said goodbye to him a few minutes after delivering and doesn't want to see him again."

"Wow. Gosh. I...I don't know what to say."

"She said it would be too hard if she didn't make a clean break immediately. But she asked if I would send her a letter every year on his birthday, letting her know how he is."

Sadness washed over me. *This beautiful baby boy isn't going to have a mom.*

Brock cleared his throat. "The nurses set me up in a little room where I can spend all day with the baby, even though I'm not a patient. He'll probably be here two days, so I booked a hotel down the block. I reserved it for a week, because I don't want to bring him on a plane until I'm more comfortable with him."

"Are any of your brothers there or coming down to keep you company?"

Brock shook his head. "Elvin and Trev offered, but I told them not to come. Though Elvin insisted he'll fly down the day I'm flying back so he can take the trip with me. I told him it wasn't necessary, but he's doing it anyway. His wife, Linda, also has a menu of meals she's food prepping for the week I return, and she's going to stop by twice a day to check in on us."

"Sounds like you have everything covered." *Without me.*

We talked for a little while until a nurse came into Brock's room. "Hi, Mr. Hawkins. We should probably do a diaper check. Would you like some help?"

"Uh... I should try to do it on my own. But if you don't mind sticking around, that would be great. It'll be the first time I've ever changed a diaper."

"Sure. No problem."

Brock's attention shifted to me. "Do you want me to call you back?"

I smiled. "And miss the debacle of your first diaper change? Not a chance. Set the camera up so I can watch."

He smiled and shook his head, but set the camera up a few feet from the portable plastic bassinet so I could see the full room.

Before he started, he stretched his neck left then right and took a deep breath. The nurse stayed in the background, looking over his shoulder. After a few minutes of fiddling around, Brock turned to her. "How'd I do?"

"I'd never know it was your first time."

He wiped his forehead. "The sweat wasn't a dead giveaway?"

She smiled warmly. "You're doing great, Dad."

"Thanks, even if you're lying." Brock ran his hand along the baby's legs. "He's really warm. Should I leave the blanket off for a bit?"

"They like to be wrapped tight, but the heat in this little room is pretty suffocating. Maybe leave it off for a few minutes before putting it back on, and I'll call building maintenance to see if we can get the temperature lowered."

"Alright, thank you."

The nurse left, and Brock took the baby back into his arms before picking up the phone.

"Oooh," I said. "Now that he's not swaddled, can I have a tour?"

Brock's brows pinched. "A tour?"

"Yeah, I love baby fingers and toes. I want to see them."

He zoomed in to show me little Patrick's hands and feet. For a nine-and-a-half-pound baby, he didn't look very chubby. His arms and legs were long and lanky. I suspected he was going to be a big boy, like his daddy. "He's perfect, Brock. Absolutely beautiful."

"He is, isn't he?" Brock looked down at the baby and rubbed his cheek tenderly. The baby seemed to smile up at him, though I wasn't sure that was possible yet. "Did you just see that?" he asked.

Considering my ovaries were currently exploding, I certainly had. "He loves his daddy already."

Brock sighed. "*Daddy*. That's going to take some getting used to."

We talked for a few more minutes, but I didn't want to monopolize the important bonding time between father and son. "Go enjoy your time with Patrick. Give me a call when you can."

"Alright."

"Congratulations again. You're going to be a great dad."

♦ ♦ ♦

The following day, melancholy set in. I was sad that Brock had this new chapter of his life starting that I wasn't part of. Yet I was also terrified of becoming part of it. I wasn't ready to be a mom, wasn't sure I ever would. And it wasn't fair to be in their lives unless I was in it for the long haul.

This morning was my meeting with Giovanni, which was a welcome distraction. Unlike my initial meetings with the venture capitalists, our talk today wasn't all about numbers. Giovanni had real vision, and we spoke about long-term goals, rather than focusing on ROI. And as we wrapped things up, Giovanni told me he would invest. I was convinced he would be a much better business partner, yet I hadn't received a formal decline on my loan application with the bank yet, and ultimately, my first choice would still be to take full ownership back myself.

"Is it alright if I take a week or so to think about things? I have a lot going on right now."

"Of course. I wouldn't want a partner who didn't think things through thoroughly." Giovanni stood and smiled. "Do you need to rush back to the States, or can I interest you in seeing some of the sites of beautiful Milan? My wife would love to take you to her favorite shops where the goods are all handmade. And I would be happy to give you a tour of our leather-manufacturing facility. Perhaps we can end the day with a wine tasting at our favorite grower?"

My gut reaction was to decline. I needed to get back home. Brock just had a baby, after all. But then it hit me that I wouldn't be going to see Brock. At least not until I felt certain I could commit to them. So instead, I forced a smile. "Sure, why not?"

# CHAPTER 30

*Brock*

"Jesus Christ." I rocked the baby back and forth, but it didn't stop him from crying. Beads of sweat dripped down my back, and I could feel the eyes of the passengers sitting nearby boring into me. I looked to the woman sitting to my right. "Sorry."

She gave me a bullshit smile and whipped to the next page of her magazine. I should've asked her to switch seats with my brother before we took off. Elvin was seated two rows back, and I could've really used his experience right now. I had no idea what the hell was wrong with Patrick. He'd been fine when we boarded, and he'd fallen asleep while we were on the runway, but as soon as we took off, he started wailing. I looked down at his red face and rocked some more. "Shhh... It's okay, little buddy. Everything's gonna be fine."

A few minutes later, we leveled out at flying altitude, and the captain made an announcement that we were free to move about the cabin. I thought about getting up and going back to see Elvin, but what if we hit turbulence and the baby got knocked from my hands? No, no… I needed to stay seated and belted in.

But *thank God*, a few minutes later my brother appeared in the aisle at my side. "Kid's got some set of lungs."

I sighed. "I don't know what's wrong with him. He was fine until we took off. I tried to give him the bottle, but he sucked once and then let the formula dribble out of the side of his mouth."

"Hand him over. Let me give it a try."

I shook my head vigorously. "No way. It's not safe. What if we hit turbulence?"

Elvin looked amused, but I definitely wasn't. He leaned toward the woman sitting next to me. "Excuse me. Would you mind changing seats with me? I'm just two rows back in a window seat, same as you."

The woman couldn't unbuckle fast enough. She grabbed her bag from under the seat and practically ran to row fourteen. Elvin parked himself next to me and put his hands out for the baby.

"Buckle first," I snapped.

My brother reached for the seatbelt, shaking his head. "Jesus Christ. You're not going to wrap the kid in foam padding, are you?"

After a click, he held his hands out again. "Come visit Uncle E, buddy."

I passed Patrick to him, and Elvin rocked back and forth a few times. To my utter amazement, the baby stopped crying. "Seriously? What was I doing wrong?"

He laughed. "Maybe he felt the stress radiating from you. Babies tend to be sensitive to the emotional cues of their parents. They pick up on anxiety from movements and body language."

"Then I'm screwed because I can't imagine not being stressed the first—I don't know—eighteen years of his life?"

"He probably started crying because he felt the pressure in his ears from takeoff. Do you have a pacifier?"

"I do. But I tried the bottle and he didn't want it."

"Sometimes they want to suck but not drink. Give it to me."

I handed over the rubber pacifier I'd wrapped in a paper towel and within a minute, Patrick had nodded off to sleep.

"He's also warm," my brother noted. "It's hot in here, and I can still feel your body heat on him through his blanket. I'm going to unwrap him and let him breathe for a minute while he sleeps."

"Uh...maybe you shouldn't—"

Though it was too late. Elvin peeled back the first layer of my "swaddle" and his eyebrows jumped. "Are you shitting me, bro? *Duct tape?*"

I hadn't been able to get the stupid swaddle to stay closed the way the nurses had, so Patrick and I took a walk to the hardware store down the block, and I duct taped the layers of swaddle together to keep it closed. "That was the best I could do. And don't curse around my kid."

"I'll show you how to swaddle once we land."

I let out a heavy breath. "Can you show me how to be a father? Because I have no damn clue."

Elvin smiled. "You're going to be great. You might not know everything, but you found a way to get the job done, didn't you?"

"I'm terrified I'm going to screw up."

"So you've said. And I've told you that's a given. But you'll both survive it. I screwed up plenty with my kids. When Ethan was two weeks old, he woke up screaming in the middle of the night. I decided to be a hero and get up for a change, but it takes me a while to *really* wake up. Ethan drank powdered formula, so I went into the kitchen and mixed him a bottle. But he wouldn't stop fussing while I fed it to him. Turned out, I'd mixed my protein powder, so he was drinking Muscle Milk. Another time, we got this fancy new jogging stroller. The thing had everything—cup holder, shock absorbers, place to clip your phone. Anyway, I decided to be the ultimate adventurer and take the baby to the nature trail around Sizemore Lake. As I was walking, a squirrel ran across the path in front of me, and I thought I'd snap a picture with Ethan and the furry guy in the frame together. So I started running after the squirrel, into the wooded area. It was a jogging stroller with beefy tires and shocks, so I figured it was meant for off-roading. But a hundred feet in, I hit a rock and the stroller lurched forward. Ethan, who was strapped into the damn thing, somehow flew out like he was launched from a cannon with no helmet. Luckily, he landed in a bush, and didn't bash his head on a rock, but he still got a couple of good scrapes and was bleeding." Elvin pointed at me. "And if you ever tell Linda that story, I'll put itching powder in all your boxers like we did to Axe for his sixteenth birthday. Linda thinks I was carrying him and some asshole cyclist whizzed by and knocked us over."

"Are you trying to make me feel better? Because those two moronic stories just made me feel worse. What if my kid lands on the rock instead of the bush?"

Elvin chuckled. "Then you'll duct tape his head shut."

The rest of the flight went by without incident, and Patrick was an angel as we waited for our luggage and drove home. I'd taken an Uber to the airport since I'd had no idea how long I was going to be gone, but Elvin had parked in short-term parking, so he drove me to my apartment.

"I need to grab my house keys from the bar," he said. "I forgot them when I stopped in the other night. Linda's not fond of being my doorman."

"Alright, well, thanks for making the trip. I really appreciate it."

"No problem. But why don't you stop in at the bar with me? I'm sure the regulars would love to see the baby."

"Maybe tomorrow. It's already been a long day."

Elvin put a hand on my shoulder and steered me to the bar entrance. "Five minutes."

I sighed. I didn't want to argue since he'd done so much for me. I was holding the baby, so Elvin opened the door. I took one step in and…

*"Surprise!"*

Holy shit. The bar was packed with people. At first I was confused. *What the hell is going on?* It wasn't my birthday. But then I scanned the room and found a blue glittery sign draped along the back wall. *Baby Shower.* I hadn't moved from inside the doorway, so Elvin prompted me to step in farther.

"Sorry," he said. "But this shit is a rite of passage."

"Yeah, for the *mother.*"

"Well, you're *Mister* Mom. So put on your best pageant smile and let the ladies coo over that cute little peanut."

Over the next three hours, half the town of Meadowbrook met Patrick. I didn't love the idea of so many people being around my week-old son, but I tried to make the best of it by reminding myself of an article I'd read during one of my late-night baby-raising reading binges this week. It said recent studies showed that infants are born with a stronger immune system than most people think. Though to be safe, I didn't let anyone except Elvin and Linda hold him. By the time people finally left, I was ready for an early bedtime.

I looked around at the plethora of gifts. "Where am I going to put all this stuff?"

"At your cabin."

"I guess I could store some of it there."

"I meant *use* it there. You might not have noticed with the big haul you got, but there weren't any gifts from me, Trev, Fritz, Mad, or Axe."

"Okay..."

"Our gift is two weeks."

"I'm not following..."

"The six of us are going to finish your house. I know you wanted to do it all yourself, but I'm guessing right about now you would agree that it's more important to get that house done than to build it alone. We all cleared our schedule for two full weeks, and Linda is going to help out with the baby. A bunch of our buddies are going to come each day, too. We already set up a nursery in one of the rooms at the cabin using Ethan's old crib and stuff, so you don't have to bring supplies back and forth on the days you want to bring him. Babies don't do much but sleep the first few months anyway."

"I can't ask you all to do that."

"You're not asking. I'm telling you. And it's a done deal. We're starting next Monday, so get your shit in order by then."

I looked around at all the boxes of baby stuff—all the *very large* boxes. Elvin was right. The apartment upstairs was too small. A kid took up space. So I nodded. "Thank you. That would be great."

Elvin clapped his hand to my shoulder and glanced around at all the packages. "Looks like you have everything you need, and then some."

I nodded, but I knew that wasn't quite true. *Everything except what I need most: February.*

# CHAPTER 31

*Brock*

A couple of days later, things hadn't gotten any easier. My eyes were groggy because I'd barely gotten any sleep last night. I needed coffee—stat. But I had to clean up my son first.

Just as I'd put a fresh diaper under Patrick, a blast of liquid shot up at me.

"Ugh! You little bugger. You pissed in my eye!"

He wriggled his arms and legs as he lay on the changing table I'd managed to squeeze into a corner next to my bed.

"You're lucky you're cute." I reached for a baby wipe, patting my eye before I looked down and saw brown freshly splattered.

"Aw, man. What the heck?"

When it rained, it poured with this kid.

"I swear sometimes you do this on purpose. The second I get a new diaper out, you get me. It's a game to you, isn't it? Like Whac-A-Mole."

Oak stood at the doorway and barked. Poor guy

didn't know what had hit him since I'd brought Patrick home. My *other* son was not too happy about the new living situation.

"I hear you. I know you need to go out," I told him. "But I have to get your brother settled first."

He barked again, this time with more fervor.

"Yeah. Yeah. Hold your horses."

Oak had been especially difficult since I'd yelled at him for pulling one of Patrick's diapers out of the trash yesterday. God only knows what he wanted to do with it, but thank fuck I caught him before finding out. Anyway, I hadn't meant to yell at him so badly, but the whole thing had freaked me out, and now I was paying for it with his attitude today.

He plopped to the ground and groaned.

I hadn't factored in how inconvenient it would be taking a dog out with a baby. Sometimes Oak wanted to go when Patrick was sleeping. And when the baby was awake, I had to put him in the carrier and take him with me just to go out for five minutes.

I made a mental note to ask around for a dog walker. The back of my apartment was fenced in, but Oak never liked to do his business without taking a walk. The new cabin would have a bigger yard; maybe he'd like that better. But the move wouldn't happen as fast as I'd hoped, even with my brothers helping me finish the cabin starting next week. The construction now took a backseat to Patrick, just like everything else in my life.

Still, it was a gift to experience raising this little mini-me. As hard as it was, I wouldn't trade a single second. The way he looked up at me on occasion, like I was his entire world, more than made up for the tough parts. I supposed I *was* his entire world, which was crazy. That didn't seem right. He deserved more than just me.

I managed to get Patrick cleaned up and into the carrier to take Oak out. Thankfully, the dog didn't get freaked out by his shadow this morning. Chasing him down the street with a baby strapped to my chest wasn't ideal.

The second we got back to the apartment, I was about to finally pour myself a morning coffee when Patrick started crying. It was time for his formula, so I fed him before getting caffeinated. Headache be damned.

After he finished his bottle, I set him in his mechanical swing just off the kitchen. He immediately started crying all over again.

"What's wrong, man? You can't still be hungry!"

I picked him back up, and he stopped crying.

"I see what you're doing." I shook my head. "I can't keep holding you, you know. I need to have my coffee so I have energy to deal with the rest of the day with you. I can't drink it with you in my arms because I'm afraid I'll burn you. Can you at least give me five minutes?"

I tried again to put him in his swing, but he cried even harder.

Lifting Patrick into my arms again, I rocked him. "I'm doing the best I can, little dude. But if Daddy doesn't have his coffee soon, we're *both* gonna be crying."

Someone knocked on the door.

I didn't care who the hell it was—the mailman, even—they'd be holding my son for five minutes so I could make my damn coffee.

With Patrick in one arm, I opened the door to find my brother Trevor.

He grinned. "Hey, I was just—"

"Here." I handed him the baby. "Take him. Rock him for a bit."

My brother awkwardly bounced Patrick back and forth while I headed straight for the coffeemaker.

Thankfully, Patrick didn't cry. At least he didn't insist on being held only by me. That gave me some hope for the future, that I'd actually be able to hire help when I was ready. I wasn't quite there yet. Elvin had said Linda would watch Patrick next week so we could all work on the cabin, but I couldn't imagine leaving him for an entire day. I'd have to play it by ear.

Trevor tilted his head. "You okay?"

"I will be once I get some caffeine in me." I opened the cabinet and grabbed a pod. "You want a coffee?"

"No. I'm good. Just had one. You look tired," he added after a moment.

"Let's see... No sleep. No coffee. That'd do it, wouldn't it?" I watched eagerly as the coffee dripped out of the single-serve coffeemaker. I grabbed the mug before the gurgling even stopped and downed half of it.

When the mug was empty, I headed for the bathroom.

"Where are you going?" Trevor asked, still rocking Patrick.

"To take a shower. I gotta take advantage while someone's here. You good?"

He shrugged. "I guess."

As I headed to the bathroom, I hollered back at him, "He just ate, so he shouldn't need anything."

When the door closed behind me, I let out a long, deep breath. Just being alone in here felt like a vacation.

For a moment, I felt human again—like myself, without a little human attached to me.

After I exited the shower and dried myself off, I thought about the last time I'd checked social media. A couple of days ago I'd seen February tagged in a bunch of photos by the wife of that Italian investor. She'd looked so happy with a drink in her hand and a beautiful landscape behind her. Seemed like heaven. That was the life she was meant to have.

I returned to the living room and saw that my brother had placed a sleeping Patrick in his bouncy seat.

"Damn. How did you get him to sleep?"

"I did absolutely nothing but look at him. And that's probably why he relaxed."

"What do you mean?"

"You're a ball of stress, Brock. You're rubbing off on him, which is why he can't calm down. It's like a domino effect."

"*You* calm down when you haven't had sleep and get pissed on."

He wriggled his brows. "How do you know *I* haven't gotten pissed on recently?"

I rolled my eyes. "I don't even wanna know..."

Trevor chuckled. "But seriously, you should try to relax."

"I've got a better idea. Why don't you get your ass over here once a day so I can shower in peace? I don't really need much. But ten minutes of quiet goes a long way."

"I can do that for you, brother. Might not be at the same time every day, but I can do it."

"I'll take anything you can give. I'm desperate."

After Trevor left, I realized it was almost noon, and I hadn't eaten anything.

My refrigerator was filled with casseroles and other dishes people around town had dropped off. I probably should've frozen some of them. My brain didn't seem to have the capacity to choose what I wanted to eat, so I reached for a random one without even knowing what it was.

Just as I'd closed the fridge, the doorbell rang.

*Great.* That was gonna wake up Patrick, and I'd never have a chance to eat.

When I opened the door, I nearly fell over at the sight of her.

*February.*

# CHAPTER 32

*February*

Brock's eyes widened. "Oh my…God."

Before he could say anything else, I leapt forward and wrapped myself around him. It felt so amazing to be in his arms, even if the reason my heart raced was a bit different than usual. I was a little scared about what would meet me inside.

And when I pulled back to look into Brock's eyes, the first thing I noticed were the bags. He was still the most beautiful man in the world, but he looked more worn than I'd ever seen him.

He blinked. "What are you doing here?"

"I changed my flight on the way back from Italy. I couldn't stay away. I needed to see you. Needed to meet him." I exhaled. "Is this okay?"

"It's *more* than okay. I just might not be able to give you the time you deser—"

"Brock, never mind me. You need to rest." I placed my hands on his cheeks.

"I'm okay…" he insisted.

"No, you're not. I can see that you're exhausted. You have bags under your eyes. Have you slept?"

He looked down. "Not really."

I patted his cheek. "Go take a nap."

"That's crazy. You just got here. You haven't even met my son."

"Well, introduce me so I can watch him while you nap."

He lowered his voice. "He's sleeping, actually. Which is rare these days. So maybe this *is* a good time for me to get a little shut-eye." He took my hand and smiled. "Come here."

Brock led me over to his sleeping baby in a little seat on the ground near the couch. He'd grown so much in just the few days he'd been alive. The resemblance to Brock was even clearer now. Patrick's little chest rose and fell as he breathed in and out, looking so at peace.

Smiling, I bent to get a closer view, examining his perfect nose and rosy complexion. I looked up at Brock and whispered, "Go get some rest. I've got it."

"Listen, I'm not sure if you know what you're getting yourself into here."

"I'll be fine."

"There are some diapers and wipes here on the end table, right on top of the changing pad."

"Got it." I nodded.

"I have to warn you, he has pretty good aim, so be careful if you have to change him. You might want to shut one eye."

I chuckled. "I'll be okay."

"I should probably be shot for leaving you to take a nap right after you got here. But it's too damn good an offer to pass up." He leaned in and gave me a firm, hard kiss. "When I feel human again later, I'm gonna find a way to make it up to you."

My body stirred.

After Brock lay down, I sat on the couch next to where Patrick was sleeping, praying he didn't wake up. As much as I wanted to help Brock, I didn't *really* know what I was doing. But I would've done anything so he could rest, even if it meant learning the ropes fast.

At one point, I peeked over at Brock to find he was sound asleep. That brought me great joy.

When I returned to my spot on the couch, though, Patrick started kicking his legs, and I knew my reprieve was over.

Growing nervous, I licked my lips. When he opened his eyes and saw me, he started to cry.

*Oh no.* I lifted him, bringing him over to the corner of the house farthest from Brock so as not to wake him. Bouncing him up and down gently, I said, "I can only imagine how scary it was for you to see me and not your daddy when you woke up. I know you don't know me, but I promise it's okay. I'm a good person."

After several minutes of rocking back and forth, Patrick finally stopped crying.

"Are you hungry?" I cooed.

I didn't want to wake Brock to ask him the last time Patrick had been fed, so I took a chance and reached for one of the bottles. Thankfully, Brock had containers of ready-to-pour formula right on the counter. I read the instructions on the back of one of them to make sure I wasn't missing anything, and it seemed pretty straightforward. Just open and pour. After taking one of the clean bottles out of the drying rack next to the sink, I used my free hand to open the formula and pour it.

The moment I placed the nipple in Patrick's mouth, he took it as if he had a vacuum attached to his little lips. The bottle was empty in no time, and I gave myself props for taking a chance and feeding him without having to interrupt his father.

Using my common sense, I held him up straighter and patted his back until he let out a burp.

"What do we do now?" I asked, placing a gentle kiss on his forehead.

It took only a few seconds before he answered in the form of a loud vibration against my arm that I surmised was an explosion.

"Oh no," I muttered. I'd been hoping to avoid changing him.

I'd only been here a matter of minutes, but it was easy to see that caring for Patrick was a full-time job. Carrying him over to the diaper supplies on the end table, I took a deep breath and tried to remember how I used to do this when I babysat as a teenager.

"You can do this..." I murmured.

Placing the mat on the floor, I put Patrick down and braced myself for what I knew was coming. Call it muscle memory, but once I got started, it was all pretty easy. Though, I'd no sooner had that thought than urine shot up into my face. I couldn't help but laugh. Brock had warned me.

After I cleaned up both of us, I took him over to the couch and held him in my arms. I could've sworn he smiled at me. Or maybe it was gas. Probably the latter.

We sat there examining each other for several minutes. As he looked up at me, probably still wondering who the hell this strange woman was, I thought about how this little person had changed the course of my life, whether he knew it or not. Despite the impact on my relationship with his father, Patrick deserved to be here, deserved to have a dad as wonderful as Brock.

"I won't hold anything against you, little man. The timing was less than optimal, for sure. But you're gonna make your daddy so proud. I just know it. And I'm so glad we have this quiet time to get to know each other without anyone else around. I'm not scared of you anymore, and I hope you're not scared of me."

"What are you two talking about?" Brock's voice startled me.

He looked so handsome in his black T-shirt and gray sweatpants, and best of all, he looked rested.

"Hey, you." I smiled up at him. "How did you sleep?"

"Like a rock, thanks to you." He sat down next to me, placing his hands around my cheeks and bringing me in for a kiss. My nipples stiffened. Apparently, it didn't matter if I was still holding his son, my capacity to be turned on by this man knew no bounds.

Brock took Patrick from me. "What did I miss?"

"A bottle, a bowel movement, and...an I-told-you-so."

Brock smiled. "Ah! He got you, eh?"

"Yeah. But it was fine." I shrugged.

He arched a brow. "You mean that?"

"I actually do." I smiled.

"Well, you know, I thought you were amazing before you walked in here like a white knight and took care of my son. But now, Red? You're gonna have a tough time keeping me away from you tonight, if I can ever get him to sleep again." He set the baby in a little seat across from us and waited a few seconds before looking back at me and grinning. "I think he's actually gonna give me a break and stay in this seat."

Brock returned to his spot on the sofa and pulled me over to straddle him.

"I fucking missed you so much." He groaned.

"I missed you, too."

He lowered my face to his and kissed me passionately. Tasting him again was heaven. Brock grunted into my mouth as he pushed his tongue inside. I felt myself growing wet, which felt wrong with the baby right there. After several seconds of being immersed in our kiss, I forced myself off of him, wiping my mouth with the back of my hand.

"We should stop."

"Why?" he asked, his eyes hazy and lustful.

"You know why."

"Patrick doesn't understand."

"I know, but..."

"Are you staying tonight?" he asked.

"I was planning to."

"Well, Patrick's crib is on the other side of the room. And I fully plan to fuck you properly. So we have to figure something out, even if I take you on the damn kitchen counter."

A chill ran down my spine.

He turned toward me and brushed the backs of his fingers against my cheek. "Tell me how you ended up here. What made you come?"

"Honestly? I had a panic attack while on a boat in the middle of Lake Como."

"Seriously?"

"Yeah. They had to bring the boat ashore, and I promptly said goodbye to a very worried Giovanni and Francesca."

"Are you okay now?"

"Yes. It all just finally caught up with me. I couldn't get on a plane here fast enough. I needed to see you. Needed to meet him."

"How long can you stay?"

I laughed. "I have no plan because I wasn't even supposed to be here. But I don't intend to leave until after tomorrow."

"Well, I'm so happy to have you here, even if it's only for a couple of days."

"I want to help you," I insisted.

"Isn't it enough that my son pissed in your face? I think you've paid your dues."

"I didn't mind it."

"If you don't mind stuff on your face…" He flashed me a mischievous grin. "I think *I* can work with that, actually."

I tugged at his hair. "Good to know becoming a father hasn't taken away your perviness."

"Actually, I might've gotten worse. I realized this morning that I'm hornier than ever. I thought about you in the shower earlier, never imagining that my fantasies could come true today. You'd better be ready for tonight."

# CHAPTER 33

*February*

"Wow." Brock stood in the bathroom doorway and looked me up and down. "You look smokin' hot."

After deciding to stay for the weekend, I'd had the brilliant idea to invite his brothers over for dinner on Saturday night—something I was now regretting as I stressed about getting ready. I smoothed the black leather skirt I'd paired with an emerald green silk blouse. "Is this too much? Should I change?"

Brock hooked an arm behind my back and yanked me flush against him. "Out of your clothes? Yes."

I smiled and rested my hands flat on his chest. "I'm serious. Am I overdressed? And do we have enough food?" My idea of hosting was generally picking items from a menu at a restaurant that did the cooking and cleaning up.

"You look beautiful."

"Thank you." Though I hadn't asked *how* I looked; I'd asked if I was overdressed. But before I could clarify, an odd aroma wafted through the air. "Do you smell that?"

"The roast cooking?"

"No, something else." I wiggled out of Brock's grip and let my nose lead the way. The stench grew stronger as I moved toward the kitchen, and my eyes nearly bulged from my head when I saw the oven. *Flames!* "Oh my God!" I ran to the baby while screaming to Brock. "*Fire, Brock! Fire!*"

I wasn't about to stop for a closer look or attempt to put it out. Instead, I scooped poor sleeping Patrick into my arms and bolted to the door. He woke with a scare, and Oak followed us in hot pursuit. From the landing outside, I watched as Brock pulled a fire extinguisher from under the kitchen sink, opened the oven door, and sprayed. Thirty seconds later, he set the extinguisher on the floor. "It's out. It was contained to the pan. You can come back inside." He pulled the still-smoking roast out of the oven and placed it in the sink. Fanning away the smoke, he shook his head. "I think I ruined your dinner though."

I walked back inside with Patrick and Oak, leaving the door open behind me to clear the apartment of residual smoke. "What the heck happened?"

Brock grabbed a fork from the sink and moved the charred roast around in the pan. He lifted what looked like burned paper. "I think you might've forgotten to take out the pad that's packaged under the roast to absorb juices when you put the meat in the oven."

"Oh my God." I closed my eyes. "I'm such a dumbass. Why, oh why, did I think I could cook a meal for eight people?"

"It's actually nine now. Fritz asked if he could bring some woman he's been seeing. Sorry. I forgot to tell you."

I let out an exasperated sigh. "No biggie. Nothing to feed *eight* or nothing to feed *nine*—doesn't really make a difference, does it?"

"It's fine. We'll order pizza."

"But I really wanted to make a good first impression with Linda."

Brock's attention shifted to the baby in my arms, and his eyes went soft. "You just ran from the apartment like a bat out of hell carrying this little guy, without even thinking. Your first gut reaction was to take care of Patrick. Trust me, that's all it's going to take to make a good impression with Elvin's wife. Linda's gonna love you."

"Did someone say my name?" A voice came from behind us.

I turned to find Brock's brother Elvin standing in the open doorway next to a pretty brunette who was holding the hand of a little boy. She smiled warmly as she entered. "You must be February."

I smiled back, though inside I was kicking myself in the ass for what I had on. Linda was dressed in a pair of jeans and a simple navy sweater. *Of course she is.* I was an idiot for putting on this fancy outfit. I was in *Meadowbrook* after all, not a restaurant in Midtown. Great, now I'm overdressed *and* set our meal on fire.

Elvin fanned the air. "What happened in here? You trying to set the mood with a fire without a fireplace?"

Brock cleared his throat. "I accidentally left the absorbing thingy on the bottom of the roast. It caught fire."

I generally owned up to my mistakes, but just this once I was going to let Brock take the hit. I looked over at him and mouthed *thank you*. He winked and wrapped an arm around my shoulder.

Meanwhile, Elvin set two big casserole dishes on the counter. "Linda made a couple of apps—taco dip and stuffed mushrooms."

"The dip needs to bake for twenty minutes at three-fifty," she said. "But the mushrooms just came out of the oven, so they should be ready to serve."

"Did someone say *stuffed mushrooms*?" Trevor walked in the still-open door. He set a big foil-wrapped tray down on the counter and lifted the lid from the one Linda brought. Popping a mushroom into his mouth, he smiled and shut his eyes. "Mmm... When are you going to divorce my dumbass brother and marry me, Lin? You know the way to my heart is through my stomach, and I love these things."

Elvin rolled his eyes. "Ignore him. He sees a woman with a baking dish and automatically proposes."

Trevor smirked. "My new lady made stuffed manicotti. She's Italian and makes a mean Sunday sauce."

Linda looked to me and put out her hands. "May I?"

It took me a second to realize she was asking to hold Patrick, who was still in my arms. The fact that I'd forgotten I was holding him was a testament to how comfortable I'd grown taking care of a baby over the last two days. "Oh sure. Of course."

Just as I was about to pass him to Linda, Patrick burped and spit up. It splattered all over my silk blouse. But I just smiled. I was actually relieved to have a reason to change before anyone else arrived. I wiped his mouth and kissed his little forehead, handing him to Linda as I silently thanked him for helping me out. I pulled a pair of jeans and a sweatshirt from my bag and went into the bathroom to change.

Brock slipped in with me and closed the door behind him. "I came to see if you were good." His eyes dropped to my lacy bra, and he grinned. "But now *I'm* feeling pretty damn good."

I smiled. "I'm okay."

"I hope Patrick didn't ruin your blouse."

"I couldn't care less."

Brock studied me a moment. "You mean that, don't you?"

"Of course." I pulled off my leather skirt and yanked on the comfy jeans. "I was happy for an excuse to change. Why didn't you tell me how overdressed I was?"

He shrugged. "I was too busy taking in how beautiful you looked."

"I want to fit in, not stand out."

"Sweetheart, you could wear a potato sack and you'd stand out in any room." He cupped my cheeks and tilted my head up so our eyes met. "You're different than a lot of the folks around here, but that's nothing to be ashamed of. You stand out in all the best ways."

My insides melted. "For a man of few words, sometimes you know the right thing to say, Brock Hawkins."

He kissed my forehead. "Come on, let's get this dinner over with so I can have you all to myself again."

That evening, I learned a thing or two about the Hawkins men. For one, they could really eat. Not only did they devour half-a-dozen dishes that people brought, they also polished off four pizzas, three bags of chips, two containers of dip, and two cases of beer. Patrick, for his part, had been in good spirits all night, considering he'd been passed around from person to person. Only in the last fifteen minutes had he started to get fussy. Linda tried rocking him, but that didn't help. Brock changed his diaper and attempted to give him a bottle, but nothing seemed to console him.

"Would you mind holding him for a minute?" Brock asked. "I left his yellow blanket in the car. Maybe he wants that. He sometimes grips it in his little fist while he sleeps."

"Of course. Go ahead."

Brock passed me the baby, but before he could finish pulling on his flannel, Patrick miraculously stopped crying.

Linda smiled. "Looks like he didn't want food or a blanket after all. He just wanted a certain someone."

This little guy was doing me all kinds of favors today. I looked down at his sweet little face. "Must be beginner's luck."

"Or you have the magic touch." Linda glanced over at Brock, who was currently looking at me with a face I couldn't put my finger on, yet I liked the way it made me feel inside. "With *both* these Hawkins boys."

♦ ♦ ♦

Eventually the crowd thinned out, and it was only Elvin and his family left. Patrick was sleeping in his bassinet, and Elvin and Linda's son, Michael, was knocked out on the couch. I finished loading the dishwasher while

Brock went downstairs with his brother to get some boxes of baby clothes out of Elvin's truck.

Linda took a seat on a stool on the other side of the counter and motioned to the last bottle of wine. "Should we open that?"

I smiled. "I've been dying to, but I didn't want you to think I drank too much around the baby."

Linda laughed. "I like my wine, and I'm not one to judge. Plus, children are the *reason* alcohol was invented."

She grabbed the bottle opener and deftly removed the cork. Pouring two glasses, she pushed one over to me before taking a big sip. "I have to say, I've never seen Brock look so happy."

"He's really a natural with Patrick, isn't he?"

Linda set her glass down. "He is, but I don't think that's the only thing making him glow. He couldn't keep his eyes off you all day." She paused and ran her finger along the bottom of her glass. "Did you know I used to be an actress?"

In fact, I did not. "Really?"

Linda chuckled. "Don't look so shocked. I wasn't a very good one. But I was in some commercials and stuff, a few small-budget films."

"Does that mean you're not from Meadowbrook?"

She shook her head. "L.A."

"Wow. How did you wind up in Meadowbrook?"

"My best friend from college was getting married, and the bachelorette party was in Vegas. One afternoon, we all went to a pool party, and I ended up talking to the only guy wearing a flannel with his swim trunks. Elvin was there for his friend's thirtieth birthday."

"That sounds about right." I laughed. "Though I had no idea you weren't from here."

Linda lifted her wine glass. "Seems like a lifetime ago, but I've only been in Maine for six years."

"Do you still do any acting?"

She shook her head. "When I first moved here, I got involved with a local theatre group. A lot of the participants were younger and didn't have too much experience, so I would help them out and show them techniques I'd learned over the years. It made me realize I like teaching acting even more than I like acting. My degree is in theatre, but I'm currently working on getting my Master's in Education. I'm hoping to teach high school theatre here someday."

Her story got me thinking. "If you don't mind me asking, how was the transition from living in L.A. to living in Meadowbrook?"

She smiled. "Bumpy. Elvin and I had been seeing each other for about six months when I came out to stay for a three-month trial period. I went back home when the time was up."

"Oh wow. What brought you back?"

"I realized I could adjust to driving twenty minutes for a Starbucks, but I couldn't adjust to not seeing Elvin every day. I missed him."

I took a deep breath but stayed quiet.

"Are you...considering moving to Meadowbrook?" Linda asked.

"I have no idea what the hell I'm doing. I'm crazy about Brock, but I've also spent a decade building a business I really love, and that business isn't easily relocatable. Before the baby, we were going to give the long-distance thing a shot and alternate visiting each other. But now, things are obviously different." I paused before meeting Linda's eyes. "Do you ever have regrets for giving up your dream?"

She shook her head. "Never. I'm happy. Life is different than I'd pictured for myself, but having Elvin and the kids is better than any dream I could've imagined."

Linda's words should've made me feel better, should've made me believe it wasn't impossible for things to work with Brock. Yet it made me feel like something was wrong.

Patrick let out a mewl from the other side of the room, so I went over and picked him up.

Linda smiled. "I know it's only been a couple of days, but he really seems to adore you. I swear, those little monsters imprint faster than a wolf from *Twilight*."

She'd meant it as a compliment, but her comment weighed heavily on my heart. Babies need consistency. Forty-eight hours ago, I'd flown into Brock's arms, so happy to see him, and now...I suddenly felt the urge to run.

It was almost ten by the time everyone left. Brock got Patrick ready for bed and tucked him in, then brought the baby monitor out to the living room. He sat on the couch next to me and hoisted me from my spot to straddle his lap.

"Talk to me. What's going on in that head of yours?"

"How do you know something is going on in my head?"

He frowned. "You can't hide your feelings for shit. Lay it on me, Red."

I sighed. "I don't want to give up you or my business."

"Why is it one or the other?"

"A child needs consistency. Tomorrow morning I'm going to fly back to New York and work sixty hours in four days to make up for being away. Next week, I have to fly to the West Coast to meet with the production team. After that, I have to start gearing up for Fashion Week. And then it will be time to—"

Brock crushed his lips to mine. After a minute, I felt the stress drain from my body. The knot in my neck loosened, and my shoulders lowered from my ears. This man could probably make me forget my name. Too soon, though, he pulled back. Brock stroked my hair tenderly. "I hate that this is all on you, and that's the only thing I can do to make you relax."

I smiled sadly. "I don't know what to do, Brock."

"I know, sweetheart. Things got complicated real fast, and now I can't do the things I committed to you that I would—like come to New York or meet you halfway trying to make this work out. There's so much more on your shoulders now, which isn't fair. And it's not just me you'd be taking on if you decide to stick around." Tears filled his eyes. "I will understand if you need to walk away. I'll fucking hate it, but I'll understand. I care about you enough to let you go, if that's what you need to do. I just want you to be happy. Because you deserve it, February. You really do."

It broke my heart when a tear rolled down his cheek. I wanted to reassure him—but I didn't want to make promises I wasn't sure I could keep. So instead, I followed his lead and crushed my lips to his. Maybe this was all we had now, the ability to make each other feel good physically.

♦ ♦ ♦

The ride to the airport the next morning was somber. I'd told Brock I'd take an Uber so he didn't have to bundle up Patrick for the ride, but he'd insisted they take me. We drove the short distance making small talk, while big questions loomed and so much was left unsaid. Brock pulled to the curb when we arrived at the terminal. The baby was in his infant carrier in the back, so after I got out, I opened the back door and gently kissed his cheek. "Be good to your daddy, little one."

Brock stood at the back of the truck with my suitcase. He looked like he wanted to say something, but instead he pulled the handle up and gave me a chaste kiss. "Text me when you get to the office so I know you made it safely."

I forced a smile. "I will."

Awkwardness set in. Should I say, *I'll see you soon* or *Nice knowing you?* Eventually, I settled on "Goodbye" and turned to walk toward the terminal.

Halfway there, Brock called after me. "February! Wait!"

I stopped and turned back. He jogged to catch up and set his hands on my shoulders. "I love you, sweetheart."

The words knocked the wind out of me. I was absolutely, positively, head-over-heels in love with this man, too.

But that's not what I told him. Instead, I pushed up on my toes and brushed my lips with his. "Take care of yourself, Brock."

# CHAPTER 34

*Brock*

I shut off my drill and turned to Trevor. "I don't know if this was a good idea."

We'd just gotten to the cabin ahead of our other brothers to get started on today's work.

"You fucked up the wood?"

Putting the tool down, I sighed. "I'm not talking about that. I'm referring to Patrick staying with the sitter today. He was pretty fussy this morning. It seemed like he was trying to get me to stay."

Trevor rolled his eyes. "He'll be fine."

For the first time, I'd left Patrick with a sitter other than Linda. Elvin's wife had to take care of their sick son, so she was out of commission until further notice. Elvin had also caught something and didn't want me to catch it and give it to the baby. Patrick had yet to get sick, and I wanted to keep it that way. So I was all for them keeping their distance.

Linda had suggested I try a local single mom whose kids were in school during the day. The woman was probably more experienced than I was, but I still felt guilty for not being there while we worked on the cabin.

I shook my head. "It's too soon. He just got used to Linda watching him. Now he's with someone totally unfamiliar. What if he thinks I'm trying to pawn him off on people?"

"I don't think Patrick is getting all analytical about it like you think he is." My brother stopped sanding the wall for a moment. "Look, the sooner he gets used to other people watching him, the better off you'll both be. It's good for your mental health, too."

The thing was, I *liked* taking care of him myself and felt like I was missing out anytime we were apart. If I could've been home all the time with him, that would've been fine by me, so long as I got a couple of quick sanity breaks here and there. But the damn cabin needed to be built. We were outgrowing my apartment fast. And I couldn't just let my businesses crumble. So I supposed my brother was right. I had to get used to giving up some control with Patrick, if I didn't want all of the other parts of my life to go to shit.

"I've seen that Tori before," Trevor said, referring to the babysitter. "She's pretty cute. I should ask her if she cooks Mexican." He winked.

"Oh yeah? You ready to be a father to her kids, too?"

"Not quite." He chuckled.

"Then don't waste her time."

"Yeah, that's probably wise." He reached for more sandpaper. "So how did you leave things with February?"

My stomach was in knots just thinking about it. February had been constantly on my mind, but this was the first time I'd be forced to talk about what had happened when she left last weekend.

I swallowed. "You mean after I told her I loved her, and she didn't return it?"

His eyes widened. "Whoa...say what?"

"It was a split-second decision and so fucking stupid. I blurted it out just as we were leaving each other at the airport. She didn't say it back. It was the pause heard around the world. She told me to 'take care of myself'."

"Ouch." He cringed. "That's the equivalent of telling someone to go jerk off. What does 'take care of yourself' even mean?"

"It doesn't mean I love you. She didn't know what to say. I caught her off guard." I ran my hand through my hair. "I realize that wasn't the most opportune time, but..."

Trevor finished my sentence. "*But* you meant it. And you've always been someone who follows your heart. So you did what felt right at the time. Don't blame yourself for being true to your feelings. If you hadn't said it, you might've regretted it. Now you know the outcome."

"I guess," I muttered. "But a lot of good that did me."

His brow furrowed. "You don't think she feels the same?"

"The answer seems pretty clear to me. Wouldn't she have said it back if she did?"

"Fair question, but there are other reasons she might've not said it at that moment."

"Like what?" I reached for the power drill but stopped short of turning it on.

He shrugged. "She was leaving town. Maybe she didn't feel like the time was right...because everything was rushed."

"That's a bit of a stretch, don't you think? What better opportunity to return the sentiment than when someone says it to you? She didn't reciprocate because she doesn't feel the same." I sighed. "I think she cares about me, but I'm not sure if *love* is what she feels."

"Okay, well, if she doesn't return your feelings, it's a good thing you're finding this out now. Right? Look at it that way."

"Nice try attempting to put a positive spin on my humiliation. But only time is gonna heal this."

Trevor walked over to find his coffee. "Maybe she's doing you a favor, allowing you the freedom you need to find a good woman locally who wants to be a mother to Patrick."

That was laughable. "Oh yeah, as if the perfect person for me just happens to be here in Meadowbrook out of everywhere in the world? Said woman's been here all this time, waiting in the wings?" I rolled my eyes. "Just because something is convenient doesn't make it right. I won't *ever* settle, Trevor. No matter how badly Patrick needs a mom. A woman his father doesn't love is never gonna be the right choice, no matter how good she might be to him. Love is one thing you don't compromise on, you know?"

Trevor nodded. "I guess you'd still be with Nina if you were open to compromise, huh?" He set his mug on the ground. "Speaking of which, do you think Nina would've changed her mind about raising Patrick if you had proposed to her back when she was giving you that ultimatum?"

"I have no idea. But in any case, things are the way they're meant to be. Nina wasn't the one—even before she gave up her son. And especially now, knowing what she did? *Definitely* wasn't the one. That only solidified what I already knew."

"I'd say you dodged a bullet, but you *did* knock her up."

"And I have no regrets about my son, thank you very much."

"Nor do I about my handsome nephew." He grinned. "Anyway, the perfect women for us are out there somewhere. We just need to be patient."

I'd thought February *was* the perfect one for me. But wouldn't the perfect person love me back? Her reaction—or lack thereof—showed that I'd been seeing everything through rose-colored glasses, expecting more from this situation and continuing to hang on to false hope for far too long. Maybe this was the wake-up call I needed.

Trevor resumed sanding the wall. "Well, if it doesn't work out between you and February, I'm truly sorry. It's not easy finding that kind of spark." He laughed. "Lord knows, *I* haven't been able to find it here in Meadowbrook."

"It ain't from lack of trying, Trev. That's for damn sure. Pretty certain you've dated three-quarters of the town."

"I've had some damn good meals along the way, too." He winked. "Just not head over heels for anyone."

"I'm better off alone if I'm not absolutely crazy about someone. My son will grow up watching me. I want to teach him to always reach for the stars. Never settle."

"It's too bad February has that job…because you're definitely crazy about *her*."

"See, I don't feel that way about her career," I explained. "One of the things I love about her is her drive. Her career is part of who she is. I just wish there were a way for me to fit into the equation." I looked away. "But maybe what we had wasn't meant to last forever. As humans, we're trained to think that in order for someone to matter in your life, you have to marry them or die next to them. But maybe sometimes people just come into your life and change you for the better. Then they move on and spread their magic to someone else."

"You're getting introspective in your old age, brother." He chuckled and whacked me on the arm. "But are you really believing your bullshit right now? It's okay for this situation *not* to have a bright side. It can just be shitty with no solution."

"Well, that it is. But I gotta find a way to pick myself up. And if that means lying a little, so be it. My son needs the best version of me. I can't give that to him if I'm walking around every day with a damn broken heart, pining over a woman I can never have."

I finally turned on my drill, vowing to get to work and try to stop thinking about her.

♦ ♦ ♦

When I got back to the house that afternoon, the moment the babysitter placed Patrick in my arms, all was right in the world again.

"I missed you so much, little buddy." I kissed his forehead.

He cooed. I told myself he was telling me he'd missed me, too.

"How was he?" I asked her.

"Really fussy after you left this morning, but it got better as the day progressed. He ate great, but he's due for another bottle soon."

"I never imagined how difficult being away from him would be. Every time I've left him has been tough, and so far it hasn't gotten any easier."

She smiled. "Trust me, it will. The best part of my day is dropping my kids off at school, heading home to make a fresh pot of coffee, kicking my feet up, and giving myself a half hour before I have to start the day. You'll come to relish that time apart one day. But when they're tiny like this, it's hard. I know."

Tori looked to be about my age. She was a friend of Linda's, and my sister-in-law had mentioned that Tori was divorced. That's really all I knew about her.

"How old are your kids now?" I asked.

"Five and three. A boy and a girl, in that order."

"Nice." I smiled.

"Their father and I split when I was pregnant with my youngest."

"That must've been tough." I rocked Patrick. "I'm sorry it didn't work out with your husband."

"*Ex*. And don't be. He cheated, and I'm better off without him."

"Ah." I nodded. "Then I would agree, yes. You're better off without him, though I'm sure it's not easy on the kids."

"We make it work."

As silence filled the air, I felt a little awkward because she seemed like she expected me to say something else. Meanwhile, I was just ready to be left alone with my son. The longer she stayed in place, the more I got a vibe that maybe she was interested in more than babysitting for me.

*Is it my imagination?*

"Before I forget like a dumbass, here…" I reached into my pocket to hand her some cash.

When she still wasn't getting ready to go, I added, "I can't thank you enough for watching him. Think I'm gonna give him a bottle now."

Finally, she walked ever so slowly toward the door. "You have my number if you ever need anything after hours."

"Yes. Thank you. Hopefully I won't have to use it."

"Well…I mean, if you ever want to just *talk*, too. I'm here. Doesn't need to be an emergency."

*Talk. Right. Great.* "Okay." I smiled politely. "Noted."

After she left, relief washed over me. *Finally alone again with my little boy.*

I fed Patrick a bottle before he fell asleep in my arms. Appreciating the break, I placed him carefully in the playpen I'd set up and cracked open a beer.

Oak came over to comfort me as I sat leaning back in my kitchen chair.

Reaching down, I rubbed between his ears. "Hey, buddy. I was so busy with your brother, I didn't even ask how *your* day was."

He dropped to the floor and rolled around as I scratched his belly. "You're such a good boy, Oak."

He growled.

A moment later, I got a FaceTime call.

*February.*

My pulse sped up. I answered as quickly as possible to avoid waking Patrick.

"Hey..." I said in a low voice.

"Hi... Is everything okay?"

She looked so beautiful, wearing a red dress with matching lipstick. She had on a simple strand of pearls.

"Yeah. Everything is fine. Why do you ask?"

Was she able to see it on my face?

"You look a little down," she said.

"It's been a long day. I was working, and Patrick was with a new sitter. It sucked to leave him."

She tilted her head. "How did that go?"

"Seemed to go well. I'll probably use her again."

"Is this a good time to talk?"

I peeked over to make sure Patrick remained sleeping. "He actually fell asleep after I gave him a bottle, so you called at a good time."

"Good."

"Did you call for a specific reason or just to check in?"

"Just wanted to see how you were doing."

As silence filled the air, we stared at each other. I don't know what came over me, but I felt it was time to cut the shit and get to the point.

"Actually, I can't stop thinking about what happened when we parted ways a few days ago. What I said. And what I maybe *shouldn't have* said."

Her face turned red. "Brock, I—"

"Wait. I'd like to finish. Okay?"

"Okay..." She swallowed.

"I've been stewing over it, you know? Not because you didn't return the sentiment. But because I *never* should've said those words." I exhaled. "I never should've put you in a position where you had to respond to that. I was sending you mixed messages to begin with. Earlier,

I'd told you I'd understand if you walked away. Then I go and tell you I love you? I can understand why you'd be confused. And I appreciate the fact that you didn't say anything you don't really mean in return. If you were ever to say those words to me, I'd want you to mean it. And if you don't, you don't."

"Brock..."

"It was fucking stupid of me. And I'm sorry."

To my surprise, her eyes began to water. I hated that I'd made her cry, but I was crying inside right now, too. As much as I tried to remain strong, I was fucking hurting. Because I was losing her.

I finally let her get a word in.

"It's all I've been able to think about, Brock. And to think you believe I didn't say it back because I don't feel it too is killing me. That's not it at all. I held back out of fear, afraid of the message it would send if I were honest about how strong my feelings are for you. I've come to realize that *my* feelings are not necessarily what's most important right now. What's important is protecting you and Patrick. Having spent those couple of days with you made me realize how difficult a situation this is. Imagine if he got attached to me, only to have me not there anymore. I wasn't expecting to feel so connected to him. And honestly, that scares me."

"I respect that, Feb. I respect that you think before you speak and that you've been contemplating how our actions will affect my son."

She sniffled. "Where do we go from here?"

"I can't imagine a life without you in it." I paused. "But if you don't think you can commit to being part of my son's life, there really is no choice but for us to take a break. Even if we tried to keep our relationship separate from everything else going on in my life, that's not realistic. There is no separation between Patrick and me. We're a package deal. Anyone in my life is in *his* life by default. He's already lost his mother. It's too much of a risk to have him fall in love and lose you, too. Because he *would* fall in love with you, Red. Just like I did. It's impossible not to."

She closed her eyes for a moment.

"So, maybe what we do is take a step back right now," I continued. "Remain friends. And do the best we can with that." I shook my head. "I don't know."

She kept nodding for a while and finally said the words I didn't want to hear.

"I agree. That's what's best. For real this time."

My heart clenched. "Not sure I know *how* to do this, but we'll figure it out."

"Yeah." She wiped her eyes. "Me, neither."

We hung up a few minutes later, and I stared into space for the longest time, trying to make sense of how I was supposed to be friends with this woman. It seemed like torture, but never seeing her again and losing her entirely wasn't an option. But friends or not, we'd just broken up. For real this time.

And that sucked.

# CHAPTER 35

*February*

*Knock. Knock.* Oliver stepped into my office before I could even look up from the computer screen. He held my daily planner in his hands. "I need a favor, boss lady."

I shut my laptop and leaned back in my chair. "What's up?"

"My friend Matthew needs some business advice. He's a former attorney who was miserable at his job, so he quit and started his own import/export company. He has family in Turkey who are in the handwoven-rug business, so that's what he started with, but he's now expanded to high-end textiles like cashmere. Anyway, his business is booming, and he wants to take the next steps and expand by buying into a manufacturing facility. But he's having a hard time getting funding since he's only been in biz for a couple of years."

I smiled. "That sounds vaguely familiar…"

"Exactly. That's why I was hoping you would talk to him. Tell him about how you found your funding and the pitfalls he should look out for."

"Sure. Why don't you put him on my calendar for lunch one day?"

Oliver smirked. "Already did. You're meeting him at one o'clock this afternoon."

I shook my head. "What if I'd said no?"

"You love me too much. I knew you wouldn't."

"But if I did?"

"Then I would have been forced to give you my puppy-dog eyes." Oliver stuck out his bottom lip in a pout and fluttered his lashes over a set of pleading peepers. He pointed to his face. "I'm impossible to say no to."

I laughed. "Get out. I have work to do before this lunch meeting."

Three hours later, I walked into Gramercy Tavern to meet Matthew. Oliver had described his friend as impeccably dressed, tall with olive skin. Not very much to go on. I looked around, but the height description didn't help since most people were seated at tables.

The hostess greeted me. "Hi. Can I help you?"

"Yes, hello. I'm meeting someone for lunch, but I'm not too sure what he looks like. His name is Matthew Reis. Maybe he's checked in?"

The woman's eyes gleamed. "Lucky lady. He's already seated, but he let me know he was waiting for someone." She grabbed a menu and gestured for me to follow. "Right this way."

Matthew was at a table in the back of the restaurant. He stood when we approached. *Oh my.* I didn't have to wonder what the *lucky lady* comment meant. This man was absolutely gorgeous. Chiseled jaw, bright blue eyes that popped from his smooth, tan skin, and slightly messy hair that made me wonder if he'd just had sex before coming to meet me. And don't even get me started on the broad shoulders. He did a quick sweep over me, and when he smiled, cavernous dimples appeared. *Seriously?* Those should be illegal on a man who looked like that. The way he checked me out made me almost certain he wasn't gay. Why had I assumed he was? Because Oliver is gay? That was pretty dumb, but yeah—*not* gay.

"February." He extended his hand. "Ollie described you perfectly."

"With Oliver, I'm not sure that's a compliment."

Matthew smiled and stepped around the table to pull my chair out.

"Thank you." I sat and settled my purse on the back of the seat. "The last time Oliver sent me to meet someone I'd never met, he described the man as a human espresso."

Matthew's brows pulled together. "Was he short with dark skin?"

"That's what I thought. But he turned out to be Nordic—six foot four and blond. Apparently, his description meant the man talked too fast and could make your heart race. He's not the best at providing a visual."

Matthew chuckled. "He described you as a hurricane in high heels. But he also mentioned that you were beautiful with red hair, so it wasn't hard to figure out who you were."

I felt my cheeks grow warm. "So how do you and Oliver know each other? I didn't get a chance to ask him."

"I represented his friend Will in his divorce."

"Ah." I nodded and picked up the white napkin on the table, draping it across my lap. "From Daniel, the husband who wouldn't put up the shower curtain."

Matthew's smile widened. "He might've mentioned that once or...three hundred times."

He folded his hands on the table, and I couldn't help but notice the big, chunky watch on his wrist. Audemars Piguet Royal Oak. Expensive, but not ostentatious. I also noticed that his hands matched the watch—large and manicured. Matthew was exactly the type of guy I used to go for—*before*. My heart sank remembering the man who'd changed my type. Though maybe...maybe things with Brock were difficult because I was trying to fit a square peg into a round hole? Matthew was definitely a round peg, and there was something comforting and safe about a man who *fits*.

Matthew lifted a glass of water. "So Ollie tells me you're originally from Brooklyn."

"I am. Park Slope."

"I grew up in Prospect Heights."

"Neighbors, huh? Do you still live there?"

He shook his head. "I stupidly sold seven years ago before the prices went berserk. I live on the Upper West Side now. But I do miss it. I don't get back often enough."

"I was there recently to meet a client," I said. "At a place called Weather Up."

"I know it well. Great place. They make a drink called Robert De Niro's Waiting that I love."

"That's what I had! It was delicious."

"A successful businesswoman from Brooklyn who drinks scotch? Do I propose now or wait until we get Ollie's blessing?"

I laughed, and as we ordered lunch, Matthew and I got to know each other a bit. It turned out we had a lot more in common than growing up in nearby neighborhoods. We were both divorced, both our exes had gotten involved with friends of ours after we split up, and we'd even gone to the same undergraduate college, though he was a few years older than me. It made me wonder if Oliver had already given his blessing, and this was a setup disguised as a business meeting. Though, after the food came, we got down to talking actual business, and it seemed Matthew did need some guidance. I was candid about my experiences taking on investors and suggested a few venture capitalists I wished I'd considered originally.

At some point, my phone illuminated, and a message from Oliver flashed on the screen. He wanted to know if he should push back my four o'clock appointment. I thought it was a little premature to start rearranging my schedule, at least until I pressed the button and looked at the time on my phone—*three forty-five*.

"Oh my gosh," I said. "Can that time be right? We've been sitting here for more than two-and-a-half hours?"

Matthew looked down at his watch. "I guess so."

"I must've lost track of time. I have a four o'clock meeting back at the office."

Matthew raised his hand to call the waiter. "Sorry. I didn't mean to take up so much of your afternoon."

"It's fine. But I should text Oliver back so he can let my appointment know I'm running a little late. Excuse me a minute."

After I thumbed off a message, the waiter brought the check. I took cash out of my purse and went to put it on the table.

Matthew shook his head. "Please. Allow me. It's the least I can do for picking your brain for hours." He smiled. "Plus, I really enjoyed your company."

His comment was innocuous enough, but something in the way he looked at me told me it wasn't as innocent as it seemed. Maybe I should reciprocate and tell him I had a good time too—push myself to keep my options open... I wasn't sure, though, and I didn't have time to debate it. I needed to get to my appointment. So I just stood and pulled my purse over my shoulder. "Thank you for lunch."

Matthew stood, too. "I really appreciate your time. I'm going to contact the VC you suggested as soon as I get back to the office. Would it be okay if I reached out to you with other questions that might come up as I go through the process?"

"Sure. Of course."

He pulled his cell phone out and handed it to me. "Put your number in, and I'll shoot you a text so you have mine."

After, he extended his hand with a smile. When we shook, his eyes dropped to my lips for the briefest of seconds. It was so quick, I thought I might've imagined it. Or maybe *I'd* been the one who'd looked at his mouth. Whatever the case, I suddenly felt the urge to bolt. I lifted my hand in an awkward wave and didn't even wait to walk out of the restaurant with him.

"Okay, well, bye!"

♦ ♦ ♦

It was almost seven before my afternoon meeting ended, but Oliver marched into the conference room less than ten seconds after the vendor had gone.

"I thought he was never going to leave!"

I swept together the samples the salesman had left behind. "We had a lot to go through. Is everything okay?"

Oliver's hands went to his hips. "What did you do to my friend?"

I blinked a few times. "Who? Matthew?"

"Yes, Matthew." Oliver turned his phone to show me the screen. "He's *blowing up* my messages."

"Oh no. Did the call with the venture capitalist I referred not go well?"

"Capitalist *schmapitalist*. The boy is smitten!"

"Smitten? You mean with me?"

Oliver rolled his eyes. "I know. It's very unfair he isn't gay, right? Yes, you! Who the hell else would I be talking about?" He swiped up on his phone and scrolled through dozens of messages. "But if he can't be mine, I guess being yours is the next best thing. Look at all these texts! I've never seen the guy so ga-ga over a girl. He's usually the recipient of the ga-ga. He wants to know if you're single. I wasn't sure how to answer."

I frowned. I hadn't yet told Oliver about my last conversation with Brock. He knew about the awkward airport goodbye, but not that we'd formally called it quits. I sighed. "Brock and I ended things two days ago."

"That's great!" Oliver lifted his cell and started to text.

I reached for his phone. "No, it's not. I love him, Oliver. Matthew was very nice, but I don't think I'm ready to jump into something new."

He gave me a sympathetic smile. "Oh honey, you don't have to marry him. Just go out and enjoy the ride. It's the best way to move on."

But I didn't *want* to move on. I wanted *Brock*. I just wasn't sure I could handle everything that now came in that package.

# CHAPTER 36

*February*

Two nights later, I decided to call Brock. We hadn't talked since we'd ended things, but I missed him like crazy and wanted to see how he was doing with the baby. It didn't feel right to completely abandon him, and it was clear to me that wasn't what I wanted. But all the complicating factors remained, and I still wasn't sure what I could ultimately commit to... So I talked myself into believing my call was just friendly, as we'd decided was best—not that I *needed* to hear his voice. But I poured myself a glass of wine to settle my nerves before hitting the FaceTime button.

Brock answered wearing a soaking-wet T-shirt, which clung to his amazing, thick body.

I licked my lips. "Are you working at the cabin this late?"

He turned the phone, and Patrick's cute little naked body filled the screen. Brock was giving him a bath in the sink. It made my heart squeeze. "Oh my God. He's adorable."

"He likes to splash his old man. Hang on a second, let me prop the phone up in the dishrack. I need both hands with this slippery little fish."

I couldn't stop smiling as I watched the two of them together. Patrick's legs were jumping all around, and he made this cute little squeaking sound.

"Watch this," Brock said. He leaned over and put his mouth on the baby's stomach and blew a big belly fart. Patrick went crazy, his arms and legs flailing around as he screeched in laughter. It made my heart full to see them happy together, and it hurt like hell that I wasn't there, wouldn't be part of that sweet little family. I hated myself for being too afraid to take a chance with them.

"He is so precious, Brock."

"He had a checkup yesterday. The butterball is almost eleven pounds already. The doc was nice, but she told me babies don't usually laugh or smile in response to interactions for at least six to eight weeks." He raised an eyebrow. "You can't tell me my boy isn't reacting to me."

"He definitely is. I think doctors tend to give averages and probably lean toward the long end of things when they give people milestones, so parents don't worry."

Brock lifted Patrick's foot, pressed his lips to it, and blew again. The baby shrieked in delight. There was no mistaking the smile on his face. "Is he that happy all the time?"

"For the most part. Though he tends to be happiest when he's naked." Brock winked. "Takes after his pop in that way, too."

I couldn't stop smiling. I watched as Brock finished his son's bath, dried him off with an adorable green, hooded dinosaur towel, and dressed him in footie pajamas. This was supposed to be a friendly check-in phone call, yet I think I fell a little more in love instead. But that still came paired with a spike of fear.

He set Patrick in a bassinet in the living room, and thirty seconds later, the little guy was fast asleep. Brock sat down on the couch and let out a big sigh. He looked happy, but tired. "He knocks out after all the bath excitement."

"I can't blame him. I love a good bath, too." Brock didn't respond, and it felt awkward. "Is this okay?" I asked. "My calling, I mean?"

"Yeah, of course. I'm just not sure how to do the friend thing with you. You said bath, and I pictured us in the tub together, you sitting between my legs, resting your head against my chest."

That sounded amazing. Clearly, I wasn't sure how to manage this new friend zone either. "I wasn't even sure I should call. But I've been thinking about you guys and wanted to see how you were holding up."

Brock smiled sadly. "I think about you a lot, too." He cleared his throat and looked away. "Anyway, what's new in New York?"

"Same old, same old. There was a rat in my subway car this morning."

"Jesus Christ, I don't know how you do it."

I laughed. "That was a little much, even for me. It was trapped and running from person to person."

"Did you make a decision on the investor guy from Italy?"

I nodded. "I did. I'm going to accept his offer. I have a call scheduled for tomorrow morning to talk to him about some things, but I don't think any of them are dealbreakers."

"So that means you'll be totally rid of the board of directors that have been giving you such a hard time?"

"Yep. I'm a corporation, so I need to have a board, but it doesn't need to be outsiders who don't know anything about my business."

"That's good. Though the board did one smart thing."

"They did?"

"They sent you to Meadowbrook."

I smiled. "That's true. I have them to thank for bringing you into my life. And in hindsight, I think I actually needed the mental break. So yeah, I guess they did *one* good thing." I paused. "How about you? How are you juggling all your businesses with the baby?"

"I hired someone to cover my shifts at the bar. Terrance was our local sheriff for thirty years. He retired six months ago and was going stir crazy at home. Said he was getting a job or a divorce, so he started yesterday. I think he could be good for the place."

"Oh, that's great. That leaves you with only two full-time jobs then—building log cabins and being a dad. Actually, it's three if you count building your own cabin, too. How's that going? Your brothers were supposed to start helping you with that, right?"

Brock nodded. "They did. And even though they've been working their tails off, I've realized it would take forever to finish at the rate I'm going. So this morning, I bit the bullet and put a full-time crew on at my place to help finish up."

"Oh wow. I thought you wanted to do it all yourself? That was your dream. You'd put every stone on that big fireplace and cut every log."

"I did, but what I want now takes a backseat to what Patrick needs. This apartment is bursting at the seams already. I want him to have a home." He shrugged. "I guess dreams change. It's funny because I don't even remember why it was so damn important for me to build it myself anymore. Everything seems unimportant now except making things good for my son."

That stabbed my heart a little, and it must have shown on my face.

"I didn't mean *you* were unimportant," Brock clarified.

"It's fine. I get it."

We talked for another half hour, until Patrick woke up and started to fuss. "I have to feed him. You want to hang on while I go make a bottle?"

"No, you go do what you need to do." I smiled. "It was really good to talk to you. I'm glad everything is going well, Brock."

He was quiet for a beat, then simply nodded.

"Give me a call when you have time," I added.

"Actually, I'm going to christen the baby next week. It's not going to be a big thing. Just my brothers and a few friends, some six-foot heroes and beer at the bar after. But I thought maybe..." He raked a hand through his hair. "I understand if you can't. I just wanted to put the offer out there."

"Can I get back to you?"

"Yeah, of course."

After we hung up, melancholy set in. The silence of my apartment felt really loud, and after another glass of wine, I decided to call it an early night. But ninety minutes after getting into bed, I was still staring up at the ceiling, thinking about something Brock had said. *Dreams change.* Had mine? I'd been hung up on building an empire for as long as I could remember.

What was I reaching for anymore? My company was successful. I owned my apartment. I lived a good life. Maybe I wasn't Christian Dior or Louis Vuitton, but I had a brand with value, a brand I was proud of. What more would I need to feel like I'd made it? To be able to stop running toward something and enjoy where I was?

I chewed on my lip. Had *my* dream changed? Could I give up my life here and be happy being a stepmom? Would I be content living a simple life in Maine? Pushing a stroller on long morning walks instead of drinking my third cup of coffee while taking business calls from Europe at eight AM? Could I give up everything I'd worked for?

*Dreams change.*

I supposed they could. But had mine?

With that thought still rattling around in my head, my cell buzzed from the nightstand. For some reason, I felt in my bones that it was going to be Brock. He was going to say something that made all the tough questions a little easier to answer. I just knew it.

Though when I picked up the phone, the message wasn't from Brock at all.

It was another handsome man.

> **Matthew: Hey. I had a great time at lunch the other day. Would love to pick your brain about a few things. Could we possibly meet for lunch again one day next week?**

I stared down at the phone, trying not to let myself think this was a sign—God was trying to redirect my attention. Though it felt even more like that when the next text came in.

> **Matthew: Or maybe dinner?**

# CHAPTER 37

*Brock*

"Don't kill me," my brother Axe said as he walked into my house one afternoon.

I patted Patrick's back to burp him. "No guarantees on that. What's up?"

He crossed his arms as he leaned his back against my kitchen counter. "So...I follow your girl February on social media."

Alarms went off in my brain. "Okay..."

"Some guy tagged her in a post."

My fist tightened. *Some guy?* "What kind of post?"

"It was a location check-in. Some fancy restaurant. Might not have meant anything, but I just thought I should tell you. I stalked the guy's page. Looks suspicious."

"Suspicious in what way?"

"Like good-looking, rich suspicious."

*Great.* "Well, she and I aren't officially dating at present. We decided a week ago to just be friends. So while I appreciate the information, who she dines with isn't my business anymore."

Axe frowned. "Oh crap. I didn't realize that."

I nodded. I was pretty sure I'd remained calm on the surface, but damn. On the inside? This news was killing me. I warned myself not to overreact. Having dinner with someone didn't mean anything. And if it did, I didn't have a right to be upset anyway.

After Axe left, I had the worst time concentrating for the rest of the day. I kept messing things up around the house. Instead of warming Patrick's formula in a pot of water like I normally did, I dunked it into the tomato soup I was making for myself. Then later that afternoon, I accidentally threw my phone into the dryer while doing laundry. Thankfully, I caught my mistake before it was too late.

As dinnertime approached, I enjoyed a rare moment of rest with Patrick asleep in the playpen. I turned to Oak, who'd been staring at me.

"This is crazy, right? Why am I so worked up that she had dinner with some dude? If she and I are gonna be friends, I can't be reacting like this."

Oak rested his chin on my leg.

I rubbed between his ears. "I know you think I'm pathetic. Why sit here and theorize about what it meant when I can just *call her* and ask, right?"

He yawned.

"You know what?" I scratched his head again. "You're right."

Taking out my phone, I stood up and went to the bathroom so as not to wake my son.

February looked alarmed when she answered. "Everything okay?"

I normally didn't call before her workday was over.

"Sure, yeah." I cleared my throat, and an awkwardly long pause ensued.

She narrowed her eyes. "What's wrong, Brock?"

"Are you dating someone?" I blurted.

Her eyes widened. "No. What makes you think that?"

I shook my head. "Never mind."

"No, wait. Why did you ask me that?"

I sighed, surrendering to my humiliation. "My brother Axe follows you online and saw you tagged in a post, out with some guy. He got a vibe that it might've been more than a business meeting. It's none of my fucking business, though."

She shook her head. "There's absolutely nothing going on there. It was a business dinner. His name is Matthew. He's a friend of Oliver's. He might have been interested in more with me, but I know for sure that isn't what I want."

Even as relief washed over me, I pulled on my hair in frustration. "I can't be reacting like this, Red."

When I looked back at her, she was smirking. "I don't know. I kind of like it."

I chuckled. "You like torturing me?"

"I think your jealousy is sexy."

Her tone lit an unwanted fire inside of me. "Well, I'm sorry for overreacting."

"I'm sorry to have caused you to overreact. This isn't going to be easy. There's no playbook for how to go from lovers to friends, when neither of us is really ready for that."

"That's for damn sure."

The christening was coming up in a few days. She hadn't mentioned it, so I figured she probably wasn't going to make it. I didn't bother asking for an update. I didn't want her to feel pressured.

"Well, I already ate up enough of your time," I told her. "I'll let you go."

"I'll always make time for you, Brock."

I smiled, wishing I could reach through the phone and taste her lips. "Take care, Red."

After I hung up, I sat on the edge of the bed, staring at the wall. Oak looked over at me from the corner of the room.

"Did you enjoy me making an ass of myself?" I groaned. "I shouldn't have listened to you. All that call did was make me look like a jealous prick."

He barked.

"I know. I know. That's what I *am*." I laughed at myself. "Now I miss her even more. Thanks a lot."

♦ ♦ ♦

The following day, I went to the local farmers' market with Patrick in tow. It soon became clear that if I planned to go to a public place with my son, I needed to be prepared for extra attention left and right. I'd never had trouble attracting single women in this town. But Patrick attached to my chest was a new, unwanted magnet.

As I sampled some homemade smoked sausage, Tori, my one-time babysitter, materialized next to me.

"Hey, Brock."

"Oh, hey, Tori."

I hadn't called her again after I'd gotten the vibe that she might've been interested in more than just babysitting Patrick.

"I'm surprised you haven't needed me to babysit again."

I wiped my mouth with a napkin. "My sister-in-law has that pretty much covered lately. But thank you for offering to help."

"Well, you know, you can always call me for *other* reasons."

"I got that." I nodded once. "Thank you."

Then some other woman I didn't recognize interrupted our conversation as she hovered over my son. "Isn't he the most precious thing? Looks just like you, Brock."

"Thank you."

"I hear you could use some help?"

Tori walked away, seeming annoyed.

"No, I've got it covered," I told the woman. "But thank you."

"Well, I'm certified in CPR. Here's my card if you ever feel overwhelmed."

I glanced down at the card. Her name was April, which comes *after* February. April was certainly attractive, but she didn't hold a candle to the preceding winter month, if you know what I mean.

At one point, hoping to escape April's clutches, I turned toward a table where a woman was selling pickled turnips. But it wasn't the turnips that caught my attention. It was the gorgeous woman staring back at me. She'd apparently been quietly observing my interactions.

"Excuse me," I muttered as I abruptly left the conversation with April.

My heart squeezed. "What are you doing here?"

February grinned. "Didn't you invite me to Meadowbrook for Patrick's christening in a couple of days?"

"Yeah. But I assumed you weren't coming."

"Well, that's why you should never assume." She winked.

I inched closer but managed to stop myself from kissing her. "I'm glad you made it, Red."

"I wouldn't have missed it."

She kissed the top of Patrick's head and rubbed the back of her hand along his cheek. "I missed you, little buddy."

"We missed *you*." I placed my hand briefly over hers. "How did you find me here?"

"I wanted to surprise you. After I dropped my stuff off at the hotel, I went to your place, but you weren't there. So I texted Trevor to see if he knew where you were. He told me where to find you."

*She's staying at a hotel.* For a second, yet again, I'd forgotten we weren't together anymore. *She won't be sleeping in my bed tonight.* How's that for torture?

"Where are you staying?" I asked.

"At Brooks Inn."

"Not a lot of places to choose from here, I suppose. Although it's weird that you're in town and not staying with me."

"It's best, don't you think?"

"No," I groaned. "I think it sucks. I want you in my bed."

She smiled. "You're nothing if not honest, Brock."

"We can be friends until kingdom come, Red. I will *never* not want you in my bed."

Her eyes lingered on mine as she murmured, "I get it."

"You do, do you?" I said seductively. It was impossible not to flirt with her.

"Yeah, I do."

"I'm gonna make you dinner tonight."

She rubbed the top of Patrick's head. "How are you gonna manage that and take care of him?"

"I'm getting better at balancing everything. He likes to watch me cook now. He sits in his little seat. As long as I talk to him, he's good."

"How about *I* entertain him while you cook?" she suggested.

"I think he'd love that."

"Good," she cooed as she pinched his cheek.

"I really appreciate you coming." *And I'd like to show that appreciation by making you come again later.*

"Like I said, I wouldn't miss it for the world."

"I'm happy you came a little earlier so we can spend some time together."

"That was the plan." She smiled up at me. "I'm gonna go back to the hotel and freshen up, though, before I head to your place."

"All right. Don't take too long. I hate wasting precious time when you're here. You should've just stayed at my apartment."

All I wanted right now was to break every friend-zone rule.

"I'll see you in about an hour?" she said.

"Sounds good, baby."

*Baby.* Once again, I couldn't help myself. But I wasn't even sorry. Maybe I was undoing whatever progress we'd made since the friendship declaration, but my feelings for this woman were just as strong as they'd always been. And I couldn't deny it. I *wouldn't* deny it.

On the way back home, I detoured toward the grocery store to pick up some stuff to make for dinner. I'd changed Patrick on the bed of my truck before we left the farmers' market, so he'd be good to go for a little bit.

I felt a bit giddy, knowing I'd get to spend time with February this evening. My mind raced as I thought about what to make for dinner. I peeked into the backseat at my son, the happiest I'd been in a while, knowing the woman who still had my heart was nearby.

The moment my eyes returned to the road, I saw it veering toward us.

And then? Everything went dark.

# CHAPTER 38

*February*

*What the heck is taking him so long?* I'd been sitting in my rental car in Brock's driveway for almost half an hour now. When I'd arrived, the only one home was Oak, and he wouldn't stop barking, so I went back to wait in the car. I checked my watch for what must have been the tenth time. It had been just about four o'clock when Brock said he'd meet me here in an hour. And it was currently five minutes to six. Turns out I'd taken almost ninety minutes at the hotel to get ready—shaving my legs and doing a little grooming touch up *other* places. You know, to have dinner with a man who was only a friend, and I *wasn't* planning to sleep with. That thought made my eyes roll.

Maybe Brock had underestimated how much time stopping at the store would take him. Everything probably took twice as long with a baby in tow. I hesitated to call him in case he was driving, but after *another* half hour went by, I finally gave in and dialed.

As the phone rang, a feeling I didn't like settled in the pit of my stomach. The call went to voicemail. I attempted to talk myself down.

*He's probably driving from the supermarket and doesn't want to answer with the baby in the car.*

*Maybe he ran into one of his brothers and they got to talking.*

*Did he say an hour? Maybe I misheard and he said two.*

Though after fifteen more minutes passed, calm went out the window. I got out of the car and went into the bar.

A few older gentlemen were sitting around, and a guy I'd never seen before was behind the counter. He smiled at me. "You're not from around here…"

I smiled back. "No, I'm not. I'm a friend of Brock's. I was supposed to meet him here more than an hour ago, and he hasn't shown up yet. Any chance you've heard from him?"

The man finished drying a glass and slung a towel over his shoulder. "Nope. I left him a message a half hour ago myself. The back refrigerator isn't working, and I wasn't sure which repair shop he wanted me to call."

I frowned. "Oh. Okay."

The guy studied me. "You look pretty worried."

I shook my head. "I'm sorry to bother you. I'm sure I'm just paranoid, and he's going to be here any minute."

The bartender reached over to the cash register and swiped a cell phone from inside the drawer. He gestured with it. "Let me put your mind at ease. I was the sheriff in this little town for thirty years. Still got all my connections on speed dial." He hit a few buttons on his cell, and it started to ring on speakerphone.

"Meadowbrook Police Department. Officer Langston speaking."

"Kenny," the bartender said. "Still taking too long to answer the phone, I see."

The guy chuckled. "And you still got nothing better to do than bust my balls, even after you retire. What's going on, Sheriff Ronin?"

The old man smiled. "Need a favor. You haven't heard anything about Brock Hawkins, have you? It seems he's gone MIA for a while, and that's not like him."

"Shit. I forgot you started bartending over at Brock's bar, or I would've reached out as soon as the call came in."

The sheriff's smile wilted. "What's going on?"

"Brock was in an accident."

♦ ♦ ♦

I ran through a set of double doors and up to the window. "I'm looking for Brock Hawkins. He was brought in by ambulance."

"And you are?"

"I'm his...friend."

The woman shook her head. "I'm sorry, but we're unable to give out—"

A familiar voice interrupted, and I turned to find Trevor. He laid a hand on my shoulder and waved to the woman behind the glass. "I got this, Fran."

Brock's brother steered me away from the window.

"Is he okay?" My heart pounded. "Is Patrick okay?"

Trevor nodded. "They're both going to be fine. Definitely a little shaken up, but it seems like nothing too serious. Brock has a broken clavicle and will probably have two black eyes from the airbag, but Patrick doesn't have a scratch on him, thank God. They just took Brock upstairs for a head CT as a precaution, but he's talking and acting pretty normal, which is a good sign. He yelled at the nurse that he wasn't leaving the baby with someone he doesn't know, so he seems like his usual grumpy self." He thumbed toward a door that I assumed led to the examination area. "Elvin's in the back with the baby now."

I couldn't stop shaking. "How long until they have the scan results?"

Trevor shrugged. "Not sure. But he's in good hands. I really think he's going to be fine."

"What happened? What caused the accident?"

"Guy driving in the opposite direction fell asleep at the wheel and veered into oncoming traffic. Brock swerved to avoid a head-on collision, but his truck went off the highway and crashed into a tree on the side of the road."

"Oh my God."

He nodded. "They brought the other guy in, too. Didn't have a scratch on him. Apparently, he woke up and avoided colliding with anything. Not sure he'll be that lucky a second time if they let Brock anywhere near him. He looked ready to kill someone when the cops told him what happened. The guy's wife was also in the waiting room, and I heard her on the phone. She said he'd been working double shifts all week. Doesn't make it right, but that explains it. At least it seems it was a true accident—no drinking or anything involved."

I didn't even realize tears were falling until Trevor shook his head. "Don't cry. I suck at lady tears, and if my big brother finds out I didn't stop you from getting upset, he's going to do more damage to me than he did to that tree…which is no longer standing, by the way."

I wiped my cheeks and sniffled a laugh. "I'm sorry. I guess my emotions got the best of me."

He wrapped an arm around my shoulder and squeezed. "Come on, let's go sit down."

We went to a quiet corner of the waiting room and sat. "I didn't realize you were even in town," Trevor said.

"I came for the christening."

He nodded and opened his mouth to say something, but then shut it.

"What?" I asked.

"Nothing." He shook his head. "I was about to stick my nose somewhere it doesn't belong and thought better of it."

But it was too late; I was curious. "What were you going to say?"

Trevor sighed. "I was just going to point out that you were pretty upset about the accident, yet you two aren't a couple anymore, supposedly."

"It's complicated."

"Is it? Because to me, it's not. If you're not sure whether something belongs in your life, you just close your eyes and imagine it's no longer your *choice* whether it's in your life anymore. If that makes you feel like a panic attack is coming on, you pull your head out of your ass and act before that choice is taken away from you."

"But…"

"Close your eyes."

"What?"

"Just humor me. Close your eyes for a minute."

I wasn't much in the mood for games, yet I took a big breath and shut my eyes.

"Now tell me the first feeling that hits you when I say each thing."

"Okay."

"Your fancy purse company gets bought out by a big chain that pays you a lot of money."

It surprised me, but my shoulders relaxed.

"Whatcha feeling?"

"I think I feel relieved."

"Good. Let's try another one. Brock gets engaged to another woman, and you won't see him or Patrick ever again."

A wave of nausea rushed through me. I slapped my hand over my mouth and opened my eyes. "Oh God. That makes me sick."

Trevor smiled and shrugged. "See? Simple."

Fifteen minutes later, Elvin came out from the back. I stood. "How is he?"

"He's about as patient as a tornado in a trailer park."

I smiled for the first time since knocking on Brock's door and getting no answer. "Can I see him? Do you think they'll let me go back?"

Elvin nodded. "Let me talk to Fran who works the desk. She's friends with Linda. Besides, I'm pretty sure there isn't a better medicine for my brother than you."

Elvin gave Trevor a quick update—clear scan, no unusual bloodwork results, and BP normal—and said Patrick just had a bottle and fell asleep. After he walked over and spoke to the woman at the desk, we went back to the examination area together. I was a ball of nerves as we passed several patients who looked pretty sick.

When we got to Brock's suite, Elvin put his hand out. "I'm going to go call my other brothers. I'll give you two a few minutes alone."

I didn't even answer him. I was too busy running to Brock.

"Oh my God!" I threw my arms around him. "Thank God you're okay!"

He held me so tightly, it was difficult to breathe. When he pulled back, he cupped both my cheeks and drew me in for a kiss. "Fuck doing the right thing," he grumbled. "Life's too short, Red. Today was a reminder. Unless you tell me to back off, I won't be pretending I can handle you not being in my life. I'm too damn in love with you."

My chest felt full. "I'm in love with you, too."

♦ ♦ ♦

The following morning, I sat in my hotel room, staring down at my phone. Brock and Patrick had stayed overnight in the hospital for observation—something Brock was *not* happy about. But he'd hit the airbag hard enough that he had two black eyes and a broken clavicle, so staying for eighteen hours and having a follow-up head scan seemed like the safe thing to do. His brothers and I reminded him that it was best for both him and Patrick, so he really couldn't say no, though I suspected that was exactly what he would've done if the baby wasn't involved.

I hadn't slept well last night, too busy tossing and turning, trying to figure out what to do with my life. This morning, I still didn't have any answers, but I'd done enough soul searching to figure out part of the problem.

I had unresolved issues that had nothing to do with Brock. So I took a deep breath, scrolled through my contacts, and pressed call when I got to *Dad*.

The phone rang once, twice, and I felt more and more panicked. I wanted nothing more than to hang up, but my desire to figure things out with Brock was stronger than my need to run away. I thought I was about to get a reprieve when the fourth ring came, but then my dad's voice came on the line.

"February?"

"Yeah, uh, hi, Dad."

"This is a nice surprise." He paused. "Is everything okay?"

"Yes. Well, pretty much."

"Are you home or at the office?"

"I'm actually up in Meadowbrook, visiting Brock."

The last time I'd spoken to my dad, I'd told him I'd started seeing someone. He didn't know about Patrick or anything else that had gone down recently, and this was definitely not the time to fill him in.

"Oh? Things between you two getting serious then?"

I didn't have to ponder that answer. Things between Brock and me had been serious from almost the first day we met, whether I wanted to admit it or not. "Yeah, they are."

"That's good. I'm happy if you're—"

I interrupted him. "I need to ask you something, Dad."

"Anything."

"Do you have regrets in life?"

"About hurting you, definitely."

"No, that's not what I meant. Do you have regrets about cheating on Mom? For leaving her?"

"I didn't leave your mom. She asked me to leave."

"That's semantics."

"Maybe. But it's an important distinction. Because if your mom could've forgiven me for being a terrible husband, I would never have left. She's the love of my life, and that's never changed—divorce and all."

I felt a lump in my throat and swallowed. "Yet you cheated on her and hurt her anyway."

The line went quiet for a long time. "I did a lot of things I'm not proud of, February. And over the years, I've asked myself many times why I would do such a stupid thing."

"And..."

"I think I acted that way because I was immature and had low self-esteem. Feeling wanted by someone who wasn't my wife made me feel like a man." He blew a breath into the phone. "That's embarrassing to say, but it's the truth."

"Okay..."

"Do you have any other questions?" Dad asked.

"I don't think so."

"Do you mind if I ask you one, then?"

"I don't know. I guess it depends on what it is."

"What prompted this call today? Are you afraid this new guy is going to cheat?"

I sighed. "No. I think I'm just afraid of getting hurt again. The two men I counted on most left me."

My father's voice cracked. "I'm so sorry I hurt you, sweetheart. I wish you could find a way to forgive me. Not because I deserve it, but because *you* deserve to not let the hurt control your decisions anymore."

♦ ♦ ♦

A day after Brock and Patrick were discharged, I notified work that I had a family emergency and would be out of the office for at least the next week.

The christening had rightfully been postponed, and I wanted these next few days to be restful for all of us.

The realization of what he'd been through in the past forty-eight hours seemed to hit Brock in waves. Even though he and the baby had managed to escape the accident almost unscathed, I'd noticed him deep in thought a lot since we returned home and could only imagine the fear in his head about what *could've* happened.

He seemed to be having one such moment right now as he sat next to me on the couch, looking up at the ceiling while Patrick lay sleeping on my chest.

"I spoke to my dad yesterday," I said, interrupting his thoughts.

"Yeah?" He turned to me. "How was that?"

"He told me I deserve to not let hurt control my decisions anymore. And he's right. So much of why I cling to my independence is because I don't want to get hurt. It's a shield."

Brock reached for my hand. The love I felt for them both practically burst through me, along with a clarity I hadn't experienced before now.

"Brock, all this time...I never really left you."

"How do you mean?"

"Even when we were apart, you were all I thought about. No part of my heart actually left you. We were supposed to be just friends, but my feelings for you never changed. It didn't matter what I tried to tell myself about the status of our relationship, I still loved you. And I think for the first time in my life, I understand what love is—an unwavering feeling you can't shake just because you want to or think you should. It's not something you can control. It just *is*."

"Yeah, Red." He smiled. "I've learned the same thing over these past months."

"I don't want you to think I'm saying this because of the accident. This was how I felt long before that. I've just been afraid to accept my feelings because that would mean making some major life changes. But I see now that I don't have a choice. Because living without you isn't an option."

Brock looked down at his son. "What about him? Because there is no me without him."

My chest tightened. "Do you think he'd be willing to accept half a mother?"

"What do you mean *half* a mother?"

"I mean, if I keep my business, I'd be traveling back and forth a lot. I don't want to give up anything, Brock. I don't want to give up my career. I don't want to give up you. And I don't want to give up Patrick, either. I want it all. But that means not being perfect at any one thing. I'll be trying my best, even if spread thin. Do you think he'd accept that?"

Brock looked at me for a moment. "Red, you've been gone for weeks, and look at him right now. He's so relaxed with you. He trusts you. You comfort him. If he's anything like me, he'd take half of you over a whole of anything else any day."

My heart filled with hope. "I want to do this. I want to do the best I can for all of us."

He nodded and squeezed my hand. "You don't

need to be anything for him and me, other than *you*. I love the independent woman you are. And I was fully prepared to raise him on my own. So you wanting to be in the equation? That's a huge bonus. And I promise you don't need to give us *all* your time. You just have to love us." His eyes glowed. "Think you can do that?"

"I can do that." I sniffled. "I love you, Brock."

"I love you too, Red. So much."

I rubbed my hand along Patrick's back. "And I love him, too."

"I know you do. I can see it in your eyes when you look at him. It's the same way you look at me. That's how I know." He paused. "But you also need to promise to take care of yourself in the process and not get too stressed about the logistics. You don't need to be everything to everyone. We just need to enjoy each other with whatever time we have together and let go of trying too hard to fit all the pieces of our lives into a perfect box. They'll fall into place on their own in due time."

I shook my head. "I don't know if I can totally avoid being stressed. It's in my nature. So is perfectionism."

Brock caressed my face. "I'll tell you what. When we move into the cabin, and you're feeling overwhelmed, I'll put a ladder by the window of our bedroom. I know a bar in town. You can sneak out for a breather whenever you want. As long as you come back." He smirked. "Deal?"

I beamed. "Deal, Lumberjack."

# EPILOGUE

*Brock*

Six Years Later

February's voice shook. "I'm freaking out that I'm not gonna make it."

"Okay, breathe, Red. You still have some time."

"Traffic isn't even moving!"

February had just landed after a quick trip to London. She was only fifteen minutes from the exit to get to our town. But if traffic didn't move, there was a good chance she'd miss Patrick's presentation at school.

I moved to the hallway outside the auditorium and spoke quietly. "I bought you some time. I asked the teacher if he could go last. She said no problem. That'll get you an extra half hour."

Our son's kindergarten class was putting on an event where each kid presented a little speech. I knew what Patrick had been practicing, but the specific subject matter was a surprise for February.

"I told him I'd always be there for the big moments," she cried. "I haven't missed anything yet. I don't want him to think I'm a liar."

"If there's anything he's learned from being your son, it's that you have to be flexible in life and that it's okay if we don't always do everything perfectly, as long as you try. He sees how hard you hustle for us, and he knows how much you love him. That doesn't change just because you get stuck in traffic one time."

She sighed.

The past six years had certainly been a balancing act for my wife. February never technically left us again after that visit when the car accident happened. She came back to Meadowbrook almost every weekend after that for a while. Eventually, when Patrick and I moved into the cabin, I turned one of the rooms into an office for her, and she worked remotely whenever she could. Sometimes that looked like three days out of the week and other times, two weeks in a row. In the summer, we spent more time in New York, since February never gave up her apartment there. We'd found a way to make it work, thanks to my wife's determination.

When Patrick was two, February and I had made it official, getting married in a small ceremony in Meadowbrook, followed by a big party in New York the following summer. The separate wedding celebrations were representative of our two worlds, which had somehow managed to blend harmoniously against all odds.

We decided sometime after the wedding that it was probably best if we didn't add another baby into the mix, given all of Feb's traveling. She wanted to give Patrick as much of her attention as she could and knew that wouldn't be possible if she had to juggle two kids along with her crazy schedule. I respected that, though I still held out hope that someday we'd have a baby together.

Waiting for her to arrive at the elementary school, I nervously sat through each presentation, checking my phone for text updates. The second-to-last kid was just about to finish his speech when I heard the frantic click of February's heels.

I turned to find my frazzled woman scurrying down the aisle of the small auditorium, bag hanging off her shoulder, hair uncharacteristically disheveled. Her cheeks flushed as heads turned amidst a bunch of whispers. I lifted the jacket I'd been using to save the seat next to me to make room for her.

"Thank God," I whispered. "You're just in time. He's up next."

She let out a long sigh of relief before continuing to catch her breath.

As the teacher introduced Patrick, I filled with pride. He walked over to the podium and searched for us in the audience before looking down at his paper.

February offered him a thumbs-up in encouragement as he cleared his throat. I smiled to myself. She had no idea what was coming.

Patrick spoke into the mic. "When Miss Green asked us to write about our hero, I knew I would either write about Spider-Man or my mom."

The audience laughed.

"I decided to write about my mom. So here goes..."

He looked down at his sheet and read.

"My mom is cooler than your mom." He paused. "Your mom makes cookies. My mom makes sparkly bags in the shape of a frog's head."

February chuckled.

"Your mom tucks you into bed at night. My mom FaceTimes and tells me stories, even if she's an ocean away. But sometimes? She falls asleep before I do."

February beamed as she muttered, "This is true."

"Your mom drinks coffee. My mom drinks fancy lattes my dad can never remember how to order."

I smiled as I squeezed February's hand.

"Your mom wears sneakers to drop you off at school. My mom wears heels that get stuck in the mud outside."

Everyone laughed.

"Your mom makes you eat your vegetables. My mom brings me cake from New York and lets me eat it before dinner."

February's mouth dropped open. "He just snitched on me."

Patrick continued. "Your mom makes pancakes. My mom accidentally burns them into the face of Jesus."

"That really happened," February whispered. Her shoulders shook with laughter.

He sighed. "My mom might be a little different than your mom. But she loves me just the same." He looked up for a moment. "I chose my mom over Spider-Man because my mom chose *me*. And that's why my mom is my hero." He nodded. "Thank you." Patrick rushed off to exit the stage.

Tears filled her eyes. "I can't believe I almost missed that."

Our little boy found us in the audience and hugged February before returning to his seat at the front of the room.

She wiped her eyes. "You think he meant it, or is he just kissing up because tomorrow is his birthday?"

"If that's true, he learned the power of schmoozing from *you*."

The following day, we celebrated Patrick's sixth birthday with a party at the cabin. The house had been filled with family and friends all day, along with a giant inflatable bouncy house out back. It was an interesting sight when Oak decided to join the kids on that thing.

After everyone finally left, I decided to do something I'd never done before: write Nina a letter. Patrick's birth mother had asked that I write her each year on his birthday, but up until now, I hadn't honored that request. She didn't deserve it, and I'd decided if she wanted to know about him, she should reach out to us.

But this year, it felt right, almost therapeutic.

After Patrick went to bed, February took a shower while Oak sat by my feet. I took out my laptop and typed.

*Dear Nina,*

*I'm sure you're surprised to hear from me when I haven't written you these past six years. Maybe it's taken me this long to put aside my pride and give you an update on the beautiful boy you gave birth to.*

*If you've ever worried you left him motherless, you should know that hasn't been the case. I was fully prepared to raise him as a single father, but I met the love of my life shortly before I found out you were pregnant. She understood from the beginning that Patrick and I were a two-for-one deal and has helped raise him as her own.*

*February was adamant that Patrick know the truth about our family as soon as he'd be able to understand. When he was about three, we sat him down and explained as best we could that he didn't grow in his mom's belly. We let him know that this didn't mean she was any less his mom. His reaction was to tell us he wanted to go to McDonald's Playland. Not sure if he fully gets it even now, but he knows February chose to be his mom and that giving birth doesn't make you a mother.*

*He has the best of both of our personalities. He loves building things like me and is smart and witty like her. You'd be proud of the boy he's become. He is safe, happy, and loved.*

*Thank you for giving birth to the best thing that ever happened to me. In retrospect, he was the best surprise of my life. It's matched only by the surprise I got this morning—that he's about to become a big brother. Something neither my wife nor I expected. Not entirely sure how we'll manage that yet, but if there's one thing I've learned: where there's a will, there's a way. I no longer think anything is impossible nor subscribe to self-limiting beliefs.*

*You left town because you wanted something bigger. I hope you found your peace. My own "something bigger" came without me having to go anywhere at all. She wears six-inch heels and likes an extra dry martini, shaken not stirred, with a lemon twist, dash of orange bitters, and two bleu cheese olives.*

*Take care,*

*Brock*

# ACKNOWLEDGEMENTS

Thank you to all of the amazing bloggers, bookstagrammers and BookTokers who helped spread the news about *Denim & Diamonds*. We are so grateful for the book community and all you do to support authors!

To our rocks: Julie, Luna and Cheri – Thank you for more than a decade of friendship and always being there for us.

To our agent, Kimberly Brower – Thank you for helping to get our books into the hands of readers internationally.

To Jessica – Thank you for always being the grammar superhero of our stories.

To Elaine – An amazing editor, proofer, formatter, and friend. We so appreciate you!

To Julia – Thank you for polishing our words and making them shine.

To Kylie and Jo at Give Me Books Promotions – Thank you for making sure our books find their way into readers' hands!

To Sommer – Thank you for giving Brock's story a face that's way better looking than we could've imagined!

To Brooke – Thank you for organizing this release and for taking some of the load off of our endless to-do lists each day.

Last but not least, to our readers – You could've spent your time anywhere, but you chose to spend it here—with these characters, this story, and us. That's pure magic, and we are endlessly grateful for your trust.

Much love,
Penelope and Vi

# OTHER BOOKS BY PENELOPE WARD & VI KEELAND

The Rules of Dating
The Rules of Dating My Best Friend's Sister
The Rules of Dating My One-Night Stand
The Rules of Dating a Younger Man
Well Played
Not Pretending Anymore
Happily Letter After
My Favorite Souvenir
Dirty Letters
Hate Notes
Rebel Heir
Rebel Heart
Cocky Bastard
Stuck-Up Suit
Playboy Pilot
Mister Moneybags
British Bedmate
Park Avenue Player

# OTHER BOOKS BY PENELOPE WARD

The Rocker's Muse
The Drummer's Heart
The Surrogate
I Could Never
Toe the Line

Moody
The Assignment
The Aristocrat
The Crush
The Anti-Boyfriend
Just One Year
The Day He Came Back
When August Ends
Love Online
Gentleman Nine
Drunk Dial
Mack Daddy
Stepbrother Dearest
Neighbor Dearest
RoomHate
Sins of Sevin
Jake Undone (Jake #1)
My Skylar (Jake #2)
Jake Understood (Jake #3)
Gemini

# OTHER BOOKS BY VI KEELAND

Indiscretion
Someone Knows
The Unraveling
Jilted
What Happens at the Lake
Somethimg Unexpected
The Game
The Boss Project
The Summer Proposal
The Spark

# OTHER BOOKS BY PENELOPE WARD & VI KEELAND

The Rules of Dating
The Rules of Dating My Best Friend's Sister
The Rules of Dating My One-Night Stand
The Rules of Dating a Younger Man
Well Played
Not Pretending Anymore
Happily Letter After
My Favorite Souvenir
Dirty Letters
Hate Notes
Rebel Heir
Rebel Heart
Cocky Bastard
Stuck-Up Suit
Playboy Pilot
Mister Moneybags
British Bedmate
Park Avenue Player

# OTHER BOOKS BY PENELOPE WARD

The Rocker's Muse
The Drummer's Heart
The Surrogate
I Could Never
Toe the Line

Moody
The Assignment
The Aristocrat
The Crush
The Anti-Boyfriend
Just One Year
The Day He Came Back
When August Ends
Love Online
Gentleman Nine
Drunk Dial
Mack Daddy
Stepbrother Dearest
Neighbor Dearest
RoomHate
Sins of Sevin
Jake Undone (Jake #1)
My Skylar (Jake #2)
Jake Understood (Jake #3)
Gemini

# OTHER BOOKS BY VI KEELAND

Indiscretion
Someone Knows
The Unraveling
Jilted
What Happens at the Lake
Somethimg Unexpected
The Game
The Boss Project
The Summer Proposal
The Spark

The Invitation
The Rivals
Inappropriate
All Grown Up
We Shouldn't
The Naked Truth
Something Borrowed, Something You
Beautiful Mistake
Egomaniac
Bossman
The Baller
Left Behind
Beat
Throb
Worth the Fight
Worth the Chance
Worth Forgiving
Belong to You
Made for You
First Thing I See

**Penelope Ward** is a *New York Times*, *USA Today*, and #1 *Wall Street Journal* Bestselling author. With millions of books sold, she's a 21-time New York Times bestseller. Her novels are published in over a dozen languages and can be found in bookstores around the world. Having grown up in Boston with five older brothers, she spent most of her twenties as a television news anchor, before switching to a more family-friendly career. She is the proud mother of a beautiful girl with autism and her amazing brother. Penelope and her family reside in Rhode Island.

### Connect with Penelope Ward

Facebook Private Fan Group:
https://www.facebook.com/groups/PenelopesPeeps/
Facebook: https://www.facebook.com/penelopewardauthor
TikTok: https://www.tiktok.com/@penelopewardofficial
Website: http://www.penelopewardauthor.com
Twitter: https://twitter.com/PenelopeAuthor
Instagram: http://instagram.com/PenelopeWardAuthor/

**Vi Keeland** is a #1 *New York Times*, #1 *Wall Street Journal*, and *USA Today* Bestselling author. With millions of books sold, her titles are currently translated in twenty-seven languages and have appeared on bestseller lists in the US, Germany, Brazil, Bulgaria, and Hungary. Three of her short stories have been turned into films by Passionflix, and two of her books are currently optioned for movies. She resides in New York with her husband and their three children where she is living out her own happily ever after with the boy she met at age six.

### Connect with Vi Keeland
Facebook Fan Group:
https://www.facebook.com/groups/ViKeelandFanGroup/)
Facebook: https://www.facebook.com/pages/Author-Vi-Keeland/435952616513958
TikTok: https://www.tiktok.com/@vikeeland
Website: http://www.vikeeland.com
Twitter: https://twitter.com/ViKeeland
Instagram: http://instagram.com/Vi_Keeland/

Made in United States
Orlando, FL
29 July 2025